IMMORTAL RETURN

IMMORTAL RETURN

PRIMORDIALS OF SHADOWTHORN

Immortal Return.

Copyright © 2021 by Jessaca Willis

ISBN: 978-1-953072-03-0

ASIN: B0924XD9NN

All rights reserved. No part of this publication may be reproduced, distributed, or transmitted in any form or by any means, including photocopying, recording, or other electronic or mechanical methods, without the prior written permission of the publisher, except in the case of brief quotations embodied in critical reviews and certain other noncommercial uses permitted by copyright law. For permission requests, write to the publisher, addressed "Attention: Permissions Request," at the address below.

Any reference to historical events, real people, or real places are used fictitiously. Names, characters, and places are products of the author's imagination.

Front cover art by Evelyne Paniez, www.secretdartiste.be
Editing by Sandra Ogle from Reedsy.
Proofreading by Kate Anderson.

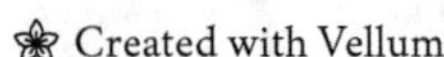 Created with Vellum

BOOKS IN SERIES

PRIMORDIALS OF SHADOWTHORN

Shadow Crusade, Book 1

Blighted Heart, Book 2

Immortal Return, Book 3

N
NW NE
W E
SW SE
S
The Capital
Unresting Mountains
ARCATHAIN
Varenholm
Aesyil Keep
ILLASHORE
Pits of Bagamore
O c

Castle of Nigh
THE FORMER SHADOWTHORN
The Dark Sea
The Eyve
The Claimed Coast
FORGOTTEN FOREST OF EYVE
n
THE BROKEN REALMS

To my family,

I may not verbally express my love often,
But at least I dedicate my books to you.

That's gotta mean something, right?

RISE WITH ME

THE FORMER SHADOWTHORN

Everything I've been led to believe is a lie.

Magic does not *only* belong to the mages, nor is it inherently evil.

Shadowsteel does not kill Primordials—in fact, it awakens them, and sets them on a murderous, potentially unstoppable rampage.

And demons are not *just* creatures of destruction.

Or at least, the one before me isn't.

Ryven stands hunched at the waist, his corded body overcome by the Blight and twisted into something caught between beast and man. No matter how long I scan and assess him for signs of anything remotely human, very little of him remains. He has become nothing more than predatorial hunger and carnal instinct. His long, ape-like torso is shrouded in dark, wiry fur, the pair of black, leathery wings at his back stretching around him as endless as the night sky. His talons are so sharp they indent the earth where he stands, but his teeth—the two fangs that hang over his withered lip—are sharper still, glinting with the saliva that had pooled on his tongue when he'd been imagining what it would be like to taste me.

His nasally breath rumbles from his scrunched batlike nose

as I take one cautious step after another, daring to venture near him. My hand is flat, frozen where it's extended from my arm, and I'm not sure if I truly believe he'll sniff me or if I'm willingly handing him my arm to be devoured. I'm not even sure the distinction matters. At this point, I just need him. I need to know he's still in there and that there's still a chance that he can be saved. The static charge in the air tells me there is. The invisible pulse of magic that's tethering us togethering and sizzling with each of my shaking advances gives me enough of the confidence I need to keep pushing forward. Ryven will not hurt me. He won't. Not as long as our eyes remain locked, my druid power leeching into him like an eternal command of obedience and demanding that he not strike.

Somewhere behind me, my friends have finally arisen from where they landed after the gust of wind knocked them down; the gust of wind that I had become to barrel over everyone and stop the battle before it truly had a chance to begin. The demons they fought are clamoring to their feet as well, and soon the sounds of shadowsteel blades and snarling roars echo heavy in the air once again.

But the battle at my back is a muffled, distant thing compared to the violent thrumming of my heart. It pounds, a cold and iron ball, heavy in my cavernous chest, as it slowly climbs into my throat and wedges itself there until I can hardly breathe. Hardly swallow.

My hand is so close to Ryven now that I can feel the heat of his breath on my palm as it spurts from his nostrils. But when he doesn't flinch, neither do I.

I press my hand to his batlike nose. His black eyes blink, and I swear a bit of that familiar russet color returns to them. I'm too relieved to recoil at the slickness I find there as he leans into my touch.

"Ryven…" I breathe, the word almost too heavy for me to

heave from my throat, but I manage it. It is a pitiful apology. A doubting promise. A weak command.

He has become the very thing he begged me to prevent him from becoming. He is the monster we both sought to free him from. And it's my fault. If I had simply done as he had asked, as he'd pleaded, if I would've had it in myself to kill him before the last of the Blight's toxin could tarnish his soul, he would've died with dignity instead of becoming the abomination he is now.

But looking into his eyes, despite the immense sorrow and guilt that wells inside me, threatening to consume me entirely, a part of me also can't help but marvel.

He is one of the shadowcreatures I've been trained to fight, to kill, but he's also something more. Under the influence of whatever druid power I'm using, he is docile. More than that, I can see the remnant of him reflected back at me from his eyes —eyes that continue to brighten with shades of brown that shimmer like flecks of gold beneath the black murky depths of his pupils.

If I had simply slain him as he'd requested, there'd be no more hope. Ryven would be dead and I never would've forgiven myself. But looking into his eyes now, I know I was right to hesitate because he is not gone. Not fully. Not yet anyway. And as long as he remains somewhere inside the creature he has become; I know there is a way to save him. There has to be, just like there was a way to save me.

The only question is how?

I press my forehead against his, the wiry hair somehow soothing as it grates on my skin, and we listen to the sounds of the battle fade behind us. The snarling of demons is punctured by the squelching of swords as they tear through stomachs and throats, until a single harrowing cry pierces the air, signaling the last demon has fallen.

I realize too late that I might've been able to help, that with my druid magic, I might've been of some assistance rather than standing here with tear-stained cheeks as I clutch the chest of the man I'd failed. I can only hope to the gods that we didn't lose anyone else during these moments I've stolen, when I have been too heartbroken and weak and afraid to move...

Footsteps approach almost as soon as the battle ends, and I back away from the shadowcreature Ryven has become to stand protectively between him and the Crusaders searching for me. For him.

When they breach the trees surrounding us, most stare in horror as they behold him, their faces dripping with black demon blood, necro-ink running down their noses. They raise their shadowsteel weapons, and Ryven growls in my ear, a noise that reminds me that not even my druid magic can keep his more primal instincts tame.

"Stop!" I throw my arms out, ignoring the scathing, disbelieving looks I receive from each of the Crusaders who have emerged. "As long as you do not attempt to harm him, he will not hurt you."

I meet every one of their gazes, silently challenging any of them to dare try anything otherwise. The few I don't know very well watch me like I'm mad, which is understandable because I can't say I would be doing anything different if put in their shoes. Until today, until just *now*, I never knew such a thing as commanding a demon was possible. In the short time I'd spent with Ryven and my aunt Imryll—two of the only druids I know, aside from my sister Kalli and my cousin Alphonse—neither of them had ever mentioned such a power. I would've thought something like that would've come up, especially as Ryven and I faced a giant shadowspider, the lunar hydra, and countless other demons of the Shadowthorn. In fact, it doesn't make sense why it hadn't. If he had been capable of commanding any demon he came across, or even just the ones who had been druids before—the behemoths

LOST

THE CLAIMED COAST, THE FORMER SHADOWTHORN

We follow Imryll in silence as our path through the woods becomes hazy. At least, I'm told it does. While I have no trouble seeing the thick oak tree trunk and the daffodils and hyacinths that have started to bloom as the season has finally shifted out of the miserable cold and into the refreshing welcome of spring, the rest of our party protests that the air is too thick to see through. The Crusaders squint as if they're walking through smoke. They curse as they bumble into each other, trip over errant roots and rocks, and rile one another up with their suspicions.

By their descriptions, the forest has disappeared behind a gray film of the unknown. The haze is worse than the darkness that had even shrouded the Blighted lands, preventing everyone from seeing much farther than the reach of their own arms. Everyone, except the druids, it would seem.

Alphonse, Imryll, Kalli, and I walk unhindered, guiding the blinded Crusaders along. They act as if they are cattle being led to the slaughter, but without the ability to see where they need to go, they follow us regardless.

We form a chain, two by two, and each person rests one hand upon the shoulder of the person ahead of them.

Fear spiders up my spine at Inigo's clamped hand. His grip is too rigid, too daunting, as if he might yank me back and pummel my face at any moment.

I remind myself that if that was truly something he wanted to do, he'd likely wait for a better time than now. It is unlike a predator to act when they do not have the advantage. No, if he plans to come for me—and I have no doubt that he doesn't—it will be when no one is near, when I have no awareness of him, and when he can strike and take me down without any chance of using my magic to interfere.

Through the trees ahead, something glints. The density of the forest makes it difficult to tell what it is, but I've spent enough time in the woods and around water to recognize the reflection of the sun off a lake's surface. Only, if my calculations are correct, it's no lake we're walking toward, but the expansive and mostly unchartered Varenholm Ocean.

Even before the Shadowthorn began to spread and the Great Rift happened, it's my understanding that few fishermen and explorers traversed these waters. The ships that set sail on the southeastern shores rarely returned. Terrifying stories of cannibalistic sirens, sea monsters as large as the ocean itself, and torrential, unrelenting storms kept most away from the treacherous ocean.

I wonder if that was part of the druids' spell too, if any of those stories held merit or if they were rumors spread to keep humans away from the Leviathan resting here.

As the clay shore on the other side of the trees becomes clearer, I realize it won't be long before I find out.

Imryll is the first to break through the thin trees, the sun shining down atop her silver head of hair, tresses glistening like a frozen waterfall down her back. The Crusaders appear to be blinded all the way up until they break through the clearing too, squinting and shielding their eyes from the bright sun overhead as they regain their lost sense of sight so suddenly.

who don't fit the mold of typical demons—then why hadn't he done so?

Sympathy cracks through Silver's expression, Güthric's too, as they realize who the shadowcreature is behind me.

Fox, however, seems to be the only one who isn't some shade of horror or sympathy. She smirks at me with a kind of impressed bemusement that almost makes me forget her betrayal of me and my sister, and convinces me I can trust her again. Almost.

But it's Dimitri's gaze, sharp as daggers, that bores into me. Shadows and warning flicker over him, as if he is seconds away from saving me from my foolish self like he has done so many times in our lives. It's a role he'd played quite often when we were children; my sense of danger and judgment had always seemed a bit...off. I was grateful every time he caught my wrist moments before I would plummet from the tree we were climbing, and for his cautionary words to watch my step as I walked by a piping hot pot of wax.

But I'm no longer that blundering, careless girl. My decisions are based on intuition, sure, but they're no less grounded in reason than his are. It's not a monster at my back, jaw unlatched and ready to devour; it's Ryven. A shadowcreature, I'll admit, but one who I appear to be in control of thanks to my power. And in this, in matters of druid magic, I might know very little, but I still know more than Dimitri, and I know that as long as I command the shadowcreature that Ryven has become, we have nothing to fear from him.

As the Crusaders finish congregating, stopping a safe enough distance back, my aunt Imryll is the only one to come forward. But she doesn't move as if she thinks there is a threat. She stares between the two of us with the wide-eyed wonderment of a scholar.

She looses a breath, a hand moving airily to reach out for Ryven before coming back to press against her thin lips. "You...

have spoken to him." A faint smile breaks through. "Miraculous."

Kalli appears at my aunt's side not a moment later. Her hand clutches a shadowsteel short sword, slick with inky blood, that she must've plucked from a fallen Crusader. She uses her shoulder to wipe at an equally dark smudge on her cheek before addressing our aunt. "Is that possible?"

Her wary, piercing gaze never leaves Ryven. If she distrusted him before, this new demon form will be even more challenging for her to accept.

Imryll shakes her head, another breathy laugh easing from her throat. "If you had asked me yesterday, I'd have told you it wasn't." My aunt continues approaching Ryven and I, her hand held out as if she'd like to touch the shadowbat's nose, but even in her wonderment, not even she is brave enough to risk it. "I told your mother her children would make for strong druids. An Elder's line is never weak."

"That's what this is? Elder magic?" I ask.

She tilts her head, wincing a little as she assesses him. "Perhaps. Or it might be a symptom of your previous predicament."

I frown, unsure of her meaning, but my sister is quick to follow.

"So, since Halira was blighted, she can now talk to demons?"

My aunt simply says, "Perhaps."

Behind us, bushes rustle. Feet pound in the nearby distance as more demons race toward the commotion. Despite the Shadowthorn falling, apparently the demons that resided there remain. I suppose only time will tell how long they can survive without the darkness to hide in, or if they have now been unleashed upon all of Arcathain. Maybe the Shadowthorn had been a tether, but now that it's gone, they are no longer shackled to the darkness.

Even though I'm fairly certain that if they found us I might be able to command them just as I have Ryven, I have enough uncertainty in my ability that I don't think it's worth the risk.

Turning to Ryven, my gaze hardens as it falls on the shadowbat, and I try something truly bold. "Find the demons who are coming for us and send them away. Make sure no others come." Then, just before he can take off, the heaviness of fear anchors in my belly. There is still much I have to learn about being a druid and commanding a demon, and I don't know how long my hold on Ryven will last once we are apart. But the demons thrash closer by the second, and I'm afraid I have no other option but to trust my instincts that our bond will hold. Still, I add, "Return to me when you're finished."

The shadowbat voices his understanding with a raspy shriek before leaping above the trees. It's not long before his terrifying roar shakes the earth as I hear him land before the throng of approaching demons and challenges them to stand down. I'm too busy keeping my vigilant eyes on the trees he's disappeared behind, biting my nails to the quick, to notice the fear and awe with which the rest of the group is watching me.

"What have you done?" Dimitri's voice looms behind me like an avalanche waiting to bury me.

I scoff, whirling on my friend. "You say that like I've done something wrong." Before my trembling can become noticeable, I clench my fists and cut the space between us. "What I've done just saved our lives and is about to save more."

He points with his chin behind me. "That *thing* can't be trusted. It's a *demon*, Halira. I can learn to accept that not all magic is evil. I can even learn to accept that druids share this realm with us—even if I'd never heard of them before that horrible day you fled Arcathain." Hurt, or something like true pain, flashes behind his eyes, and Dimitri does nothing to curb it. "But do not expect me to believe that demons are anything but evil. They have hunted our people for generations. They terrorize villages. They eat children, and the elderly. Brothers and sisters. They killed your parents."

He strikes the chord he meant to pluck, but he has no idea just how right and wrong he is about *this* demon.

My finger darts toward the direction of Ryven's snarling. "That *thing* was a person. He was a…a friend. If he hadn't given me the breath of life, if the demon toxin had been allowed to spread deeper into my heart—into *my* soul—that is exactly what would've become of me too. Would you still want to kill *that thing* if it were me?"

"Yes."

There is no pause, no hesitation. Duty has been forged into Dimitri's bones since the day he was born, and he will never apologize for it. But a muscle twitches in his sharp jaw.

"I would," he continued. "Because that's what I've been trained to do. It's my job to defend Arcathain from demons. To protect our people from dying in a bloodbath if those creatures went unchecked."

I shake my head, slowly inching away from him. But the longer I spend in the comfort of my own mind, the less shocked and horrified I am by his response. Of course, he would feel no moral obligation to do anything different. The principles of a Crusader are simple: kill demons; end Qaeus' reign. Few would likely be able to find the nuance between the right and wrong they've been taught, let alone someone as rigid as Dimitri.

"We have a bigger problem here," Alphonse reminds us, using the cape of a nearby Crusader to wipe away the slick dark blood from the sword in his hand. It's strange to see him with another weapon, and I wonder who among the fallen he plucked it from to defend himself and his people. "We have a Primordial to contend with. It marches toward our citizens as we speak. We came to the druids for answers. Did they provide any?"

A shadowcreature crashes through the spindly branches of the canopy in a gust of wings and fury before I can respond. In unison, we whip around, the Crusaders' drawing their weapons and readying to strike while I feel for the currents of wind around me. But the moment my gaze snags on the two familiar russet eyes before us, I hold up my hand and stop everyone before they can lunge.

Ryven's eyes dart around us, as if he can still sense danger nearby. Processing his caution, his readiness, reminds me that there are more than just demons who roam these woods. The night he and I spent in the Eyve, the howls that sounded from the forest as long as the moon was in the sky had ricocheted through my bones and embedded themselves in my night-mares. Night will come again soon, and not even Ryven, with all the prowess of a shadowcreature, will be able to protect us from the horrors that will flood this forest then.

"Well?" A particularly gruff Crusader sneers from the crowd. The disdain he casts my way makes my skin crawl. There's no doubt that if we were alone right now, he'd have no guilt about ringing his sausage fingers around my druid neck until I gasped for my last breath. His lip pulls back, a scar running jagged just above his mouth, twisting his scornful expression lopsided. "Did we come all this way for nothing or did these *druids* give us something useful?"

I resist the urge to glance back at Ryven, forcing myself to instead hold his stare. I will not allow him to intimidate me. The Halira who cowered before bullies is gone. "They did not. They do not know how to imprison or slay the Primordial. Or at least, they were unwilling to share."

The large man scoffs.

Dimitri shoots a menacing glare at the Crusader, arms crossed as he steps between us. "That's enough, Inigo."

"Yes." Alphonse waves his hand. "Agreed. Bravado is so pedestrian." My cousin strides before the group as if he was never even gone, as if he's been general all this time. He slips so effortlessly back into the role of their leader, that I wonder if any of the growth I've witnessed from him these past days has been real. But just before he faces them, he flashes me a private look, one that allows his mask to slip, just long enough for me to see that he is still the same Alphonse I've come to know. "If the druids were unable to provide useful information regarding the Primordial's weaknesses, then it is time we return to Arcathain, to the Capital. We will need to warn the Magistrate. At the very least, we must warn the people of the border towns that the Primordial is coming…"

The suggestion catapults me deep into my thoughts. Although Alphonse's concern for Arcathain is understandable, returning now would accomplish nothing. We've gained no new insight or advantage. The one thing we thought could kill a Primordial—our beloved shadowsteel weapons—don't work. My axe didn't kill Qaeus, it just reunited her with the Primordial Khunas' soul and made her stronger, more formidable than ever. We have no way of killing her. That doesn't mean there isn't one though, but it means we have to keep searching for either a way to kill her and end the Primordials once and for all, or learn to contain her until we can.

As Alphonse drones on—he and Eparah strategizing the safest route back to civilization—I fall deeper into my thoughts and what I've learned these past weeks.

No one in Arcathain knows the druids exist. Even in the history books I read in the library at Nigh, the druids were not even mentioned once, whereas nearly extinct creatures like the sirens were. I tap my chin, mulling that piece of information over, but nothing clicks.

The discovery of the ineffectiveness of shadowsteel snag on my thoughts next. As Crusaders, we were trained to believe that any one of our shadowsteel weapons could kill Qaeus. But not even my axe, a weapon imbued with the power of a

Primordial, could kill her, let alone the measly swords that the other Crusaders are armed with. Even the spear that struck down the Primordial Khaymus would likely only serve to invigorate Qaeus, and further exacerbate her strength, her darkness, even her size, judging from the memory she shared with me from when the Primordials first rose from the Pits of Bagamore. They'd been smaller then, closer in size to Güthric than the behemoth thing Qaeus has become.

The birth of the Primordials is another conundrum that racks through me, one that even the druids don't seem to have knowledge of, or at least Ryven didn't. Other than recognizing them on the mural, he hadn't otherwise mentioned them, nor did he seem to know anything about the image and how the Primordials were connected to them. The Pits of Bagamore hadn't even been referenced much in any of the books I'd read while studying in the library of Nigh, but I'd been made aware of them once the druid Elders told us that one of the Primordial weapons resided there.

I nearly curse out loud, seconds away from screaming in frustration and interrupting the focused conversation Alphonse is having with the others. There are too many holes in the information I have to make sense of anything, let alone to forge a path forward. Even the things I once thought to be true I can no longer believe. There is no way to determine what's truth from lie, what's important from a rabbit hole.

But one thing stands out above all else: everything keeps pointing back to the Pits of Bagamore. The mural found on the wall bordering the Forgotten Forest of Eyve, the shadowsteel spear that is believed to have been the weapon used to slay the Primordial Khaymus. The Pits of Bagamore were on the side of the continent that the mages stole when they fled the Blight and abandoned the rest of us. It clearly holds some significance. If the Primordials came from there, it's possible they can be returned as well. Maybe all of the evil that they've brought to the land, the demons that are likely bounding over the disappeared Shadowthorn boundary and terrorizing villages as we speak, can be sent back too.

Even the evil that's seeped into Ryven.

"You've been quiet." Dimitri's voice is low, edged in concern. With one arm crossed, he caresses the stubble on his chin, a shadow of hair that must've grown since he last left the Castle of Nigh on a mission to infiltrate the Wardens and retrieve Alphonse. "What are you not telling us?" he asks at last.

Alphonse can't resist the urge to hear what I might have to say so he falls silent, the others soon following suit, even if some of them—including Inigo—initially grumble about it.

"Yes, cousin. Please do share with the class."

My throat is no longer a hollow tube of slick muscles, but a tightly bound rope that's so rough it shreds the back of my tongue as I attempt to swallow. I am no one to these people. Less than no one. I am a fugitive in many of their eyes, someone who had turned on her country and all Arcathainians to flee her own "crimes." What reason would any of them have to listen to me, let alone follow along with what I'm tempted to suggest?

Despite fearing their disregard, their palpable distrust, I swallow hard and force my lips to cooperate. "I was thinking what a grave mistake it would be to return to the Capital now."

Inigo sneers, the sound guttural and weighted with disdain. But the scar that cuts through his lip and reaches up to his nose twitches as his thick shoulders begin to bob with laughter. "Right. And I suppose we're just supposed to take the word of a criminal? A deceitful magic-user? I'd die before I ever took orders from the likes of you."

I clench my jaw to keep the hateful venom from spewing from my lips. Though Inigo bears no physical resemblance to Alphonse, there's something about the hatred in his eyes that smacks me back in time, to those moments when I cowered at my cousin's feet. He'd made me feel so small, so insignificant, so fragile. But I am none of those things anymore, nor was I ever.

Dark clouds roll in overhead, an ominous breeze accompanying them as I reach out to my power. Inigo thinks he can intimidate and belittle me? He thinks *he* holds any power over me? Then let me prove him wrong, just as I did with Alphonse.

The Crusaders surrounding me shift nervously, but despite the flicker of fear in his eyes, Inigo remains intently focused, planted in place like the warrior he is, the one who was trained to face down a horde of demons, even if it meant his life.

Behind me, Ryven looses a low snarl, a not-so-subtle but very effective reminder of what he would like to do if it weren't for my hold on him. There might be something more there too, a certain level of protectiveness that's spurred by the tether between us. Or perhaps by the connection our human selves experienced before...

As grateful as I am that he would defend me though, I wish he wouldn't all the same. His menacing nature and my ill-timed display of magic will only crystallize the negative way that these Crusaders view me and therefore any magic-user or demon they encounter. It's no wonder the humans hated the mages; soon they'll hate druids too, because magic, as it turns out, is terrifyingly powerful, especially to those who cannot wield it for themselves.

Dimitri's arms fly out, his palms slamming into Inigo's chest and knocking him back a step before I can blink. "Let her speak. She knows something she hasn't yet shared," he growls. His irritation is still palpable when he turns his attention to me. "What are you suggesting?"

Whether intentionally or not, my spine lengthens until I possess the intimidating but wise nature I think a true leader should possess. It reminds me of the way Kalli would enter a room, and though I'll never be quite as imposing as she, I lean into that idea and do my best to embody her. I have to. The truth is, these people *will* die if they choose not to follow me. All of Arcathain will be lost if Qaeus is not stopped, and we will not find the answers to stop her in the Capital.

But convincing any of them of that won't be easy.

"We will find no answers in Arcathain," I argue, shifting uncomfortably on my feet and already losing some of Kalli's steel I tried infusing in my spine. "We know that Qaeus is unleashed. We know that she is far more terrifying and deadly than any demon we've ever faced. And we know that shadow-steel weapons will not subdue her—"

"We know none of this!" Inigo barks, pushing past Dimitri and folding his bulky arms. His dark eyes, shaded by a thick brow, bore into mine. "All I know is you went into those shadows, and the Primordial soon followed. Am I supposed to take the word of someone who released Qaeus upon Arcathain after her own imprisonment and treason? Am I supposed to believe that the weapons that we've been trained to use against the Primordial are suddenly useless, just because some harlot says so?"

"Watch it." Out of the corner of my eye, I notice Dimitri's fists tighten, his jaw bite down on itself. He jerks to confront the man, but my stride is swifter.

I look up at the disgruntled Crusader with an air of coy indifference. "If you truly believe that, then go. No one is forcing you to stay here. In fact, if you don't want what's best for Arcathain, if you can't set aside your petty, childish grievances to do what's best for mankind, then no one wants you here. Only the brave and dutiful should remain."

Inigo's rotund cheeks spark a shade of red that's almost violet. His chest heaves with the unsteady rhythm of an off-beat drum, and I prepare myself to duck or leap backward from whatever attack he's about to throw my way. While I somehow have become quite capable of handling myself in a fight with a demon, hand-to-hand combat with humans is still something I still struggle with, and the only strategy I know how to use confidently is to avoid being struck to the ground, giving myself enough time to summon my lightning or wind.

Inigo holds his ground though, his gaze drifting to the unwavering stillness of his comrades, waiting for any of them to turn around and leave me here where I stand. Something volatile screams through the glower he shoots them when they don't.

"No?" I ask before he can burst in another outrage. "Very well. Then I suggest you listen and heed my warning. I alone entered the ward protecting the exposed heart of Qaeus. I alone know what occurred in there. And believe me, I understand your tendency toward paranoia, but I assure you now is not the time for it. Lives are at stake and I am not your enemy. I never have been. We trained as Crusaders to defend Arcathain. Think of me what you will, but I want to end Qaeus and restore peace to our continent as much as you."

Inigo opens his mouth to speak, but Alphonse circles closer, his hands clasped at the small of his back. "What do you propose we do then?"

My back straightens, some of my confidence returning to me as I realize the support I already have. Despite our tumultuous childhoods, Alphonse and I are on the same side now. Dimitri, too, despite having abandoned me just a few days or weeks ago, is choosing to stand by me now. Silver and Güthric followed me into the Shadowthorn, and though we were separated for a time, they're still here, looking to me for guidance.

"We only have two choices," I tell the group, speaking from the pit of my belly so that I'm loud enough that everyone can hear me. "We either need to find a new way to kill the Primordial—something more effective than a shadowsteel weapon—or we need a way to contain her." My voice wavers, but I steel myself for the absurd suggestion that's about to leave my lips, and the outcry that will surely follow. "The only people who have done either of those things are living on Illashore."

The Crusaders erupt.

There are so many doubtful, wicked, angered cries that I can hardly tell one from the next. They swell and coalesce like an ocean storm, the waves of their protests thunderous and raging and swelling against me until I start to drown in them.

"She'll lure us to our deaths!"

"She's just as bad as the mages!"

"She can't be trusted! She tried killing the general once. She'll strike again."

Alphonse takes another calm stride closer. When he holds his hand up, the Crusaders quiet, eager to hear their general put this druid—this deserter, this fugitive—in her place.

But instead of addressing the collective, he pivots so his back is toward them, speaking so softly that I have to lean in to hear him. "You have strategically left out that what you are truly after is a cure for your blighted lover."

I flinch, the truth of his words something I'm not even sure I've admitted to myself yet. But it is the hope I'm holding onto. The Elders might not have known how to cure Ryven now that the breath of life is gone, but that doesn't mean the mages don't.

Alphonse leans closer, his teeth snapped in a tight smile. "You would ask these people to risk their lives simply for a cure no one knows exists?"

"This isn't *just* about Ryven, Alphonse. What I said was true. The mages helped Arcathain kill the other Primordials and they built the wall that kept Qaeus contained for years. They know things we don't, or at least have access to magic that could help. Besides…Qaeus showed me where she and the other Primordials were created—the Pits of Bagamore, a place that is, according to the Elders, still on the continent of Illashore. That place holds significance. I don't know how it could help, but I think it could. Qaeus is too strong to be defeated simply by shadowsteel and—"

"And you know this for certain?" One of his dark eyebrows climbs up his forehead.

"I do." I shudder at the memory of my shadowsteel axe primed to slice Qaeus' heart in two, only for horrifying claws and knobby limbs to reach out from the blackened heart and the Primordial Qaeus to tear out of her vessel into her true form. "The soul that had been trapped inside my axe made Qaeus stronger. Maybe our shadowsteel weapons—the ones that weren't containing Primordial souls—were able to slay the Primordials a long time ago, but Qaeus is too powerful now. It would be like…like trying to fell a deer by notching a rock instead of an arrow—"

"Which can be done," Dimitri says, appearing beside the two of us on silent feet. His fingers drag over his unshaven chin, and he shrugs. "It would be difficult, but not impossible."

"Piss on a mage!" I say through gritted teeth, losing my patience. "So, my analogy is inaccurate. I'm not just talking about something being difficult." I glare at him, and my awareness of the hostility of the others awakens. Inigo isn't the only one watching me like he's ready to attack the moment my guard is down. I speak louder so that they can all hear. "None of you saw the mural. You didn't talk to the Elders. You weren't there with Qaeus. You cannot begin to understand the sheer power the Primordial possesses now, the limitless depths of her evil. No mere human—no druid, for that matter—is going to destroy her! But rest assured, if Qaeus is allowed to continue on her current path, all of Arcathain will be lost."

The Crusaders glance among each other, their gazes flicking to Alphonse periodically as he taps a finger atop his lips and considers me. Judging from the hungry determination in his eyes, I'm fairly certain he has already decided to join me, either out of loyalty or because few Crusaders would be able to resist the promise of glory, of ending the Primordial's reign.

But still, the others remain cautious, unable to see past my magic to be able to hear the logic in what I'm saying. The hatred Arcathainians have toward the mages, and therefore anyone who possesses magic, runs too deep.

Fortunately, it isn't the entire group I needed to persuade, but Alphonse alone.

He sweeps his long arms out, swiveling to address the concerned Crusaders with a voice that was made for politics. "Devout champions of Arcathain. You alone bore witness to the end of the Shadowthorn, to the end of the Blight that plagued our farmlands and made our villages uninhabitable, overrun with demons and fiends who hunted your friends, your families. Your names shall already be written in history among the Crusaders who rid the Broken Realms of one of the darkest threats to ever face us. The bards will write hymns and lyrics of what transpired here today.

"Alas, they will not erect statues or name cities after the ones who simply witnessed the fall of the Shadowthorn. Nay, such monuments and testaments to the triumphs of man will be reserved for the fighters who slay the last living Primordial, the very being that has evaded every Crusader for centuries. And *you* were there the day it awakened."

Alphonse slams his boot into the ground.

Thump.

"Will you run back to Nigh and prepare for the slaughter?"

Thump.

"Will you say, *I've done enough,* and return to the Capital to become fodder to the war that awaits on the horizon?"

Thump.

By now, the Crusaders start to look alive. They shift on their feet where they stand, cautiously glancing to one another as if to gauge each other's commitment against their own.

"Will you fail the vows you made when you entered the Castle of Nigh?"

Thump.

"Will you fail the Crusaders who fell before you?"

Thump.

A few of the Crusaders slam their fists against their chests. "*No, sir!*" they answer.

"Are you afraid of facing Qaeus?"

Thump.

"*No, sir!*" More join in, the response growing more forceful.

"Then tell me," Alphonse bellows, "are you the protectors of Arcathain?"

"*Yes, sir!*"

"Will you do what is necessary to defend our people?"

"*Yes, sir!*"

"Will you be by my side as I slay the Primordial Qaeus?"

"*Yes, sir!*"

Every Crusader chants it now, even the ones nursing wounds from the brief battle, the ones who will shortly die from the demon toxin invading their bloodstreams. Even Dimitri pumps his fist into the air and answers. Even Sai, who the Crusaders left for dead in Ashenvale. Even Inigo.

Even me.

"Of one country!" Alphonse shouts.

The Crusaders reply with bone-chilling unison: "*Of one blood!*"

"We are Crusaders!" Alphonse bellows, pumping his fist with the sword into the air. "We know no fear! We know no bounds! We will stop at nothing until the Primordial is in the ground, and Halira will help us."

The whooping fizzles like he's just doused the crowd with a bucket of ice-cold water.

He drops his sword, voice quieting as he implores them. "Hear her, Crusaders. If I can forgive her—if she can forgive *me*

—if the two of us can work together for a common good, then I know you can come to terms with this alliance as well. We are not enemies in this fight. We are allies."

My heart flutters. For much of our lives, I've hoped at best to find indifference between Alphonse and I. But to have arrived to actual harmony, comradery, even alliance? It's surreal. I might not even believe it were true if it weren't for the hand he clamps down on my shoulder, and the look of support he flashes me when our gazes connect.

To my surprise, the Crusaders around us begin nodding. It's begrudging, of course. Not even one of Alphonse's speeches would be able to undo generations of hate and fear that have been ingrained in Arcathainians. But it's a start.

Bowing ever so slightly, Alphonse holds out his arm for me.

I'm so stunned by the turn of events, by the fact that Alphonse is standing by my side and these Crusaders are willing to at least hear me out, that there's a moment where I don't know what to do. I stand there like a fish out of water, my mouth bobbing silently and making a fool of me. But someone steps closer behind me, warmth exuding from the large body that belongs to a monster but contains the soul of a friend. It's all the reminder I need of what I am fighting for.

I clear my throat. "As I was saying, the answers we seek aren't in Arcathain. But they might be in Illashore. Our best chance at ending Qaeus' reign is for us to go to Illashore, to seek out the knowledge that the mages took with them when they fled."

"And how exactly do you propose we do that?" Inigo snorts his disapproval. The hefty weight of him shifts from one hip to the other as he folds his arms over his bulging chest. "Illashore isn't exactly a hop and a skip away. It's across the entire bloody ocean. Should we all expect a ride from your new demon pet?"

Sheepishly, I glance over my shoulder to the shadowbat. Although Ryven has always been large enough to haul me into the air when necessary, even now that he has completed his transition, I'm not sure how long he'd be able to carry me, not to mention a small legion of Crusaders. Especially not across the entire Varenholm Ocean. Even if he could fit two or three of us in his much larger arms, he'd still have to take a dozen trips just to transport every last one of us, and there's no telling how long that would take considering I have no reference for the distance between Arcathain's coasts and Illashore's. Never mind the fact that I wouldn't trust half of these people and the malicious fear in their hearts to be alone with him anyway.

Surprising us all, Imryll strides forth, a confident glint in her eyes. "If you are certain you must go to Illashore, there is a better way to travel than in the clutches of a demon, and I can show you the way."

THE FORMER SHADOWTHORN

"W-what are you talking about?" I stammer, folding and unfolding my arms as if they've never been more out of place than from where they're attached to my torso. Worst yet is knowing that the more confusion I show now, and the more disjointed I acknowledge we are, the easier it will be for the Crusaders to fall back into their skepticism. But my questions can't be helped. Not when so much rides on them. "Why would you know a way to Illashore? I thought you said the druids didn't get along with the mages."

Imryll's chin lifts. "We did not. However, that does not mean we left our enemies to their own devices without keeping a wary eye on them."

Dimitri waves his arm, indicating around him to the gathered Crusaders and misfits. "I think I speak for everyone when I say the time for being cryptic has long since passed. If you have something you'd like to share, please do so."

My aunt's gaze whips to Dimitri with palpable disdain. Were it not for the dozen onlookers, and the earth-shaking roar that sounds in the distance as the sun sets and the behemoths awaken, I have no doubt that she would've struck him right where he stood, summoning her vines to hang him from the trees until he begged to be released.

"Please, Imryll," I say, a gentleness to my tone. "What is it you know?"

She huffs at Dimitri but returns her attention to Alphonse and I. "We sent envoys to Illashore, frequent at first, though I'll admit once the Shadowthorn came, our means of doing so were compromised. But for as long as we were able to, we kept watch on the mages and assessed their intentions."

"How?" Alphonse asks. "How did the druid envoys travel to Illashore?"

"After the wall fell, before the Shadowthorn consumed it, there was a sacred place called the Claimed Coast."

My face scrunches. "Claimed by what?"

"I've never heard of such a place," Alphonse says. "In Arcathain?"

Her head dips in reply. "That's because it was kept hidden from Arcathainians for fear of what your kind would do if you stumbled upon what resides there."

Swallowing the dryness in my throat, I ask again, "Claimed by what? What resides there?"

Imryll's keen gaze pierces mine, but she continues as if she hasn't heard me. "If ever a human were to wander too close to the Claimed Coast, there were spells meant to keep the area guarded. Some of them would summon a pack of wolves, others would make the forest so thick with overgrowth that it became impenetrable without knowing the correct path. Each spell prevented any non-druid from reaching the Claimed Coast."

"Why not spell it like they spelled the wall between Arcathain and the Forgotten Forest of Eyve?" Kalli asks. "When non-druids near that boundary, they don't trigger wolves and overgrowth."

"Because that spell is concentrated on a single point," our

aunt snaps. "On one hole in a wall. The magic sheltering the Claimed Coast spans acres of land. No magic is powerful enough to veil an area of that size without losing potency over time, or need I remind you of what became of the original spell the mages imbued the wall with? The one that fell within only a matter of decades."

Darkness roils inside me, her sharp tone one I'm no longer accustomed to stomaching. But my sister appears unfazed, simply nodding her understanding and leaning into her next line of questioning.

"So why forbid humans to enter?" she asks, eyes narrowing as they always do when she hasn't quite yet cracked the puzzle she's working on. "If it was through the Claimed Coast that the druids kept watch on the mages, what threat could humans pose to them? Were they honestly afraid that the Arcathainians would ask to accompany them on one of their spies' ships?"

"*Ships?*" Imryll's brow hikes to her white hairline. "No one said anything about ships. The Claimed Coast was kept sheltered from the humans because we feared what they'd do to the creature that resides there."

Murmurs sweep across the people I've come to trust—Silver and Güthric, Alphonse, Dimitri, my sister, my uncle, Sai—but a more alarmed outcry spurs from the rest.

"*Creature? What kind of creature?*"

"*Is it a demon?*"

Inigo's baritone voice booms over them all. "If such a beast was kept from us, I can only surmise that it's one we would've wanted dead? Tell me, does this *creature* feast on humans, as well?"

If he meant to be intimidating, the effect falls short on my aunt. Whether he knows it or not, she's a woman who can command the very forest around us. I've only glimpsed her powers a handful of times, but my imagination is ignited by the flare of challenge that sparks behind her glacial eyes.

A tree nearby creeks, but Inigo is too busy standing triumphantly, foolishly believing he's bested her, to even fear that she might be seconds away from felling it upon him.

To my surprise, and slight disappointment, she doesn't. Instead, Imryll merely levels him with a single deadly look. "Only on those who mean it harm."

Inigo sneers, stained teeth flashing below his contorted lip.

Since nothing good or productive can come from anything else that might leave his lips, I thrust myself forward before he has a chance to breathe the heinous retort he's formulating.

"And for those of us who don't mean the creature harm; it will take us to Illashore?"

She nods, her silken, moonbeam hair falling past her shoulders. "It should, yes. Granted, it has been many years since the druids have encountered the creature. Once the Shadowthorn expanded to the coastline, we were cut off from the Leviathan, and so there is no telling if it still lives or if it has moved on—"

"Hang on," Fox blurts. I almost hadn't even noticed her from where she'd kept herself nestled behind the other Crusaders. But now she steps forward, her auburn hair seeming to glow in the dying light of day. "The *Leviathan*?" she snorts. "The beast that prowls the Varenholm Ocean, sinking any ship that should dare venture too far out? It's nothing more than a myth."

A loud crack sounds, rustling the trees and making the crispy leaves at the ends of their branches crackle against each other. I glance behind me to see Güthric, fist-deep into one poor tree in particular, his chest heaving with restraint. Beside him, Silver watches him, as pale as the moon as she assesses how to approach him. Eventually, with a timid tilt of her head, she reaches out a hand and gently rests it on his hulking shoulder. He flinches at the touch, as if he'd been so consumed by whatever dark place he'd withdrawn to that he hadn't even seen her there.

Finally, abashedly, he withdraws his fist, turning to the rest of us with solemn quiet as he rubs his knuckles. "Not myth."

The group remains quiet for a breath. If their thoughts are anything like mine, they're busy wondering why mention of the Leviathan would bring about such a profoundly volatile response from Güthric.

But before anyone can muster the courage to ask him to explain, Imryll speaks. "Your friend is right. The Leviathan is real. The only question is whether it has survived the Blight."

"Why wouldn't it have?" Dimitri folds his arms. "The Shadowthorn stopped at the coastlines. It never infected the oceans, nor the lakes or the rivers. It stayed on the land."

"Be that as it may, there is no guarantee that the Blight left the Leviathan unaffected. When the dark Shadowthorn first began its spread, did Arcathain not see a swift decline in many of their woodland species, and a sudden insurgence of others? While predators lost access to their prey as animals scattered across the realm, the fortunate ones thrived in unforeseen numbers. Some plant species are now extinct, while new ones sprouted from the tainted soil in their stead. We cannot presume to know the far-reaching impacts of such a devastating event."

I turn to look at Ryven, at the creature he's become. Though the stain on the land has rescinded, whatever toxin had infiltrated living beings has certainly remained. I shudder at the thought of what the Blight could've done to a menacing creature such as the Leviathan, when it has turned druids into formidable monsters.

"So where do we find this Leviathan if it survived?" I ask at last, trying not to dwell too much on all the things we still don't know or understand. "Where is the Claimed Coast located?"

Her chin lifts. "There is a peninsula to the southwest of here. No more than a few days' journey away."

"A few *days*?" Inigo barks, scowling between the others. "We don't have a few days. The Primordial will be upon Arcathain by then. Those people need us now!"

Adrien steps toward the Crusader to pat his shoulder, a condescending albeit slightly sympathetic smile tugging the edge of his lips. "I hate to break it to you, but they're talking a lot longer than *a few days*. If we're to travel to Illashore, it'll be…well—" A disbelieving laugh catches in his throat, and he stares back at Imryll expectantly. "I don't actually presume to know, but I imagine someone here does."

She dips her head, low and respectful. "On the Leviathan, it would take no longer than a few weeks."

"A few *weeks*!"

The cries of outrage come from more than just Inigo now. The Crusaders bicker among themselves, riling one another up as they discuss how cowardly it would be to abandon the people now, how gullible they'd have to be to allow themselves to be lured willingly to a beast like the Leviathan, how dead they'd be if the Magistrate ever learned that their unit had chosen to pay a visit to the mages of Illashore instead of standing to fight and defend their own country.

Dimitri's own outrage doesn't surprise me, but I do startle when I notice Eparah's, her brow bunched and nodding emphatically to Inigo and some of the others around him. Before everyone knew what I was—before *I* knew—if I had ever considered sharing my secret druid nature with anyone, it might've been with her. From the moment we'd met, she'd struck me as someone who could be trusted, someone willing to protect those under her wing, regardless of whether that choice would go against protocol.

But that was weeks ago now. That was before she'd discovered someone among her ranks who was suspected of being a mage, and before that same person had struck down and allegedly killed her general.

Even now that they know I'm only a druid—not a filthy

mage—even now that they've found Alphonse alive and breathing, I still catch the distrusting glances she casts my way, see her lips move as she whispers what I can only presume to be terrible ploys to end me to her fellow Crusaders.

Through the roar of grievance, it's nearly impossible to hear the howling of the shadowcreatures that continue to stalk closer, creeping out from the Labyrinth to prowl along the Eyve's borders now that night is upon us.

But one sound finally bellows over them all.

"That's enough!" Alphonse roars, slamming the heel of his boot into the gray soil.

The Crusaders' mouths clamp shut at the direct command from their superior.

"We have no other choice!" he continues, arms outstretched and parading before them. "Don't you see that? Our country, our people are as good as dead if we don't do this. We are the only Arcathainians with knowledge of the druids, of the inadequacy of shadowsteel against the Primordial, and we are the only ones who the secrets of the Leviathan are being shared with."

He rakes a hand through his long, dark hair. "I understand that the very idea of doing such a thing grinds against your every nerve—I can sympathize with the jarring sense that everything you thought you knew was wrong. Do you think that I, the Magistrate's son of all people, have not been raised to hate magic and demons as much as the rest of you?"

The begrudging whispers are not enough to prove they are convinced. Most of the Crusaders here came with Captain Eparah to retrieve Alphonse's body. Upon finding the map that led to Qaeus, they'd stayed in the Shadowthorn to avenge him and his cause. These are his most loyal subjects, and even they remain hesitant. Probably because he's so different from the man he'd been the last time they saw him. The Alphonse they knew wouldn't have been caught dead working alongside someone who could wield magic; he certainly wouldn't be suggesting anything other than leading an attack on the Primordial that they've been searching for and planning to kill for decades.

But Alphonse knows his Crusaders. He understands what inspires them, what fuels them, and he is not afraid to manipulate them if it means saving our country. Even though his viperous tongue has sliced through me more times than I can count, I've always known one of his strengths to be the way he wields words like a sword.

He stops his pacing, clasping his hands behind his back and standing tall as he looks out over them, over his underlings. "However," he begins. "Above all else, I was raised to win."

His voice, low and unwavering, sends a tremor through me. It does the same to most of the men and women standing before him, reminding us all of who he is and what he is supposed to represent to us. Even I, someone who has fled the country and has no intentions of ever returning to the Shadow Crusade, regard him with reverence—ironically, far more than I ever did while being a Crusader under his command.

"Qaeus cannot prevail," Alphonse insists. "And I see no other choice but to do as Halira suggests and seek *real* answers, ones that might stand a chance at helping us save our people by embarking on a quest to Illashore.

"Besides," he continues, speaking so quickly that he practically cuts himself off. "Why do you think the Magistrate was gathering the Crusaders and taking them to the Capital? This is privileged information that I shouldn't be sharing with you, but the Magistrate plans to attack Illashore. If anything, us arriving first and making ourselves ready for battle—not to mention finding the secret to killing the Primordial along the way—is exactly what our country needs from us. I beseech you, do not make me lead us in another invigorating chant. I'd hoped your loyalty to your country would last longer than a few minutes. Remember who you fight for, remember that the only way to protect your loved ones is by serving your country. And that now, the best way to do that is to follow my lead."

The Crusaders consider him quietly. Unnervingly so. The silence gives way to the screeching and yowling of the shadow-creatures that are dashing madly toward us. Behind me, Ryven snarls over his shoulder before leaping through the thick trees. The hands of the Crusaders dip down toward their shadow-steel weapons if they didn't have them in hand already, clutching them so tightly that if their arms were to be severed right now, I have no doubt that it would take three men to pry the weapons from their dead grasps.

Finally, Captain Eparah steps forward. Her gaze is fixed on Alphonse as she pounds a fist over the white phoenix insignia on her chest. "I do not trust the druids, nor do I trust this demon that Halira has allied herself with. But I have always trusted you, General Alphonse. If this is what you believe must be done, then I know it to be true. You would not lead us astray."

One by one, the rest of the Crusaders nod their agreement. But it's Inigo who Alphonse and I keep our eyes on. His neck remains stiff, his glower as cold as the catacombs of Nigh on a winter night.

"What about you?" Alphonse asks, striding toward the large Crusader and planting himself in his shadow as if he were his equal in size. "Will you come with us? Or is this where we say our farewells?"

Inigo's scarred lip twitches into something saccharine and hateful, but he manages to utter through his gritted teeth, "At your command, General."

Alphonse nods, once, either oblivious to the unspoken threat, or refusing to give it any more power than it deserves. "Good. Then, Imryll, if you would please tell us what we need to know."

"And I shall," Imryll replies.

But a powerful roar shakes the earth, cutting off her words and demanding the attention of all of us.

"We can't stay here," I say to Alphonse. "The creatures of the Labyrinth are coming and—"

"I know," he replies. "But to flee now would be foolish. It's far easier to defend a stationary camp than one that's on the run."

"What are you suggesting? That we just stay put as those... those *things* draw nearer?" I know it's not fair of me to call them that, considering that every one of them is very likely a druid who had an unfortunate encounter with a demon, but I can't bring myself to call them what they are either.

Imryll watches me with cool impassivity. "Unless you want to lead these people to their deaths, I see no other option. We stay the night here and we fight."

CREATURES OF DARKNESS

THE WALL, THE FORMER SHADOWTHORN

We walk Kalli back to the border of Eyve so that Imryll can send her across to gather the supplies we'll need for our journey. My sister is hesitant to leave us at first, but between the druids present in our company—myself, Imryll, Kalli, and Alphonse—my sister is the only one who isn't needed here. My aunt's expertise as a druid is too valuable, her skill with the elements too useful for us to let her leave before the shadowcreatures arrive. Even I have shown promise with some of my more offensive powers, whereas my sister is still mostly capable of utilizing her magic to shapeshift into her animal forms. And Alphonse, well, he has shown no signs of druid magic, but he is currently the only one whom the Crusaders will listen to, and it is imperative for the rest of the evening that they do exactly as instructed if we're all to make it through this alive.

Imryll makes quick work of summoning her vines and tree roots to offer us what little protection they can. They crawl up from the earth like rigid snakes, slithering down the stone wall that surrounds the Forgotten Forest of Eyve, and keeps the druids hidden from the rest of Arcathain. They won't stop the horde of monsters that terrorize the border at night, but hopefully they'll slow them enough for us to fight them back as they come.

It dawns on me now that without the Shadowthorn, I wonder how long it will be before a human stumbles over here and discovers the shattered wall between the Eyve and Arcathain for themselves. How long will it be before Arcathainians try to enter? How long will it take for them to discern the magic keeping anyone but someone of druid descent out?

Vines of ivy and wisteria arch over the heads of the Crusaders who are backed up against the towering wall. The foliage weaves as it reaches for the sky and climbs up the stone surface, forming a bramble hut large enough for the twenty or so of us to be sheltered through the night.

Unfortunately, not all of us will have the pleasure of resting though. Not for many hours. Fewer still will never know mortal rest again. Those who were slashed and bitten by demons earlier have already succumbed to the Blight and perished. No amount of bravery or druid healing magic could've saved their non-druid blood from the demon toxin once it reached their blood system.

As my aunt finishes creating the safe haven—a precaution we're hopeful we won't need to rely on, seeing as it's only created from vines and would likely be easily destroyed by any one of the behemoth shadowcreatures I saw in the Labyrinth—Imryll and I sprint in opposite directions, headed away from the Eyve and back into what had recently been the Shadowthorn.

Her goal is to create as many barriers as she can between us and the behemoth creatures. My goal is much the same, to slow the shadowcreatures down using my wind and lightning…if I can still muster any. Even if I can't, even if my reserves are tapped, neither of us are to fight the creatures directly. After all, these aren't *just* demons. They were druids once. Malicious and volatile as they may be now, killing them wouldn't be much different than killing a living person.

Of course, if it comes to that, we are both prepared to do what must be done.

At least, that's what I keep reassuring myself.

But as I send another cyclone of air at the shadowhound snarling and snapping its unhinged jaw at me, as my last surge of power sputters at my fingertips, all I can think of is Ryven. He is trapped inside a shadowcreature not too dissimilar to this one. Beneath his slick, obsidian skin, behind the eyes that are as dark as death itself, he's trapped inside. Who just might be stuck inside this shadowhound, clawing and screaming for their freedom? How long have they been condemned to such a fate? And when, if ever, will they find their release?

The bluish-black beast slams into a nearby tree trunk with a yelp that claws at my already fissured heart. Even if it appears to be nothing more than bones and shadows, something inside it was once a living person with hopes and fears, a family. It scrambles back to its legs, one of the only places on its body with any flesh on it. A sheen layer of something grotesque glistens along the muscles, making it look as if it has no flesh, only sinew and lean muscle that are as black as night.

The shadowhound bares its razor teeth, and I feel like if it could speak, it would be asking me what my final words will be. Because I can feel the lethargy sinking deep into my bones and burying me at the bottom of an ocean of exhaustion, and because I know once I reach the bottom, I'll have no more reserves of magic to pull from, I speak the words that I'd like to be remembered by:

"I don't want to hurt you," I try reassuring the shadowhound, cautiously crouching as I try both to catch my breath and convince it that I am not its enemy. Not unless I have to be.

My lungs strain against each inhale, as if the air around us has already been depleted. It's possible I've already overestimated my reserves. Without wind to knock the beast back, and without enough strength to summon lightning, I will have no choice but to use the shadowsteel saber that Fox insisted I take with me, her only weapon.

"Please, don't do this," I beg, my arms spreading wider, taking on a non-threatening stance. "Stand down and I won't have to hurt you."

The shadowhound blinks, almost looking human for the briefest of moments. It shakes its sleek, square head, its pointed ears lying flat against its black skull, and I swear its steps falter. In disbelief, my knees straighten while I watch the shadowhound in awe as it slowly bows its head, snarling the entire time, but casting its vicious red eyes away from me.

I balk before embarrassment floods through me. It's only been an hour or so since the Blight finished consuming Ryven, and I'd already forgotten what I'd been capable of. Demons are animals, as are the shadowcreatures that the druids unfortunate enough to receive a poisonous blow become, and as such a druid can command them. Or, at the very least, I can.

With the arrival of a throbbing twinge in my temple, I collapse to my knees. A low, almost silent growl rumbles from the shadowhound's throat, but I command the beast before it can seize whatever opportunity it has to attack.

"Go. Return to the Labyrinth from which you came, and do not leave again until tomorrow's nightfall."

Begrudgingly, the creature skulks away. There's a moment when it's condemning howl echoes up and above with the moon that I wonder if I should've been harsher in my instructions, if I should've told the shadowhound to never leave the Labyrinth again. After all, now that the Shadowthorn has fallen, these woods may soon have human inhabitants again, but as long as the behemoth shadowcreatures of the Labyrinth exist and guard the neighboring lands, no one will be safe here.

Better yet, I should've told the creature to fight with us, to stand and defend the people behind me until the sun rose.

I shake my head, trying to clear away the ache infiltrating my skull and making it all the more difficult to think. The truth is, I don't even know if my command will hold on the creature now that it's gone. For all I know, the moment Ryven disappeared is the moment the demon side of him regained control. Or perhaps it has nothing to do with distance. Maybe it's only a matter of time before my sway lessens, or until the demon inside can fight its way back to the top.

I haven't allowed myself to think about it, but for all I know, Ryven is long gone, fled the moment he left my sight, and now there is no saving him.

Something sloshes and slurps in the darkness. In this section of the woods, the branches are impenetrable to the moon's silvery beams and the stars' brilliant glow, so I have nothing but my ears to rely on to gauge the danger barreling toward me. I stagger backward, feet nearly tripping over one another as I try making my way back into a clearing so that I might be able to see.

But I'm too slow and the shadowcreature is much faster.

Sharp, red eyes blink through the darkness. Not two, like most creatures would have. But dozens. Thirty, at least.

My heart thrashes in my chest, and I swear I feel it shatter against my ribs, taste the blood that pumps freely from it in the base of my throat. I keep staggering back, my fearful gaze darting from one crimson eye to the next, and the next, and the next. Each one has a different shape, a different angle. Some watch me with lethal intent, while others search the trees almost aimlessly, as if they don't yet know I am here.

In the pitch-blackness of night, I can't make sense of the creature charging toward me. The eyes blunder forward in the same trajectory, with the same speed, as if they belong to a single creature, but they're too spread apart to be anything that

I've ever seen, and that alone makes me quiver. They can't be just *one* monster.

I don't have enough energy or strength to face one shadowcreature, let alone thirty.

Finally, I reach a place in the woods where there's a break in the trees, the branches overhead having been torn down by a pack of demons, or perhaps by the very behemoths that hunt us now. The moon shines bright through the clear sky, no clouds or haze for it to fight through now that Qaeus has awakened, the Primordial abandoning her post, and thereby eradicating the Shadowthorn.

The demon sloshes forward and into the light, revealing itself, one slippery tentacle at a time.

My inability to guess the shadowcreature's form comes as no surprise now. The beast before me is like nothing my frightful eyes have ever seen before.

The behemoth is a slick and writhing knot of wormlike limbs. It is a horrendous living nightmare that, would any Arcathainian know of its existence, it would've been at the center of every cautious tale we were ever told about the Shadowthorn. Mere demons and fiends barely compare to its horrifying presence, its hungry menace.

My feet move quicker now, putting as much distance between myself and the reaching arms as possible. Some of them, I notice, have mouths with jagged teeth that nip at everything around them. Others are barbed. They reach and slice through the air as if desperate to puncture something, anything. And I have no doubt that, were I to be nicked by one of them, becoming a demon would be the least of my problems.

At least half of the shadowcreature's eyes train on me, but the others move of their own accord. I can't tell if this beast is one being, or many. If the druid who fell to such a demise has metastasized like a disease, churning and mangling into this horrific beast, or if it has always been something so ghastly and horrendous.

For me, I hope it is the latter, otherwise I'm not sure if I'll be able to command it.

I hold out my arm, palm pressed flat against the air. "Stop."

But the shadowcreature only continues to advance, its slimy limbs crawling across the forest floor, dragging itself closer and closer. It clutches the nearby tree trunks, the weaker branches cracking as it propels itself along.

"S-stop!" I say again, my voice stronger now, but also more frantic. "Don't come closer. I do not want to harm you."

Only I realize, I do want to harm the thing. Every instinct in me tells me to slay the monster before I lose my chance. It's what I have trained for. It's what I've been told is necessary my entire life. What chance do we stand against beasts like *this*? Ones whose teeth are like shards of glass. Ones that have so many coiling arms that they could snatch a hundred Crusaders up and still have enough limbs to bite and sting and move with. One that surpass even a child's wildest imaginings of the horrors that lie beyond the Shadowthorn—or I suppose now, the former Shadowthorn.

But one glance at the saber shaking in my grasp is enough to tell me that I won't be able to kill this thing, even if I wanted to. At best, I'll be able to hack away ten or so of its tentacles before it wraps ten more around me and squeezes me to death.

Perhaps it's instincts, perhaps it's my training, but as the monster approaches, as my back slams up against the rough, warm back of a tree, I ready my saber to strike.

But the tree behind me clutches my arms and swings me aside. Spinning and staggering away, I steady myself just in time to see that it was no tree I'd collided with, but a shadowbat.

Ryven pitches forward, membranous wings tucked against his knotted back and permitting him the swiftness of an arrow cutting through a clearing. He is fluid shadow, and the monster hardly has a chance to register him before he's upon it.

Before the oily creature can wrap Ryven up in its snakelike vises, the shadowbat leaps into the air, his wings spreading wide and catching the wind to carry him high above the monster's amorphous head. It grabs for him with every snapping and writhing tentacle available, but they all miss by seconds, as if they're on a time delay. Having thirty eyes, some that face the backside of the shadowcreature, must throw off its perception. The more that are trained on me, the easier a time Ryven will have doing…whatever it is he has planned.

With the flowing sleeve of my black blouse, I wipe the sweat away from my brow before careening after them.

"Hey!" I shout, the shadowsteel saber waving perilously above my head. It glints in the moonlight, its reflection beaming one of the sets of eyes that looks my way. "Over here!"

I slice through the first black tendril that reaches for me, the oily thing shriveling at my feet before I dodge the next. I weave in and around the tightly knit trees, using my small size and agility to my advantage as the shadowcreature struggles to squeeze through the openings that I slip through with ease. Its arms get tangled in a particularly low knot of branches when it tries grabbing for me.

While it directs its attention to tugging its slick arms out from the bramble, I glance up at Ryven to see what he's doing, what his plan is. We can't fight the shadowcreature forever. At least, I can't.

But as I strain to see past the black branches to the shadowbat flying in the night sky, the moonlight catches on his wing as he dives for the behemoth's head. He careens between two wriggling tentacles—one with a great glowing eye on the end, the other barbed and oozing green from the sharpened point. Ryven barely manages to dodge both before either can latch onto him. But instead of veering upward and away, he dives backward, over the limbs that have collided into themselves. He snatches another less menacing tendril nearby. I watch with confusion as he uses the third tentacle, slippery as it is in his struggling claws, to rope around the other two, tying them into a knot, all the while dodging the thrashing barb.

He's doing the same thing I was, attempting to tangle the shadowcreature up in itself, thereby eliminating one of the advantages it has on us.

We spend the next hour or more ensnaring the creature in its own tentacles, in the canopy of bare branches and thick tree trunks, and anywhere else we can tie the beast up. Ryven weaves in and out of the behemoth's raging, snakelike arms, while I take care of its legs until it is no more than a crippled, stationary knot of sodden noodles.

By the time we're finished, I'm panting. The delirium of exhaustion settles over me, somehow making my head feel as if it has been made of glass and that one wrong move could crack me. Sleep has never beckoned me more, but the night has only just begun.

Another howl sounds in the night and my eyes snap open. I hadn't even known I'd shut them, but they blink wide now, fear of what's lurking in the unknown like a bucket of ice water to my senses.

Ryven floats down toward me, our gazes meeting for the briefest of moments as he hovers nearby protectively. The ground rumbles, and I shift on my feet, staring out into the darkness and awaiting the howling beast to emerge.

But the next roar that ripples through the trees sounds farther away, not closer, despite the rumbling approaching.

My wide eyes flick to the trembling earth.

The soil bursts beneath my feet just as Ryven barrels into me. With his arms encasing me against his bristled chest, he can't fly. As debris is flung from the ground, his wings instead act as another layer of protection as the two of us crash away from the shadowwyrm erupting from the earth.

We're scrambling to our feet as the massive creature beaches itself, only dodging its thick, heavy body by mere seconds before we would've been crushed. The weight of it crashing down makes the ground roll again. I lose my footing, falling to my knees and then my face, too exhausted to catch myself.

I glance up at Ryven and notice that he's still clutching my hand. His claws are surprisingly gentle atop my pale skin, unlike the vicious paws I've seen tear through my neighbors, my parents.

I never want him to let go. Having our hands entangled is like holding on to a tangible kind of hope.

To my dismay, Ryven releases my hand abruptly, spinning on his heels to face the dreadful shadowwyrm. But something dark comes careening out of the shadows. A demon with its mouth unhinged flings itself atop Ryven before either of us can even register its arrival. The two of them clamber before me as I watch helplessly. I try pulling myself up, but my muscles protest as if I am suddenly made of the heaviest of stones, as if the tree roots had climbed from the earth to wrap themselves around my ankles, my legs, my body, and pinned me to the cold forest floor.

Ryven reaches for the demon's snapping jaw. The demon twists away, Ryven's hand coming down on the creature's neck instead and giving the evil beast an opening at his arm. Teeth sink into Ryven's dark flesh. The raw, painful sound that escapes from his throat pierces my heart.

I try again to move. I muster enough strength to pull myself to my knees, the damp earth wet beneath me, but it takes everything in me not to topple over.

Behind me, the shadowwyrm inches closer. I feel its heavy presence like a wall of doom closing in on me, one I want to ignore. If I am to die, would it be better to watch it happen? To see the behemoth open its jaw and devour me between the hundreds of teeth that line its gaping hole of a mouth? Or would it be best to watch as my friend is torn to bits, while the same is done to me?

I don't make any conscious choice, but I feel myself twisting around to face my demise. The image is worse than I imagined. Despite the darkness, I can see every ring of teeth inside the shadowwyrm's mouth; I can practically feel each one of them serrate my skin as the beast will surely devour me whole.

A twig snaps to my left, my neck snapping along with it. Movement flickers, but shadow upon shadow makes it difficult to discern what the movement might be and what foul beast might be lurking in the darkness. It's not until I hear the man screaming that I know for certain someone is there.

With a broadsword in hand, a Crusader clad in black leather charges toward us. His snarl is so deep, so hateful, that it takes me a moment to recognize the man coming to our rescue.

Dimitri lunges for the shadowwyrm, his blade sinking deep into the creature's ribbed flesh. The wyrm wails, a screeching pitch that is quiet, but irritating to my human ears, unlike to the demons behind me. Ryven and the creature he'd fought writhe where they lie, clutching their ears as if they might bleed until they fall off.

The wyrm pitches upward. It towers over me, and suddenly my ability to move is restored. I crawl onto my shaking legs and stumble farther away, too focused on survival to watch where Dimitri has gone.

The shadowwyrm slams itself back down. The rumble isn't quite as powerful now that it's farther away, and I manage to clutch a tree to keep myself upright, twisting around in time to spot Dimitri pop out from the shadows, shadowsteel glinting in the moonlight.

He crams his sword into the wyrm's belly. The creature writhes again, but this time Dimitri pulls out another blade, one that had been slung over his back. I don't recognize it other than that it's clearly another shadowsteel weapon, and therefore must've belonged to one of the Crusaders with us.

He reaches higher, digging the sword into the wyrm's side, a few feet above the last wound. The behemoth seems too disoriented and wounded to do much of anything. It screeches and tries sloshing forward, but its movements are slow, dazed.

Dimitri uses his blades to climb all the way up to the wyrm's back, and it's not until then that I remember with sickening clarity exactly *what* the creature is beneath him. A terrifying monster, sure, but it wasn't always. Every one of the large shadowcreatures were once druids, my forgotten people.

As the wyrm slithers away, Dimitri stands atop it, both blades in hand.

"Dimitri! No!"

He sinks both swords into the back of the shadowwyrm's neck. It bucks, but Dimitri holds tight, and once the behemoth has crashed back to the ground, Dimitri wrenches his swords down deeper, pulling them apart and severing a gaping hole into the back of the beast's neck.

The wyrm whines and groans. It flails in staggering, slithering motions until its great body comes to a sudden halt.

My eyes well with tears, raw grief clawing at my tender heart. That could've been Ryven. That could've been *me*.

Dimitri pulls his swords free, wipes them on the back of the shadowwyrm's neck, and hops down. I'm upon him before he gets to sheath his swords.

I shove his shoulders, hard. "You killed it!"

He's too confused by my outrage to steady himself. His back collides into the motionless beast behind him, its gelatinous body reverberating from the impact. And for a single, painfully hopeful moment, I actually convince myself that it's still alive.

That the monster that had once been a druid might still be breathing, somewhere beneath all that grotesque, corrupted flesh, and that they might be able to be saved.

But once Dimitri shoves himself off the wyrm's corpse, once its body stops jostling, the creatures stills again. For good.

With irritated force, he shoves his broadsword into the sheath at his waist. "Of course I did, and I'd do it again. That *thing* would've killed you—"

"I don't care!" My shrill voice carries through the forest, as fragile as the dead and Blight-wreaked branches clawing the canopy above us. They're so mangled and malnourished, they look as if they could snap off at the slightest brush of wind.

Dimitri watches me for a long moment, the hard set of his brow unreadable. I prepare myself for the argument to come, falling into our old, bristling habits as easily as I breathe. But when he returns his second sword to its place on his back, he does so gently, the lines of his face softening.

"Are you all right?" he asks.

The sound that escapes me is nothing close to resembling the derision I meant it to. I'm too tired to fight him, too exhausted by the very idea of bristling at every possible turn just to feel the thrill of arguing with him. Whatever remnant of energy I have left, I must reserve. The night is not over yet.

Besides, he wouldn't understand what I have to say. To him, the shadowcreatures are vile and wicked. Just like the mages. Presumably, just like me.

"I'll be fine," I say, pushing past him on wobbling legs.

He catches my elbow, steadies me. "You don't *look* fine," he says, his voice impossibly soft and tender, especially for him. I blink up into his eyes. In the dim light of the moon, the sage-green irises look more silver than anything, dazzling down on me like liquid stars falling from the sky. "You look as pale as the day you…as the day I thought you were going to die."

The ache in his tone sears my cheeks and enflames my

chest. I wrench my arm from his grasp if only to put some distance between me and his mesmerizing gaze. My stomach dips when I close my eyes and find myself haunted by his intoxicating regard, silvery flashes sparkling amid a sea of darkness. I don't want to acknowledge whatever feeling this is, and instead I do anything to distract myself from it.

Glancing back to where I'd left Ryven, I take note of the amorphous shadow lying at his feet, the slain demon. I would've thought he'd join us once he was finished, or perhaps that he would've gone back into the forest to secure the border. But he just stands there. Waiting. Watching.

Even in the darkness I can feel his dark eyes upon me, and they send a ripple of guilt coiling around my stomach that I also don't want to acknowledge.

"You should rest," Dimitri says.

"I can't." I am all that stands between our travel companions and the monsters of this realm. As if proving my point, another horrifying roar sounds from somewhere beyond the blackness. "There's only a few hours until daybreak. I'll rest when the sun is up."

Dimitri's laugh is humorless, his eyes flitting up to the sky. "We'll be on the move then."

Something snaps inside me. "Then I'll rest when we reach the Claimed Coast." Before he can counter with his own argument, I remind him, "If I stop fighting now, nothing will stand between the shadowcreatures and our friends. Everyone will die."

He just shakes his head, quiet for a moment as he rubs at his temples. "You're not the only trained fighter here, Halira. We're all Crusaders. Well, most of us—" He glances momentarily back to Ryven, and the very air changes, becoming heavier and darker somehow. "Take a break and allow someone else to relieve you. We will all need our strength come tomorrow."

"I said no."

Frustration rumbles low in his throat, and a second later, his sword is drawn.

"What are you doing?"

He turns his back to me, knees braced. "What does it look like I'm doing? I'm getting ready for the next battle."

"You don't have to—"

Dimitri snorts. "Just because you won't listen to reason and try to get some sleep, doesn't mean I'm leaving our defenses to you. You can hardly stand."

My hands snap to my waist, closing over my hips. "I'm standing fine, thank you…" But the swift movement makes my head feel light and detached again, and I wobble.

"Yeah, I can see that," Dimitri says dryly, his head shaking as he returns his attention to the black forest. "Look, if you won't leave, at least sit down until the next demons are upon us. Get what little rest you can in between the fights." After scanning the darkness and finding nothing of danger out there *yet*, Dimitri straightens and returns his gaze to mine. The moonlight cuts across his face once more, making his eyes glow and my stomach dip again. "It's not a weakness to take a break. It is a strength to know one's limitations. Humility saves lives. Pride gets people killed."

I roll my eyes. Leave it to Dimitri to lecture *me* on pride. He is one of the proudest people I know, always choosing to do *what's right*, even if it means damning the ones he supposedly loves.

There it is again. That twisting, bitter sensation that tugs at the heart inside me that feels too raw to be beating still.

Thankfully, I can't dwell on it too long because Dimitri isn't finished with his lecture.

He takes a step closer, his chin angled down so that we are looking each other straight in the eyes.

"I understand you want to protect everyone. Believe me, I do. But no one can rely on you if you collapse."

I'm rendered speechless. I don't think I've ever heard such wisdom come from Dimitri's lips, even if he is still being a bit condescending and hypocritical. If the situation was flipped, I have no doubt that he'd stubbornly refuse to back down, just as I am. Then again, maybe our time as Crusaders and everything that has come afterward has changed him. I know it has done something to me.

Gently, his hands clasp over my shoulders. For a moment, my breath hitches. Our proximity is too...too familiar. The evenings we would spend locked in each other's arms are too fresh for me not to think about how soft his lips had been, how hungry his kisses could become.

He guides me backward, and I allow it, my eyes never leaving his thin lips. I wet mine almost unconsciously. I don't know what I'm doing, or why I would even think I wanted—

My back bumps against something rough, and Dimitri releases me. The twisting ache in my chest releases as he slowly backs away from me.

"Sit. Rest. When the next battle comes, you can jump to your feet and join me."

Air returns to my lungs, sharp and heavy. I allow the weight of it to pull me down as I sink back against the tree and slide to the cold forest floor. I should be relieved—I mean I *am* relieved. Dimitri and I, we were never...I hadn't realized it at the time, but looking back, our romantic entanglement had only been an outcome of loneliness, of desperation and longing to live even the slightest amount before either of us died.

I think.

But even as immature and heedless as it was, what we felt, I'd thrown myself into it wholly. Dimitri had always been my best friend. He'd been there to comfort and shelter me in my darkest times. I knew he'd protect me no matter what. He was a good man; he always has been. And once we were at Nigh, I guess I just... I believed he was right for me. I believed he would be the only man for me because, to be quite frank, I didn't expect either of us to live past our eighteenth birthdays.

I had convinced my mind and my body that he was what I wanted because I thought he was the best thing for me. And I suppose that kind of self-brainwashing doesn't just disappear overnight.

At least, that's what I keep telling myself because the alternative, the idea that my feelings might've been true, is far too painful to consider.

Without realizing it, my eyes become heavy, and I drift off to the eerie quiet of the night.

DAWN

THE FORMER SHADOWTHORN

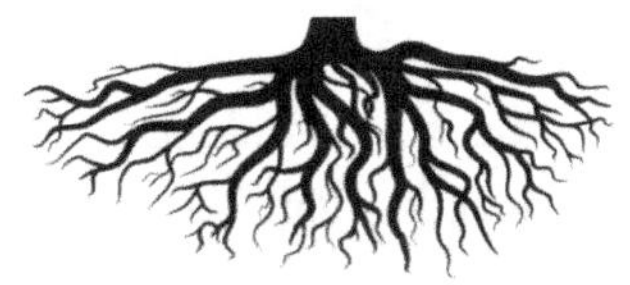

From dusk to dawn the foul stench of blighted blood soured the very air surrounding the Eyve. My teeth stung every time I forgot to inhale through my nose and accidentally ripped my mouth apart to grunt or gasp and tasted the metallic, putrid scent that lingered everywhere and only worsened the more we fought. It didn't matter that we didn't slay a single one of those creatures, the Blight wreaked on them like the stale stench of death clings to the terminally ill. It's a rot that's bone-deep and permeates the skin.

That foulness clings to Dimitri and I now as we travel through the Shadowthorn with the rest of the Crusaders. They won't tell us as much, but I can tell by the way they keep their distance throughout the morning, by the way their noses crinkle and their eyes water that the reek is intolerable. They weren't trained to handle it. They can't stand it.

Or perhaps it's the knowledge that while they were tucked safely behind Imryll's den of bramble, the rest of us were fighting off the creatures that they can't stand. Dimitri and I fought until we had no more sweat left to drip, until we were so bone-weary that even the battle fever that emboldens any warrior was barely enough to keep us from dozing during the quiet moments between one monster fight and the next.

If the sun hadn't risen when it had, banishing the beasts back to the Labyrinth and sparing Dimitri and I from facing the truly horrific lunar hydra that had been swiftly approaching, I'm not sure we would've survived the night.

The hour of rest I claimed before the camp was ready to move was hardly enough to soothe any of my aching muscles, let alone chase away the battle-induced paranoia that at any moment I could have to fight again, but as we stumble through the Shadowthorn, the sun shining as cheerfully as a lark's peaceful song, I remind myself that there isn't anything left to fear here. At least not during the day.

I'm still not used to how bright the sky is now that the Blight has dissipated. I'd almost forgotten how white the clouds could be when they're floating in a sea of baby blue, undisturbed and so…free. The Shadowthorn not only marred the skies from inside its vast expanses, but the grayness had also eventually seeped outward, infesting the skies of Gravenburg and every other bordering town. The last time I saw a blue sky like this that wasn't in the Eyve, was like over a year ago, before the Shadowthorn was close enough to cast Gravenburg in its dark net.

It's difficult not to refer to the land now as the Shadowthorn still, considering the havoc that's been wreaked on the soil, on the trees, and on the few towns and villages we've passed in the recent days since we left the Eyve. Despite the Blight having lifted, this place looks nothing like the Arcathain I know and love. Instead, it's just a cruel, twisted version, a nightmarish memory of our once thriving country.

So, I'm not too surprised that I'm not the only one grateful for the distraction my uncle provides us as he shares one tantalizing story after another.

Although, this one in particular seems to be purely for the amusement of one, and the embarrassment of another.

Fox cackles, throwing her entire body into the robust laughter that bubbles out of her.

Alphonse merely glares, his cheeks bright pink. "I think you've said enough, *Uncle.*"

"No, he hasn't." Fox brushes a tear from her eye, her grin stretching from ear to ear. "Please, Adrien, do continue. I love hearing how inept Alphy had been at, well, everything. You should've seen him when we were on the training grounds. He acted as if he had no flaws at all—"

Alphonse clutches her elbow, tugging her back so that she spins into his chest. The movement is so forceful that I flinch, prepared to chastise him for being so rough. But Fox's grin only widens, a ravenous hunger swelling behind her big, blue eyes as she stares up at him. She springs to the tips of her toes and crushes her face against his. Alphonse stiffens at first, peering over the top of her head to the many witnesses around them. Back at Nigh, they had to keep their—whatever it is—a secret, likely ducking into abandoned rooms and shadowy nooks to catch a few private moments together. It wasn't exactly encouraged for superiors to fraternize with their underlings, let alone recruits. But whatever hesitation he was prepared to bolster, he releases it almost instantly, sinking deeper into her kiss, a breath easing from his tight chest as he melts into her.

I have *never* seen him so at ease before. I can't pretend to know what brought them together, but whatever it was, I can see how much it means to both of them now. I can almost understand why Fox gave me up back at Nigh to be with him.

Almost.

Fox pulls away, and when her long lashes blink up at him, I can't help but watch as he strokes her cheek, tucking a lock of fiery red hair behind her ear. It's like I'm seeing him for the first time. Her as well, but it's different with Alphonse. Our entire lives, my cousin has been nothing but ruthless, pompous, and wicked. But even after having spent time together in the Shadowthorn searching for a cure, and witnessing *some* of his obsidian walls fall down, I still never expected to witness this level of bliss and vulnerability from him.

With his arms around her waist, the two of them walking together and somehow never tripping over each other's feet, Fox twists her neck back toward Adrien.

"Tell us again how awful he was at sneaking around."

"The worst!" Adrien barks. "Even before he made it a habit of attempting to stowaway on every ship and carriage I departed on, you could always see his scrawny limbs sticking up from under the luggage, or hear him giggling inside a barrel of mulberries. It was almost as if he wanted to be caught, even though he'd wail every time for his favorite uncle not to leave him."

Alphonse's face becomes a shade of red even brighter than a tomato. "I was five."

Adrien tilts his head. Fox giggles.

It's been years, almost closer to a lifetime from the feel of it, since I've even dared think about times from that long ago. Alphonse and I were so young then, I can hardly even remember the days when he actually enjoyed being among family. Yet Adrien recalls those moments as if they occurred only yesterday. And he does so with such profound fondness that it leaves my chest feeling cold and hollow afterward. What would our lives have been like if he hadn't been forced into hiding? How pleasantly different all of our lives would've been if it had been Uncle Esmond who'd been shoved to the outskirts instead of Adrien.

"I was a child!" Alphonse insists, his low growl of a voice somehow making the situation all the funnier. "Hardly the formidable warrior trained in stealth that I am now."

"Here we go." Adrien rolls his eyes.

"What? If I wanted to sneak aboard a ship now, I could."

"Oh, I believe it."

Only, there is something mocking in Adrien's tone that makes us all laugh harder, drowning out the sounds of Alphonse's desperate protests. My laughter is a bit bitter than everyone else's. This is a side of both of them that I never knew. By the time I was old enough to be thinking about stowing away with my adventurous uncle, Adrien had already been mostly ostracized from the family. My father still permitted him occasional visits, but they were infrequent at best so as not to be caught harboring a fugitive wanted for this crime or that by a dozen or more towns.

I'm not sure why I'm so jealous of the memories they share. It's not like Dimitri, Tor, and I didn't get into plenty of our own shenanigans when we were that age, and older.

I glance to my oldest friend now, surprised to catch his steady gaze. A smile has cracked through his expression, as if he, too, is remembering some of our fondest childhood memories. Like the time we spent an entire month collecting discarded boards, nails, and other miscellaneous trash, just to build our own makeshift hovel in the middle of the forest behind our town. Or the time the three of us jumped into the lake fully clothed and then chased each other back home, through every home in the Wallows, earning us a menacing glare from everyone—and an entire week's worth of amends while we cleaned our neighbors' homes afterward.

I'm smiling back at him until the memories crystalize, their clarity enhancing the more I give in to them. I don't remember him smiling quite like he does now. The Dimitri from back then had always been frowning as the rest of us frolicked, too concerned by the ethics of our choices and the consequences that would surely follow. Even then, he'd been too afraid to simply live, to make mistakes and learn from them, to ever truly be present. Sure, he'd chase us around, but mostly just to remind us that what we were doing was wrong rather than to join in our enjoyment.

Almost involuntarily, my eyes flit overhead, to the shadow that remains directly above me at all times. If anyone understood the value of living, it was Ryven. After spending all his childhood and most of his adolescence cut off from Arcathain, him and his best friend had decided to venture out into the world. Even after losing Ahl'Ro to a horrific death…well, he'd spent a good number of his days lamenting and blaming himself, but I'd glimpsed the real him the night we spent at the Ushines waters. I saw the spark of life that shone behind his dark eyes every time we leaped into the air and he spread his wings wide. He didn't care about the *rules* or what was expected of us. He didn't care that I'd left the Wardens on a reckless quest to save my own life. He didn't stop me. Albeit he tried convincing me of my rash foolishness, but he didn't stop me, even though I had no doubt that he could've. Ryven understood that sometimes people needed to do things, not because they were right or wrong, but because they simply needed to.

I wanted to invite him to join us. On more than one occasion, the urge had come to me, but I'd always hesitated. I might feel comfortable around him as he is, but I am more than positive that the others want to keep him far, far away from them.

Besides, I know he'd insist on remaining vigilant up above. Not that he could speak, but I could already see the look he'd give me if I were to invite him to walk among us and share in our laughter now.

The smile falls from my lips when I realize at least one of us should probably remain alert down here as well. After all, if we'd learned anything about the Shadowthorn this last week, it was that even though the darkness had crept away, taking the fiends with it, the demons still remain.

I charge ahead to get a better view of our surroundings,

doing my best to ignore the conversation happening behind me.

But now it's Sai's laughter that has become infectious. "You are a glutton, Mr. Devonshire."

Adrien blows through his lips. "A glutton, sure. But I haven't been a Mr. Devonshire since I was a young buck. Come to think of it, the last time anyone called me that might've been that very night."

"Tell me," Sai continues, his voice sounding strangely low and heavy. "Did you force all your lovers to call you Mr. Devonshire then?"

"The lovers? Gods no. It was their wives who shouted it, chucking my trousers at me while they chased me down the bustling streets of the Arcathain Capital."

"And you wonder why Father disapproved of your visits," Alphonse snorts.

Adrien barks a laugh. "My dreadful brother Esmond could've cared less about who I bedded. It was the coin purses that always came up missing in my presence that he disapproved of."

I can't see Alphonse's face, but I can tell from the flatness of his voice that he's rolling his eyes. "Would it have killed you to make an honest wage?"

I glance behind me just in time to see Adrien cock his head, considering. "Yes. I believe it would've."

"Scoundrel," Sai says, and I can hear the sly grin in his tone.

"You don't know the half of it," my uncle replies.

I glance over my shoulder just in time to see their eyes light up as they gaze across to each other. Sometimes I forget that Sai and Adrien already know each other. After we left Ashenvale, Adrien and the Wardens rescued Sai and took him back to the compound to be healed. He's been with them for a few weeks now, even though judging from the way they talk, as thick as thieves, you'd assume they'd known each other for far longer.

They're definitely the chummiest among us. In the reprieve of Adrien's tales, the group falls silent once more. The Crusaders watch the thicket of trees, returning to their previous levels of alertness and terror. The necro-ink they applied this morning is beginning to drip and smear, the fight we only recently endured leaving them sweat-slicked and covered in demon blood. It's almost impossible to see where their leather armor is soaked in it, until they walk in the sunlight, the black sheen glistening like oil.

Behind them, dressed in a shockingly white robe, strides my aunt Imryll. She leans over to whisper something at my sister, but her eyes slide to me. Abruptly, I snap forward so that neither of them mistake me for trying to eavesdrop, but even as I do, my ears still strain. Kalli looked…strange. Her expression rarely shows anything but indifference and occasionally disdain, so it was difficult to determine what the slight crinkle of her brow meant. Was my sister actually…worried? Not much could penetrate her concerns. Kalli found immense solace in being able to problem solve difficult and seemingly impossible situations. So if something frightened her now, I knew it couldn't be good. Then again, if it was that disturbing, I would think she would, at the very least, tell me that she was concerned.

No matter how hard I try to hear them, it's of no use. Not only are they too far away, but Adrien has started another tale. Unsurprisingly, this one begins with another dashing young man of somewhat impressive status—far more impressive than Adrien or any of us, anyway.

He tells us of how they met at a card table in a tavern, the baron instantly charmed by Adrien's utter beauty—his words, not mine—and quick wit. The night was one of pleasure and passion, and all it cost the young baron who was new to his title was his prized cane.

"Tell me, Uncle," Alphonse begins. "Does it bring you enjoyment knowing you outwitted and swindled a good man? Someone disabled, of all things."

The laughter that erupts from Adrien's lungs seems misplaced, not only to the question but also considering our position. I'm not the only one among our party to glance nervously at our surroundings.

"*A good man?*" Adrien repeats. "Tell me, how well did *you* know the Baron Gilbert Bouldre?"

Before Alphonse can respond, Silver cuts in. There's something sharp about her tone. "Baron Gilbert? Of Ashenvale?"

"The one and only."

Sparing a moment from my vigilant tree-watching, I angle my head to look at the tall, raven-haired woman. If ever there was a living, walking, breathing embodiment of beauty, she was it. Even now as seething anger leeched from her hazel eyes.

Adrien's arms gesture toward her, wide. "Ah. See? *She* knows the man I speak of. Gorgeous as he was, Baron Gilbert was no delicate lily. Before you castigate me for what I pilfered from him, why don't you ask *her* if he had any use of such a thing."

I stare intently as Silver shakes her head, curious to see where this story is going.

Alphonse frowns. "He wasn't...he didn't use... But, why would a man possess a cane if he had no use of it?"

"I'm so glad you asked," my uncle sings. He sneaks a wink at Sai while Alphonse rolls his eyes again, bringing a devious smile to both of their faces. "You see, my reputation preceded me. At least among the commoners. This must be part of the story that your father never shared with you, for fear that you'd see the vague nuance between right and wrong."

Dimitri bristles beside me. "What nuance can you possibly claim? You stole something from a *baron*."

Arrogance ripples off Alphonse and he casts an approving nod toward Dimitri.

"Simple, simple children." Adrien sighs dramatically. He quickens his pace enough to catch up to Alphonse and, bending his arm, leans his elbow against Alphonse's shoulder. He barely reaches it, but he remains there regardless. "Is it truly stealing if the cane never belonged to the baron to begin with?"

"What are you talking about?" Alphonse shrugs my uncle's arm away.

"There was an elderly woman living in Ashenvale. Her husband had given his life to the Shadow Crusade. He fought valiantly, even managed to survive a few years of missions into the Shadowthorn. But, as all Crusaders do, eventually he fell, leaving his wife with little to manage. When she couldn't pay her taxes, the baron took her cane from her—from an elderly woman whose back had started to bend forward, whose knees were too weak to hold her weight on her own."

"I remember that," Silver says. "A few of the townspeople petitioned the baron to return the cane to her. We even gathered up the funds she'd been short, but he refused."

Adrien dips his head. "In comes me, a dashing, roguish fella who knows the skill of sleight of hand."

"If the baron was misusing his power, then the Magistrate should've been informed," Dimitri argues.

My uncle pats him on the shoulder, a mockingly rueful sigh easing from his lips. Instead of arguing otherwise though, Adrien continues walking, surpassing us all, myself included as even I had become engulfed in his story. I always did.

The silence stretches, and one by one the members of our group begin walking again until Silver's voice pierces the quiet.

"He never could find it, you know? He tore that poor woman's home apart."

Adrien answers with a flash of a crooked grin tossed over his shoulder.

"Where did you two hide it?" Silver asks.

"Hide it?"

"The cane. You retrieved it for her and returned it, knowing he'd come back for it. Where did you advise her to keep it hidden?"

An airy laugh hisses from Adrien's lips. "Nowhere. We burned the cane. It was a difficult decision for her to make, destroying one of the only heirlooms her husband left her and therefore something of great sentimental value. But she knew she'd never be able to keep it after what we'd done. The baron would never allow it." A wicked grin curves his mouth. "We did save one part though, a small chunk of the wood that we had whittled into a doorstop. I'm told he kicked the thing on his way back out the door, never once suspecting that the very thing he'd searched for, he'd come into direct contact with."

Silver's lips purse together. "What you did for her was a great kindness."

A derisive scoff gusts from Alphonse's lungs. "*What he did for her?* Stole a scrap of wood, destroyed it, and made an even smaller scrap of wood?"

"It was more than that," Silver tells him. "He brought her peace. She had been distraught knowing that one of her prized possessions was in the hands of someone so...callous. She blamed herself for losing that final piece of her husband. It might not seem like much to you, *General,* but what your uncle did meant the world to that poor woman."

Out of the corner of my eye, I watch Adrien lower his head in gratitude. Something warm emits from Sai and the gaze he lets linger on my uncle. It feels too personal, too private, and so I resist the urge to stare, but still, I watch them from afar. I try thinking about whether I've ever seen Dimitri looking at me that way, or Ryven. If I've ever watched either of them with so much glowing pride or appreciation.

My cheeks flush when I realize I have. The day Dimitri received his Crusader patch comes to mind. His pride, his fulfillment had been infectious. I knew how much it meant to him to achieve such an honor in his eyes, to have finally secured himself a new place in the world, a family, and I'd been overwhelmed by delight for him. Thinking back on it, I think I'd been more excited for him than I was for myself, which should've caused me concern even before everything went awry, but it hadn't. Being happy for Dimitri had been enough for me. It didn't feel like enough anymore though.

Things had been different with Ryven. My joy had been mine. When we'd soaked in the Ushines waters and marveled up at the stars, when we'd leapt from the top of the Eyve canopy and dove down into town with his wings spread behind us, something light and electric had stirred inside me. For the first time in my life, I felt alive. I no longer felt like I was trying to fit in or follow rules that I thought I was expected to follow. I was simply enjoying the moments that presented themselves.

Adrien glances up, his voice so low that I'm surprised it drags me out of my thoughts. "If we had a professional wood smith such as yourself, we would've made something far more precious than a doorstop from that cane. One of the many reasons I should've found you sooner."

The smile is tight on Sai's face, nowhere near as warm as the rest of their exchanges. It baffles me so much that I forget that I'm trying not to stare at them and instead look straight on.

Adrien's sly expression wilts. "Forgive me. I didn't mean to—"

Sai shakes his head, the smile deepening but still never quite reaching his eyes.

Now I really do avert my attention away from the two of them. Although I can't translate the exact meaning of their unspoken language, I recognize the intimacy of it, the vulnerability. Though they've only spent a short while together, far shorter than the time Sai and I spent training at the Castle of Nigh, they seem to have already developed a deep understanding of each other. I don't know what stories they've shared, but I've always known there were many that my uncle hadn't shared with me yet, and likely quadruple as many that Sai hadn't.

My gaze settles on a sparse group of saplings, to the absence of the wind between their branches.

It's been quiet for too long, the forest. Even with the conversations that ebb and flow from the others, there's something eerily still about the woods we're walking through. It's different from what it feels like when demons are near. The ravenous beasts scare away any of the birds and squirrels that might've dared to live inside the Shadowthorn, their songs and chittering dying the moment they come within a mile of them, but I'd hardly describe the forest as falling silent. The demons snarl, their stomachs gurgling for blood and thereby giving themselves away before they even have a chance of closing the distance on us with our knowing.

This quiet, this stillness, it's different. Not a single woodland critter rustles the leaves from their branches, and come to think of it, neither does the wind. The air is stagnant, but heavy, like a pit of quicksand just waiting for an unsuspecting victim to wander through it.

Magic is alive and thrumming here. I can feel it weighing over my black leathers, feel it sparking against the bare skin of my face.

Imryll said we were getting close. This morning, when we packed up camp, she said we'd arrive at the Claimed Coast in the early afternoon, and to expect something...strange.

Since the day is already halfway done, and since the sensation of this place snugly fits into the description of *strange*, I have no doubt we are approaching our destination.

"Stop."

My aunt's voice is so forceful, so resonate, that it feels like a whip to our backs and everyone stills. Twisting around, I watch her stride forward, Kalli tailing close behind. She doesn't have to squeeze through the Crusaders standing shoulder to shoulder. One look at her and they practically leap out of the way. They might respect Alphonse enough to support his decisions, they might even actually believe that the only way to save Arcathain is by going to Illashore, but they have not yet come to terms with accepting that druids are different from mages.

Neither Imryll nor Kalli glance toward me as they make their way to the front of the group. Resisting the urge to bark at them, I clutch my hands into fists and march behind them.

"This is it. This is the barrier that kept humans from discovering the Leviathan. If we are to reach the Claimed Coast, we'll have to break through it."

"Break through it?" I ask, stepping forward and coming around Imryll so that she can see me, so that she has to acknowledge my existence. "How do we do that? You said yourself this boundary has stood here since…since long before the Shadowthorn ever came into existence. And it's kept humans out all this time. Presumably demons too judging from how confident you are that the Leviathan still stands. How will we get everyone through?"

One of Imryll's slender brows ticks high. "I never said the barrier was impenetrable, but I can understand why you would think it so. Your experience with such spells only expands to the shield around the Eyve and the one that had protected Qaeus' heart. But the spell here is different. In fact, you may have noticed, we're already inside it."

The Crusaders, the ones who had accompanied Captain Eparah and Dimitri into the Shadowthorn to avenge their fallen general, shift uncomfortably. It's almost an imperceptible movement, but Dimitri seems to move closer, leaning into the hip closest to me protectively as if he has any defenses against the magic around us that he distrusts so much. I can't say I blame any of them. For our entire lives we've been told magic is evil—sometimes, I'm not even sure it isn't, especially now as the hair on the back of my neck tenses in response to the humming power surrounding us.

"Anyone may cross through the magic here, as long as they know the signs to follow."

I should gape at my aunt. I should still be so shocked by all of the things I'm learning about magic that this should be the last straw that my back is able to withstand. But instead, it's as if I'm completely unfazed and have known this all along. My only concern...

My eyes flit up. Ryven's dark shadow circles above us.

My aunt's hand clasps my shoulder. "Don't worry. He will be able to follow us. When our people set this magic in place, demons did not exist. The barrier does not reach past the tree-tops, I can assure you. I've flown here many times. Come."

My attention refuses to obey, lingering a moment longer at the winged demon-man. I swear I catch his gaze at every rotation, his eyes never leaving mine.

It's not until Fox walks past me, her elbow thrown into my gut, that I finally return my awareness to what's happening on land. My glare is readied. If she has a problem with me then she really has lost it because I've never done anything but be there for her. But my anger fades when I catch her looking over her shoulder at me, a cautionary kind of bulge to her eyes as she throws her gaze even farther behind me.

Twisting around, I find Dimitri as he marches in line with the others. He's not staring back at me, but that almost makes it worse, especially considering I can tell he had been by the stiffness of his back and the way he stubbornly refuses to look at me.

Fox must've thought she was doing me a favor alerting me to Dimitri's attentive gaze, unless her cruelty runs even deeper than I imagined.

Considering Inigo is among the rest of the people marching behind Dimitri though, I quickly follow in line with him.

Now Dimitri finally deigns a look over his tense shoulder. "Your aunt knows what she's doing?"

"I certainly hope so, otherwise we're all doomed."

A tight, clipped sort of laugh eases from his lips.

Behind me, Inigo's low whispers send a chill up my spine. He speaks too quietly for me to discern any of what he's saying, but somehow, I know he's talking about me.

I jog ahead a few steps until I'm right beside my old friend, my old lover. "Why do you ask?"

Dimitri shrugs. "Just wondering how alert I should remain."

Now I'm the one to let out a dry laugh. "Like you had any intention of remaining anything *but* vigilant as long as you're in the company of magic-users."

A muscle tenses in his jaw and he only glances to me briefly before staring forward again. "You're right. I don't trust them."

"If by *them* you mean druids, then what you really mean is you don't trust *me* either."

He shakes his head, brow furrowing and darkening his face with shadows. "That's not true. I know *you*. I don't know...*her*." His lip pulls up with disgust as he gestures to my aunt. I swear she hears him because her ear twitches in the slightest motion. "If you were leading us to this place, if you knew what awaited us on the other side, and if you still said it was safe, I'd have no fears. But I do not like being led by some stranger."

"She's no stranger," I snap. "She's my aunt. She's part of the only family I have left. You don't have to know her to be able to put your trust in her. Simply knowing that I trust her should be good enough."

He cocks his head toward me, one brow arched. "Do you? Do you trust her? She and Kalli have been keeping their distance from the rest of the group for days now, speaking in hushed whispers, acting suspicious. I know you've noticed it too. I've seen the way you're watching them, like something is up and you're just waiting for the avalanche to come. Something isn't right and you know it."

I fight the urge to bite my lower lip. What Dimitri's suggesting, I don't want to admit I've wondered the same thing. Thinking these paranoid thoughts to myself is one thing, but admitting them out loud is entirely too painful to consider. They are my family. Granted, Imryll, I've only known for a few short weeks, but Kalli? We may have our differences, but never once have I thought she had malintent toward me, and I don't want to start now.

At first, I'd been able to convince myself they were just getting to know one another. I'd imagined that Kalli felt more of an instant connection to our aunt because of how much she resembled our mother, and how easy it would be to long for that connection again. Not to mention, they spent the last week or more traveling together, so it wouldn't be a surprise if they had bonded. I told myself it was just immature jealousy that had me feeling so paranoid.

But now that someone else has voiced the fears that have been niggling at the back of my mind these past few days, I can't resist the pull and succumbing to them. What other reason would they have to talk privately without me? Why the nervous glances to make sure no one is within earshot? Why making sure they're at the opposite end of the group from me when these conversations occur?

The only conclusion I've been able to draw is that they're plotting something…something they don't want me to know.

Dimitri's hand resettles on the broadsword sheathed at his hip. "Your silence says it all."

I clamp my mouth shut, unwanted and worrying thoughts infiltrating my mind.

I'm so preoccupied that I don't notice him watching me. "I don't like that you don't have a weapon." He smirks when I look at him. "Not that you were ever very good with one."

When we were younger, this was exactly the sort of comment that would earn him an elbow in the ribs. But we've grown up since then. *I've* grown. I no longer *need* a weapon—though, I'll admit I do feel naked without one. But I have something much more permanent, a weapon that no one can take away.

Inhaling the fresh scent of the damp woodlands, I fill my lungs with air. Magic sizzles inside me, imbued in the air more so than anywhere else I've been. Typically, there is the buzzing sense of life in everything. Ryven said that each druid senses magic in their own way, and for me I pick up on the life of it all. The animals, the winds, the leaves. But that vivacity is different here, stronger.

I don't need to exhale to summon the winds, but it feels good to do so, like it's a more direct connection to the air itself, allowing my breeze to be strong, and more precise.

Dimitri's shivers as the gust blasts over his bare neck, the longer, golden hair on the top of his head becoming disheveled. He braces himself, as do the others behind us. Most of them stand outside the torrent, receiving only the ricochet of the wind I'm directing at him.

He holds his arm up to shield his face, but a moment later, I let the magic cease.

Hesitantly, his arm falls to his side and we all begin walking again, our steps a bit quickened to make up for the distance Imryll has gained on us.

Dimitri angles his disapproving gaze at me. "I see you've become quite comfortable with *that*."

I roll my eyes. I'm so sick of feeling this way around him, like I've somehow offended or wronged him when all I've done is exist. "Yeah, well, it only took me eighteen years, but I've finally learned to embrace myself."

He has no judgmental response, no callous retort to shame me with. But his brow twitches with the slightest indication that he might actually feel...remorseful.

"You've...been this way all that time?"

Sideways, I sneak a glance at him. "Yes."

"But you never said anything. To me."

Suddenly, I feel the need to shift inside my own skin. My cheeks burn with something like regret or sorrow, but only enough to make the rage simmer away. "Can you blame me, what with the way you look at me, even now? Our whole lives we were raised to hate magic. I spent most of those years convincing myself that the things happening around me were impossible imaginings, the hallucinations of starvation or enduring too much of the winter's cold. It wasn't until we reached Nigh that I truly started to wonder. There were too many inexplicable things—"

"Like what?" he asks. When I stiffen beside him, he eases out a painful, almost apologetic sigh. "I just mean that I want to know. I'm sorry you ever felt like you had to hide part of yourself from me. I'm sorry I never noticed. I'm sorry for...the way I reacted. I never meant to—"

"It's fine," I say, taking a loose strand of hair into my hand and coiling it around my finger. There's something about the way I'm able to anchor my grip on the soft tress that makes me feel secure, comforted.

"It really isn't. I—I have no excuses that don't make it sound like I'm trying to justify it. We *were* raised to hate magic, to hate the mages, but I was also raised to be loyal, to defend the ones I love, and I just…I left you."

Something pinches in my chest, a warm, liquid sensation twisting inside me. I've been so preoccupied with curing myself of the Blight and now finding a cure for Ryven that I've had very little time to dwell on how much Dimitri's betrayal had stung. It wasn't just that he'd left me; it was the way he'd looked at me when he found out I was a druid. Out of everyone in the entire world, I never thought Dimitri, of all people, could grow to hate me. He had always been by my side, and I'd taken that loyalty for granted until that agonizing moment.

Without realizing I'm doing it, I reach for Dimitri's hand. The calluses are rougher than I remember, as if the past few weeks have worn on him like another ten years as a butcher's ward. His coarse palm is abrasive against mine, but it still fills me with the same soft, fluttering warmth I felt every moment we'd stolen before dawn in Nigh, his hands laced in mine, our bodies entwined, the two of us awaiting our deaths and making the best of our lives until then.

Dimitri's sage eyes meet mine, his pupils wide as his chest hitches. I recognize the guilt, hear his silent protest that he does not deserve my gratitude even though he speaks none of it. If I were a better person, I'd insist he was mistaken. But a bitter twinge in my heart is like chains to my lips, and instead, I merely squeeze his hand one last time before disentangling our fingers and parting with the warmth that had bloomed inside me at our touch.

The water is calmer than I expected. My family would visit Drayfil Shore from time to time, the beaches always a churning beauty of seafoam and salt. As a child, I'd always thought the ocean was mad at us for something, or perhaps angered at the mages for disturbing it when they broke the continent and sailed away with our lands. Thinking back on it now, perhaps I was right. Perhaps my druid powers could sense that the ocean was upset. Not in the emotional way that humans experience, but simply in the disturbed way of nature, when a winter lasts too long or begins too soon, and it throws off an entire population of birds' migration, mating, and egg-hatching patterns. Maybe the ocean was still adjusting to the missing piece of land that it had grown accustomed to lapping up against.

Maybe that's why it's so still here. This coastline was never disturbed during the Great Rift. The mages took only the westernmost corner, and even if they had tried to steal away whatever secrets reside here, I have no doubt that the druids had magic in place to thwart any plans such as those as well.

Dimitri and I are next. He staggers forward, eyes squinting so tightly they might as well be closed. I jerk my shoulder out from under Inigo's burning grip, all too pleased to feel him stumbling behind me as he staggers into the blindingly bright coastline.

It must be high noon, judging from where the sun sits high overhead. It's the only reason the Crusaders find it so bright. The clay is too dark to reflect the bright rays, but the still waters that stretch as wide as the eye can see might as well be mirrors to the sun's light.

Squinting, I look above, searching the bright sky for any flickers of shadow. I catch a glimpse of him as he soars through the cloudless blue before he veers down to the earth. He lands with alarming precision beside me, somehow as gentle as a butterfly despite his massive form. I didn't think it would be possible for him to be any larger than he had been. Before the

Blight took over him entirely, he was already sculpted from rock, his shoulders broad and hard, his stomach rippling with taut muscle. When we'd first met, it had been difficult to keep myself from being distracted by his shirtless existence, one forced upon him the day his wings grew in.

A liquid warmth pools inside me at the thought, but then I blink and see him as he is now. The fire cools like water to hot coals. I did this to him. It's my fault he is so close to the brink of demonhood. If I had been smarter, cleverer—if only I had thought to trick him into taking the breath of life for himself before he ran away, leaving me no choice but to ingest it for myself. Another knife twists in my gut when I remind myself that I *had* thought about it, but forcing his hand had somehow seemed...wrong. I'd been foolish though. There was nothing wrong in saving someone you cared about, and he'd realized it sooner than I had.

I'm not sure how to greet him anymore. The Ryven I knew is still in there, I'm sure of it, but there's so much guilt and resentment and sorrow and hope between us that I become too overwhelmed to speak any time he's near.

Then, of course, comes the gazes of the others. They watch us whenever we're near, as if they're waiting for him to devour me. Most of them would be all too pleased to have been proven right: that demons and magic cannot be trusted.

I flash a rueful smile that only ticks up one side of my face before returning my attention elsewhere.

Dimitri stands beside me. I avoid his fixed gaze as he watches me, his scrutiny too burdensome to bear, and instead I twist to find Imryll and Kalli striding down the beach toward a dock I hadn't noticed yet.

My feet move before I'm even aware of my haste to catch up to them.

"Wait up," I call, well aware of the bite in my tone. "Aren't you forgetting the rest of us?"

Kalli's steel-gray eyes cut to mine, and I glare back, but it's our aunt who answers.

"I assumed those who were interested would follow."

I almost remind her that almost all of our party has spent the last hour being blinded by fog only to then be blinded by light, but ultimately I decide against wasting my breath. "What are we doing?"

Imryll twists around. "I thought I'd been fairly clear about what we were doing."

Shaking my head doesn't even begin to clear the flush of my cheeks. "I know *what* we're doing. I meant—"

"Where is the Leviathan?" Dimitri barks.

He's so surprisingly close behind me that I gasp, my heart racing in my chest.

Glaring back at him, I see that he's not the only one hot on our heels, but it appears that the moment I spotted my sister and aunt and began racing after them, so did the others.

Dimitri's gaze turns worrying when he settles it on me. It seems to warn that the thing we've been worried about, whatever secret plan Kalli and Imryll have in the works, is about to be revealed, and he's not sure we're going to like it.

"Where do you think a Leviathan would be?" Imryll asks once we've all congregated around the wooden planks that she and Kalli stand upon. The dock is so short that I'm not even sure it can be called a dock, only five boards holding it together, all of which appear to be tied with thick, sea-gorged ropes to poles that jut from the clay and water.

Güthric lumbers forward, his thick finger outstretched toward the distant horizon. "In water."

He seems to be about just the only one among us who doesn't irritate Imryll just by breathing.

"Correct. But a creature such as the Leviathan does not stay idle long. We will need to summon her."

"Her?" Dimitri's eyes bulge.

"How do we do that?" I ask.

"It's quite simple. Something precious and safeguarded must be offered to the waters. The Leviathan will come if she deems it a worthy contribution."

Slowly, I can feel consternation crinkling my brow. I know who I'll find in my company, but I look among them anyway. We are Crusaders and fugitives, people who left behind their lives and committed to a short and harsh existence. We do not carry a single precious item of value among us, aside from the shadowsteel blades that I doubt any of them will toss into the salty waters.

Despite knowing we have nothing to give, I still search my persons, as do a few of the others once they see me looking. My eyes catch on the silver chain dangling from my neck, to the small vial I had forgotten I was still carrying.

I take the glass into my hand, the edges sharp and cool to the touch. With the absence of the breath of life, the vial no longer holds its subtle luminosity, but I still feel the energy from it sparking at my fingertips. For an untold number of years, this vial contained the dying breath of the first Queen Siren. After the humans and mages hunted their kind down and forced them into hiding in the Dark Sea, this was one of the few items that remained in their possession, certainly one of the most precious. They kept it safeguarded for centuries, maybe longer.

Tilting my head, I pull the necklace up and over my ears, guiding it from around my neck as my long tresses lift before sliding through.

"Something like this?" I hold the necklace out for my aunt to see. The empty jar shines in the sunlight.

Imryll nods, stepping down from the planks and extending her arm for me to take her place. It takes me a moment to move. I'm too struck by the magnitude of everything that's come before this moment, everything that's happened to me since the day my parents died. Leaving Gravenburg, the Wallows, training to be a Crusader, all of that had felt surreal at the time, clouded behind a haze of grief that never felt like I was actually living those moments, but observing them from afar. The rest though? Fighting demons and the behemoth in Ashenvale, being accused of being a mage and deciding to flee, embarking on a quest to find a cure for the Blighted… Those moments were vivid. They made my heart thrash against my ribcage like it was trying to burst out. They made my skin prick as every one of my senses was brought to life—and that's just it. Those things, they made me feel *alive*. Despite all the heartache and betrayal and misery, I have never felt more alive, more in the right place than I have in these past few weeks.

But now, after everything, I hesitate. Perhaps it's because this feels different than every other choice that's led me here. Leaving Gravenburg to travel a few days north was difficult, but it was hardly the same as crossing an ocean into enemy territory. Trekking through the dangerous Shadowthorn couldn't be avoided. If I had sat and done nothing, I could've died. My aunt and Kalli might never have found a way to retrieve the breath of life from the sirens.

This is different. Because, although Arcathain is in danger by the Primordial Qaeus' rampage, my family and I could return to the Eyve and be safe. We do not need to cross the ocean to ensure that we will survive. In fact, doing so puts our very lives at risk.

That's when I look at my sister and notice the slight curve to her eyes, the ones that watch me as if she's moments away from speaking an apology.

Crossing this ocean to do what's right might be something I'm willing to do, but I'm suddenly not so sure she is.

Something warm presses against the low dip of my back, and I glance up through my lashes to find Dimitri standing beside me. A reassuring smile softens the usually hard details of his expression. It seems to say that he is here for me, no matter what happens.

My lips purse before I brave the dock. I hold the vial out from my chest.

"Do I need to say anything?" I call over my shoulder.

"No."

I wait for Imryll to elaborate, thinking she might provide some details as to how this will work. But when she says nothing, I realize the time has come, and my fingers release the silver cord and the vial attached to it.

THE CLAIMED COAST, THE FORMER SHADOWTHORN

The small glass container hits the water's rippling surface with a plunk. The shallow depths of the ocean swallow it before it's even reached the clay below, and the vial is carried out with the next gentle tide.

But then the waves still.

If I thought this beach had been eerily stagnant before, it is nothing like the unnaturalness I'm witnessing now. The waves appear to have stopped midstream, the white, frothy bubbles rising to a crescendo only to have stopped just as they were about to reach full bloom.

One look at my aunt tells me that this is to be expected. She stands, hands clasped before her, looking much the way Alphonse does when he is feeling superior.

But before her unfazed serenity can soothe my own trepidation and unease, her glacial eyes widen.

I whip back around, expecting to come face-to-face with a monster whose existence defies anything my imagination could've summoned to my nightmares. Instead, I see only an ocean of blue, the waves rolling once again as if they'd never even stopped.

"What just happened?" I ask, striding back toward the

others, my boots clunking on the sodden boards beneath my feet. "You said to offer something that was precious and safeguarded. I did just that. Did the Leviathan reject my offering?"

Something like guilt pinches my chest. I had planned on returning that vial to the sirens once this was all done. It wouldn't be much, returning the empty remnants of something they'd once held dearly, but it was the least I could do for the aid they provided. I suppose once they're allowed to return to the oceans though, maybe they'll find the vial someday, resting at the bottom of a trench.

Imryll sighs, shaking her head. "Your offering was sufficient. However, there is more than just one of you seeking voyage. Is there not?"

The Crusaders murmur among themselves, and my breath nearly catches.

"Do you mean everyone here has to offer something?" As Imryll nods, I glance out at the dozen or more people with us, to Silver whose long, gray skirts are tattered at the hem from all of the travel, to Sai and the boots that are beginning to wear and peel back from treading through the mud. Every last one of them looks at each other as if the very notion that they might have anything of value to give is ludicrous. And it is. "We don't have enough to throw away into the ocean. You know who we are, right? It's not the wealthy who throw away their lives to join the Crusaders or abscond to the Shadowthorn."

"Precious and safeguarded. Those are the only requirements?" Kalli's voice is low and calculating, harsh compared to the swaying, lulling sea.

Imryll bows her head, but she looks to my sister with the intrigue of a mother watching her baby bird spread its wings for the first time. She'd known it would come to this, and she knows the solution around it, but she wanted to see which one of us would figure it out first.

Of course it's Kalli. While I've spent the last few moments

bristling, arguing, and convincing myself that all was lost, her brilliant mind had been at work.

"Secrets." Her words are like arrows cutting through the air. Everyone stills, even me whose already provided an offering. "Those of you who do not have possessions you cherish will share a secret."

She turns on her heel while everyone else remains stunned and motionless. No one speaks as Kalli crosses the planks, unclasps the cloak from her shoulders, and holds the black, wool fabric before her. She brushes a hand over the white phoenix sigil but doesn't linger long. Almost carelessly, as if the cloak means nothing to her when I know it means the world, she tosses it into the ocean. The dark wool sinks quickly, leaving her only a few moments to watch as her token and a symbol of her past life, the one she'd worked relentlessly for and was forced to abandon because I'd been caught using my druid powers, is gobbled up by the sea.

"Who's next?" she asks, striding back to Imryll's side, her head held high. It's not really a question. The command in her tone is felt by everyone, and soon the rest of the group is forming something that vaguely resembles a line.

Taking a page from Kalli's playbook, Alphonse offers his General sigil. I've never seen him more at war with himself, like the detailed patch was the one refusing to release his palm as he tried chucking it into the water. It wasn't until Fox cleared her throat loudly enough that he looked back at her and found her reassuring nod, before he finally released the item.

Fox is next. I watch her, wondering what she could possibly have to offer, and remember too late about the necklace tucked under her blouse at all times. She takes a deep breath, but like my sister, she doesn't dally before throwing the chain and the ring around it as far as she can. She'd already turned her back to the ocean by the time the jewelry hit the water, flinching as if she could hear the inaudible plip as it hit the surface.

Dimitri is next in the vague line, his hands curled into fists so tightly that his knuckles are turning white. How long had he been standing like that, seething, struggling? He'd made it seem so easy when it was my turn, but I suppose watching someone else offer up something of themselves is different than doing it himself.

I start to move toward him, but Dimitri grits his teeth at my aunt. "I have nothing to give."

Imryll's head tilts to the side, her slender chin raised in that slightly condescending way. "I doubt that. I am quite confident that all men have secrets, ones that are kept near them at all cost. Now is the time to part with one of them, unless you prefer to remain here."

His square jaw tenses harder, his shoulders so rigid I fear they may snap right off him, but he turns toward the sea. His footsteps are thunderous on the dock, louder than anyone who went before him and not because of his size. Dimitri has always been made of lean, compact muscles. He has the body of a famished laborer, true to his upbringing, and though we spent months training at the Castle of Nigh, it will take a lifetime to retrain his body to retain anything more than only what it needs.

From where I stand amid the others, the gentle waves lapping against the shore, the occasional groan of leather as the Crusaders shift uncomfortably beside me, I cannot hear what Dimitri is telling the ocean. From this angle, his jaw is visibly moving, lips parting in a reluctant whisper, but his words are meant for only him and the Leviathan.

"You will need to speak up," Imryll tells him, something cold spiking through my chest. "If your voice is to be heard by the Leviathan who could be hundreds of miles away, you will need to speak louder."

His glare at her is one of simmering fires and sharpened daggers. I can tell by how long it lingers on her that he's debating his options. It's then that I remember that none of these people are being forced to go. They *could* stay behind, if they so choose. But the way Dimitri's sage eyes drift to meet mine tell me that he's already left me once and he's not about to do it again.

He stares out across the watery horizon once more, chest rising with a deep breath of commitment before his voice comes booming. "I...am in love with—"

Beside me, Fox nudges my ribs and says through the side of her mouth, "As if that's a secret to anyone."

I hadn't even noticed her next to me. In fact, I'm certain she wasn't. Her vibrant tresses, as bright as the falling leaves of autumn, are not easily concealed from a sea of Crusaders in black.

By the time I'm done scowling at her, I look up to find she's distracted Dimitri too. He looks...contemplative, caught, like he's having to readjust course against his will. Had that truly been what he was going to offer? Granted, we'd never actually said the words to one another, but even long before we'd been involved in...that way, it was obvious that Dimitri and I loved each other. We grew up together, fending for ourselves and protecting one another during every cruel summer and harsher winter. Love didn't have to be romantic, and our love for each other was no secret.

His fists open and close at his sides. It takes him a long while before he musters the courage to speak again, his head hanging from his shoulders like the weight of the world rest upon it.

"Part of me was relieved," he begins, his rugged voice surprisingly loud and clear for someone so clearly ashamed of what he is about to admit. I nearly flinch when he turns away from the ocean, his gaze cutting to mine and pinning me in place. No longer does it feel like a sacrifice he's making to pay his way for a ride, but an intimate conversation that was meant for just the two of us. "When your parents died, I was selfishly relieved because I knew it meant that nothing was keeping you in Gravenburg anymore. I knew you had no reason to stay but every reason to join me at the Castle of Nigh, and that made me so grateful because... because I wasn't ready to lose you..."

The waves peel back, pausing like the curling, sleepy leaves of jasmine in the middle of the night. But it's more than the waves that still. The air becomes so stagnant it's heavy. The humming breath of life I usually feel in everything around me quiets, leaving me dizzy and disoriented. My lungs don't even want to work, the burning ache too painful to breathe against.

But in a single moment, the waves uncurl against the shore, the air sways again, and life returns to everything around me. My chest remains raw and tattered though as Dimitri walks down the dock, his eyes cast downward and his jaw clenched. He makes a point of standing on the other side of the Crusaders from me, and I am equally enraged at him for thinking I'd want him so far away, and relieved that I don't have to face him just yet. Some rational part of me understands what he was saying. Dimitri loved my parents; they raised him as much as any other adult in his life, so I know he wasn't actually glad they were gone. Still, to find any joy in their departure feels wrong, and for that reason, my feet remain where they're planted.

The Crusaders take turns, walking out to the ocean and offering the trinkets and confessions they have to offer, the water seeming to freeze with every offering provided. I'm so consumed by my own retorn heart that I miss whatever Silver gives that causes her to collapse to the dock in tears. I can only imagine it was something of great importance to her, maybe something that had belonged to her late husband or the child she lost.

Güthric is the one to retrieve her. He had been next in the rotation, but instead guides her to the side to cradle her in his massive, bear-like embrace. She finds comfort quickly there, burying her wet face against his chest as he strokes her raven hair.

Near the dock, Adrien clears his throat. The soft tilt of his mouth tells me he's hoping to bring some levity to the situation that has become far darker than I think any of us imagined it would. "A roguish man like me carries no secrets, I'm afraid, but I never dreamed that would be to my own detriment. Remind me to conduct myself as an enigma from now on."

He reaches into his tunic and pulls out a map. I'm not the only one to startle when I see the vellum with a dark splash in the center and what appears to be the Primordial Qaeus in the middle of it.

"What?" The grin he flashes at the Crusaders is wicked, devious. "You didn't expect me to have but one map, did you? The one you stole was only a spare, in case we ever found ourselves robbed in the dead of night."

Sai purses his lips in thought. "As I recall, it was daytime."

With a lavish, exaggerated wave of his hand, my uncle tosses the map over the dock, the item drifting down to the waters as he returns to the group. He flashes Sai a devious grin.

Arms folded, gait as heavy as a lumbering ox, Inigo barrels forward, making Adrien have to practically jump out of the way. He leans over the dock, pauses, and then spits. "The water's unchanged," he growls. "It doesn't look like your contribution is good enough."

Adrien's sly expression falls. He storms back to the shoreline, squatting at the end of the dock as he leans over to retrieve the sodden map from the sloshing ocean below.

"Piss on a mage," he exclaims, waving the vellum to flick as much of the moisture off as he's able.

"A secret it is then," Sai says, smirking.

Adrien scowls at him, and a chuckle bubbles up within me. It feels foreign at first, and I realize it's been days since I've been able to truly laugh. Not since we left the Eyve and Ryven disappeared so that I would be forced to take the breath of life...

The reminder of that dreadful moment snuffs out the momentary joy just as Adrien sighs.

"Oh!" One of his hands shoots into the air. "Ah-ha! I've got it! When we were children—Esmond, Oddo, and I—we were... handfuls, to say the least."

The sound of my father's name is enough to make my skin turn cold. I can't remember the last time I heard someone speak it. Was it my mother the day they died? Across the group, I notice that Alphonse is having a similar reaction to hearing his father's name mentioned so casually as well. It is different for him though. Whereas my father is dead, Esmond still lives, charging back to the Capital as we speak with reinforcements for his plans to infiltrate Illashore. I can only hope that whatever he has in motion will serve to distract the mages from our own arrival. They're bound to determine that an entire legion of warriors is far more dangerous than this ragtag bunch of fugitives and nobodies...right?

"There was one time in particular," my uncle continues, stroking the wisp of brown hair dangling from his chin. "Someone had run through the cottage in shoes that must've been made from mud. Naturally, our mother blamed dear Esmond, for it was he who'd been tasked with cleaning the filthy stables. But Esmond was convinced Oddo was responsible. They'd been in some petty argument earlier that day, and he thought it was Oddo's way of getting revenge on him, by making it seem as if Esmond had destroyed our home and violated our mother's rules about leaving our boots at the door.

"Here's the secret though: it was me. I hadn't meant to keep it a secret, but the finger was never pointed at me, and well, it was admittedly fulfilling to see them argue about it." He pauses, getting swept away into the memory and barking a sharp laugh. But the smile fades all too quickly, almost as if it's swept off his face and swallowed into the stilling tide below. "I'd meant to tell Oddo. He would've found it amusing now, looking back, but… Well, I suppose that opportunity has come and went."

The two of us meet eyes, and I feel my own sorrow reflected in his gaze, hollowing and grave.

He rubs his forehead, shielding part of his face, but once his hand finally falls, his smile has returned.

"What about you?" he asks Sai. "What dismal skeletons do you harbor from that past of yours?"

I've never seen Sai grow so tense. The two of them, really, it's difficult to imagine a time when I've seen either of them when they weren't forcing a smile or a laugh. Even in some of the most despairing times, we've always been able to rely on Adrien to bring levity, and Sai to act as if he is unfazed.

But Adrien's choice of words has a visible impact. He lowers his head as he crosses the shore, and I can't help but glance at Imryll to see if she knew this would be such a miserable endeavor. When the druids of the past came here, did it always end in so many tears and heartbreak? Considering she remains as unmoving as stone, I may never know.

"I wish I could think of something other than my most shameful secret," Sai says quietly. "But I suppose those are the secrets we hold tight to." He resituates his feet, clasping and unclasping his hands in front of him. "I don't much enjoy remembering this moment, so I'll be quick, and I expect no one to bring it up after."

The hush that falls over everyone is deafening. No one dares utter a word, but our silence must be agreement enough because he sucks in a breath.

"My brother. He's why I joined the Shadow Crusade." When

the tide continues swaying back and forth between the vast ocean and the coastline, he sighs and carries on. "We were artisans. We had our own shop. People—*wealthy people* came from all over Arcathain to request our services. We even worked for the Magistrate on more than one occasion—"

Alphonse snaps his pale fingers. "I knew I recognized you! My father had you brought to the Capital to get measurements for the conference hall."

"Shh!" Fox punches his arm.

"Ow." He rubs at his arm, but noticing her glare, reluctantly he closes his mouth.

It takes Sai a moment to resume, as if he's far away in the memory. "It was lucrative work, better than anything we could've ever hoped for." A laugh escapes him, making him blink rapidly. "Here I said I was going to make this short."

"You don't have to," my uncle says softly, joining him where he stands. The sun remains high overhead, but as it's started its decline toward the horizon, it's left a blazing trail of light reflecting off the ocean's surface behind them. It illuminates the two of them in a halo of light, and my uncle takes Sai's hand into his own.

There's something about seeing the two of them together, supporting one another during a dark moment that makes me turn toward Dimitri. My breath catches as our eyes meet. I wonder how long he's been looking at me, waiting for me to finally acknowledge him and his confession.

A sad sort of smile curves the edges of my lips, and I can't tell for certain from this distance, but I swear his lip quivers.

Sai sucks in another breath, this one sounding more painful than the others. "The Shadowthorn came. My brother—Maxwell was his name, ironically enough—he wanted to leave. The demon scourges were becoming more frequent, and he didn't think the Crusaders could defend our borders much longer. But I insisted we stay. We were in the middle of completing an order from a duke that would've kept us fed for a month. It would be enough to allow us to flee."

He glances back down to the dock, but the waves continue to slide beneath the planks at his feet. The Leviathan refuses his offering, still, as if there is more to his confession left to give.

"It's my fault he died. The demons came while I was in the shop, and Maxwell was at the market to purchase a new rasp for some of the finer details...and the demons attacked. I didn't even know for hours, so lost in the work..."

He can't even finish his sentence before sobs rack their way through him. He spasms with each one. My uncle inches closer, gathering him into his arms as the ocean finally stills, Sai's offering accepted. Not wanting to disturb them in this moment of such tender caring and consoling, I avert my attention to the waters that pick back up where they left off. I don't know what I'm waiting for exactly, for the ocean to empty itself, for geysers to form like reverse waterfalls, but I stare out into the expanse and search for any signs of the large creature we've been promised.

My heart thunders beneath my skin; I feel it all the way down my legs, my arms. Something must be seriously wrong with me to be so excited about facing such a formidable crea-ture, but few things have ever thrilled me like this.

But nothing happens. The waters never move. The ground doesn't rumble as if something enormous is coming.

I look to Imryll who appears as equally as confused as I am. She shakes her head. I glance to the others, wondering if maybe we've forgotten someone and then my eyes skim over to Güthric.

"Güthric, you never went."

He curls his head up from where it rests atop Silver's hair and frowns, pulling himself away from her to stare out at the sea. But he doesn't walk toward it. Not at first. After a stint of silence, Güthric whips around and hoists Silver up into his hulking arms.

An uncharacteristic shriek bursts from her lungs as she flails in the air, pinwheeling her arms until she catches his neck. "Güthric!"

He lumbers onto the dock, the gorged planks bowing beneath his heavy stature.

"What are you doing?" she squeals when he stops at the edge.

Güthric looks down at her, his golden blond hair thick and unruly down his back. It's with utter honesty that he speaks. "I only have you."

Silver softens in his grasp, I can see her melt into him, even from this distance. Then she tenses again when he begins heaving her upward. "Güthric! No—"

But just before he can release his hold and toss her into the frigid, salty waters, something changes in the lulling motion of the waves.

And the ocean moans.

FROM THE WATER

THE CLAIMED COAST, THE FORMER SHADOWTHORN

The cataclysmic moment is less of a sound and more of a sensation. The ocean ripples. Like a flag blowing in the wind, the water rumbles with an unnatural and quivering vibration, each writhing wrinkle creeping toward us, and only us, on this very spot on the beach.

With Silver still clutched against his chest, Güthric staggers backward, putting as much distance between him and the expansive ocean as possible. He keeps backing away until he puts every last one of us between him and the monster coming. It's survival instincts, ones I understand just by looking at the other Crusaders who have also started to take unconscious steps away from the livening sea.

But I remain frozen in place, awestruck and eager to behold the sight that's remained hidden for decades.

Darkness bleeds beneath the ocean's surface. Even with the sun shining overhead, even from this distance, level with the tide, I can still see the shadows that creep just below the water's lining, and suddenly my heart is pounding again. The darkness, the creature's body below, is far larger than anything I've ever seen. Larger than any tree that's sprouted from the soil. Larger, still, than the eel that dwells at the bottom of the rivers of

Ushines. Larger even than the Castle of Nigh with its hundreds of corridors and dormitories and chambers.

Like a crack of thunder, the ocean opens its maw. Water pours in sheets down the cavernous abyss that appears, and a moment later, the Leviathan rises with a mighty, earth-shattering roar.

Its slick neck stretches so high that it could rival the Primordial Qaeus in its magnitude. Its body is long and whale-like, aside from the jagged spines and tentacles that jut from its scaly skin in every direction. Its face though isn't whalelike at all. From atop that thin, long neck, the enlarged face of a crocodile stares down at us, one whose teeth are longer, thinner, and far deadlier. The Leviathan couldn't just swallow a human whole; it could guzzle down a small village, all of us standing here before it. A small part of me worries that we've just offered ourselves up on a platter, but that voice is swiftly drowned out by the wonder soaring beneath my skin.

My feet move of their own accord, dragging through the clay beach, aimed for the shadow encroaching as the Leviathan continues its journey toward the shoreline.

Dimitri catches my elbow and pulls me back, the sudden jerking motion whipping me from my state of wonder just in time to see Ryven snarling at him. Before the demon-man can lurch and possibly tear Dimitri limb from limb, I yank my arm free of his grasp and hold my hands out to Ryven.

"I'm all right," I tell them both.

My back turns cold. A shadow casts up and over me, covering Dimitri and everyone else behind him. Slowly, and with immense excitement, I turn around to gaze up at the Leviathan beached on the shore.

It towers over us so high that I'm sure it can't tell us apart from the grains of sand. It lowers its reptilian head to look at us, but then I realize it has no eyes. There are slits of darkness in various locations atop its skull that could indicate some other source of sight—sensors for heat or sound or echolocation—but I can't tell which. I just know it's watching us, assessing the ones who have summoned it.

I wonder how long it's been since it was beckoned to the land, how long since it's seen a druid, or a human, for that matter.

Its swiveling head stops, and a piercing screech belts from its horrifying jaw. It writhes and stomps, the ground quaking beneath the blubbery body meant for water, not land. Without knowing what it saw, it's hard to say for certain what upset it. Maybe it still isn't satisfied with our offerings. Perhaps we still forgot someone—

Ryven.

I glance over my shoulder at him, as if I can dare ask him to offer something to the Leviathan before it flees. The words fall limp on my tongue. His sharp bat nose is scrunched up more than usual, his fangs opened wide in a hiss as he and the Leviathan screech at one another.

Suddenly, I no longer have to guess what's upset the giant water creature.

Imryll steps forward, her arms up in the air. She beseeches the Leviathan with soft chirps and coos that sound like nonsense at first. But as the Leviathan calms, and its shrieks dwindle, allowing my ears to *truly* listen, the sounds my aunt makes start to take on new meaning.

"We mean you no harm, Leviathan. We have offered you our most precious and guarded belongings in exchange for passage to Illashore. Will you grant it?"

The creature bucks, but its flippers only rise a short distance before the dense body of it brings it crashing back down. Not a single one among us stands tall, but Dimitri is quick to offer his hand for steadying regardless.

"I...smell...death."

It takes me a moment to register who has spoken, who the

unfamiliar feminine voice in my head belongs to. The Leviathan talks in languid syllables, not too dissimilar from the way one floats in a lake, calm and drifting. But there's malice buried in her tone. Malice and fear.

"The creature you speak of is not dead, but one created of evil. We believe the answer for his salvation resides on Illashore, along with the key to saving all of humanity."

The Leviathan swivels her long neck down beside my aunt like a predator on the prowl. Her mouth cracks open, just far enough to show off her impressive deadly teeth, freshly crushed shark bones still stuck between some of them.

"The creature...will stay... It can offer nothing to me."

Imryll turns her gaze to mine, sorrow settling in her expression.

Something heavy and cold sinks in my chest. There will be no counterargument. This is what the Leviathan demands, and we are in no position to insist it do anything other than what it wants. I have the distinct feeling that if we were to even try and bargain for Ryven to come, the Leviathan would flop back into the water and ignore any future offerings we might provide. We would never see the creature again. We would never make it to Illashore.

I can feel my heart splintering. Leaving him behind now feels too much like betrayal. I made him a promise and I need to keep it. I don't know what will happen if I leave him here. Will the demon side of him take over? Will he roam the lands, lost to me forever and remain trapped inside the monstrosity that has consumed him?

Without another choice though, what option do I have?

But when I look toward Ryven, his dark, leathery wings are already spread. I reach out for him, a pleading wail bursting from my throat as he catapults into the sky, but I'm too late.

Once again, he's left me. Once again, he's made the difficult choice that I didn't want to.

I steel myself when I hear the snickering whispers of Inigo and his friends. I will not show weakness in front of them, especially not one of heartbreak. Now is the time to follow through on my promises, not crumble in the face of uncertainty and obstacles. No matter where Ryven goes, no matter how long we are separated, nothing will prevent me from following through on the task I've set out to accomplish. If it takes me the rest of my years, I will scour every crevice of Arcathain and cure him. But first, I need to actually find the cure.

"There. He's gone. May we please get on with this then?" The venom in my voice surprises even me, especially considering who I'm directing it at. I'm either fearless or foolish—my sister, judging from the sudden flash of the whites of her eyes would call me the latter.

Imryll dips her head at the beast but her words are for me. "It seems you already have an adept understanding of communicating with beasts, so I have no doubt you'll be able to instruct the Leviathan on where to take you."

"Sir," Inigo's gruff voice drones in the background, as I'm struck by something about my aunt's words.

"You're not coming with us?"

Behind us, I almost don't even hear Alphonse reassuring the brute that going to Illashore is still our safest and most effective strategy in securing the realm. He reminds him that the Magistrate is gathering his army as we speak, and will soon be traveling across the ocean as well. If anything, we are only doing exactly what the Magistrate would be ordering of us; we're just doing it quicker.

I'm distracted by the direction of Imryll's gaze, those cool eyes slipping past me to something that I'm realizing with increasing worry I don't want to acknowledge. Suddenly, all of their hushed conversations are beginning to make sense.

"You're not coming either," I say to my sister.

Her lips are already pursed so tightly, it's almost as if she doesn't even have a mouth. And that would be better because I don't want to have to listen to whatever *logic* is about to come spewing from her lips.

But instead of poised arrogance, Kalli's lips curve, shocking me thoroughly, and almost somehow worrying me more than anything. "You are about to board a Leviathan, a creature that, up until a week ago, you never knew existed. You will travel to the stolen land of the mages, a fractured piece of the old continent that no human—nor druid—has set foot on in decades. This is a reckless mission for someone who has always been guided more by their jittering heart than someone guided by rationality, planning, intention."

I won't stand here and be ridiculed by her from her high horse. Maybe when we were younger, she could've gotten away with speaking to me like this, but I've been through too much since Gravenburg. I'm not the pushover she and Alphonse once took advantage of. I know my decisions might always seem brash, but they're no less calculating than hers.

I open my mouth to tell her just that, but she holds up her hand, her eyes pressing shut. "Please. Let me finish."

Only because of the softness with which she speaks, making it sound more like a plea than the commands I'm used to hearing from her, do I oblige.

"This quest of yours, there is reason behind it. I can see the value of seeking out the mages and the knowledge they might possess. But it is *your* pursuit, not mine."

I look from her to the raven perched on her shoulder. It leans into her cheek, and she strokes its oily feathers with more affection than I've ever seen her show any living being.

"What are you saying?"

She doesn't answer and my ribcage cinches around my heart.

"But you—you gave an offering. To the Leviathan!"

Kalli's white dreads sway around her face as she shakes her head and lowers her eyes. "That was not an offering. It was a statement. A declaration of which side I am on."

"I don't understand."

"I'm saying, dearest Halira, that you should follow your heart, and I will follow mine. The Magistrate is gathering his forces. He plans to launch an attack on Illashore, one that could, at the very least, impact your plans of requesting their aid with the Primordial, and of course, with Ryven."

The ache in my chest floods out into the rest of my being, making it difficult to hear her at first. But slowly, her intent settles on me. "You plan to return to the Magistrate then?"

"I am not returning *to* him. But he needs to know that—"

"Know what? What will you tell him? Have you forgotten that we're both fugitives now? He could execute you—"

"He will not." Her tone grows icy cold, as do her steel gray eyes as they snap to mine. "Despite the poison our Father fed you for years about the callousness of our uncle, he is someone who can be reasoned with, if he believes it to be in the interest of his people."

Alphonse scoffs, pushing forward through the worried-looking crowd as they continue to gape up at the Leviathan's offered tentacle. "I beg to differ. You might've had the pleasure of working alongside him for a few years, but I've known him my entire life. He is stubborn in his convictions."

Kalli's shoulders remain stiff and pulled back. "That may be so, but the Magistrate and I speak the same language. His conviction is to restore his country and preserve what he can of humanity. If I go to him with a proposal of how to do just that, he will listen."

Like a striking cobra, I spin around to face my aunt. "And you're encouraging this?"

"It is what Kalli believes she must do. Would you want

someone to stand in your way when your mind was made up on your calling?"

My fingers curl. I'm too distraught to hear this level of reason, especially since I thought hearing it from Kalli would be bad enough; now I have two of them to deal with.

"Why didn't you tell me sooner? Why have you both been so secretive about this?"

Kalli's lips thin again as she glances to our aunt. "Because I was asking her for a favor, one she countered with a less than preferable bargain, and I wanted to be certain I was accepting it before I told you anything."

"What favor? What bargain?"

"She wanted me to join you," Imryll says plainly. "But she does not know what she asks. You two were not raised by our people, so you cannot comprehend the enormity of such a request. I have no plans of accompanying you to Illashore. With the Shadowthorn destroyed, I have a greater purpose at the Eyve, and that is where I desire to be."

"Then what was the bargain?" I ask, growing irritated.

"The bargain is," Kalli begins, dragging her finger up to the raven's talons. It steps onto her hand. "You will go to Illashore. You will seek your answers, and my raven will join you. He cannot aid you if you are in trouble, but he will help us stay connected. Whenever you need to speak to me, send him away. He will find me.

"But, in the instance that you find yourself in danger, you will summon Imryll the same way you did back in Nigh."

Two memories flashes before me, the first that dingy cell that Imryll had torn apart to release her nieces. I wasn't even sure when I'd said her name what to expect. A spell? Some kind of protection? I hadn't imagined it could be a summoning, let alone one that would call upon an aunt we never knew existed.

The second image to flash in my mind's eye is the name of my aunt whispered on my mother's dying lips.

"She is bound to you, thanks to our mother," Kalli says. "If you are ever in danger, Imryll will come. She has no choice, but she has also agreed to it. It is the least she can do since she will not accompany you directly." She sends a scathing look at my aunt who remains unmoved.

"But what about you? I don't care about your raven—" I glare at the bird trying and failing at settling on my shoulder. "I don't care about being able to summon our aunt. I care about the danger you're putting yourself in."

"And what about you?" My sister's eyes grow sharp, a small flicker of amusement flashing somewhere behind her gray irises. "Are you not doing the same? Some would argue you're putting yourself in more danger than I am, but I am not foolish enough to try to convince you to do anything other than what you've already decided you'll do."

"Don't call me foolish," I grit out under my breath.

She sighs, her hands grasping both of my arms. "I'm not." She holds me there for a moment, searching my face until my stubborn gaze finally caves and meets hers. She looks so much like our mother from this close that the next inhale I take is sharp. "We both have tasks to complete that we believe will be useful. Yes, it will be dangerous for both of us. But doing nothing is possibly more so."

And there it is. The strike of reason that cracks away my steel armor.

If I stayed on Arcathain, I have no doubt what would become of Qaeus. The Magistrate is too distracted by his lust for vengeance to respond quick enough to save anyone, not to mention we have nothing that can be used to bring down the Primordial. Kalli believes her path to be one of equal importance, and who am I to say that it isn't? Having the Magistrate on our side, aligned with our cause, could prove invaluable if it works. And having him against us, having him arrive with cannons loaded and archers readied as we are in the middle of negotiations could ruin everything.

My head bows when I sigh, and my forehead presses against Kalli's.

"I will be fine," she reassures me, but it's an empty promise, one I repeat just to mock her and how utterly unbelievable she sounds.

An amused grin graces through her usually impassive face, but all traces of it are gone by the time she stands straight again.

She holds her arm out, indicating to the tentacle I'd almost forgotten was resting on the ground behind me. The Crusaders have gathered around it, but they still stare at it with distrust, not a single one of them having braved it while we were speaking—

"This is amazing!" someone shrieks, drawing my attention above. Shielding my eyes and straining against the brightness of the sky, I peer up to get a better look at who has already boarded the Leviathan's back. With the sun still hanging almost directly overhead, all I catch is a flash of fiery red. "It's like a ship up here, but on the back of a sea monster—no offense."

I am next to brave the Leviathan's tentacle. I stand atop the spear-tip-shaped flesh, and it squelches beneath my feet. I'm too busy staring at my sister, trying to memorize her steel-cold eyes, the freckle above her brow, and the way her white ropes of hair are adorned with a few silver bangles. I want to sear everything about her into my mind, for fear I will never see her again.

I'm still staring at her as the Leviathan hoists me up to its back, but from this surprising and majestic height, I'm distracted quickly. The magnificent hull on its back beckons me, as does the hand that extends out to help me aboard.

"What is this?"

Fox beams at me, her toothy grin almost childlike. "I told you," she says. "It's like a ship up here."

I'm barely steady on my feet before the Leviathan removes its tentacle, seemingly preparing to retrieve another member of our party, but I hardly notice. My gaze roves over the vessel I'm standing on, the one constructed by something black and shiny, something that almost looks alive. There are no sails—the Leviathan would have no need for them—but otherwise the rest of it looks exactly like the deck of a ship. A lookout stretches high from the back of the deck atop an elevated platform. There is a cabin beneath it, I realize, and another set of stairs that leads below.

There will be time to explore later though, I remind myself. I only get one farewell.

But when I look over the edge back down to the beach, my sister and aunt are already gone.

A BEAST AWAKENS

VARENHOLM OCEAN, THE CLAIMED COAST

Before I can think better of it, I lean farther over the ledge. Desperately, I search the surrounding area for the two heads of white hair that belong to Kalli and Imryll, but though I find neither, my eye catches on the black wings of a raven and the white wings of a snow owl just before they disappear behind the trees. My cheeks sting with held back tears. I don't understand how they could just leave—I wasn't ready yet. I feel like we didn't even get to say—

"Halira!" Dimitri's voice catches my attention, and I swivel around, finding him boarding the ship just down the deck. Fox rolls her eyes, and when he turns his back to her and races toward me, she makes a face at him. "Be careful. You could fall."

His hands hook under my arms, and he spins me away from the ledge. My heart flutters, a light, buzzing sensation that sets my whole body afloat—or maybe that's just from my feet being lifted off the ground.

When he sets me back down, we're so close I can smell the familiar scent of wood on him, the one that had followed him his entire life, and always lay dormant beneath his other pungent aromas: the blood of cattle, the sweat of hard labor. I much prefer this one. It reminds me of our childhood, of racing through the woods behind the Wallows.

His chest rises and falls in a deep and steadying rhythm. I stare up into his green eyes, the ones that make me think of herbs and salt and—

Something black flickers across the sun behind him and my throat catches. Ryven soars through the clouds out in the vast sky, and it dawns on me: he hasn't left, he's just keeping his distance.

My awareness returns to the proximity of Dimitri's body, to where his flat stomach presses against mine and I can feel the pulsing of his heart. His fingers stroke my arms absentmindedly and my stomach dips.

A short, nervous laugh bursts from my lips, and I shove myself away from him. "You know you have nothing to worry about, right?" I remind him. "If I fell, I'd just...*whoosh*." I gesture with my arm for effect though it's obvious from his pained expression that he needed no interpretive dance.

He sinks into the heels of his shoes. "Right. I forgot. You can...do things like that now." He's quiet for a moment before asking, "What does it feel like when—"

"Hello!" Fox sings the word, but there's more irritation in her tone than anything jubilant. "Are you two going to help me, or what?"

We both turn to find her helping someone else off the gelatinous tentacle. The Leviathan has dozens though, and she's begun using them. The three on this side are all occupied by Crusaders now. Dimitri and I exchange a brief look that says, *We best get to work*, before we each race to one of the struggling travelers, aiding one after another up onto the ship on the Leviathan's back until every last one of us is here.

As the others gather near the back of the deck, I make my way closer toward the Leviathan's neck. The glorious creates raises her head from the ground, swiveling it around so that she can look at me. For a moment, I fear I won't be able to communicate with her. The noises my aunt made are ones I can't mimic, at least not with any coherency. Unlike her, I wasn't raised with the druids, apparently learning ancient Leviathan.

But then I remember what she told me before I left, and I think about the way I've communicated with Ryven.

"You can understand me?"

"*Yes,*" the creature says, a gust of fishy breath wafting over me.

I try not to inhale through my nose. "That's all of us. We're ready to go."

"*Where do we travel?*"

I stiffen. "To…Illashore."

The Leviathan doesn't reply immediately, and I start to worry that we loaded everyone up here just to find out that it can't make such a long journey. "*Yes...to Illashore...but where?*"

"Oh." I understand her conundrum more clearly now. I remember seeing maps of Arcathain from before the Great Rift. The section of the continent that was stolen was not insignificant by any means; it was probably as large as the Eyve itself, maybe even larger now if the mages used their magic to tamper with it.

But now I'm the one to hesitate. I sneak a cautionary look over my shoulder at the others. They're too preoccupied marveling at the deck or arguing with one another that this is a mistake or exploring to notice me speaking with our ride. I know what they'd want me to say. Their sole purpose is to find the mages and destroy Qaeus. They'd want to be taken to the mages immediately. According to our history books, the mages once ruled themselves under a council, and there's been talk among us that if we were to request their aid now, it would need to be done through their council.

But I have a promise to keep.

"We are headed for the Pits of Bagamore. Can you take us there?"

The Leviathan's inhale is a sharp hiss. *"No."* All sense of hope plummets into my belly. But she continues. *"The Pits of Bagamore...are inland..."*

"Oh..." My shoulders slump again, but my mind is quick at work. We've come too far—some of us having sacrificed too much—to give up so quickly. "But you can take us to Illashore and leave us as close as we can get?"

"There is a shore—"

"Great! That's wonderful. Thank you."

The Leviathan sighs, a sound robust and heavy with centuries' worth of exhaustion as she returns her head upright. I don't have time to announce to the others that we're about to leave. The Leviathan lumbers on the land, its blubberous body wiggling to turn back around toward the sea. The ripples of every rocking motion fill the deck with a tremor. Everyone staggers and stumbles. I wobble on bent legs until finally deciding it's useless and succumb to the ground. Whatever the deck is made of is cool to the touch, refreshing. It makes my hands feel wet, but the moment I pull them away, I find my fingertips are still dry.

Before long, the Leviathan has corrected its trajectory, but the wiggling continues as it shimmies back into the ocean. I hadn't actually thought about what would happen to us once we reached the water. Seeing the boat-like container on the Leviathan's back, I assumed it would be like drifting at sea, but I suppose I never asked.

I guess we're about to find out.

It takes a while for the rocking to stop, even long after the Leviathan is back in the water. I realize it's because the ocean was too shallow before for the creature to swim, its impossibly large body still dragging on the ocean floor even after we leave the coast. I drag myself to one side of the deck, leaning against the taffrail in an effort to get comfortable.

Eventually, after what feels like hours, the jerking back and forth gives way to a gentler sway, one that mimics the ocean we find ourselves drifting in. The noises of the woods fade, replaced by the wet sounds of fishes jumping up from the water's surface, of the occasional gull squawking overhead, of the constant rhythmic groaning of the vast body of water that surrounds us on all sides.

I realize I'm hunched in a strange position, one side of my body cradled in my clutch. My hands are pressed against my stomach, atop the same spot where I'd been bitten by a demon not too long ago.

Tentatively, I unclasp my leather waistcoat and peel up the thin fabric of my blouse underneath. My breath actually hitches when I behold nothing but soft, pale flesh, all signs of the dark infestation of evil that had seeped out from fang marks: gone. Suddenly, the phantom pain that had me wincing and curling into myself ceases.

It doesn't seem real that the Blight is gone. I keep thinking that I can still feel it inside me, dormant and lying in wait until it is sparked again. The thought sends a shiver through me, and somewhere distant I swear I hear Ryven's mournful cry.

Just as I'm lowering my blouse, a calloused hand catches my wrist. The instinct to fight flares in me like a stoked fire. I look over, ready to throw my fist into Inigo's already crumpled face, when I meet kind sage eyes instead.

Dimitri lowers himself from his knees to a sitting position, his grip unrelenting but gentle. Sorrow etches into his expression as he gazes upon my exposed stomach.

His throat bobs. "I watched that demon sink its fangs right through you," he says, voice hoarse. "It's a miracle you're alive."

Miracle doesn't feel like the right word. My survival wasn't happenstance or a fluke; it was a gift from the very person who needed it more than I did.

After realizing he's still holding my wrist, he lets go and scoots beside me. "So, what's the deal with you and that demon-guy anyway?"

Fire blooms from my chest, the flames climbing my neck and singeing my cheeks until I'm sure there isn't a bit of my flesh that isn't bright red. I don't want to talk to Dimitri about Ryven. It seems…wrong. I'm not even sure what I'd say anyway. I could say I owe him my life, but it's more than that, and I've known that for a while now. *A while* seems like a joke though. I've known Dimitri for almost our entire lives, and I've only known Ryven now for what? A few weeks? If it took me eighteen years to realize I had a romantic interest in Dimitri, what makes me think I could possibly have one for someone who is practically a stranger after less than a month?

The briefest shadow drifts over the ship, but when I look up, all I see are clouds.

I change the subject. "What you said on the beach, I… understand." He tenses beside me, but I continue. "I know you weren't glad my parents died. I know you loved them. The confession you gave, the feelings you had, I…I can understand them. I want you to know that."

He sniffs. "It was wrong for me to feel that way."

"No one can help how they feel," I argue.

His head snaps up again, his green eyes penetrating against my skin. "How do you feel?"

The simmering heat in my face threatens to rise again, but I remind myself that there are too many possible answers to that question for him to mean the one that I fear he does. "About what?"

"About all of this?" His arms gesture to our surroundings. "We're on the back of a Leviathan, somewhere in the middle of the Varenholm Ocean, on our way to Illashore to seek the mages who we've been raised to detest." He glances at me out of the corner of his eye. "Not to mention…your aunt and sister left. I know that couldn't have been easy."

Now I'm the one to feel my shoulders turning to stone. I avert my gaze to anything but his face and the sympathy I know I'll find there.

"You left that demon too, and I saw the way you called after him. Like you were…"

It's like warm water rushes over my ears, drowning out the familiar sound of Dimitri's voice and forcing my thoughts to Ryven. The day has been too testing—the entire past month has been nothing but one challenge after another, and I no longer have the patience to deal with any of it. For weeks I wondered how Dimitri was faring. I wondered if he regretted his choice, if we'd ever see each other again, if he even thought about me after he'd left me in the Shadowthorn.

But he did leave me. That was his choice, not mine.

"*You* left *me*, Dimitri. Remember?" His mouth gapes open, but I fill the brief moment of silence before he can. "I was dying. I was forced into hiding in the Shadowthorn, and I didn't know if I was going to survive."

"I—I know," he stutters. His warm hands search for mine. "That's why I left. Your uncle, he said—"

"You were going to leave before!" I shout, yanking my hands away. "And why? Because you thought I was a mage! Not because I'd actually done anything wrong, or harmed someone, or…or…was no longer the person you wanted, but because you discovered I had magic."

His mouth hangs agape. "I-I'm sorry. All I can say is I'm sorry. I was afraid and it was foolish. I told you—"

"You don't understand. You were the one person I thought I could rely on. You were the one thing in my life that I thought I'd never lose—except in battle. But never did I dream you'd walk away from me while we both still lived. I'd never even considered it..."

With his lips parted, a thousand thoughts screaming from his throat but never quite making it past his mouth, he finally sighs. "I've never been like you, Halira. I'm weak minded. I'm not...free-willed like you are. I do what I'm told because that's what is right. Or at least, that's what I've always thought. But I'm...I'm *trying*. I'm trying to learn and adapt and become... better than I was. It took making the biggest mistake of my life to learn that sometimes what's right is the same thing you've been told is wrong all your life."

My throat becomes a shriveled-up thing that's been left in the sun too long. But I manage to squeak out a few words. "And what mistake was that?"

"Leaving you there that day. I should've stayed with you. Or I should've brought you back with us—I don't know. But what's been painfully obvious to me ever since I left those woods was that I should've never left your side."

An ache builds inside me, its warmth coiling out from my chest as if it were calling to him. From lowered lashes, I lift my gaze to meet his. The sage-green eyes I expect to find are different than I remember. Perhaps it's the reflection of the ocean, but they appear more vibrant than ever before, the golden flecks inside them dazzling like jewels.

Before I can do something stupid, I focus on what he said just before and grin. "So am I the *wrong* thing in this scenario or—"

He shoves my shoulder hard, and for a moment, it feels like old times again. Before Nigh and the Shadow Crusade. Before the Shadowthorn was at our front doors, a constant reminder of the doom that awaited us and our families.

Our laughter fades in time into an uneasy silence. Doubt and uncertainty and hurt fills the space between us, a dozen questions and accusations swimming around us like sharks waiting to strike. Talking about our past, what we meant to each other, is a conversation I'm not ready to have yet. And so, I let my mind occupy itself with one of the many concerns that has been clawing at me, and I bring Dimitri there with me.

"We were told shadowsteel would kill a Primordial. It's the entire reason why we trained with it; why the Crusaders fight with it. Why didn't it work on Qaeus?"

Dimitri shakes his head, golden hair shining in the sun. "I don't know. But you're sure it didn't work?" Noticing my irritation, he adds quickly, "I mean, it was shadowsteel you struck it with, right?"

I nod, and the two of us slouch against the deck's railing again.

"Maybe the mages will know," he offers. "They did help create shadowsteel, after all."

"You don't think…that it was all a lie, do you?"

The sound that leaves his lips is one of pure derision. I'm not sure he's aware he's doing it, but he's started stroking the length of his scabbard, a cool look of vengeance seething behind his eyes. "I wouldn't doubt it. But we did kill the first three. I don't know how we could've done that without the shadowsteel the mages made, and why those same weapons would be ineffective on Qaeus."

Frowning, I chew on my lip. "Some people believe that she's become too powerful to be slain. History says that many Crusaders faced her, and the more who perished by her hand, the stronger she became."

"The other Primordials slaughtered us too, though." Dimitri tilts his head, considering. "I don't know. I think we're missing something."

"I think we're missing a lot," I counter. "Like, where did the Primordials even come from? Have they been malevolently roaming the realm for all eternity? And if so, how have we survived this long? How did anyone survive them before shadowsteel was created? How many years had passed before we began killing them? Were there demons then too, or did those come later?"

A long sigh eases from Dimitri's lips. "I wish I knew."

I watch him from the corner of my eye for a moment. It feels good to be able to talk to him again. We'd always operated differently from each other, but unlike with my sister, Dimitri and I could actually speak without irritating the other. It still happened, granted, but the other times when it didn't, when we could talk to each other about anything and everything, I felt as if the realm was right.

Or at least as right as it could be with a crazed Primordial loose.

Thinking of Qaeus that way sparked something nearly forgotten, something I haven't shared with anyone yet for fear of how they'd look at me. Dimitri still might doubt my sanity, or my ability to discern truth from lie, good from evil, but sharing this time with him emboldens me.

"I was able to speak with Qaeus, right after she became… what she is."

Dimitri watches me through widening eyes, but he doesn't speak. He lets me tell him on my own terms.

I swallow through the trepidation. "She seemed…good. At least, at first. It was like there were two sides of her, each one warring with the other, and the darkness was winning."

"Okay…" he says after a long moment. "What do you think that means?"

"I don't pretend to have any clue. I'm just talking through it all, in case something sparks for either of us."

His brow furrows, mind working in overdrive. "You don't think she was always evil."

I flinch, shame making me avert my eyes. The moment he says it, I can hear how ridiculous it sounds. The others would be right to distrust my judgment. The Primordial has wreaked havoc on our lands for generations. Her demons hunt us down and feed on our bodies. Every Arcathainian has lost someone to the demons or worse, including myself. How could I ever even suggest that—

"Maybe you're right."

Choking on air, I struggle to find words. "Excuse me?"

Dimitri shrugs. "I said maybe you're right. It would make sense, in some ways. It's like you were saying earlier: could we really have survived all this time if a monster like that—four of them—lived to devour us? Think of how many people die every day from the demons at our borders. Think of how many Crusaders we've lost in the Blight. We would've been extinct by now if those bloodthirsty monsters had been here all along. So either—"

"Either they were created for evil, or they were once good," I finish for him.

"Maybe even both."

"*Ahem.*" Fox clears her throat, drawing us both out of our exceedingly interesting conversation.

She fixes her gaze on me, hardly even acknowledging Dimitri's presence, and already my chest is tightening. I still can't decide whether to trust her or not. I know where that blind loyalty got me in the past.

"Sorry to interrupt you," she says. "But some of us are going to play a game of Maximus, and wanted to extend an invitation." When I don't immediately accept, doubt and hesitation clawing my throat, she adds, "Could be a lot of fun to lose some fake coin." A playful smile cuts across her face, but it abruptly falls when she swivels to address Dimitri. "Since I'm trying to make amends to my friend here, I feel compelled to invite you as well."

Dimitri glares back at her, even as he speaks to me. "I told you not to trust her. Once a liar and a thief, always a liar and a thief."

She balks. "Excuse you. If you really think we should play a game of Whose-Betrayal-Hurt-Worse, please, be my guest."

It's another scratch, another incision along my aching throat that trails to the tender flesh of my beating heart, and it's too much. Something akin to blood, warm and metallic, fills the back of my mouth, and all I want is for it to stop. I don't want to feel this pain. I don't want to have to think about their betrayals every time I look at them. I don't want to relive the unbearable agony of realizing Fox had condemned me to my death and Dimitri left me to die in the Shadowthorn. I just want things to be as they once were.

And maybe it's for that reason that I ignore the instinct screaming inside me to run away from the both of them now. Who would've thought that any of us would ever see one another again? Who'd have thought I'd survive the Blight, the Shadowthorn, and find myself on the back of a Leviathan with my oldest and newest friends?

Warmth exudes me the more I think about being reunited with the people I thought I'd never see again, some of whom I was sure would die without me ever getting to say goodbye, and so, instead of denying her, I hear myself say, "Count us in."

TO SAIL THE SEAS

VARENHOLM OCEAN

As we stand, the Leviathan bucks ever so slightly, presumably rolling with the sway of the ocean. It's nowhere near as jostling as the motions were when we were first starting our voyage, but Dimitri curses under his breath and looks as if he's about to buckle to the ground. His face becomes as pallid as the moon.

I flash him a teasing grin. "Is the great Crusader Dimitri afraid of being tossed into the ocean?"

"Piss off," he growls, batting away the hand I offer.

I roll my eyes and grab his bicep anyway. "Don't be such a mage."

The rocking settles, and he returns to his feet with a scowl that I realize as soon as the sun shines on it is more playful than anything. "You better stop saying that, if you hope to ingratiate to those cretins."

I open my mouth to retort, but my teeth snap shut. He's right. I can't imagine that using that colloquial phrase would engender much trust or respect from the mages, and if they're as haughty and arrogant as our history books make them appear, I wouldn't put it past them to deny us outright for saying anything that could be perceived as disrespectful.

"I'll work on it," I promise him, the two of us following the path we saw Fox take as she strolled off to alert the others that we'd both be joining them.

We find a half dozen of our fellow travelers crammed below deck and gathered around a table that appears as if it might fall apart if one more person rests their elbows atop it. I'm not surprised when I notice Inigo and his friends are missing. Though much of their disdain has been targeted at me, I'm not the only fugitive among us who has been on the receiving end of their ire. Güthric was known and beloved by the Crusaders before we fled. Silver, less so, but still. It's obvious that some among us recognize her and don't approve of her departure. But it's perhaps my uncle who has received the dirtiest looks. If it hadn't been for his frequent storytelling, I'm not sure the others would've even known who he was and how many times he'd stolen from the realm, tricked the Magistrate and made him look a fool, or otherwise participated in shenanigans befitting a ruffian. None of us dared point out that they were technically rogue Crusaders now as well, especially after how much effort Alphonse put into reassuring them that this was in alignment with the Magistrate's will. Why he even bothered was beyond me.

By the time Dimitri and I take our seats, a game has already been dealt.

I smile across at Sai and the familiar, worn cards in his hands. "You've had these on you the entire time?"

He shrugs, a sly smile tugging at one side of his face. "You expected something different from me?"

I'm about to remind him that he was tossed around like a ragdoll in Ashenvale, and that the cards could've easily been flung from his satchel or wherever he kept them, but after what he said about his brother earlier, and the gruesome end he met, it feels wrong to bring up any encounters with the shadowcreatures. Especially now, while people are clearly trying to distract their minds.

"Anyway, as I was saying before I was so rudely interrupted —" Alphonse squints his eyes in my direction. I had been so wrapped up in trying to find the group that I hadn't even noticed they were amid a conversation when we arrived. He gives a theatrical clearing of his throat. "Never in my three years of Shadowthorn missions had I ever seen such a beast. Its eight crooked legs, the heavy body that hung low to the ground as it prowled, the bones… It's a sight that will forever haunt my mind."

"How did you survive?" Fox asks, inching so close that she's practically on his lap.

His discomfort at her public display of affection is obvious, but the question strokes his ego too much for him to do anything but answer her.

"How does any Crusader evade death? With bravery and—"

My head falls backward as I guffaw, the burst of laughter bright and echoing between these strange, glistening walls. "Bravery? You ran away like a scared child, practically screaming and mewling like a babe."

He straightens in his seat, lifting his head higher. "It's a general's duty to survive—"

Now it's Dimitri who snorts. "Not while abandoning his people to their deaths."

Güthric barks a loud laugh that is more boisterous than the moment entails. He slams his hand on Dimitri's back in good jest, and it's the first time I've noticed just how excited he is to see his old friend. He followed me—well, Silver, more likely—into the Shadowthorn out of loyalty to the both of us, but I'd never wondered what it had cost him.

As the chuckling dwindles between Adrien, Sai, Fox, and Silver, I glance at my cousin. His gusto is all but gone. He sits, slumped on the bench, a dark cloud raining down upon him.

The old Alphonse would've deserved such scorn and ridicule. I'd even wished it upon him on numerous occasions. But even if he was still the arrogant man who couldn't admit his faults for fear of being judged, he had made some changes, ones that I appreciated more than he would ever know.

"He made up for it later," I say, silencing the group. Alphonse's eyes flick to mine with ever-shifting reservation and hope. "We found a Labyrinth on our way to the Eyve. The monsters we fought outside the wall? Those all came from that horrid place of nightmares. We were forced to enter to—" Realizing my purpose in telling this story is to paint my cousin in a more generous light, I decide to omit the reasons that led us there. "Well, we were forced to enter, but leaving was no easy task."

My uncle sets his cards flat on the table, a devilish grin spreading on his face as he leans back in his chair. "This sounds like it's about to be more exciting than the time the Wardens and I attended the annual masquerade at the Capital, and slipped jimsonweed into the—"

"Shh!" Fox hissed. "Let her tell us how heroic Alphy was."

Heat returns to Alphonse's gaze.

My uncle pouts, and Sai leans over him and whispers something in my uncle's ear that makes his entire expression warm.

"You were saying?" Fox prompts.

"There were a lot of shadowcreatures in the Labyrinth. We outran most of them, but just as we were reaching the exit, a giant wyrm burst from the ground. I faced the creature, commanding it back to the depths from which it came, but the endeavor took the last bit of strength I was clutching onto out of me. I fell unconscious. If it wasn't for Alphonse dragging me out and away to safety, there's no telling which of the monsters chasing us would've devoured me."

Fox springs closer to my cousin, wrapping her arms around his neck and dragging him down to her until their lips crash.

Seeing them together now, it's difficult to imagine them ever being able to refrain themselves before. But I remind myself that things were different then. That was before Fox learned that the man she—I'm assuming—loves was dead.

She's not the only one. According to Dimitri, discovering such a thing about the person you cared about really put things into perspective. He had been different since our reunification outside the Primordial's heart, and I'm not sure what that means for us exactly, but I don't have to think about it now.

Despite assuming the dark conversation would be of no interest to our friends, they keep asking me and Alphonse questions about our time in the Shadowthorn. I tell them about the Eyve and the three druid Elders that offered us helpful, if not cryptic, guidance. I describe to them in vivid detail the beautiful Ushines streams and rivers, and the serene lake. I skip over the pleasant evening Ryven and I had spent there, not only to spare myself the twinge in my heart at the thought that we might never share a moment like that again, but also because something had felt sacred about that moment, like Ryven was sharing that spot with me and only me, and I'm not sure I want anyone knowing about it either. Fast-forwarding to the next morning, I tell everyone about the eel that had dwelled deep below the surface, the one that swallowed us whole to grant Ryven and I the temporary gills that allowed us entrance into the Dark Sea.

I leave out the rest of our time at the lake, staring up at the stars, bathing in the warm spring, and when the ache in my chest becomes too raw, when I swear I can hear the low agonizing groan of a forlorn demon soaring somewhere above the ship as we are propelled through the sea on a Leviathan, I veer the conversation back to some of our more harrowing adventures and avoid anything having to do with the strange, aching warmth in my chest.

I tell them of my journey to the Dark Sea, of meeting the

long-forsaken sirens and the angler fish guarding their most prized possession. We talk of the Labyrinth and the Blight sickness, and the behemoths stalking outside the Eyve and what happened with the Primordial Qaeus.

Alphonse chimes in whenever he can, getting particularly boastful about how he heroically survived the dingy dungeons as a druid prisoner. But, when the group teases him about his wrongful imprisonment, it seems as if he's actually being genuine when he admits that he has done far worse for far less.

I'd almost forgotten what it was like to be surrounded by friends, to share stories, and tears, and laughter. Glancing around the table now as Silver bests Adrien with a particularly low primero hand, guilt sifts through me for feeling so happy to have them here. Where we are heading, it will likely be dangerous. The mages left our homeland and abandoned us without ever looking back; only beings of pure loathing could ever do such a thing, and we are almost certain to face their ire upon our arrival. We could have to fight. We could have to kill. Some of us could die. Then again, I doubt it could be any more dangerous than being Crusaders sent into the Shadowthorn to fight a Primordial that no one can slay.

The dwindling laughter is punctured by the sound of wood creaking, before the bench Güthric is sitting on buckles beneath his weight and crashes. The sudden slant of the bench takes Silver with it, the raven-haired woman falling into his arms as Fox and Alphonse slide into the two of them.

Laughter rises from the small room like a chorus. Güthric bellows, tossing his head back while Silver tries to stand from the refuse.

"Well, that's just great," Fox growls, climbing up from the splintered bench and wiping her hands on her leather breeches. "Now where are we going to eat or congregate and entertain ourselves?"

Dimitri grunts as he helps Güthric to stand. "I'm sure we can figure something out."

My uncle rounds the table and squats down to examine the rubble. I don't know enough about woodworking to know whether the damage that's been done to the bench is irreparable, but Adrien lifts the long board with an optimistic frown. "I can fix it."

My eyes bulge with disbelief. "My father never said you were a wood worker."

His laugh is clipped and airy. "Far from. I've never touched a board or a nail or a hammer a day in my life. But," he adds with a shrug, "it's not like I don't have the time to learn. Traveling across the ocean will take…well, a while, I imagine. I'm sure I'll be able to figure it out."

There's a groan from the other end of the table. "You'll need help. It's not as simple as hammering a nail into a board. You have to take into account weight distribution, the angles of the supports, the thickness of the wood."

My uncle's honey-brown eyes drift up to Sai whose already examining the thing like he's building it in his mind. "It is very generous of you to offer. Shall we begin those lessons now then?"

Rather than standing there watching the two of them work, we all clear out to explore the other nooks and rooms.

But before I leave, my uncle winks as he digs into the pocket of his tattered trousers and pulls out a nail. He twirls it between his fingers, smirks, and mouths, "Exactly as planned."

A NEW DRUID

CABINS, LEVIATHAN, VARENHOLM OCEAN

A sound that should be too quiet to awaken me jars me from my sleep. My eyes are heavy as they blink through the darkness of the bedchamber. Despite sleeping on this exact same cot for a number of days now, with this same dingy, salt-roughened blanket pulled up to my shoulders, it still takes me a few weary blinks before I remember where I am.

Out at sea.

Atop a swaying Leviathan that never seems to sleep or rest.

Headed for the land of the mages.

It feels more like I'm falling into a dream than waking from one. Aside from a few family trips to Drayfil Shore or to visit my uncle at the Capital, my entire life was spent in the same small, drab town, never even daring to dream of what might lay beyond our borders. Even while I was training to become a Crusader, I never thought I'd see any new side of Arcathain other than one of the border towns that would soon be devoured by darkness, let alone did I think I'd discover the Forgotten Forest of Eyve and then set sail across the Varenholm Ocean to go to Illashore.

But I settle back into the acknowledgment that all of this is true. This is the life I've chosen for myself, the path I've set out on, and suddenly I recognize the airy flapping that had nudged me from the depths of my slumber.

I swing my legs over the side of the cot, squeeze my feet into the boots laying discarded below me, and race up the stairs to the main deck.

The moon hangs low on the horizon, like the dark sky is moments away from swallowing it and casting the rest of the world into oblivion. No one ever told me how beautiful it was to be out at sea at night. I'd thought the stars in the Eyve had been dazzling, but here? Here they illuminate the sky with the slightest purple and blue hues. I can see them for miles and miles, thousands if not millions of them burning in the ether above.

It always makes me catch my breath, every time I come up here. But just as I've done every morning, I try not to dally.

I turn right and take the stairs to the upper deck at the front of the ship. The night sky blends in so thoroughly with the vast, dark ocean that I can't even tell the difference between the two. I almost can't even see the Leviathan's flippers and tentacles, the ones that always protrude from the water and cradle the ship I'm standing on now. The large shadow of corded arms and legs and leathery wings balancing on the ship's edge merges almost seamlessly with the darkness.

Ryven doesn't react to my presence, but I know he senses me the moment I arrive. Perhaps even sooner.

I fill the space beside him, sucking in a deep breath when his warmth hits me. Unlike the frigid harshness of the morning, the heat of his proximity melts into me, turning the ice that had begun to cling to my bones to puddles.

I stare up at him, but his black eyes remain fixed on the horizon ahead.

"I'm sorry you have to go," is all I can think to say. It's all I ever say. Because out of all of the circumstances I am powerless to change, it is the easiest to accept. The Leviathan still does not approve of his presence, but after a few pleading conversations, I was able to convince her to allow him to sleep here during the nights. Without the small reprieves from travel, I'm not sure how far he would've been able to make it. And despite wanting to implore the Leviathan to change her stance on him all together, I fear asking for anything more would only make matters worse.

Ryven's eyes, as black and glistening as two cores of onyx, flick to mine for the briefest of moments before he turns his face farther away. He doesn't like allowing me to see him. I'm sure by now he's glimpsed his reflection, and I can't blame him for being horrified or embarrassed; I know I would be, even though I don't want that for him.

In the same breath that I reach out for him, I draw back. He's not a pet to be stroked, I keep reminding myself. I want to give him comfort, but I never know how.

"I'm sending the raven back to Kalli today," I say to him, attempting to break the awkward silence. "Maybe by now she'll have found the Magistrate, or at least by the time her raven finds her. Maybe she'll have news about whether they'll be joining us, how many ships they'll bring, and how long it'll take for them to meet us there."

I leave out the part where she might send no message in return. If the Magistrate has imprisoned my sister or worse, the raven may never find her. But I tell myself that can't be the case. At the very least, I know my sister is still alive. Her bird would know if she had met her end.

The taut muscles of Ryven's back rise and fall as he listens. He keeps his dark wings tucked against him like a shield.

I bite my lower lip. Things had been so easy between us before. I'd spent much of my life feeling numb and dead inside, and then I met him, and it was like I was alive for the first time. I miss the way he'd look at me and my skin would burn. I miss the way he'd take me into his arms and we'd spring into the air or dive over a cliff, and I'd cling on to him like he was the only thing I needed to be grounded.

"Ryven…" I start, the word a breathless whisper. A raw ache settles in my chest like a hot coal.

But my shaky voice is cut off by the sudden extension of his wings. Before I can tell him how much I miss him, how sorry I am that he's no longer human, or that I wish he'd taken the breath of life instead of me, his knees bend, the deck rumbling beneath the might of his leap as he springs into the sky. He disappears into the darkness almost the moment his clawed feet leap from the ground, leaving me once more in the bitter cold.

Boots thud against the hollow deck behind me. I turn around to discover that I'm not as alone as I thought I was.

Crossing my arms and sinking into my hip, I force a smile at Dimitri. "Do you always sneak up on women in the middle of the night?"

He points over his shoulder at the purpling horizon. "Saying it's the *middle* of the night seems a bit unfair." Dimitri smooths a hand over the top of his head, fixing the disheveled locks of his hair as he walks toward me. His expression shifts. "Have a nice talk with your *demon?*"

"He's *not* a demon."

Dimitri's hands shoot into the air, but I catch the roll of his eyes as he turns toward the taffrail and leans over it. "Fine. How was the conversation with the *not*-demon?"

I scowl at his back. I don't know why he's asking considering he can tell exactly how the conversation went. He had to have seen Ryven leave just as he arrived. Come to think of it, maybe that's *why* he left. I shake away that hopeful thinking though. Every time I even tried broaching the topic of Ryven's demon side, or what I intend to do to save him, he always fled. I'd been worried at first that he'd left for good, but he always came back. Regardless of whether he believed it possible—which I was certain he didn't—for some reason, he *always* came back. He either had more hope than he was allowing himself to admit, or something else was keeping him here.

I dared not hope for the latter.

The sun moves quickly now in the early minutes of daybreak. In a matter of a few short minutes, the deep purple brightens into the soft pink of rose petals as it climbs across the sky. As the silence settles between us, I join Dimitri at the edge of the boat, propping my elbows onto the slick rail as I watch the horizon separate from the water, until I can once again see as far as the ocean stretches. There's no land in either direction; there hasn't been for days, not since we left Arcathain.

"What will you do if your plan doesn't work?" he asks, mirroring my stance on the strange obsidian-like rail. "If the mages don't have the answers you seek. Will you be able to do what needs to be done?"

Something cold snakes its way along my spine. "What needs to be done?"

He stands and turns toward me, the moon casting his shadow over me. "You know what I mean."

That cold sensation ignites like a flame to a fuse. My brow tightens. "Nothing *needs* to be done. Ryven is as docile as a house cat. He's not like other demons—"

An incredulous burst of air eases through Dimitri's lips. He starts pacing the upper deck, shaking his head. "Is that really how you think he wants to spend the rest of his life? As a demon?"

I open my mouth to speak, to remind Dimitri that he doesn't know him like I do, but the words slide back down my throat. A crippling heaviness weighs over me. He's right. Of course, that's not what Ryven wanted. He said as much before he made the full transition into…into what he is now. But this possibility, the very notion that I might not be able to save him, it's something I never let myself consider. The mages have to know how to save him. They simply have to.

Dimitri's throaty sigh breaks the silence. He throws his arms around me, and I feel so helpless and broken that I don't even question nestling myself against his chest. I breathe him in, the familiar scent of pine and earth still buried beneath the sea salt that coats us all by now.

Something soft presses against the top of my head, the smallest tug pulling on my heart.

"Come on," he says into my hair. "Alphonse was awakening when I left the room. He's probably ready for you by now."

Unfolding myself from Dimitri's warmth, I glance to the far side of the vessel and spy two figures: one dark-haired man and a fiery-haired woman wrapped around him.

A pathetic groan gurgles from my throat.

Dimitri laughs. "You're the one who offered to help him."

"Yeah, but I didn't think it meant having a constant audience with the friend who betrayed me."

He tilts his head, the sun catching in his golden-brown locks. "I told you not to—"

"Don't." I'm already down the stairs before he can finish, leaving him behind and taking the space I need to clear my head.

The ship sways as I cross the deck, a random dip of the water misting me as I climb the stairs on the other side.

Fox giggles something into Alphonse's ear as his hands rove over her surprisingly curvaceous backside. For someone so short and thin, someone who likely spent as many days hungry as Dimitri and I had, I'm surprised to notice how much meat she's stored back there.

When I catch myself staring, I clear my throat. Alphonse's

hands jolt away, the rest of his form turning as rigid as a tree in her grasp. Fox whines in his ear as he shoves her away.

"What took you so long?" Alphonse snaps.

My jaw unhinges, practically slamming into my collarbone as frustration rolls over me.

"Give her a break," Fox coos, sliding beneath Alphonse's arm. She traces circles over his chest, playing with the low V shape of his collar. "She wasn't doing anything we weren't. Halira just needed to see her men before her day started."

My ire becomes blinding. *Men.* She said *men,* and I couldn't tell if she was trying to provoke me or if she simply is tactless that she fails to see just how infuriating she is being—they both are.

Clouds shift overhead, the pale purple sky darkening once more.

Alphonse lowers his arm from Fox's shoulder. "Halira… might I suggest you take a breath?"

My teeth grind together, and I spit, "I *am* breathing." In fact, my pulls of the crisp, salty air are deep and steady, each one emboldening me, making me feel stronger, bigger.

Despite her brief protests, Alphonse shoves Fox down the stairs, leaving the two of us alone. He leans down to stare me in the eyes, his head crooked and the faintest concern etched in his usually flawless expression. "Is this part of my training? A lesson in losing control and lashing out on people who have done nothing wrong?"

"*Nothing wrong?*" I roar, the sky quaking. "If anyone has ever wronged me, it's the two of you!"

His hands are splayed as he continues to approach. "And we're both trying to make up for it." When he sees my nails are still digging into my palms, he takes a cautious glance up to the gray sky, and then one to the water around us. "Do you really think it's a good idea to summon lightning right now? What if you struck the Leviathan? Then how would we get to Illashore?"

Clarity returns to me like a curtain being drawn to reveal a blinding light. My clenched hands relax at my sides. My call to the storm ceases.

Alphonse's shoulders slump forward with relief, but it's not long before he's standing tall again. He's always towered over me, nowhere as near as much as he stands above Fox, but enough to make me feel small in his presence. This time when he stands before me, a hand floating to my shoulder, I still feel like the scared little girl I always was, but it's different this time. My fear is not directed at him. I'm not cowering away; I'm looking up to him for support.

"I'm sorry," I say, my voice cracking so that my words aren't much more than a whisper. "I don't know what happened—"

"It's not difficult to guess."

Confused, I stare at him.

He tilts his head, the long black sheet of hair somehow managing to stay tucked behind his ear. "You cannot tell me that you truly have no idea how numerous emotional tragedies might be weighing on you. Your best friend betrayed you—as did I, as you were so gracious to remind me. The man you loved abandoned you when you thought you were moments away from death. You then didn't die, but instead discovered a secret about yourself that your family—your *dead* family—had kept from you all your life. You met the people you descended from, even met another man whom you connected with only to have him ripped away from you as well. And now you find yourself stranded on the back of an ancient beast, surrounded by brutes who used to be your equals but no longer want anything to do with you, friends who you don't know if you can trust, an ex-lover, another ex-lover, and you have no assurance that this painful journey will be fruitful in the slightest."

He pauses long enough for his brow to arch. "Yes, who would possibly be influenced by any of that?"

I smile through the tears assaulting the back of my throat. "Some days I feel so exhausted by it all, I don't know what to do. Some days, I see Fox and I feel nothing. She might as well be a stranger I'm meeting for the first time. Other days I just want to"—my fists clench again—"punch her in that sly smile of hers."

"That may just be the effect she has on people."

I snort a laugh, but whatever amusement flickers inside of me is swiftly snuffed by a bitter clenching claw.

Alphonse's gaze remains fixed on me, seemingly reading every nuance in my expression. "So, how is our blighted friend doing these days?"

I sigh, the air shaky in my lungs. "I don't know. He's a demon, but...he's also not. He's still in there, even if he tries hiding from me. But I worry the more he keeps his distance, the more he becomes..."

After a stretch of quiet, Alphonse finally prods me. "Becomes what?"

"Lost. He won't even talk to me, won't even let me look at him."

"Yes," he says gently, thoughtfully. "But can you blame him?"

Closing my eyes, I shake my head.

"If I were to become an abomin—" Seeing the scathing glare I cut at him, he corrects himself. "If I were to become a *half-demon-druid-man-thing*, you can bet I'd hide my face as well. It's no wonder so many of them congregated at the Labyrinth."

A wrinkle forms in my forehead. "What do you mean? None of those creatures have the awareness of their former selves anymore. They're lost in the demons that ravage them."

He shrugs, ducking when one of the Leviathan's tentacles reaches up from the water, casting us in shadow before splashing back beneath the sea. "Sentient or not, they must be able to recognize something, perhaps their distinctness from the other demons that prowl the Shadowthorn, or maybe, deep down beneath the *ravaging* darkness, perhaps part of them does know. Perhaps that's why they linger outside of the Eyve, drawn to it as if they know they belong on the other side of that wall."

A new burning sort of sadness fills my chest. "I...I don't think you're helping."

His smile is mischievous, if not a bit rueful. "I beg to differ. The sky no longer looks like it's about to fall down upon us."

I punch him in his shoulder, an instinctual reflex that's almost always been reserved for Dimitri. The two of us stare at each other for a moment, a flicker of emotion flashing over him that I can't quite place, but if it's anything like mine, it's nothing short of astonishment. How strange it is to have reached this place, where Alphonse and I, of all people, can tease each other in good jest. He has years of pain to make up for, but it's moments like these that make me realize I'm better off allowing him the opportunity to try, rather than holding past grudges against him.

The same is probably true of Fox. She could've refused to apologize. She could've pretended like she never liked me, and joined some of the other people on this ship in keeping their distance, but she didn't. Every morning I find her up here waiting with Alphonse. Every morning she greets me, she tries holding a conversation. What she said earlier was insensitive, no doubt, but I don't think she meant for it to be. She's still reaching for any sort of connection between us, and while we were at Nigh, one of our most frequented topics had been my conflicted feelings about Dimitri. It dawns on me now that her ear had always been willing to listen, but in all that time she never even hinted at what was transpiring between Alphonse and her. I don't know whether to feel slighted about it, my emotions already spent from my previous display of magic.

"Well, my apologies for not having sage wisdom to offer in an unprecedented moment such as this," Alphonse says, drawing a begrudging snort of laughter from me again. His theatrics shift after he accidentally bumps his arm against the hull. He wipes the nonexistent grime onto his salt-kissed breeches. "Now, are you going to stand there feeling sorry for yourself, or will you guide me in fruitless lessons on druid magic so that I can feel sorry for myself instead?"

WE ARE SURVIVORS

LEVIATHAN, VARENHOLM OCEAN

"It's no use!" Alphonse shouts, throwing his hands in the air and kicking a crate with some of our provisions in it. It's one of the heavier ones of grain we haven't touched yet, and the hollow thud that thumps at the contact of his boot tells me all I need to know about the pain likely stinging his toes now. His fury rises. "Druid lineage or not, I cannot do magic."

"You've hardly even tried."

His lips part with a hiss. "Beg your pardon? Have we not been at this every day for the better part of our voyage? Have I not spent hours here, today alone, trying to—to—whatever it is you call it?"

"Summon the wind?"

His eyes narrow to slits. "Do not patronize me."

Rolling my eyes, I set aside the cloth I'd fastened to one of the splinters of wood from the broken bench—one that Adrien and Sai had assured me they didn't need—and stand before my cousin. "I'm not trying to patronize you. I'm just surprised to hear you sound so…"

"Annoyed? Surfeited?"

"Defeated," I finally say.

"Surfeited was a more accurate description," he grumbles, leaning back against the crate.

The sight of him slouched and…*surfeited*…is such a stark comparison to the man I knew a month ago, the one who pushed us during training until we were unconscious on the ground.

"If you were one of your Crusaders right now, what would you say to yourself?"

Still scowling, he glances up at me. "I do not care for your tone."

"I'm being serious. If I had just given up and tried to sit down in the middle of a training session, you would've sicked Güthric on me."

He scoffs. "Not that it ever did anything for you."

I roll my eyes. "Stop. This self-pity, it's not getting you anywhere."

"Neither are your lessons."

For some reason, that statement stings more than it should. It's not like I'm an expert in this stuff. I've only known for a few short weeks what I am, what I'm capable of. Even if I had encounters with my magic at varying moments in my life, I never knew how to control it, how to summon it, let alone how to *become* it like I do with the wind.

If Imryll were here, she would be able to help him. Ryven, too, if he were his normal druid self again and allowed to stay aboard the ship. He might be able to offer some insight into how Alphonse's powers manifest for him.

But neither of them are here. Instead, right now all I have to go off is what the magic is like for me.

I sink onto the corner of the crate beside him, scooting him over as the two of us sulk.

"You're right," I sigh. "I want to help you, but I don't know how."

"It's like I said, maybe there is no helping me. Maybe I can't sense that—that spark of life like you can."

His choice of words reminds me of something Ryven told me. "It's not the same for everyone, you know? Ryven said that some people feel it like an energy, and others can smell it or taste it. We just have to figure out what your catalyst is." Biting my bottom lip, I think back to our childhoods. "You don't remember anything strange ever happening to you or around you?"

One of his eyebrows inches toward his dark hairline. "If I so much as showed even the slightest hint of magic, you know very well what would've become of me."

The right thing to do here would be to argue, to insist that no father would ever harm their child in that way, regardless of their perceived offenses, but that lie serves us no purpose here.

"Nothing?" I ask again.

He shakes his head, returning his sorrowful eyes to the tips of his unpolished boots. We sit there for so long, listening to the swaying of the ocean and the people aboard who are going about their work, that neither of us notice when Fox walks up on us.

"I hope it's not a bad time, but can I steal Alphonse back? It's well past lunch and—"

He jumps to his feet. "Gladly." He strides toward her, but stops halfway to look back at me. "I appreciate your efforts, Halira. I do. But perhaps we face the hard truth that these sessions are getting us nowhere. If I did have any druid powers, it might be best to wait until our return to Arcathain where I might find a more practiced druid to guide me."

Absentmindedly, I nod, bearing down on the wrenching of my chest. It takes me a staggered moment to realize why I'm so saddened by this conclusion. It's not that I take offense to it—I know I still have a lot to learn myself. But I guess I've simply enjoyed having this time with my cousin, where our roles are reversed, where there is no vitriol between us as we work together to improve ourselves.

"Will you be joining us for a meal?" he asks.

I look up, grimacing when I find them entwined in each other again. I know it's more than just my bitter feelings toward Fox that has my chest tightening this way.

The smile I summon is forced, but I pretend neither of them notice. "That's all right. You two go without me. I still need to send Kalli's raven to her, and…do a few other things."

Because it's not entirely a lie, the two of them have an easier time of leaving me to head to the lower deck.

Standing from the crate, I use the tumultuous storm inside me and channel it into the sky. A sudden gust of ocean air sweeps over the deck, causing those of us still up here to anchor ourselves to our heels and grab on to anything nearby. A few of the Crusaders glower my way, making my skin prick with the sudden sensation of danger, and reminding me that there are worse things than not being able to spend time with my cousin.

I scurry down the stairs and into the main cabin, closing the door behind me.

Kalli's raven squawks at my arrival, the bird spreading its black wings and gliding across the room to my shoulder. I scratch the space between its eyes, just above its smooth beak. When we first left Arcathain, I tried letting it fly freely while we were out at sea, but the poor creature seemed to grow more and more distraught the farther away from land we became. Or rather, the farther away from Kalli.

"Are you ready to see your master?" I ask the bird.

It ruffles its feathers in response, seeming to become a little more alert, more eager.

"It'll be a long journey for you, but there are plenty of stops along the way for you to rest."

And there were. Thanks to the mages for severing our

continent and drifting across the ocean with our land, the sea had been littered with the smallest of islands, chunks of barely inhabitable land that had broken off during the transition. They were becoming fewer and farther between, but none were more than a day's journey apart; most less than that. They weren't ample land, but they would be enough for Kalli's bird to rest. At least, I hoped they were.

"Do you still have my note?" I ask the bird, well aware that it won't respond. I don't know if it's because I haven't learned how to speak with birds, if my druid magic only extends to demons and Leviathans, or if it has something to do with the bond this raven has with my sister, but I have never been able to translate anything from it.

I glance to the raven's leg, finding my note secured in the twine there. Even if it falls out during the journey, it's not like Kalli couldn't figure out why I'd send her bird back to her. She has to know that I haven't stopped thinking about the danger she's putting herself in.

Then again, if her raven returns with no note, she might assume the worst.

I give the twine a good tug, finding it more secure than it looks. The raven fidgets. "Well, if you're ready, let's get you a full belly before I send you back to Kalli."

We find Güthric and Silver where they always are at this time of day, hoisting up the nets from their fishing efforts from the day. It's never much. I imagine that if there were schools of fish swimming nearby, the Leviathan likely required an ample amount in her diet to sustain her endurance. But every day enough made it into the net to keep the rest of our bellies sated.

Güthric's muscles bulge, sweat glistening on his bare back as he pulls another net up and onto the deck. Only a few dozen fish scatter in the net when it lands on the floor, the deck suddenly slick and difficult to stand on.

"Hey!" I wave when I catch their attention.

Silver nods before bending with a basket in hand to scoop the flailing fish inside. Güthric waves so vigorously the whole vessel seems to rock.

"Am I interrupting?"

"Not at all," Silver says, reaching for the last few fish. Their slippery fins make the task harder than it should be, but nothing deters her from her task.

It's been strange seeing her work like this. Silver always struck me as someone who was too elegant for the work of Crusaders, even if she did come from Ashenvale, a town hardly known for its wealth and prestige. Still, there had always been something about the way she carried herself that made her seem too good for the life she'd chosen. But the longer I watch her, the more I realize she's not afraid of getting her hands dirty. Never has been.

With the last fish in the basket, she stands and hoists the wicker onto her hip. She hardly looks at me as she strides over to stand behind a small table, the wood stained red. She sets her basket down, grabs the knife from her belt, and points it at us. "Is it time to feed that black beauty again?"

I nod, my throat going dry. "I'm sending word to my sister."

Silver reaches into the basket and pulls out a silver fish, one of the larger ones from today's catch. She sets it atop the bloodstained table and—

Thunk.

The sharp metal blade cleaves clean through the fish's head with one whack. It doesn't take long for the oily slickness coating my gut and the nauseating sway of the ocean to win over what little restraint I have over the contents of my stomach. Kalli's bird flies from my shoulder as I chuck myself over the side of the vessel and vomit down into the sea. It's not until I'm done that I start to feel bad for the Leviathan below me, or the rest of the sea creatures who have to swim with *that* from now on.

I come back up, wiping my mouth as the raven lands back on my shoulder.

Silver remains unflinching and unapologetic. She has a job to do, one that all of us rely on her for, and she can't stop just because some druid can't stand the sight of animals being slaughtered. I don't blame her for it, even if every whack of her knife twists my stomach into a tighter knot.

Instead, I pierce my gaze into the center of her eyes and wait for her to finish. For every swing of her knife, I think instead of the training grounds and how some of the Crusaders trained with their swords. Every time the squelch of a fish head severing from its body would threaten the contents of my stomach, I'd instead think about the demons we were trained to kill, the ones we slaughtered before they could do the same to us.

Once all of the heads and guts were removed and tossed into the ocean, Silver set to work cutting one fish in particular into long chunks. She cupped them into her hand when she was done and offered it to the raven who ate without hesitation. I could either watch with disgust as it devoured the creature that had just moments prior been alive, or I could watch with amazement. Before our time at sea, I don't think Kalli's raven had ever eaten fish before; I didn't even know they could. But this bird was learning to adapt to ocean life, as were the rest of us.

"You're taking to this line of work rather easily," I say to Silver as she cleans her knives.

As far as I am aware, before we set sail, Silver hadn't even been on a ship, let alone had any experience netting and gutting fish from one. Her life had been that of a wife, of a mother, tending to the homestead and socializing with the other wives of Ashenvale. But she'd been up here on the deck every day with Güthric, learning from him as he went about securing us fish to go along with all the rice and dried fruits my aunt sent with us.

Güthric grunts his agreement, flashing Silver a proud grin before gathering the tray of fish and taking it below deck.

Silver watches him leave. "It's not much different from anything else I've experienced in my life. Childbirth, preparing game from a hunt, the bloodletting, slaying demons while we were in the Shadowthorn. It's all the same. In the end, it's nothing more than flesh and blood, and those who survive and those who don't." She turns to me, a certain powerful essence, a quiet strength about her. "No matter what we face, we are survivors. We adapt. We do what must be done to live another day. It's of little importance that no human has crossed the Varenholm Ocean before us."

The raven-haired woman retrieves the net from the ground, tidying it as she walks back to the table to place it into the basket.

"We are survivors. Remember that, Halira, and it will serve you well."

NEVER ALONE

LEVIATHAN, VARENHOLM OCEAN

Kalli's bird ruffles and wiggles on my shoulder as Silver disappears below deck to start preparations for dinner. I get the sense that the raven is awaiting my permission to leave. I have no doubt that it can sense my trepidation over its departure. It is the only thing I have of my sister, and I fear once I release her bird I'll lose what little connection I have to her.

But that's fear talking. There is no other way for us to communicate, and truth be told, I probably should've sent the raven days ago.

I give its soft feathers one more nuzzle with my cheek before bobbing my shoulder and setting the bird into the air. The gentle breeze that chases it is of no natural cause, but rather one I create to aid in what little way I can while it travels. But once the raven is out of sight, once I can no longer see or feel the wind I'm commanding, I let go of my magic, and the air returns to its normal stasis.

With nothing else left to do, and at the boisterous insistence of my rumbling stomach, I decide to head below deck to try and find myself a bite before dinner is served soon.

I find Adrien and Sai in the common area, the two of them

hard at work on the bench they agreed to repair. It's clear even to me, someone who knows little to nothing about woodworking, that such a project should've been completed days ago. It would've been too, if it had just been Sai's expert hands re-sanding the edges and hammering the boards back together.

But my uncle has interrupted Sai's every attempt to repair the bench on his own. Even now, Adrien steps in and takes the newly decorate board from Sai. I'm too far away to see the details of the artwork from here, but I've been by numerous times to admire the great oak tree with a vastly-spreading canopy of leaves that's now etched into the light wood. It's no wonder the Magistrate hired Sai and his brother to design some things for the Capital; he truly knows his craft, even after going without it for however long.

"Yes, so you've told me," my uncle replies, holding the board behind his back and out of Sai's grasp. "I'm aware that you know what you're doing, but how shall I ever learn if I'm just left to watch?"

Sai's smile flashes white and blinding, the kind of grin that says he's holding nothing back. "Gods forbid we finish this bench within either of our lifetimes."

"I'll have you know, haste is not always of the utmost importance." When it appears Sai has acquiesced, my uncle places the board back on their workstation and proceeds to share a story about how if he had hurried in his robbery of the Keep of Amendell, they would've been caught and hung because a guard would've been standing right in front of their escape route. But since they exercised a bit of patience, my uncle was still walking around with his head to this day.

Some artisans might've found his constant…assistance annoying, but I hadn't seen Sai take a single drink since we were in the Wardens camp, not even when the Crusaders passed around the wine bottles they found in the main cabin during dinner times.

But far more telling than any man's indulgences is his smile, and the way those two grin at each other, the way they draw out every seemingly simple task so that it will take hours upon hours, just to be together, says everything I need to know. It's not the return to woodworking that is giving Sai his new polished shine.

Instead of interrupting as I have many days, I continue down the hall. If food is what I am after, I'll find it in the modest kitchen. Knowing that I'd find Silver, Güthric, and—most disturbingly—all those fish filets in there, I take my time meandering down the hall, peeking through the open cabin doors to glimpse what the others are up to. I spent so much of my time these last few days training with Alphonse and worrying about Ryven that I rarely had a chance to just sit and relax with everyone else. But since the Leviathan is handling our course, and Güthric and Silver our meals, there really isn't any excuse.

But I know what my excuse is, and it has nothing to do with how busy I am or am not. I am avoiding things. I am avoiding *people*. Fox and Dimitri are just the tip of the iceberg. There is an entire gang of Crusaders who neither believe in me nor trust me, and I don't much care for sharing confined spaces with them.

If I am ever going to convince them I am on their side, I suppose we need to spend time together.

An uproarious bout of laughter spills from the next open door. I creep up, my hand on the doorknob, ready to stride inside with my head held high. But as I crack the door, Dimitri comes into view. Then Fox. Then Inigo.

Everyone is inside the small cabin, squeezed in together like sardines as they gather in the room. The laughter dies when they see me in the doorway.

I panic. It is so glaringly obvious that I don't belong that rather than do the rational thing and just slide into the room like a fly on the wall and let their entertainment continue, I back out into the hall, slamming the door in front of me, and run.

I don't even make it to the next room when the door swings open again.

"And just where are you headed off to in such a hurry?"

My shoulders bunch to my ears, but I force myself to spin around and face her. She glares at someone I can't quite see in the doorway before slamming it shut and fixing her attention to me with a cool smile.

"What are you doing out here?" Fox asks.

"I—I—" My eyes flit around the lower decks, but I find no good excuse just lying around waiting to be picked up off the floor.

"We were just about to gamble." Her grin grows mischievous and cunning. "If you were interested, we'll be betting chores. But don't worry, dumping out the latrine buckets has already been taken off the list of acceptable contributions."

The light-hearted nature of the way she speaks to me makes me want to be like that too. I really do wish I could just go back to the way things were between us. I wish I could be carefree around her again; I wish I could trust her. But I can't.

"N-no thank you. I was just…going to bed."

One of her hands plants itself on her hip. "With no lunch or dinner?"

A protest starts to form, but surprise stops it. "How would you know that?"

She shrugs. "Just one of the many skills I picked up in my life: the ability to hear a rumbling stomach and gauge how long it's been since it last had any food."

My eyes narrow on her. "You can't possibly tell that just from a stomach growl."

Fox rolls her blue eyes and sighs. "Of course not. It was a deduction, and an accurate one at that. You and Alphonse trained all morning, skipping right over lunch. Remember? And, since Güthric has lumbered into that cabin with a tray full of raw fish and barely cooked rice, then by my calculations you haven't eaten dinner yet either, just like the rest of us."

"Oh. Right..." I hold her striking gaze as long as I can, but soon memories of our past infiltrate my thoughts once more, and it becomes too painful. "Well, enjoy your gambling. I'm tired from training and think it best if I—"

She catches my elbow. My head snaps. I can't tell if I'm more shocked at how quickly and silently she cut the space between us or more irate that she feels like she has the right to touch me. After *all* that she's done.

"Look," she says, those bright eyes searing into mine. Her words come out emphatic. "I am sorry. If I could take it all back, I would."

I jerk my arm away, but she doesn't stop there.

"What do you want me to say here? I've apologized. A half dozen times. And mind you, I've meant every one of them. But I can't do anything more than say I'm sorry—"

And I lose it. "I don't want you to say anything! You're right. You've said enough. You were doing what you thought you needed to do to survive and be with the ones you—you care about." My throat becomes the heel of a boot as I stomp on the puddle of hurt and betrayal pooling there. "You can keep using your excuses. You can keep blaming your actions on the survival instincts that you adopted as an orphan fending for yourself on the streets, and don't doubt that you had to at the time. I won't discredit that hardship. But it doesn't make your actions toward me and my family excused. Because of you, my sister and I were arrested and we would've faced execution if we hadn't escaped. We were forced to run, to become fugitives, and then—and *then* I was bitten by a demon and nearly died, sending my sister and I on a death-defying quest to find a cure that neither of us even knew existed."

The room quiets to the point where I become well aware that everyone on this ship is listening to us. But I don't care. If it's forgiveness she seeks, then first she needs to understand exactly what it is she caused.

And to my surprise, she actually listens. Fox's lips don't so much as twitch as I go on my tirade, as fresh tears prick the edges of my eyes. With such a captive audience, some of my fire is lost, but none of my conviction.

"That's not even the worst of it. Look around you, Fox. How many people are here because you betrayed me? How many of our lives have been altered because you were too selfish to see that we were supposed to have each other's backs, no matter what. I saw you as…as a sister."

"I know," she says softly.

I scoff because she can't truly. She can't. If she did, then we wouldn't be in the situation now. Sisters shouldn't betray each other.

"I do," she insists, lowering her head. "I know that because of me you were infected. I know that Alphonse nearly died because he chased after you during your escape. I know that… that I've only made my tenuous friendship with Dimitri even more challenging. And I know that literally every Crusader on this ship, let alone the ones we left back home, think of me as a snitch, as someone who can't be trusted."

My lips finally clamp shut. I hadn't actually considered what the repercussion of her actions would be on herself. As Alphonse's woman, she would've been protected. But without him there, she'd just been the girl who condemned a Crusader, even if that Crusader was suspected of having magic.

"Believe me when I say that I *do* regret what I did. I let fear take control of me, and I wish like hell that I hadn't. But—" Her blue eyes flick to mine, her expression somehow growing more pained. "And please understand that this is not to excuse my wrongdoings, but it is simply a fact: we now know more about the Primordials than we ever did before."

"You've got to be kidding me."

"I know. I know how it sounds, but it's true. Our people were doomed before. If what you say is true about the shadow-steel weapons—and I believe you when you say it—then all of Arcathain would've been lost in a matter of decades. But because of everything that transpired, we may actually stand a chance of finding the *real* way to end Qaeus and her tyranny."

I can't even feel rage anymore. I'm just gaping at her like a fish out of water.

"Betraying you was the biggest mistake of my life. I never had any true friends. I should've valued the one I found, but I pissed it away. I will carry the regret of losing your trust to my pyre. But I *am* grateful that we are on *this* path now—the only true path to Arcathain's salvation. And I hope in time you can find it in your heart to forgive me because… I do miss you, you know. I mourned you when we thought you were dead. I thought I…"

She trails off, and it seems like the perfect opportunity for me to continue my fake trajectory to my room. I slam the door behind me loud enough so that everyone listening knows not to come in. I don't care if I have to electrocute this entire ship, I will if it grants me the peace and quiet I need from the warring emotions and thoughts inside me.

But all that gusto and rage is just a front, because the moment I find my bed and sink into it, the hot anger gives way to cold pain. I curl my knees against my chest and take my face into my hands. The tears come instantly, the ones I've been holding back for months now. Tears for my parents, for my imprisonment, for Ryven.

But somewhere between my racketing sobs, a foot scuffs on the floor in front of me. I am not alone.

EVIL'S TWISTED FACE

THE CABINS, LEVIATHAN, VARENHOLM OCEAN

My head snaps up, heart pounding in my chest. Inigo's grin twists at my damp cheeks.

"What do you want?" My voice is gruff, but I try mustering as much warning as I can. Something about the way he prowls through the cramped space tells me that I need to get him to leave, no matter what it takes.

The scar on his lip makes his sneer all the more menacing. He crosses his arms, tapping his chin. "What do I want? The same thing I've always wanted."

My back straightens against the wall behind me. "And what's that?"

His eyes narrow to pinpricks. "To vanquish evil."

"Stay back!" I shout when he takes a thundering step forward.

As easily as I breathe, I call to the air around us. It answers, a living thing that wraps itself around me, and I shove. A breeze billows from my outstretched hand, but it's hardly more than a caress of air across his dark, unkempt hair.

Something vile and wicked blooms inside his irises, making it all too obvious to me which of us could be mistaken for evil.

"That's the problem with magic," he says, another foot

pounding forward beneath his brawny body. "It lowers your defenses because it makes you mages think you're better than us."

"I'm not a mage!" The claim sounds pathetic even to my own ears. It's exactly the sort of trickery we were told the mages would use when facing the Magistrate for their crimes of magic. They'd beg and plead and cry, but it was every Arcathainian's duty to hold strong and never waver in their disdain.

I finally lower my hand. The wind is doing nothing but exhausting me, and though he's wrong about me being a mage, he's right about one thing. Relying on magic will make me weak. But it's not the only skillset I possess. I've fought and survived some of the most terrifying shadowcreatures. Surely, I can handle a brute like Inigo.

He takes another slow step forward, and I press onto the heels of my feet, ready to spring the moment he's close enough. He might have me by size alone, but I can be swifter. He's cornered me alone because he expects to fight a frightened, helpless girl, but that's not who I am. It never has been, even when Alphonse made me think it was.

It was never fear that kept me immobilized. It was fury.

"You may have the rest of them convinced, but you don't fool me. I see you communing with that demon pet of yours. I know your plan."

"Oh really? And what's that?"

"To lead us to the mages to be slaughtered."

I roll my eyes, thoroughly unimpressed by his imagination. "And what would I possibly have to gain from that? You know I've lived in Arcathain my whole life, right?"

The slow, knowing nod of his bulbous head sends a chill down my spine. "Oh, I don't doubt there were many of you. Sent here to ensure the return of the Primordial Qaeus, and now that your mission is complete, you're finally heading home."

Breath heaves from my lungs at the absurdity of it. He actually believes I'm a spy? Sent here by the mages at what, birth? Just to release the Primordial?

"We are just the consolation prize, the suckers who were in the wrong place at the wrong time, following the wrong people into battle. But none of that matters now. Once you're gone, the others will have no choice but to change course back to Arcathain, where we're *really* needed."

A protest forms at the edge of my lips, but he leaves me no time to say it. Inigo dives for me, arms extended, sausage fingers outstretched like a mountain lion pouncing at its prey. I refuse to be the helpless doe that's slaughtered where she grazes. I lunge forward with just as much menace in my eyes, hoping to intercept him and throw him off in whatever way I can.

But Inigo is faster than I anticipate. He's closer than I ever wanted to let him get. His shoulder slams into my chest like a concrete brick, the air gushing from my lungs as we crash into the wall behind me. My head breaks the fall, a throbbing pressure pounding between my ears in time with my racing heartbeat.

Dazed and head spinning, I try blinking out of the fog as Inigo, too, pushes himself upright. My Crusader training is of no help here. Inigo isn't a demon to be disemboweled, and even if he was, I have no shadowsteel to tear him to shreds.

Instead, Tor's voice rises from the beyond. A memory of him finding me in the mud after one of Alphonse's particularly humiliating stunts flashes before my eyes. He reaches out his hand and pulls me to my feet. Tor had always known what Alphonse did to me when no one else was watching; I could never hide my bruises or tear-slicked eyes from him. But whenever he offered to *pummel our cousin into the ground until he was nothing more than the soil we walk on,* I was always quick to decline. Tor and I both knew that involving him would only mean more trouble for the both of us.

Still, he never wanted to just let his younger sister suffer. And that day, he did the only thing I would allow him.

"You don't need to be stronger than him to win in a fight. You just need to know his weaknesses. And as luck would have it, humans mostly share the same ones."

As Inigo rises, one mighty fist cocked back, I go through the list of Tor's recommendations. My legs are pinned and of no use to me. With my back pressed into the cot, I don't have anywhere to wind my own arm, leaving any blow I could land to his jaw or eye mostly ineffectual. Besides, those are the areas people expect to be hit, and therefore they're the easiest ones to dodge.

I'm prepared to do just that, when Inigo's other hand grabs the collar of my shirt and holds me in place. Panic claws at me. Any freewill I possessed, any wandering thoughts that were trying to assess my next move, scurry back into the shadows as nothing but primal survival takes hold.

I shield my face with my forearms, but it's not enough to stop his blow. The weight of his punch slams my arms into my head, though the angle protects my tender cheekbones. I spread my arms to reassess. To react. To move. To do anything other than lie here and be pulverized, but his fist has already reformed and is striking down like a hammer.

It cracks against my jaw, a fiery, angry pain blanketing the entire left side of my face.

A knock—or rather, a pounding on the thick, hard door—startles him from the next swing he has readied.

"Is everything all right in there?" A voice filters through from the other side. I'd expected it to be Fox, but even though I can't place who it belongs to, I can tell it's decidedly male.

My tongue sloshes against something warm and metallic.

"Has it crossed you yet," I say, my jaw throbbing with every effort I expend. "That without me, no one can tell the Leviathan to change course."

I almost wish I hadn't said anything. Inigo's attention had been fixed on the door, but now he turns those menacingly dark eyes to me. "Then we kill it too. Break the ship free, and set sail on our own."

I don't know how I do it, but I manage a weak laugh. "The only one here who knows how to sail a boat is Güthric. You really think he's going to help you if you kill me?"

The cold snake of fear slithers down my spine at the widening grin than coils up one side of his face. "I'm sure I can find some way to incentivize him."

My breath hitches. Silver. He would use Silver, and with her life on the line, Güthric *would* do anything. Already he'd followed her as she fled the Shadow Crusade and turned to the Shadowthorn. He'd protected her when she fell in battle. He'd been there for her when her offering to the Leviathan had been the last heartbreak she could bear alone.

Güthric had already given too much. So had Silver. She'd fought too hard, survived too much, to be taken down by this dreadful brute.

"We are survivors. We adapt. We do what must be done to live another day."

Silver would survive any awful threat this pathetic man might intimidate her with, but he will never get the chance. Not if I have anything to say about it.

As someone's body collides into the door, the hinges unfortunately not giving way, Inigo turns his head, giving me my opening.

Tor's voice is strong and deadly in my ear. *"The ears are one of the most tender spots on the human body, and one of the most neglected."*

It doesn't take much power, but I summon every amount of

force I have as I swing my fist into the side of his head. Inigo roars, a sound that bubbles and rises from the back of his throat as the formidable blow topples him over the edge of the cot and to the ground where he lands with a mighty thud.

I don't wait to see what he does next. I don't foolishly waste time racing to unlock the door that will take me too many precious seconds to fumble with before he is back on his feet again.

I throw my body off the bed and land on top of him, straddling him as he did me. His knees won't do as much damage between my legs as mine would his, but legs are one of our most powerful and useful natural assets, and I can't afford him to gain use of them.

My arms pinwheel with mad desperation, each aching blow loosening the hold I have on my fists. But still, I thrash. I pound away at his face and neck, just as Tor instructed. Throat. Nose. Ears. Jaw. Anywhere I can land a blow, I strike, hopeful that what I lack in power, I make up for in speed and tenacity. A person can only endure so many blows to the head before they succumb to the darkness. I should know.

But Inigo is unlike any man I've ever seen. Whereas most would grow weary and disoriented, he only seems to liven. Each of my landing blows is like a jolt to his senses. Rage fills the throbbing veins in his temple and neck. His pupils dilate with intent. And before I can even trace his movement, he reaches up with one arm, snatching both of my wrists in his hand.

He laughs in my face, the hot air of his breath an unwelcomed caress against my skin. "That was very stupid."

At the same time he yanked my arms down and to his side, he grabbed the back of my head in one giant palm, and slammed my face into the cool floor. Before the pain could register, all I felt was the life of the ship, the breath of the vessel that seemed to be made from the Leviathan itself. There was something there, some useful information to be pulled upon, but then the pain flared, searing away all rational thought.

I lost count of the number of times my teeth slammed into the floor. I lost count of the number of times I tried begging the wind to blow him off me, but the wind never came. I lost count of the number of times I thought that this was the end. After all I'd been through, after all I'd survived, I would die at the hands of a bigoted, shortsighted man who was going to condemn everyone.

I don't know when, but at some point, he rolls me to my back. The weight of him atop my chest is enough to crush my ribs, but it's not until his thick fingers have laced around my throat that I learn the true meaning of struggling for air.

Blood blooms to my face, hot and pulsing. It has nowhere else to go and so it just screams behind my eyes, in my skull. My hands claw at the cold, damp floor. They pound and reach, trying desperately to push myself off the ground, to free myself from his deadly grasp, or to find something useful to strike him with. By instinct alone I reach for my brother's dagger, its absence another stark reminder that I have nothing. I am nothing. No magic. No weapons.

Everything becomes a gray, blurry mess, and I can't tell if it's because I'm fading away or because of the tears puddling my vision. I'm grateful for one thing though. At least I don't have to look at his horrid, menacing face anymore.

The door bangs ajar. If I could move, I might look to see who's entered, friend or foe. From where he has me pinned, I can hardly do much of anything.

But Inigo rises to his knees, even if his hands remain glued to my neck, muttering something menacing to the person who I think is yelling at him to stop. It's the only opportunity I have, and I don't know what I'll do with it, but I seize it.

I pull my arms up from under his legs just as he sinks back down on me. I pry at his fingers, tug and beat on his arms, but his hold is formidable. I feel another pair of arms doing the same. Friend then. But they're just as useless as I am.

In my frantic beating, my fingers graze something hard dangling from his neck. I reach for it again, my head heavy—so heavy—but I can just make sense of the vial I clutch between my fingers.

Without thinking, with the last vestiges of consciousness holding me in the world of the living, I yank the vial from his neck and crush the jar into his eyes. The glass breaks beneath my palm, a warbled roar echoing in the chamber. The pressure releases around my neck as Inigo staggers backward, and I suck a rush of air into my agonizing lungs. The breath is painful, nothing like the sweetness I expected. It's like drinking death itself. The air burns through me as my vision clears and someone pulls me over to my side.

Inigo's enraged growls are drowned out by the pale, dark-haired man standing over me.

"Breathe," Alphonse implores, blood trickling from his lip. I'm not sure how it got there, but I have no doubt it's courtesy of Inigo. "And here I thought I'd find you and Fox in a tussle."

Breathing is still too much of a struggle for me to be able to muster a smile, let alone laughter, but I meet Alphonse's gaze regardless, hoping he can decipher my silent appreciation.

"My fucking eye!" Inigo roars with the malice of a hundred demons.

Alphonse gives a gentle pat to my shoulder before rising. "After the stunt you pulled here today, you'll be lucky if all you lose is that eye."

Inigo turns toward him, snarling, blood coating his face like a waterfall.

"That's enough, Inigo."

The scar stitched in Inigo's lip twitches behind the red gush. "Not in the slightest."

Alphonse stiffens. For whatever reason, he must've believed

that this man still respected him enough to obey his orders. That was the kind of allegiance he'd had with his Crusaders. They'd risk their lives in the Shadowthorn at his command. They'd imprison one of their own. They'd feed him information, as Fox had.

But Inigo has far outgrown his loyalty to Alphonse. I knew that the moment he stepped foot into this room. Maybe I even knew it before.

"You're just as bad as her, and just as guilty," Inigo growls. "You think I haven't seen the two of you? You think we don' t know you're a mage sympathizer, and one pathetic enough to try to learn magic."

Alphonse's face contorts with confusion. "A mage sympa—"

But his words are cut short by Inigo's tackle. The man holds nothing back. He throws every ounce of him into every attack he's sent either of our ways.

Alphonse barely has time to counter, but he wedges his forearm against Inigo's shoulder, grabbing the same arm with his other hand and somehow rendering the tackle incomplete. Inigo grabs his leg and lifts, but Alphonse spins his weight to his other foot and cranks the man's large hand away from him.

I continue drawing breath in painful hacks, as I back away from the two of them.

"You led us astray!" Inigo bellows, yanking his head up and smacking Alphonse in the jaw, throwing him off balance.

Unending rage flickers behind Inigo's eyes as he releases Alphonse's leg and instead cracks him in the jaw with a solid fist.

Alphonse staggers backward, head swiveling, as another blow finds his nose. The crunch of it makes my spine tingle. Blood gushes down his face as his eyes glaze over. He won't last much longer. Another blow like that, and Alphonse will lose consciousness and Inigo will either release him to finish killing me, or he'll kill him first before returning to clean up his mess.

Crack after crack echoes in the cabin as I attempt to pull myself up. My head is as heavy as the ocean beneath us though, and it sways as much as the rising tide.

"Two mages in one night; better than I'd hoped for," Inigo mutters with sickening pride. "Any last words?"

My boots slip and slide, knees buckling as I try to straighten, but land face-first on the cot instead.

"Just a few," Alphonse groans, his voice muffled briefly by the soft bed. "I hope it hurts."

Inigo's quiet confusion is met by my own as something squelches from where they stand. I heave my head to the side to look, discerning nothing but a flash of red at first. I mistake it for blood, until it jumps back, the heavy shadow of Inigo's body staggering with it.

A female's voice pools into the room with saccharine contempt. "I never liked you anyway."

As I blink clarity back into view, I watch as Fox pulls her sword from Inigo's back and the brute slumps to the ground, Alphonse's exhausted form falling after him.

THE CABINS, LEVIATHAN, VARENHOLM OCEAN

Fox catches his waist, and my tall, lanky cousin leans into her small stature.

"Piss on a mage," she says, kicking Inigo as if she were trying to move him out of the middle of their path. But the large, dead man is unmovable. "Are you two all right?"

Alphonse meets my eyes, the question echoing in his concerned gaze.

Since I'm already here, I pull myself up onto the cot rather than attempt to stand again. Hunched but managing to sit, I brace myself on shaking arms and spit the pooling blood in my mouth over the side of the bed and onto Inigo's boots. "I—I think so."

The boisterous cheering that's practically banging on the wall from the other room makes my head snap. Did literally no one in there here our struggle? Hear us shouting and crashing to the ground?

No one but these two…

"How did you know to find me?" I say to my cousin.

His head rests atop Fox's, and for the first time since learning they were an item, I realize just how striking they are together. There's a cunning beauty to the both of them, one that few would ever dare cross. Or maybe that's just the dead man at their feet talking.

"You must've taken quite the beating," Alphonse says. "As I told you previously, when neither of you returned, I came to make sure you were both…behaving. The moment I left the ruckus occurring in that forsaken room, the sounds of a scuffle drew my attention. I came to pry you off each other." He pauses long enough to glance down into Fox's blue eyes. "Where did you run off to?"

With her hand splayed on his chest, she draws a tight circle. "To get some air. Halira made it clear she wanted to be left alone, but I wasn't ready to return to the room yet."

He cups her cheek. "Did mean ol' Halira hurt your feelings?"

She bats his hand away with a playful scowl.

"But Inigo, h-he—" I stammer, still trying to distinguish where my body ends and the swaying of the ocean begins. "How did he get in here?"

A shadow of anger falls over Alphonse's expression. "He left to get more wine, or so he said."

And still, next door, no one has yet to notice his absence. They still dance around, the hollow thuds of their boots and the drunken strumming on the guitar loud enough to drown out even the storm that had been raging outside.

"Halira!" someone gasps in the doorway. Our heads snap toward them, but Dimitri has already devoured the space between us. He's on his knees before me, cradling the sides of my face and twisting my head this way and that to examine the bulge of my jaw. "What happened?"

His gaze travels to my bloodied hand and the gashes that are only now starting to burn there. Tearing a strip of his tunic off, he wraps it around my palm, leveling his glare on the other two people in the room.

"Someone tell me what happened here."

"What does it look like?" Fox says, making no effort to hide her disapproving feelings toward him. "Inigo cornered your girl. Alphonse tried to save her, but he's a dumbass who thought Inigo still held some ounce of allegiance to him, so I stepped in and finished the brute off."

My heart twists when she says *your girl*, and I pull my hand from Dimitri's grasp. He notices, but he either can't decipher the deeper meaning or is too engulfed to focus on it now.

His gaze narrows on Inigo's lifeless form. His green eyes have never seemed darker. "We need to get rid of the body."

"No shit," Fox mutters.

But my forehead crinkles. "Why would we need to hide him? He attacked me. The others will—"

"Saying *the others* suggests that everyone aboard this ship is of one mind, but Inigo's actions prove that isn't the case." Dimitri angles his head so that we are staring at each other. "It's very likely that others agreed with his decision. Maybe they didn't know he was acting on it tonight—I think when he left the room earlier, he meant to grab some wine. But then he saw you, alone, and he took what opportunity he could.

"If there were others who believed you deserved death, that Alphonse was no longer worth following, then they will not take too kindly to learning that he was killed by one of you."

Fox smacks her lips, throwing her weight into one hip to argue, but Dimitri silences her.

"It would be just as bad coming from you. You and the General haven't exactly hidden your relationship. They'll call you a mage sympathizer."

"We're *not* mages," I growl, anger rising up my neck.

"It doesn't matter!" Dimitri glares me down, and the only reason I don't shout back is because I don't even know what I'd say. He's right. The Crusaders make no distinctions between us and the mages that robbed their parents and grandparents of their land, even though I am one of those people whose family was wronged.

Dimitri's voice is softer when he speaks. "They don't trust you and your magic because they don't understand how it's different from the mages. How could they, when they have nothing to compare it to? And if bodies start piling up at your feet—"

"Wouldn't it be better to learn who those people are? Draw them out with this tragedy?"

Alphonse and Dimitri exchange a look, but it's Dimitri who answers. "We don't want to give them another cause to rally behind. They already see you and Alphonse as the enemy. Finding their brethren slain at your feet will only make things worse. It would be better to discover them one at a time, than incur the wrath of them all."

My eyes bulge. "How many are there?"

"I have no way of knowing. But people like this don't just rile themselves up," Dimitri says, and I'm tempted to argue the point. I saw the way Inigo responded to my blows. He didn't need anyone but himself and his hatred to fuel him. However, on this matter, I think Dimitri might be right. The way Inigo spoke, he was too confident about the others following his lead and returning to Arcathain, as if he'd already spoken to many of them.

"At least we can narrow it down to us four," Fox says unhelpfully, but considering she just saved my life, I tamper my annoyance.

"More than that," Dimitri says. "Adrien's her uncle. He wouldn't harm her. Sai, I imagine, wouldn't either."

"Silver and Güthric," I say hoarsely. "They're friends. I know it."

Dimitri nods.

"What about Eparah?" Alphonse asks, and there's a deep sort of curiosity in his tone, leaving me with the impression that he's been trying to figure her out for a while. As have I, honestly. Things had been different with her ever since the

Shadowthorn, ever since the Castle of Nigh. I've hardly found the time to speak with her, and I honestly wasn't sure if that was a product of my self-isolation, or if she was the one avoiding me.

"It doesn't matter who was on Inigo's side right now," Dimitri says, standing. He takes a few sidesteps until the Crusader's body is at his feet, and he squats down to grab the man's pant legs. "We need to move the body."

"But where?" Alphonse asks as Fox guides him to a nearby cot. There's no grace to his movement as he slumps against the thin mattress, holding himself upright by sheer willpower alone. "If we move him into another room, people will still talk."

"Not another room," Dimitri says, nodding to Fox as she hooks Inigo under the arms, and the two of them lift the dead man in unison. Dimitri grunts. "We have to throw him overboard."

The middle half of the man's body sags, making both Dimitri and Fox stagger forward, nearly toppling on top of him. But by some stroke of luck, they find their balance.

The throbbing of my head has started to subside. Sound is no longer stretched and warbled in my ears, but has mostly returned with clarity. My jaw still burns, as does my bleeding hand, but as I ease toward the edge of the bed, I find that I'm not as weak as I'd been a few moments prior.

Alphonse settles back onto the bed as Fox and Dimitri shuffle out of the room, pausing only long enough for Dimitri to look to make sure no one else was in the hallway. Given the joyous commotion that vibrates from the room next to us, I doubt any of them have even noticed us missing. Silver might've if she hadn't been preparing dinner all this time.

As Fox disappears around the corner, a cold dread settles over me. What if they *do* notice soon though? What if they run out of whatever alcohol has been circling the room next door, and someone realizes that Inigo has been gone far too long? They would come looking for him, and they'd find me, beaten half to death, with a pool of blood on the ground.

Glancing beside me, my gaze settles on Alphonse's closed eyes, to the steady rise and fall of his chest. Sleep. It's what we both need after such an ordeal. But I won't be able to rest for a while, not with so much paranoia now coursing through me and sharpening all of my senses.

I hop from the bed, gently clasp the door shut behind me so that no one will see Alphonse and the bloodstained room if they happen to stroll by, and stagger my way up the stairs.

With Fox's back to the stairs, Dimitri notices me first. He's mid-swing as his gaze catches on mine, and Inigo's body lulls when his concentration breaks. "What are you doing? You should be resting."

Fox grunts at the jostle to their momentum. "Piss on a mage! Can you not just focus on anything but Halira for more than five minutes?"

My gaze fixes on the hard set of his jaw, but he stares only at Fox as the two of them heave Inigo's corpse, once, twice, three swings, before releasing him over the taffrail. The splash that follows wouldn't be easily confused for a fish breaching the surface, but fortunately, even if they had tossed him overboard on the same side as the cabins, I doubt any one of the Crusaders would've heard it.

Fox smacks her hands together, as if that will do anything to clean away the blood. "There. Now there's just one thing left before I leave the two of you alone."

My chest squeezes at the implication. But rather than drawing attention to the suggestion that we'd *want* to be left alone, I focus on the obvious. "What *one thing*?"

Fox's boots thud atop the dark deck as she strides over to me. "Punch me."

"What?"

"You heard me. I said throw a punch—and make it look believable." She sticks her chin out for emphasis.

I recoil. "I-I'm not punching you. Why would I—"

Heaving an exaggerating sigh, she reaches toward me and takes my hand in hers, forming my fingers into a fist. "*Because* we need a backstory. Look at you! You look like you just walked out of the Shadowthorn, half-chewed. No one's going to believe that Inigo fell overboard with you looking like that."

My eyes cut to Dimitri's. "Is that what we're telling people? That he just…fell?"

The stark angles of his expression never relent. "He was drunk before he left the room. It could be believable—"

"*If* you punch me," Fox finishes for him. She claps my fist with her palm, a sly crook to her grin. "It's what you wanted. Isn't it?"

I scowl. "I never said I wanted to hit you," I say, even though I can vaguely recall confessing to Alphonse otherwise.

"I know, but…I bet you did." When I don't argue with her, her grin broadens. "Come on. It'll be good for you. We both know I deserve it."

My lips part, a breath easing from between them. I glance from her sparkling eyes to my fist. "You just saved my life."

She shrugs, that playful, upbeat tone of hers never faltering. "True. But, weren't we just talking about how I endangered you first?" She must notice my jaw muscle tighten because mischief flashes behind her eyes. "Oh, I see. You need me to remind you so that the punch is justified."

"I didn't say that either."

"No, no. Don't deny it. It makes total sense why you'd rather punch the girl who uprooted your life, than the one who saved it. And I'd be happy to remind you that I am both. I am Foxlynn Abigail, your former best friend."

"Stop," I beg. The night has already been too rough. I don't have the emotional stamina to live through the ways in which she betrayed me.

But she doesn't stop. If anything, my small protest only serves to invigorate her. "After I discovered what you were, or what I thought you were, I used that information to get me close to the General."

"Stop."

The word is thicker now, stronger. It is a beast inside me awakening, and it is more of a warning than a plea now.

Fox toes her way closer, her blue eyes looking up into mine. I find no remorse there, only the giddy glee of someone who got exactly what they wanted at the expense of everyone else.

She licks her lips, leaning in so close that her cheek grazes mine, her breath becoming a warm cloud on my ear. "I bought my way to safety by telling the General that you possessed magic, knowing he'd tell the Magistrate and you'd be hung for your crimes."

My fists are iron melted onto the ends of my arms.

By the time Fox leans back, my fist is already drawn to my ear. I swing from my shoulder, as Tor had once advised, and just before my fingers crack against the hollow of her eye, the arrogant, unapologetic facade drops ever so slightly, and I see the real Fox behind the mask, the one I'd come to know and love while we were in Nigh.

Still, I let my arm fly. Maybe she's right. As petulant as it sounds, maybe this is all we've needed, a physical release of all of the pent-up frustration I've held against her.

The force sends her spinning and staggering. I stumble forward too, Dimitri catching me before I can fall. But as I hang limp and weary in his arms, I realize that maybe we were both wrong, because I feel no sense of fulfillment from such a blow. In fact, ever since I heard her voice in that room, every ill notion I've held against her has vanished.

Maybe it wasn't that I needed to lash out at her for what

she'd done to me and Kalli. Maybe all I truly needed to be able to move past it was to know that she'd never do something like that again, and that the next time my life was on the line, she wouldn't be standing with the enemy, but at my side, sword readied.

It takes Fox a moment to collect herself, but by the time she's standing again, swiveling her jaw, the two of us are smiling.

"That oughta do it," she says, rubbing the tender spot high on her cheek that's already starting to purple. "Now if you'll excuse me, I believe there is a puddle of blood with my name on it."

"And an unconscious man who could probably use some cleaning up," I remind her, thinking about how it'll look if all three of us are bloodied and bruised tomorrow morning.

She nods, still rubbing her cheek as she saunters down the stairs. It's not until she disappears in the darkness that I realize arms still envelop me.

Dimitri has not let go of my crumpled body. He holds me firm against his chest, his hands clasped and promising to never let me go again. It's the sort of embrace that would've sent my heart fluttering back when we were at Nigh. It was the unspoken death-pact we had: together until the end.

And though I still believe in the sentiment on some amicable level, I don't feel it like he does anymore.

Twisting in his arms, I face the man I thought I loved, the one who had been my only family when I'd lost them all. His sage eyes flick to the bruise on my jaw again, but it's to my lips where his hungry gaze settles.

"Dimitri…"

My voice cracks just as his lips crush mine. His mouth moves with urgent need, a fire burning inside him, but one whose flames I cannot feel. This had never been what I wanted. Before I lost everything, before we had nothing to lose but each other, I'd thought I could love him. I mean, I did; I cared about him as any friend would. But I'd confused that desperate need to belong with love.

The first time we kissed, I'd been so swept away from my loneliness that I never wanted to return, no matter what it took. I hadn't known it then, but looking back now, I can see it for what it was.

My chest aches, his lips moving in gentle circles over mine and cracking me in two. I don't want to hurt him. I never meant for any of this to happen.

I press my hand on his chest to gently shove him away, but hiss at the sharp sting that lances through my palm.

He mistakes my lips parting as an invitation, my breath hitching as a sign that I'm as lost in this moment as he is, and he plunges himself forward, deepening the kiss. My stomach churns in a tangled mess of knots that I'm not sure I'll ever be able to undo. He's tried so hard to prove that things can be the way they were, that he can change and is trying to accept me for who I am.

But it's just not enough. I know that's not fair to him, but I have no power over the way I feel.

Something as heavy as an ox thuds on the upper deck behind us. The sound draws Dimitri's mouth away from mine, and I sigh with relief to be able to taste air again.

But that relief all but sours in the pit of my stomach when I turn to find the shadowed figure looming over us.

Ryven stands at the top of the stairs, nothing of the beast in his eyes as he watches me.

Suddenly, I have no problem shoving Dimitri away; I can't even feel the pain burning in my hand as I press and shove at his chest until he finally lets me go.

"Ryven," I breathe into the night, unsure of what to say.

A low, sorrowful moan rumbles in his throat, bringing cold, stinging tears to my eyes. I'm shaking my head as I climb the stairs, two at a time, my feet unsteady and my legs still wobbling from the events of earlier. I collapse halfway up, my eyes trained on my quaking hands.

Wind whooshes up ahead. The ship rocks with a sudden, powerful jostle, and when I finally peel my eyes up from the dark stairs, the place where Ryven had been standing is empty.

RYVEN

VARENHOLM OCEAN

There is nothing but darkness for miles.

As long as I never look over my shoulder, back to the woman I left atop the Leviathan, I can go on believing that. It would even be for the best. This journey to Illashore has been foolhardy, to say the least, but even now, despite my fractured heart, Halira's recklessness brings a tugging smile to the left side of my disfigured face.

Just like that, it's gone again.

I am what I am. Disfigured doesn't even cover the half of it. Without Halira's hold on the darkness inside me, I am doomed to live out the rest of my days, not as a druid, but as a demonic bat monster, who will stop at nothing to kill and slaughter everyone who crosses my path.

If I had any sense of self-preservation left, I'd dive into the cruel ocean, let it fill my lungs, and sink to the very depths to become shark bait. Of course, the thought has crossed my mind over the days and weeks. But Halira's hope has been infectious. For a time, I actually started to allow myself to believe what she did, that we'd arrive to Illashore and the mages would cure me and save all of Arcathain.

How foolish a notion that is though. Not for Halira, who

knows no limits to where her determination and conviction can take her. But for me, I should've known.

In some ways, I did.

I'm not surprised she found comfort in Dimitri's arms, but that doesn't make the pain hurt any less. It was almost as if she'd wanted me to see. Why else would she choose that spot atop the deck, moments before my arrival, to kiss him so openly?

The knife I'm trying to twist in my chest doesn't budge though. Part of me can't believe that's true. The way she looked at me, there was true regret and fear in her eyes. No, it wasn't intentional for me to discover her. I'm not even sure she was—

Despite the way one black ripple leaks into the next, something distinct catches my eye in the tumbling waves below.

Dinner.

My wings tuck tight against my back as I dive for the ocean. The mass drifts, bigger than any fish I've seen floating atop the water's surface before. Given the round shape, I'd almost think I was looking at a sea lion, but I think we're too far from a coast for them to swim this far.

The closer I near the creature, the hungrier I become. Blood is heavy in the air. I notice the dark collection of it pooling around the limp form beneath me.

My claws stretch, aching to tear through the flesh and sink my fangs into the raw meat. As a druid, the very thought should repulse me. The lives of animals are sacred things, meant to be respected and cared for, even in death. But when the hunger settles in, I remember very little about the druid I'd been, and only the demon I've become.

At the last second, I splay my wings out wide, the updraft catching in the thin membrane. My talons grasp the shimmering skin and I careen back into the sky.

But when I glance down to behold my find, it's not the dead

eyes of a seal I find, nor that of a shark or whale, or any other creature belonging to the sea.

This thing is human. And I recognize him as one of the humans Halira has been traveling with.

My suspicious gaze flits to the horizon, to the ship that Halira's on. How did this man fall overboard, especially while there were at least two others on the deck who would've seen him and tried to help?

Slowly, I lower the two of us back down until his body floats upright in the mostly calm waters. It's only then that I notice the fresh lances, jagged and bloodied, surrounding his eye socket. There's a small bruise near his temple.

Thinking back to when I saw Halira, I realize that she had looked different too. I'd mistaken it for a trick of the light, for shadows cast by the ill-placed moon, but in my mind's eye, I can see the bruise along her chin as clear as day now. Her hand had been bandaged, as well, fresh blood seeping through the fabric.

My gaze cuts to the horizon, my wings sending a powerful gust of wind below as I propel myself toward her.

She may have made her choice, and for that I cannot fault her. Dimitri will make her happy, and that is all I want for her. But I cannot leave her now, not when it is so very obvious that others would have her killed.

A STORM ON THE HORIZON

THE CABINS, LEVIATHAN, VARENHOLM OCEAN

Every morning I awaken to the flapping sound of wings as Ryven leaps into the air. Now, more than ever, I'm convinced that he used to wait for me to arise and say farewell before leaving, because now he does no such thing. At first, I'd been tempted to wait for him at the bow all night long, until I realized that he would either have to choose to stubbornly fly throughout the night, thereby tiring himself out and prevent him from having any real rest for almost two straight days, or land and face me. Fearing he'd be as stubborn as I would, I'd returned to my cot, and breathed a sigh of relief when I heard the thud of his talons as he landed just moments after my head hit the pillow.

But I am running out of options. I need to talk to him. I need to tell him that what he saw—what he *thought* he saw—was nothing. If he would just let me explain, I'm sure I could make him understand.

At the same time, the distance he'd kept had been good for us all. Once I told my uncle what transpired that night with Inigo, he suggested that for the time being I keep my distance from the demon, and to limit my daily training with magic. It was easy enough to do when Alphonse had given up on magic anyway and the demon in question was avoiding me.

And he wasn't the only one who'd rather not face someone.

I still hadn't faced Dimitri. Every time I'd thought to, I didn't know what to say. The words all sounded so cheesy in my thick skull. *It's not you, it's me* was just the tip of the iceberg. How could I confess to someone who had been my best friend my entire life that the love I had for him didn't go beyond our friendship anymore? How could I answer the onslaught of questions that he was surely to have for me?

Of course, avoiding him on this vessel had been nearly impossible, so instead I'd focused on avoiding private encounters with him. I spent most of my time watching Adrien and Sai work on the final touches to the bench—which they had since moved on to work on the entire table, so that it would be a matching set. When it became apparent that they'd wanted more quality time alone, I transitioned to the kitchen with Silver and Güthric. Thanks to my upbringing, my mother had ensured I'd known how to wield a knife in the kitchen.

But even the kitchen could only be a safe haven for so long, and whenever they started hacking away at fish heads, I vacated quickly.

To Dimitri's credit, he hasn't actually given me any reason to hide from him. It's not like every time we run into each other, he tries gathering me into his arms, or shoving his tongue down my throat, or worse yet, talking about why I am being so strange around him. If I didn't know any better, I'd bet he already suspected something was off, but I'd been too skittish to give either of us a chance to air the awkwardness.

Despite knowing Ryven's already long gone, I kick the blanket from my legs and race to the bow. A Crusader passes me on my way up, shoulder-checking my arm with painful precision. He grumbles something about Inigo under his breath as he climbs down the stairs and heads back into the cabin, likely returning from a late-night piss over the ship's ledge.

Bumping into him makes me feel as if I've swallowed an entire desert, my throat becoming so dry as I stare dumfounded at the Crusader. Tensions had risen between everyone the past few days. Ever since Inigo's strange and sudden disappearance, the glares I'd been receiving had come tenfold. At least it was no longer difficult to tell where everyone stood. It seemed almost every one of the Crusaders who accompanied Eparah on her mission to retrieve Alphonse's body were against me, everyone except Dimitri and Fox. They were turning on Alphonse too. Their distrust of him hadn't been so bad before, but even if they wanted to believe that the big oaf Inigo had stumbled over the ship's ledge and drowned, the moment they laid eyes on the thick, purple bruises on my neck, everyone knew the lie for what it was. Fox's hands wouldn't have been able to leave such grotesque and painful marks. She wouldn't have been able to overpower me for long enough. If only Kalli or Imryll had been here. One of them could've healed the bruises before the morning had come. Alphonse and I both tried, but neither of our gifts for magic appeared to be linked to healing.

I wait at the bow long after the sun has risen, staring up into the sky and watching the clouds pass. I keep hoping that maybe I will glimpse Ryven up there among them, but truth is, I have no idea how far he goes when he leaves, nor do I know how he spends that time. Presumably he's…feeding somehow, though I didn't dare think about how. If I thought it would be helpful or allowed, I might ask Güthric to set aside some of the daily catch of fish for him, but I was honestly trying to heed Adrien's advice: focus less on the demon, and more on the people aboard the ship.

When I catch myself staring up into the sky too long, I turn my back to the ocean, heading back to the lower decks where

I'm sure Fox is still asleep. But instead, I collide with someone else. The white cotton chemise is soft beneath my fingers, but I recoil with a shiver when I think about how cold she must be.

"Silver," I gasp, wrapping my arms around my shoulders and clutching them tightly. "What are you doing up here? You have to be frozen."

She looks past me, out toward the stark line where the sky kisses the sea. She sucks in a deep breath, letting the morning air fill her entirely before exhaling. "If I stay up here too long, I'm sure I will be. But Güthric keeps me plenty warm at night. The crisp air can be refreshing."

"Oh." My voice lilts. I hope that the pink that rises to my cheeks will be mistaken for the windbreak, and not my own girlish embarrassments, let alone be mistaken for something worse, something darker that I don't even like admitting to myself. "I was just getting some fresh air myself, but I'll leave you to it then—"

Apparently sensing the thoughts I feared she would, she puts her hand on my shoulder, stopping me in place. "He will come when he is ready."

"Who?" I start to ask, but the word doesn't even become the fog that parts my lips. I have no believable reason to deny that he's the reason I'm up here, that he's the reason I'm so uncomfortable around any of my friends right now. Every single one of them—Fox, Silver, Güthric, Sai—they're all happily engaged with another, something I covet ferociously. But the man I want to be with isn't even a man right now, nor is he bothering to allow me to so much as see him.

My head bows, despair anchoring itself to my chest. "I'm not so sure he will. He thinks I…"

I struggle with the words as long as I can, but ultimately, I can't even bring myself to say it. He thinks I betrayed him, abandoned him in his greatest time of need, just as Dimitri did to me. And for some reason, that makes me feel all the rottener about it.

Silver shakes her head, more fervently than I expect her to. Her hazel eyes bore into mine, as solid as stones. "He fears the worst because he is living a nightmare without any hope of reprieve. But when our loved ones are living in fear, it is for us to be their courage in the face of uncertainty."

I hear my father's voice in my head utter some hope for bravery to fill my heart, but I shake the memory away. "I don't know how to fix it. Any of it. Not what happened with Dimitri. Not what happened to Ryven. None of it. I can't change the past and what's worse…" I don't even recognize the thought until I'm speaking it, my fears taking on a life of their own. "What if we get to Illashore and we can't find the mages? What if they're all dead and that's why no one has heard from them all these centuries? Or worse…what if they refuse to help us?"

When I glance up to search her eyes for any signs of reassurance I might find there, I recoil from the emotion I find instead. Dread? Trepidation?

Silver's lips press into a thin line. "You may not have to wait much longer to find out what will happen once we find the mages."

Fear drags its sharpened nail down my spine, the shiver of it continuing all the way through to my toes. Slowly, I turn, Silver walking along beside me, as we behold the ominous horizon.

But as I squint, it's not just land we're staring at, but something dark and heavy hanging in the sky.

A storm's coming.

UNLEASHED

LEVIATHAN, VARENHOLM OCEAN

I suppose a more accurate description would be that we are approaching the storm. Dark clouds, heavy and black, sink low in the skyline ahead, as if they belong anchored to the very sea itself.

Silver returns with just about everyone, aside from the one or two who opted to stay in bed. Among those of us here, none of us have seen a more menacing storm, not even Güthric or Adrien who had been out at sea many times. Not even me, someone who is capable of creating her own tempests.

Even from this distance, there's something off about this particular storm. The lightning sparks with an unsettling shine. The vibration in the air, the very energy we're sailing into, none of it feels natural. It's tainted, somehow. Tarnished and misshapen.

Spying Alphonse beside me, I lean into him. "Do you feel that?"

His head bobs, but it's such a vague motion that I can't tell if he's nodding or shaking it. "Something definitely doesn't look right about it. Is it magic?"

"I don't know."

One thing I do know for certain though, as my gaze travels

along the bottom of the sky, is that we have to sail through it. The shadow that's formed up ahead, it's more than just storm clouds; there's land beneath them, a large enough mass that I think we just might be approaching Illashore.

As I press forward through the crowd, my thoughts momentarily flicker to Ryven. The demon blood in him makes him strong, but I have no way of knowing whether even he could fly through this storm unaided. But I only have a moment to search the sky for him before I've reached the frontmost point of the bow.

"Leviathan!" I call, the storm clouds, still at least a few hours away, already churning the waters with violence.

The Leviathan's head surfaces a moment later, water spilling down either side of her long neck. It waterfalls onto the ship, most of the crew dashing down the stairs to avoid it, but by now I've grown accustomed to the occasional shower the Leviathan provides. This is too important to run from, anyway.

"Is that Illashore ahead?" I ask her.

Her silken voice slithers in my mind, coiling inside me like a snake. "*Yesss.*"

"Will we make it through the storm?" I shout, realizing that it's not just mist from her that's drenching me. We've drifting into a light drizzle, one that I can only guess will intensify as we grow nearer. It's alarming though just how much the storm is already impacting us when it is still so far away.

The Leviathan dips its head low as if it's looking over the horizon instead of from high above the mist. "*I do not know.*"

Something like hopelessness sinks in my belly, but I shake the feeling away before it can settle and fester. We don't need doubt right now. Doubt breeds fear, and there's been enough of that on this ship these past few days. Right now, these people need someone they can believe in, someone who can assure them everything is going to be all right.

Even if that someone can't say for certain that it will.

"All right, everybody," I shout over the splashing of the waves and the scuttling of the boots that dash across and the deck below. "We are sailing through the storm. Being a druid of the sky, I should be able to contain it enough to allow us to pass safely. I will keep the winds as peaceful as I can so the waves are gentle, and I won't let the lightning strike us. But I need the rest of you to remain calm. Get below deck, just in case it gets too unruly.

"Güthric? Adrien? Perhaps there's aid you can offer me?"

Güthric pounds his chest once and strides up the stairs to my side.

My uncle bows at the waist, long unkempt hair hanging around his ears. "It would be an honor to offer any assistance." He peeks up. "But might I remind you that this vessel might... differ from any craft I've sailed before. We ride atop the back of an ancient being. I hate to sound like I'm being fatalistic but—"

Dimitri strides forward. His chest is puffed, his nostrils flared, and he waits behind Adrien, so dauntingly still and quiet, that my uncle finally has no choice but to step aside. "I'll just...get to work and leave you two to be."

Unflinching, I meet Dimitri's gaze. "You have something to say?"

He crosses his arms. "Is it really necessary for anyone to be above deck during a storm like this? The Leviathan can handle it."

"The Leviathan cannot," I state firmly. What does he know of the abilities of creatures like her when he isn't the one capable of hearing her pleas now. I look past him to the rest of the crew gathering at the base of the stairs. "Everyone else will remain below deck, unless summoned. Dimitri is right, this will be dangerous, but we can handle it as long as everyone stays out of the way."

I make sure to look back to my old friend, my old lover,

when I utter the last bit. He fights against spitting back whatever retort is curdling his lips into a sneer, and spins around to disappear below with the others who scatter.

Finally, I'm able to refocus, and spying Alphonse across the deck, I cut the distance between us. I keep my voice at a low growl so that none below can hear me or my concern. "The Leviathan says she doesn't know if we'll make it through."

"Then what are we doing?" Alphonse says, arms splaying out. The rain has already drenched his hair, mine too, and now it's working to seep through the heavy leathers he's donned. "Let's turn around. Head back the way we came and find another way through."

One look over my shoulder is all it takes to see how far the storm reaches. "There is no other way. Don't you understand? This storm can't be natural. It's magic. It's protecting Illashore, and the only way to reach the stolen land is to get through the storm."

Already, the ship sways, the Leviathan struggling to keep us afloat and upright as she battles the crashing waves. I'd miscalculated how long I thought it would take us to reach it, but I don't have a trained eye for distance at sea, let alone one to gauge spells such as this. If the mages' magic is antagonistic as they have been described in our history books, then it could be responding to our presence, seeping out to swat us away before we reach the eye.

"And you can stop it?" Alphonse splutters, and it's not doubt in his tone exactly, but something worrying nonetheless.

"I never said that. I don't think I have the power to stop whatever spell they've put around them. It took dozens of mages to create the boundary spell at the Eyve, and hundreds to break the continent. I can only imagine it was hundreds more to create this storm."

"Then what's your plan?"

The Leviathan bucks with another wave, and Alphonse and

I stagger to the taffrail, both of us nearly falling over the edge. But Alphonse anchors himself to the rail with the crook of his elbow, grabbing me around the waist with his other arm.

I swallow a mouthful of the water streaming down my face.

"I already told you," I shout over the winds that I haven't tamed yet. "To ease the wind and direct the lightning elsewhere, away from the Leviathan."

"Then what do you need them for?"

Alphonse bobs his chin behind us to Güthric, Adrien, and Sai who must've either not heard me give the order to stay below, or simply decided he had a death wish. The three of them cling to whatever they can wrap their sodden, withering fingers around and hold for dear life.

Adrien's dripping face is bunched in a perpetual grimace as the torrential rain beats down on him. It strikes me then how odd it is to see him without Sai nearby. The two of them have been almost inseparable the entire trip; I get the impression it's been that way since my uncle rescued and sheltered him. Asking Adrien to stay up here is keeping him from Sai, and vice versa.

Beside him, Güthric shields his face with his thick forearm, and I realize the same is true for him.

I thought they'd be able to help me understand how to direct the wind to ensure a safe and straight passage through the storm, but truth is, I have the Leviathan for that. I'm only putting them at a greater risk, and causing more stress to the ones that are sheltering below.

"He's right!" I shout over the rolling clouds and churning sea. "You two should head back below deck. I'll manage up here." At Güthric's bunching brow, I say hurriedly, "I promise. Once everyone is below and I'm not dealing with anymore distractions, I'll be able to focus better. I can do this. I promise." I shift my attention to Alphonse and the dark hair that's so wet it looks like oil is slicked over his head. "You too."

Another wave crashes into the side of the boat, of the Leviathan, and we clutch onto what we can.

Alphonse doesn't lose my gaze. He shouts over his shoulder to Güthric and Adrien though. "You heard the woman! Get down below!"

If Güthric was conflicted, he shows no signs of it as he staggers toward the staircase, disappearing to the lower deck with the others. Adrien, however, hesitates. He may only be my uncle, but I imagine leaving me to combat this horrific storm feels an awful lot like leaving a babe in a den of lions.

I manage to flash a weak smile at him, one that says I've faced far worse than angry clouds.

Conflict twists his expression, but finally, with a begrudging shake of his head, he releases the broken mast and bounds for the stairs.

I glare between Dimitri and Alphonse. I can't let either of them stay up here with me. One is an incompetent liability when it comes to handling magic, and the other...well, the other is much the same. Alphonse still hasn't even brushed up against the power that's dormant inside him—if it's even there at all—and Dimitri has no experience of magic other than the few glimpse he's caught around me.

But no matter how much I stab them with my gaze, neither budges.

The Leviathan bucks again, as if to remind me that we have no time to argue. The storm is no longer just some dark clouds off in the distance; it surrounds us now in every direction. Light flashes directly over our heads, punctuating what I already know to be true: it's time.

I shove out of Dimitri's arms, spinning to clutch the railing on my arm. I try anticipating the movements of the ocean, the rise and fall of the Leviathan's swaying body, but the water isn't as rhythmic as it had been before. The ship sways and jerks. It's tossed across the black waters like a feather caught in a cyclone. Beneath us, I can sense the Leviathan's struggle to keep us afloat, but even such an ancient beast as she has no control over the erratic waves.

Magic triumphs here.

My magic.

The clouds. The lightning. The wind. The very air around us—these are the elements I have practiced with; these are the elements I have come to see as extensions of myself.

My eyes fall shut. I close myself off to the fear and panic aboard this ship and below it, and instead lean backward, drifting into that quiet, secluded place where there is no distinction between solid and not, where my flesh tingles as I brush up against my awareness of magic, of life all around me. I am nothing as much as I am everything. I am neither here nor there, but everywhere. I am one but also connected to the many.

With a belly-deep inhale, I reach up to the sky. The air is erratic, without any purpose or sense of direction. It simply moves, swirling in dizzying waves, and zagging in patterns that hurt my head.

The magic here is raw and vile. Wind is meant to blow in one constant stream. Sure, it can shift, careening from the left to the right as another gust becomes it. But here the air does not act as one entity, a constant stream of wind, but as fractured shards of glass that impale the sky and everything below it.

I use my own breath to anchor me and the irregular gusts. With each inhale I muster, I pull on the cords of wind to align them, and by the time I exhale, I breathe calm into the sky above.

The ship still rocks and I breathe again, the splintered shards agonizing in my throat and chest until I spit them back out into the world.

Another breath. This one hurts less as it goes down, and less still as it resurfaces, aligning itself in the sky as one great breeze wafts over us.

I continue breathing as if I don't have a body, but instead am the captain of the sky. I feel the wind fill my lungs like roiling rapids, feel it course through my veins as it becomes me, and I become it.

Inhale.

Exhale.

Inhale.

With each breath, something shifts in the atmosphere. For the first time since we spotted the storm clouds, warmth grazes over my cheeks, the morning sun far warmer than I ever remember it being before.

Another wave crashes, and the Leviathan tips with the ship, tossing everyone starboard. It's more than a mere stagger. The earth-shattering shove jostles me from my state of focus, and I just barely have time to grab on to the balustrade before I surely would've been flung into the churning sea.

I stare into the deep blue, long after the Leviathan corrects its bearings. Something's wrong. My hold over the sky should ease the anger of the sea, but the waves thrash even more wildly than before.

"It was working," Alphonse shouts, water spilling from his lips as he offers Fox a hand. I hadn't even realized she was up here, but I'm not surprised. They have been inseparable ever since they reunited in the Shadowthorn.

The two of them might as well stay where they are though, supine on the wet deck. It might just be the safest place for them, if they insist on remaining up here. "Can you do it again?"

Shaking my head, I too spit through a stream of rain when I cry. "It's not just the wind. It's the ocean. I have no control over it."

As if by way of mocking us, the riotous sea kicks up again.

Fox manages to rise to her feet despite her shaking legs. They clutch to the dripping bannister, to each other.

"I need your help," I shout across the deck. "My magic is of the wind, but we still don't know what yours is."

It takes my cousin a moment to register what I'm suggesting. "Are you mad? Don't you think if I had magic, we would've felt it by now?"

"Maybe." I shrug, my hands sliding to the next notch of the railing as the sea rocks us along. "But maybe not. My magic always feels the strongest when I'm in need of it, when I'm in danger."

He snorts, tossing his slicked hair out of his face with a wet smack that's lost in the torrential downpour.

"Do you remember that day in the sparring ring? When you kept landing blow after blow and you knocked me down and I was done for."

Indignant understanding flares in his gaze. "That raven was you! I'll have you know, I nearly lost an eye that day—"

Ignoring him, I continue. "The day we fled the castle and you and I fought in the Shadowthorn it was the same. I didn't know I could summon storm clouds, let alone lightning. But I needed to escape you. I needed to defeat you."

A shudder runs through him, one as much from the memory as it is the storm overhead. His eyes narrow on me. "Are you reaching your point, or just reminding me how infuriating you can be?"

"Alphonse. We need you to try and access your magic again. I can't do this alone. I don't have the power. My magic can't even sense whatever is wrong with the ocean. But maybe yours can."

His lips part to protest, but I cut him off.

"Please. If not for me...for her."

He straightens for a moment, staring into the crystal-blue eyes of the red-haired woman beside him, until the ship rocks again. The two of them slam into the balustrade, their hips surely bruising from the impact. His lips press into a thin line, and that's when I know I've won him over.

As Alphonse moves to stagger back toward the broken mast in the center of the deck, seemingly deciding it to be a safer anchor than the taffrail that has already been dunked beneath the water now ten times over, the ship bucks. With Alphonse leaning inward, and Fox's unsteady form balanced over the right side of the ship, there's nothing stopping her feet from kicking up from the deck. She's tossed overboard, heels flying over her head in the blink of an eye. One moment there, the next gone. I can't discern her scream over the raging storm; I can't even hear Alphonse's as his jaw cracks wide, and horror wells in his throat.

He races to the side of the boat, seconds away from diving in after her, when Dimitri magically appears beside him. With a firm grasp on Alphonse's shoulders, he cranes him back. From where I stand on the upper deck, their shouts become as thunderous as the sky, a menacing cacophony of yelling and screaming.

Alphonse twists and torques, his torso ripping out from Dimitri's grasp as he hurls himself back to the balustrade. This time, he doesn't dive. He stares out into the churning, dismal sea, scanning for the one sign of life that he needs. I search too, for even the slightest fleck of auburn hair, or crystal-blue eyes blinking through the darkness, or a dainty hand reaching. Anything. Any sight, any sound. But there are none.

Alphonse's knuckles burn white hot as he squeezes the railing and bellows, a sound so horrendous with agony that even the storm shutters.

Not just shutters, but recoils. The storm peels back from him, layers of waves and dark clouds clambering away in either direction. His eyes are squeezed too tightly, the roar too all-consuming for him to notice, but Dimitri and I stare in awe as the ocean falls silent.

We stop rocking. We stop swaying. We stop, all except for the forward momentum the Leviathan carries us on.

Then, something strange happens, stranger than a storm dissipating from thin air. The waters around us ripple with the slightest hue of gold. It starts from the boat, a barely noticeable flash of light, that spreads outward, over the expansive blue, illuminating everything in its wake before fading just as swiftly.

As if he can sense it, Alphonse pries one eye open. The sky is a light shade of blue again, the water dark from depth but no longer from malevolent forces, but his gaze notices none of it.

Dimitri and I exchange a glance as Alphonse chucks his torso over the edge of the ship. I inch closer, still trying to make sense of what just transpired.

Alphonse stopped the storm. Not just the churning waves, but all of it. He stopped the clouds from pouring. He cleared the skies of darkness. He calmed and soothed the climate in ways I couldn't even dream of; in ways I never even thought possible.

Ryven had said that every druid has their strengths, but my mind couldn't settle on what Alphonse's must be. It wasn't just the water he mastered, but also the sky. It must take a powerful druid to be able to break through both of the magical barriers intertwined with this place, and I only knew that because I'd tried. I could find no connection to the waters, to the waves that rocked us and the ocean that meant to devour us. But Alphonse had found that connection in a single, desperate moment.

But how?

We'd been out at sea for weeks now. Surely, if he was some master of the tides, we would've discovered it by now? And all my lessons on becoming weightless, of finding the wind and sailing alongside it, why had none of those landed with him if he had been able to sense them all along?

Not just sense them. *Control* them.

My stomach sloshes, exhaustion sinking deep into my bones, as I stumble toward them. Dimitri moves to catch me in his arms, but I divert my trajectory, hanging limply over the taffrail and peeking down to the calm waters.

One of the Leviathan's tentacles rises, a coughing woman slouched over the fleshy underside of its limb. Once she's within arm's reach, Alphonse grabs her by the belt of her trousers and one of her arms and hoists her with no effort at all. He sets her down on the ground, enveloping her in his lanky arms as she continues to cough up water.

Her wide, disbelieving eyes meet mine, but none of that fear shows in her playful tone. "Pity. And here I thought I'd be able to hold it over your head that I saved your life."

He chuckles into her hair. "I couldn't allow that to last too long. What would it have done to my poor, precious ego?"

She squirms to elbow him, but his hold is too tight.

With the waters calmed, some of the people below deck start to trickle up. Adrien is one of the first. He envelops me in a tight embrace, lifting me off my feet and jostling my stomach more than I would like to admit.

Once he sets me back down, his attention falls somewhere over my shoulder. "Land-ho, scallywags!"

I whip around to behold my mission. My goal. My destiny. My heart becomes a beating drum, and I suddenly wonder again about how Ryven fared the storm. I still see no signs of him in the sky, but hopefully since the storm has been rendered useless, he will have no problem flying through from…wherever he's gone.

A boyish grin splits Adrien's face as he leans in close to whisper, "In all my time aboard pirate ships, that's the first time I've actually had the chance to say that. Can you believe it?"

THE STOLEN LAND

ILLASHORE

Silence descends, heavy and unsettling, as we approach the long-lost land of Arcathain. I say *lost,* but it's not like we misplaced it. The approaching island—the earthen soil, the nettled trees, the chirping songbirds—all of it was stolen, ripped away from the mainland in a devastating fissure that left our country and our people scarred for generations. The mages had been our allies. They'd rallied with us to slay the Primordials, stacked bricks alongside Arcathainians to help build the wall that kept Qaeus trapped in the Eyve, and were singlehandedly responsible for enchanting the wall so that none of Arcathain would ever fear Qaeus' reign again.

But then the spell broke. The Primordial tore through the centuries-old wall and terrorized Arcathain once more. And in our people's greatest time of need, when our magical allies meant more to us than we'd ever imagined, they'd fled. They'd fissured the westernmost tip of our country, cavalier about the hundreds if not thousands of human lives lost to those cracks, and absconded.

And those of us on this ship will be the first to see this stolen segment of our home country since. Even the druids that Imryll said came to investigate were never able to breach the storm of magic protecting the place.

Shivers skitter along my heart as I behold the island's beauty. I don't know what I expected, but this wasn't it. It is like walking through the front door of my parents' cottage, like sinking into my bed after a long day's work. Home. This place is home. Not some horrifyingly foreign fortress of evil like so many of the history books depicted. I recognize its pine scent; I'm comforted by the caress of wind that, no matter how hard I search it, appears to possess no traces of the dark magic we encountered in the storm.

Home.

And yet...

My skin is pinpricked as the Leviathan slides onto the shoreline. The boisterous laughter and lighthearted conversations that had filled this ship more days than not have retreated below deck to our cabins, likely hiding beneath the beds where they will remain until we leave this place again.

If we leave this place again...

The Leviathan's tentacles reach over its back to allow us onto them. We disembark from the strange vessel and the ancient beast, each of us carrying what supplies are left—mostly boar and elk jerky that Imryll had packed specifically for this part of the journey, when our ever-flowing supply of fish would end, a few jars of pickled carrots and beets, our pots for cooking and boiling water, the buckskin canteens of water we'd collected during the rainfalls, and the pitiful selection of spices that remained. It wouldn't be enough to last for long, but I take solace in having familiarity with the land. Thanks to our survival lessons at the Castle of Nigh, most of us know what plants are edible in Arcathainian forests. Some of us—Dimitri, Adrien, and I imagine Fox as well—can even hunt if the need surfaces.

"It's too quiet," Dimitri says, the hard set of his eyes scanning the sparse tree line behind us as the Leviathan continues plucking our companions from the ship.

I nod my understanding, but I'm honestly not sure if there is truly something unsettling about this place, or if it is just generations of paranoia niggling at both of us. The mages, as we understand them, are cunning, hostile, ruthless, and powerful beings. I'd almost rather greet them here, upon our arrival, than wander Illashore, always wondering when we'd bump into one. For all we know, they could already be planning an attack. It wouldn't be too farfetched to believe that they noticed their storm spell was shattered, an enchantment that was almost definitely set in motion to ward off human—and druid—wanderers such as ourselves. They will want to know the people who broke through their magic.

So, where are they?

"Will...that be all?" the Leviathan asks me after she places the last member of our group on the damp soil.

The question is a difficult one to answer. I'd hoped to hear back from Kalli by now, to have at least some vague reassurance that she and the Magistrate were in motion and would be arriving soon to support us if necessary. But there has been no sign of the raven since I sent it away. No sign of any creatures soaring high in the sky. Other than Ryven.

Despite Illashore having a certain feel of home to it, the idea of being stranded here, in this home away from home, makes my stomach feel heavy and watery.

"Would we need to make another offering to the Leviathan to get back home? I'm not sure what more we could give."

The Leviathan is quiet for a moment before her hissing voice slithers back into my thoughts. *"There are always...secrets to be shared..."* I bite my lower lip, and pink rises to my cheeks as if it was a personal accusation. Maybe it was. *"I will...remain close by."*

A rumble reverberates through the earth as the ancient,

corpulent creature waddles back into the ocean. Once the tip of the Leviathan's slick, gray head disappears beneath the water, my gaze drifts back to the sky. White clouds bulge like flowery canopies of cotton, but few litter the bright blue sky, offering a nearly clear view of the expanse overhead.

Not a speck of black in sight.

My heart sinks into my stomach, struggling to stay afloat. Maybe he finally left us? Maybe after days of not seeing one another, my hold on the demon side of him has finally been severed and he's lost his way?

My foot rises of its own accord, as if it's about to carry me across the sea so I can scour the vast ocean just to find him.

"What do we do now?" a voice asks somewhere behind me, drawing my attention back to the gathered group of travelers. Adrien leans over, one elbow propped on Sai's shoulder. "Are all the mages dead?"

Alphonse snorts, clasping his hands behind his back. "Would serve them right if they were."

I shoot him a dagger of a glare. If we are ever going to gain their trust and aid, we will have to stop saying things like *that*.

His shoulders slouch. "Right. Hopefully, not *all* of them, considering we need someone to guide us to the Pits of Bagamore and tell us how to slay the last Primordial. Which begs the question, how do we find a mage willing to help us? How do we find any mage, for that matter? Illashore seems far more…antiquated than I imagined."

"He's right." Dimitri crosses his arms, but his eyes have not once left the trees. "They're supposed to be a superior race with unlimited magic. They severed an entire country. You'd think this place would be more advanced, but I didn't see anything for miles up the coastline as we sailed in."

"Maybe they're farther inland," Silver offers. "Many of our own cities were built away from the dangers the ocean could pose."

"Okay," Dimitri admits. "But where? This island is a small country. Where do we even begin? We can't just wander aimlessly while the Primordial runs rampant; we've already wasted precious time just by venturing this far for answers that we don't even know with certainty exist." My jaw flexes, but I bite back the urge to insist otherwise. "The sooner we find a mage, the sooner we can return to help our people."

"Well," someone croons from the trees. His husky voice sends shards of ice spiking through my veins. "I suppose if one was to announce their intentions loudly enough, a mage just might stumble upon one's path."

PISS ON A MAGE

ILLASHORE

$\mathcal{D}$imitri's sword is drawn in an instant, the rest of us spinning on our heels to face the man who'd crept so silently that none of us had even heard him. Not until he wanted us to.

When I sneak a glance at Dimitri, a muscle in his jaw twitches, and I know he's wondering how he hadn't noticed the stranger sooner. Magic is the only answer I can surmise. My knowledge of the mages' powers is about as limited as my knowledge of druids, but I know they're not limited to the natural laws of the world like the druids are. I sensed as much while we were caught in the storm. They hadn't just tampered with the wind and water, altering it until it had become a dangerous and formidable force of nature; they'd mangled the elements with something so dark it had almost been unrecognizable.

So I have no doubt that a mage such as the one who steps out of the shadows between the trees now, his long tailored tunic a brilliant shade of green that shines like dew on leaves, would be able to manipulate anything: sound, perception.

He strides forward with a level of arrogance that goes unmatched to any other person I've ever met, including

Alphonse. Whereas it had always seemed like my cousin had to think about lengthening his spine when he entered the training grounds, or carrying his head high when he rode horseback, so as to make everyone around him feel small, the grace with which this stranger carries himself seems to come as natural to him as it is to breathe.

The other armed Crusaders draw their weapons, the sharp song of metal humming on the beach as the man strides forward. He stops a safe distance away, adjusting the bulbous buttons along the front of his tunic.

"Allow me to introduce myself. Igemonar Awyn Tallis, at your service." His dark head of hair dips, but those striking eyes, sunken in his skull, remain fixed ahead on us. "And who might I have the pleasure of meeting?"

Alphonse steps forward, seemingly still accustomed to being the leader of this group, and though I have no interest in fighting him for the position if he truly wants it, I'm not sure I can trust him to be the voice of our mission.

I leap in front of him. "We come from Arcathain, and we would like a word with the mages. I'm assuming you are one?"

His already soured expression puckers more. "I know where you come from, girl. But what is of more interest to me is how in the name of magic you deduced the significance of the Pits of Bagamore?"

I glance to Alphonse beside me, wishing he were Ryven instead. Ryven had been with me the day the Elders told us about the Pits of Bagamore. It hadn't been the first time I'd heard of them. Though there had been a few tomes in the library at Nigh that mentioned the grim place, they had been cryptic enough that even then I'd been curious about them. Even more so now knowing that the mage before us believes we shouldn't know about them at all. Perhaps the mages had a hand at wiping away any mention of the Pits of Bagamore throughout history. But why? And what *significance* was he so worried we'd uncovered? Was it about the Primordials?

If Kalli was here, she'd be able to piece this mystery together with ease, and then assault the man with an overly analyzed accusation that he'd be unable to refute. But as it is, Kalli isn't here. There is only me and the fugitives and Crusaders I traveled with.

"So, there is significance to the Pits of Bagamore?" I crane my neck the other direction to find Dimitri scowling at the mage, the lines etched in his face threatening to fissure straight through him if he continues thinking as hard as he is.

The mage barks a cold, sharp laugh that fills my lungs with icy vapor. "Please. Do not insult my intelligence and I will not insult yours."

"That is definitely *not* our intent while we're here." I pin Dimitri down with a deadly glower, one that he doesn't even glance at, too preoccupied by staring down the *evil* mage.

"Oh?" Igemonar says. "You come with intent?"

My hackles rise at that, but I clamp my mouth shut on any bitter outcry that might've flown from my lips. "My apologies, Igemonar. You asked for our names, and I declined to introduce us. My name is Halira Devonshire. I should first like to thank you for welcoming the first humans to set foot on Illashore since—"

"Humans?" Igemonar's smile curves like a coiling viper. "You do not need to play coy with me. You broke through the spell guarding the island. You have a familiar." A scowl comes too quickly to my face, and he points up to the sky, to where a black speck circles in the clouds high overhead. My heart skitters at first, hopeful that Ryven might've finally resurfaced. But a new kind of hope springs forth when I realize the creature is a raven. "I know what you are, and I know why you've come, and the Council will not be thrilled to hear it.

"So, I'll ask you again. How did you do it? How did you break the spell?"

I don't actually remember him asking us how we got through the storm, but the gray and ominous clouds roll into my thoughts again, clearing all previous ponderings of what the mage knows about the Pits of Bagamore, if we should lie about there being druids among us, and just how upset the Council of mages will be about our appearance, and how that will bode for us.

Instead, I think about how I'd tried reaching up to the winds to calm them, but how powerless I'd been to the dark arcana that had been laced in the air. Ultimately, I'd been as good as useless. If Alphonse hadn't been there...

But not even he knows how he broke through the enchantment, I can tell as much by his paling skin and downcast eyes.

It's not the sort of truth you offer a complete stranger though, one who also possesses magic and almost certainly knows how to use it better than either Alphonse or me.

"That pitiful storm you had guarding the island?" I arch an eyebrow. "I would hardly call that a challenge for any druid."

Something like confusion flashes behind the mage's eyes, but it's gone so fast, replaced with cool indifference, that I barely have a chance to notice it. "Yes, I suppose not for druids powerful enough to summon a Leviathan."

The mocking nature of his tone twists my stomach into knots. Judging from the skittish glances and knuckles cracking as the Crusaders' hands tighten on their weapons, I'm not the only one who senses the danger. But how can we be so certain? Our entire lives we've been told the mages are evil, so it's only natural that we'd be on high alert. Put a doe in a meadow with a wolf and it will run as far away from the predator as it can, even if the wolf is injured or unconscious, even if it's already dead.

Thinking back to the look of betrayal on Dimitri's face

when he first beheld my magic reopens an already tender wound in my chest. Silver and Güthric could've done the same. They could've taken one look at my shapeshifting aunt, my sister and her raven, and me and my lightning and left. But rather than running from the unknown, they were willing to stay.

It makes me want to give Igemonar and all the mages a chance, at least until they prove otherwise to be distrustful.

But a worm of a thought writhes in my mind, slimy and restless.

"How do you know of the druids?" I ask, my eyes trained on Igemonar and the ever-growing crack in his mask of cordiality. "No one else on Arcathain knows of them. Or at least, not the commonfolk. None of us knew of them. But you do? Why is that?"

I pause, watching his mask of cordiality shift, ire seeping into the cracks as I hit on something profound, something tender, something I am not meant to have deduced. Arcathainian history flickers through my thoughts, every lecture I endured, every book whose dusty pages I flipped through. The mages helped to construct the wall that kept the Forgotten Forest of Eyve sequestered, but even long after it fell, most of the druids remained behind the border, limiting what few interactions humans had with them. The ones who did venture across the border, like my mother and her family, hid their druid nature for fear of being accused as a mage.

I don't quite know how all of this is connected back to whatever secret Igemonar and the other mages wanted kept from us, but now that the thought is there, I can't help but speak it. My forehead creases. "What did your people do?"

"What we had to." His response is cold and swift, a heartless lie that has been parroted and passed down over the generations. But it's his second statement that turns my skin to frost-bitten ice. "And we'll continue doing as such."

Dread builds inside me. Every instinct I've ever had screams at me to run. To hide. To flee this place and never return. Coming here was a mistake. The mages were content to let us live out the rest of our days with no interference from them, but now we've gone and prodded the sleeping bear.

My nails dig into my palms as I clear those panicked thoughts away. We had no choice but to come. With Qaeus lose, there will be no living in Arcathain for much longer, not for the humans anyway. Our only option, our only chance for survival was to come here, and I will not allow this proud mage to trick me into thinking otherwise.

There has to be others, kind mages who are sympathetic to the choice their rulers imposed on our people. The hateful Igemonar can't be the only mage we'll encounter.

"Well," he says after a fashion. "I best leave you to your quest. You have a long way to travel before reaching the Pits of Bagamore." The mage turns to walk away, his green, wool tunic hanging stiff in his wake.

But out of the corner of my vision, something resolute flashes in Dimitri's eyes. The heavy broadsword is already over his shoulder, ready to strike, before I can even reach for him, before I can urge him not to wage war on the very people who we've come to for help.

A horrified scream bulges in my throat, threatening to claw through me if I don't release it. In the blink of an eye, I can see the war that plays out. All of us dead on the beach, our gelatinous guts torn from gaping wounds, our blood dousing the soil, the verdant shrubbery, and each other. Arcathain abandoned once and for all behind an even more formidable storm spell that not even the best druids could break through.

No one would come to our aid.

No one would cure Ryven.

No one would save Arcathain.

But just as Dimitri swings his shadowsteel overhead, the tip of the blade shining in the bright sun with a promised kiss waiting to pierce through the mage's flesh, Igemonar halts. The very air around us seems to change at the flick of his wrists, the crisp vivacity of it instead roiling with something dark and desolate. Smoke blooms from his feet in billowing clouds. I can taste the ash on my tongue before it even reaches me, and I pinch my nose to ward off the acrid stench of sulfur.

From where I stand, I can just barely make out over the mage's shoulder that his lips are twitching, moving in a nearly silent incantation as he breathes power into whatever spell he's about to unleash upon us.

Dimitri freezes, sword dangling almost limply over his shoulder as he, too, senses the danger. He steps back in leaping strides, running from the smoke that creeps along the ground. It shows no signs of waning. The opaque density would have to stretch across the entire beach before it even started to spread too thinly. With our backs to the ocean, there's nowhere for us to run.

Almost involuntarily, we all shuffle backward. The ocean laps at my heels, seeping in through the soles of my boots to surround my feet with frigid pools of clarity. The water reminds me of the Leviathan, of our journey, of the storm, but most importantly, of the druid powers I'm still growing accustomed to.

And it dawns on me. Smoke's greatest enemy is wind.

I call to the sky. Through my senses, I reach up into the heavens and let the heady pull of it course through me like I did while we were on the Leviathan. But the winds are weary, as am I from my exertion of power during the storm. It's like reaching into a river and grasping at a slick fish, the tendrils of air keep slipping through my fingertips before I can tug on any of them.

All I manage to summon is a gentle caress of wind, one not even strong enough to rustle the mage's dark hair.

I'm about to shout at everyone to dive into the ocean for fear that Igemonar is seconds away from igniting the smoke, or that one whiff of it will be poisonous to our lungs, when I notice it rising up around him as well. He's barely visible through the hazy anymore, no more than a shadow is visible on the ground at night. But his voice rises, the incantation reaching a harrowing crescendo as he mutters the last few words of his spell.

The smoke flashes. I shield my eyes, once again fearing the worst. But when I open them again to the sounds of my fellow travelers coughing—still breathing—the space where Igemonar was standing is empty, only his footprints remain in the moist soil and the smoke he left in his wake, to prove that he had even been here to begin with.

My hand drifts to my shoulder to stroke the raven's rough beak. She is my only solace as we've made our silent trek through these unknown and almost certainly dangerous woods. Igemonar's warnings have left us shaken. If there were some among us who already feared coming here and doubted whether Alphonse and I were leading them to their salvations, the fire of those fears has been stoked, the flames whipping high enough to burn the very tops of the trees around us. I search the shadows for enemy mages. I keep my eyes on the Crusaders with me in search of any fists that might be sent my way—or worse.

No one has re-stashed their weapons into their holsters for hours, not since our encounter with Igemonar on the beach, and having so many armed individuals surrounding me, does nothing but make my skin buzz with adrenaline.

Wings flutter overhead and my foolishly optimistic heart whirls. I search the skies for the demon-man I've been more desperate than usual to spy. He still hasn't made an appearance since the storm, and although as we left the beach behind, I never saw the spell return to guard the surrounding sea, I still can't shake the twisting sensation of fear that's taken root in the bottom of my belly.

But it's only an owl spreading his wings and taking flight for a night of hunting.

"We should setup camp for the night," Dimitri says over his shoulder from the front of the group. "There's no telling what sort of danger prowls in these woods after dark."

Because I'm so used to associating dark wooded areas with demons, they are the first to spring to my mind, and it takes me a moment to remember that we are no longer in Arcathain. Far worse *could* be lurking in the darkness. We have no way of knowing in what ways the mages have tampered with what used to be our world. They could've created hybrid beasts far more ravenous than the demons of the Shadowthorn to help guard their lands and ward off unwanted visitors. There could be more magical traps and enchantments meant to ensnare or maim or worse.

But not even mystical creatures and unforeseen curses scare me as much as the thought of the mages watching us, hunting us. The spell Igemonar used might not have been one that killed us, but I still fear what power they have access to, and what limits they possess. If any. The others could make no distinction between druids and mages, but they couldn't sense the air like I had during the storm. Whatever unnatural magic they used, it was unlike the magic of the druids entirely. It was darkness and death. Chaos and war.

Güthric, Eparah, and another Crusader elect to take the first shift of patrolling the surrounding area for any signs of danger. If I wasn't so spent from earlier, I'd have volunteered myself, but right now I need to rest and replenish my magic so that I can actually stand a chance of protecting us if the mages ever return.

Dimitri sets out to work on creating a fire, keeping the flames low so as not to draw any more attention than it already will. Considering we're already in the thick of the woods though, anyone who'd be close enough to see the smoke wouldn't be able to track it through the towering tree canopies anyway. Still, we're not taking any unnecessary risks. Despite keeping the flames low, and the smoke at a minimum, he still inhales enough of it to send him into a coughing fit, one he's quick to muffle in the crook of his elbow so as not to make too much noise.

The rest of us gather fallen branches, thick and lush with needles, and begin stacking them over a few different makeshift shelters. One shelter uses a low-hanging branch that juts at a particularly odd, perpendicular angle from the tree trunk. Another is created from a set of closely standing, thin birch trees. A third and fourth are made for more personal, singular use, and therefore require far less branches, ferns, and other foliage to stand tall or for covering the roof.

By the time we're done, night has long since fallen. The branches Dimitri used to create the first fire have burned away, leaving behind only the glowing orange coals that periodically he stacks another branch on top of.

As much as the smoke worries me, I'm grateful for the way it masks the stench of cooking fish, as Silver prepares us a modest dinner. I'm so hungry and drained though that I don't even let myself think about it when I bite into the charred, salted flesh.

It's not until our bellies are full, and the Crusaders and fugitives alike are huddled comfortably inside their shelters or gathered closer around the fire, that soft-spoken conversation settles over the camp.

"I spotted a patch of sweet gale just before we setup camp," Silver says, clearing her throat before taking a seat on a rock, a skewered slab of fish in hand. "Before we leave tomorrow, we should harvest some. There's no telling how far inland we'll have to travel until we reach Bagamore, even with the map your sister provided."

The rolled parchment crinkles as I rotate it between my fingers. I was surprised to find it tied to the raven's foot. I'm not sure how Kalli came across it—likely through Imryll who might've taken the liberty to inquire in the Eyve—but even more surprising is the amount of effort she went to, in order to ensure we received it. I can tell from the precise inking and the thin curve of her lettering that this small map was drawn by her hand. When she had time to draw such a thing is beyond me, and only mildly irritating to consider, but the map isn't the only thing in my grasp.

A letter, one I have yet to read for fear of what news she may have. The others know of it; they saw me untie it from the raven's ankle on the beach, so there really is no excuse for wanting to wait for some privacy before reading it, but I've held onto it all day, waiting for tonight, and the privacy the evening might provide.

"There was some wood sorrel close by, too," Alphonse says as I stand from my place to excuse myself, but his words snap my full attention to him. He notices my peculiar stare. "What? You think simply because I lived a life of privilege and wealth that I ignored the lessons I received at the Castle of Nigh before my rise in the ranks? You forget, I was a Crusader before I became a General."

I snort, almost choking on the last bite of fish I'm still working on. "You were a Crusader for all of ten minutes before your father deemed you of a high enough status that you would never have to step foot in the Shadowthorn."

He flinches, sitting taller on the log where he's perched. "I'll have you know, I accompanied many men into the Shadowthorn. And though we rarely were inclined to stay longer than was necessary, and always brought enough rations to last us, I was quite attentive during the lectures about food and

survival. Milkwort, quickweed, burdock, chicory—I can identify them all. *And,* I even know how to prepare a few rather
decadent salads, if I do say so myself."

Fox takes over his teasing, telling him that perhaps he
should be on foraging and meal prepping tomorrow, and I step
away from the group with soft laughter in my full belly. The
fire they sit around is so small that I hadn't noticed its heat
reaching me where I sat, but as I put a short distance between
us, even just a few paces, where the firelight can still brighten
the parchment I'm about to read, the temperature drops to a
chilling degree.

The note is tightly bound, my fingers fumbling with the coil
of the small letter before my eyes even have a chance to strain
at the impossibly small penmanship.

Dearest sister,

*Arcathain fares worse than we imagined. Without the boundary of
the Shadowthorn, demons roam freely across the lands. Gravenburg
is all but in flames. The Magistrate and his envoy were attacked at
the base of the Unresting Mountains on their journey back to the
Capital. He lives and was easily convinced to set aside his notions of
war to sail for Illashore in search of a means to slay the Primordial.
But he has suffered great losses. There will only be sixty ships with us.
I beseech the gods that will be enough.*

See you shortly.

Yours,

Kalli

MY HEART TWISTS and coils for the loss of my hometown; for the people of Arcathain; for my sister whom I've never seen drop the title in her name before. An ache even builds in my chest for the Magistrate who faces an impossible feat: tasked with the protection of an entire nation, without having the means to do so. Or at least, he was until Kalli intercepted him, and I'm hopeful that means he will do what it takes to ensure the safety of our people. I'm hopeful he'll listen to reason and join us in seeking the aid of the mages, rather than launching an attack. Considering my sister's letter didn't warn us of any possible foul play, I'm guessing he's been agreeable to the idea, which would be surprising, if Kalli's recounting of the crumbling nation hadn't been so stark. Finding the means to defeat Qaeus is all that matters now.

As I return to the fire, I twist the scroll back into its cylindrical shape before tossing it into the flames. The parchment catches almost instantly, a flicker's all it takes before the note has disintegrated.

"What did she say?" Dimitri asks, his voice low and husky. The smoke from the fire still seems to cling to his lungs. Despite speaking quietly, in the dead silence of the evening, during a lull in the conversation, his words are far louder than he means for them to be.

Every pair of ears opens to us.

I stare into the fire, watching the embers burn every shade of red and orange and gold, but rather than shrugging him off completely, I give them the answers they deserve. "Kalli was able to intercept the Magistrate before he made it back to the Capital. She's convinced him to join us."

Firelight dances along Alphonse's face when his eyebrows shoot upward. "Will he be *joining* us, or has he simply hastened his plans for attack?"

Shaking my head, I return to the rock I'd been sitting on before I'd left to read Kalli's note. The people around me deserve to know what's happening to their homeland, but still I hesitate to tell them. There is already so much to fear, and they would be helpless to intervene in any way.

I swallow the lump that's bulging in my throat before it can deprive me of air. "My sister said that he's agreed to set aside his prospects for war. At least for now."

Alphonse's eyes narrow on me, but the hazel color is darkened by the shadows cast down by the moon, so that all I can see is the black of his irises. "My father is a persistent, stubborn man."

"Oh, now I see the resemblance," Fox quips.

But Alphonse ignores her, voice heady and calculating. "He wouldn't just abandon years of planning and preparation for war, only to veer course at the last minute. When he last visited the Castle of Nigh, he confided in me that he'd be launching an attack on the mages before the next full moon. Either he was lying to your sister and he still plans to attack, or...or..."

When Alphonse gets caught up in his worrying thoughts, I chime in for him. "*Or,* perhaps Kalli is right and he comes for one reason only: to defeat Qaeus." Alphonse is shaking his head, so I continue. "So much has changed since the night you spoke to your father. He thought you dead. That alone is enough to change a person, but now the Shadowthorn has vanished and Qaeus is free to roam and terrorize the—"

The murmurings that ripple throughout the group bring a silent curse to my lips. They start quiet, but once the people recognize their own fear and despair in each other, their concerns grow louder. They ask about Kalli's letter, about their homes, their families, and they finally start to wonder how Kalli could've convinced the Magistrate to change his mind.

Sighing heavily, my head hangs over my chest and I lean forward, elbows propped on my knees.

"We already knew this!" Dimitri's bark, resonate and strong, silences them in an instant. Even I lift my gaze to his, feeling small as he stands in the center of the circle, looking out over all of us. He's quieter when he speaks again. "Halira has told us nothing new. The Shadowthorn fell long before we left Arcathain. The Primordial's rise from slumber is what brought us here. We knew what Qaeus would do. We saw it with our own eyes that the worst was yet to come. The demons that hunted along the borders of the Shadowthorn? All of you knew as well as I, the moment you saw the Primordial's might, that it would be nothing like the bloodshed such an enormous and wicked creature would inflict."

Something starker than silence settles over us. Those who had inched to the edge of their seats, shift back. Their shoulders, tense with anticipation for a fight, relax along their backs as they listen. I hadn't even realized what Dimitri was saying was true until he spoke it, but I suppose it is why we've all come. None of us knew the threat Qaeus posed until we saw her rise. We thought we did, but we had been wrong.

But her initial moments after her slumber return to me, and I'm reminded again of how gentle she was at first. I sensed her trepidation and angst. She regretted the damage she had caused, and though I'd wanted to ask her if she could tell me how she came to be so…wretched and evil, she had little time other than to warn me.

Idly, I wonder if the Wardens of Qaeus ever knew the gentle creature she had been, if perhaps that's why Adrien and my mother—

"Where's Adrien?" I ask, doing a double-take around the circle and once again finding my uncle missing. "And Sai. Has anyone seen them?"

A sly, crooked grin inches up Fox's face. "They're fine. Don't worry. They excused themselves while you were off reading your note."

My jaw falls open at the forwardness of it. Not because I think they shouldn't, but rather because of how reckless it is.

We are in unknown territory, possibly surrounded by enemies, with no way of knowing what carnivorous creatures are in the woods around us, and they're off...off having a romantic getaway.

I'm not even sure how anyone could be thinking about such a thing right now. Or at least, that's what I tell myself as my stomach wrenches itself when my thoughts drift back to Ryven's notable absence.

He should've been here by now. When we were at sea, he always arrived right when the sun was setting, and we are hours past that now, not to mention, once we were off the Leviathan, he had no reason not to return sooner. The only reason he'd kept his distance while we were traveling was because his very presence made the Leviathan skittish and uncomfortable.

So, if we are finally on land, then where is he? Did he make it through the storm? Was he lost somewhere, searching for us, but having difficulty finding us through the thick canopy of trees? Or is he lost in another, more permanent way, his mind finally caving to the demon side of him, and stealing him from me forever?

My chest becomes a gaping wound, the cool night air painful against the tender, exposed flesh. I don't know why I miss him so much tonight, why I thought that our first evening on land would go any differently than any of the nights we shared in the Shadowthorn or atop the Leviathan. I'd wanted to be near him, but he had been distant from the moment he changed. I could understand it, but it didn't make it any easier to accept.

Through the trees overhead, thousands of dazzling stars twinkle in the black sky, reminding me of the night we stayed at the Ushines Rivers.

Before the painful set of jaws that is clamping down on my heart can snap me in two, I stand abruptly, interrupting

Dimitri in whatever dutiful ramblings he was in the middle of. Everyone's eyes snap to me but I bear through the flames searing me. My lips press into a thin line and I walk back into the night, toward the place of solitude I found when I read Kalli's letter. I need air. I need to breathe.

As if I willed it, a gentle gust wafts over me, even though I touched no part of my magic to summon it. My lungs ache as they fill, the air crisp and soothing. Once they're finally done burning, I tip my head back. Seeing the bright, big moon nestled in the dark vastness of the sky reminds me of the angler fish pet the sirens kept. If we are successful here, if we can defeat Qaeus, when this is all said and done, I'll have to face that creature again. Face them all.

A twig snaps behind me. A chill skitters over my skin like the thin spindly legs of a thousand spiders. I spin around, my white hair whipping about.

Dimitri holds his hands up. "I wasn't trying to startle you or interrupt but…are you all right?"

I fold my arms over myself and turn my back to him again. "I'm fine."

Despite my very obvious nonverbal communication that I'd rather be left alone, I hear his feet pad in the dirt. He appears beside me, his head leaning forward to try and get a better look at me. "So, are we just never going to talk again?"

"Talk about what?"

"About that kiss? About us?"

Ice spills over me, coating every inch of my skin and dousing my senses with a frigid sort of concern. My arms dig in tighter. "I—"

The sigh that eases out of him is the same one he would exhale on hunting trips when he'd lose the stag he'd been tracking. He'd spend the next hour or more, our entire way back home, grumbling about how long the deer's meat would've lasted, how many pelts he could've bartered with, and he'd be unable to smile for the better part of a week.

So, when his lips twitch with a rueful grin, confusion ripples through me.

"Why are you smiling?" I ask slowly, and now I'm the one inching forward, ducking even lower, trying to see his shadowed face.

The grin tugs upward. His words ride out on a disheartened sigh. "Because I knew you'd react one of two ways to this conversation. Either your cheeks would turn rosy and you'd bite your lips to prevent a smile of your own from giving you away, or you'd do…*that*." He tilts his chin at me, the golden hair atop his head seeming almost as dark as tree bark in the night. "Your eyes would bulge. You'd stiffen as if I'd just held a knife to your throat."

"Dimitri, I—"

He shakes his head. "It's all right. I knew that was going to be your reaction. I'd hoped you were avoiding me out of embarrassment or just unsure of how to get back to the place we were —" We would never reach that place again "—but that was wishful, foolish thinking. Somewhere deep down, I've known from the moment I saw you that things were different. That we would never be the same again. And I…" He sucks in a ragged breath, bringing his eyes to meet mine. The moonlight turns them almost silver. "I thought if I tried hard enough and showed you that I still lov—cared…that maybe you'd come back, that you'd remember what we had and what we'd been like together."

My chest aches and burns, tearing into pieces all over again. It's a pain I don't quite understand. How can it be so painful to tell someone that it's over? I'm not the one who's heart should be breaking.

"My memory isn't the problem," I say softly.

"I know. I should've known—I should've realized before I

kissed you. You made it so obvious that you were at best conflicted about us. But even that's being generous to myself." His hand cups my cheek, warm compared to the frigid night filtering over us. The gesture isn't one of attempted romance or sly maneuvering, but that of sorrow. "I kissed you the other night, without your permission. It was wrong of me, and for that I am sorry."

I press into his hand absentmindedly. My oldest friend, dutiful and good down to every fiber of his being.

But it's not until his next words that I become truly touched by him. "And I'm sorry that *Ryven* saw, and that he mistook the action as mutual."

It just might be the first time I've ever heard him use Ryven's name, the syllables sticking to his tongue like vomit. But there is no disdain in his tone; he manages to set all of that aside for this truly heartfelt apology.

I reach up, placing my hand over his, my thumb idly drawing circles over the back of his hand. "I am sorry too, Dimitri."

His brow creases. "For what?"

For this part, I have to look away. Our hands fall from my face as I take a few steps, biting my lip as I consider my next words as carefully as he has chosen his. A rustle in the trees above startles me from my deep thoughts though. I glance up, wondering if it had just been a raccoon, or perhaps the owl returning with its feast, or dare I hope that it's Ryven—hope, and dread, considering the last thing I want is for him to find Dimitri and I alone together again, lest he get the wrong impression.

Dimitri's presence behind me is palpable, his attentiveness practically bringing him to the tips of his toes at the edge of a canyon.

"For all of it," I finally say, settling my gaze back down to the forest floor. "For everything."

When I twist back around, the expression on his face has shifted, a twisted cloth of hurt bunching and darkening the shadows of his face. "All of it?"

His words are an anvil to my glass heart. "No," I breathe. "I mean, yes. But also, no. I mostly mean for everything that came…after."

He nods, turning introspective for a few heavy moments. "Do you think we could've been happy? If we had survived the Shadowthorn and retired to some small village somewhere."

It's fantastical thinking, considering the only way we could've ever retired was if Qaeus was defeated, and she never would've been if everything hadn't gone exactly as it had, if I hadn't awakened her from her slumber, and if we hadn't set forth to Illashore.

But I don't say any of that. I allow myself to imagine the fabricated alternate future, the one I'd daydreamed about a few times myself while we were still at Nigh, and say, "Yes."

"I do too." He chuckles, the sound fading into a cough. "Gods, I loathe to admit it, but I can even see me being content back in a butchery. I can see you tending to a new hive of bees and dipping candles, just as your mother trained you."

I couldn't. Not even on the days I missed my family the most. That life, that mundane existence where I'd felt nothing beyond boredom, was never meant for me.

Sadness bleeds into my smile, but I nod again. Now was not the time to continue shattering him, but to allow him whatever thoughts would bring him peace.

"If I hadn't left you, I think things would've been a lot different…" he says after another long bout of silence. "But, some mistakes can't be corrected. They can only be learned from." I open my mouth to remind him that he did nothing wrong, or at least that all is forgiven, but he speaks before I can. "I don't say that for your pity. I just mean that…I will regret losing you for the rest of my life, but I will never make that mistake again."

I get the sense that he's speaking more global now, and it's a relief to have the focus of our conversation shift from me to something else—anything else. I'm about to veer the conversation to the mages, and our plans for tomorrow, when a bout of coughing seizes him. He pounds on his chest, the crackling coming from much deeper than it had earlier in the night.

Through the trees, back toward camp, Fox clears her throat as well, giving her lungs a heavy wringing as she tries clearing whatever smoke as settled inside them.

I realize with frightened clarity that the smoke from the bonfire isn't the only smoke we've inhaled today. When Igemonar cast his spell and disappeared, the smog had been so dense that it felt like we were breathing in singed cotton.

"What?" Dimitri wriggles an eyebrow at me, his hand still fisted in front of his mouth. "What's on your mind now?"

"Nothing," I say quickly. I'm just being paranoid. The mage's spell allowed him to flee without being seen. That is all. And there is no need to make anyone else worry otherwise. "We have a long day ahead of us tomorrow. I'm just going through everything that needs to be done in my head, and all of the obstacles we may come across."

"Well, whatever the obstacles, just know that I won't leave your side this time." My stomach dips and either it makes the sloshing noise that I feel, or he's become a lot more perceptive since we parted at Nigh. "Not because I'm holding out hope for a future together, but because…that is what friends do. And we are still friends, Halira. Aren't we?"

My teeth drag across my bottom lip. "Always."

His smile doesn't reach his sad eyes. "Then, as your friend, I'll remind you that no matter the obstacle, we will overcome. We will save Arcathain. And, if Ryven ever returns, we will save him as well."

Heedless to the twisting beneath my chest and that inside his, I fling myself into Dimitri's arms. He's made this too easy on me. All this time, I feared having this conversation with him because I worried what the outcome would be. I feared he'd tell me the opposite, that our friendship meant nothing if it didn't also include our romantic partnership. But I don't know why I ever feared that at all. We've been friends for as long as I can remember. I was there for him when his family died, one by one, and he had been there for me. He might've left me once in the Shadowthorn when he thought I was minutes from death, but I can hardly blame him given how deeply he cares for me. I wouldn't have wanted to watch me perish either. Besides, he had no time to consider an alternative. The Crusaders were leaving and, with my death on the horizon, they were all he had.

He coughs to the side of our heads and I try not to worry too much about it. Because he's right. We have each other now. Again. The blip friendship was simply that: a momentary error of the otherwise formidable and long-lasting friendship we have. The two of us, we will not be broken by it. With any luck, we'll be fortified.

FROM ABOVE

UNKNOWN FOREST, ILLASHORE

Shrouded in leaves of darkness and shadow, I watch Halira from the branches above as she turns away from Dimitri. The moment she does, I'm tempted to dive down there and remind her of the monster I've become. If she is forbidding herself this one, human comfort on a whim that I may return to her in human flesh, then I cannot allow it. I do not deserve it. She doesn't.

"Do you think we could've been happy? If we had survived the Shadowthorn and retired to some small village somewhere."

"Yes."

Despite my conviction that she still can be, that she and this lackluster man can travel somewhere far away and grow old together, teeth clench against my blackened heart when I hear her admit those feelings. When I'm not thirsting for flesh and blood, I've spent the last few weeks wondering much the same, and attempting not to drown in self-pity when the answer I always came to only disappointed me.

I should leave them. I should. It's the argument I have with myself daily—minutely. The sooner I'm gone from her life, the sooner she can move on. I've managed to stay out of sight since our arrival on land, but I've seen her searching the sky for me. How long would it take before I became nothing more than a distant memory?

"Gods, I loathe to admit it, but I can even see me being content back in a butchery. I can see you tending to a new hive of bees and dipping candles, just as your mother trained you."

The mashed orifice that my nose has become crumples in the best show I can make of a smirk. This is the man who's known her all her life? This is the man whom she chose to lie with all those months ago, even though he clearly understands her so little? It takes every ounce of control I have, to clamp my sharp teeth around the scoff that tries to creep forward. I shouldn't care. I shouldn't judge her or him, but despite knowing that logically, my muscles still tense with an incessant need to dominate and destroy the pathetic man next to her. He doesn't deserve her.

Neither do I, I remind myself, and it's enough to bring me back to my senses.

At least until I see her nod. I'm so taken aback that I nearly lose my footing on the thick branches I'm precariously balanced between.

It's a lie. Agreeing to returning back to candle making, and doing so with a smile plastered between her cheeks, is a lie. It's not what she wants. It never has been. That life held no meaning for her, and anyone who truly knows her, truly understands her, would know that.

But more importantly, if she's lying to him now, in what other ways has she been less than straight forward with him?

They keep talking while my foolish and self-deprecating thoughts devour me. But finally I come back to the present.

"We are still friends, Halira. Aren't we?"

"Always."

Friends. Friends. But why? Why can't she just accept him

and move on? Why can't she allow herself this after everything she's already sacrificed?

Dimitri diverts his cough to the side, and when he does, her eyes flit up to mine. I'm frozen still as our gazes snag, unsure if she can see me, sense me, or if she's somehow not looking at me at all, but perhaps guided by intuition. By whatever force has brought us together and kept us that way. These wretched demon eyes offer no enhancements, and from this distance it should be no more like looking down upon a fox. But my lungs quiver beneath the silver pools of her eyes, the moonlight casting them in an eerily bright glow. The color silver will forever be changed for me, forever will it remind me of her silken hair, or her piercing eyes, of the fierce way in which she wields a blade.

The moment passes too quickly, Halira pulling her attention back to Dimitri and damn near dragging me down from the tree as she does it. They separate from the embrace and head back to the camp, but I am left alone, like one of the guardian gargoyles that overlooks the castle in Nigh where the Wardens would have me steal necro-ink. For now, it is a title I can carry with pride, watching over her and her friends as they rest peacefully for the evening.

But their slumber is anything but peaceful. Very few among them sleep through the night, tossing and turning as their lungs wage war against something thick and hoarse inside them. All but Halira and Alphonse. The only druids among them.

My wings spread wide, and I drift nearer. Perched atop the crooked branch of a tree that leans over one of their shelters, my concern grows as I scent the darkness here. Something isn't right. These people survived weeks out at sea without so much as a sniffle or a chill, but now every single human is ill.

Magic is at work here. I can sense it like I sense the moonlight trickling over my peaked ears like a stream of cool, silver water. The mages will come for them. Not the humans, but for the druids. For Halira. And despite her already powerful displays of magic, outnumbered she will be rendered utterly useless.

My grotesque lips peel back, and I curse to myself. They need more power. They need a druid to help defend them, one who knows how to manipulate the elements with deadly precision, one who can transform into the most vicious of creatures.

I can linger above like a silent protector, I can even scour the land for any signs of the mages approaching, and maybe even take a few of them out before they eviscerate me with their dark magic. Or worse. My people don't remember much of the mages' powers, but tales of magic capable of obliterating autonomy still linger in our histories. For all I know, they could shove my awareness back into the shadows and allow the demon to rise. They could turn me against Halira and unleash me upon their camp while they sleep. Even if they didn't, the moment they subdue her, I could become feral again.

As long as I am at Halira's mercy, I am at the mages' as well. As long as I am a shadowcreature, I put everyone at risk.

But I've glimpsed the black pits the Crusaders travel toward. From my safe distance away, high in the sky with the clouds in my face, as we've traversed Illashore, I've seen the Pits of Bagamore just ahead, the place where the answers to my cursed heart supposedly lie.

It'll take the Crusaders less than full day to arrive there. But me? I could be there by sunrise if I left now. I could intercept them on their way tomorrow, hopefully before the mages finish closing in. I can't smell them in the air, so they aren't close yet. And once Halira and the others start traveling again, they'll continue to keep a steady distance between them and the mages.

The time to go is now.

I hesitate no longer and bound from the tree, heedless to whatever thrashing is audible from the camp below, hopeful none can be discerned over the incessant coughing. My wings have never felt stronger, the journey over sea hardening them to the arduous nature of flight.

But it's not the flight itself that become grueling. As the hours stretch, as I cut through the night sky and put more distance between Halira and myself, the more ravenous I become. The demon consciousness is awakening, clawing its way to the surface while the veil between us thins and thins quicker by the minute.

The same thing occurred the night I witnessed Halira and Dimitri kiss on the deck. It hadn't been as strong of a sensation, as severe as this time, but it had been a prelude to what would occur should the two of us be parted for any extended period of time or too far a distance.

There is no other option though. To turn back now would delay whatever salvation I will find at the Pits of Bagamore. It would delay whatever aid I can provide in the battle to come. And that knowledge alone is enough to fortify me. I jam my elbow into the demon's throat and slam him back against the wall of my mind.

Every time we fly over a village or a town, he struggles against me. A few times, I even lose my hold, plummeting the both of us from the sky so that I might hunt and feed on the platter of mage flesh presented to us. The hunger is gnawing and primal. It cannot be fought. It drives me down toward the sleeping towns, my stomach clawing to feed, the heady allure of blood all but driving me mad.

Only the sight of the silver moon snaps me back. It reminds me of eyes like pools of liquid silver, and I'm reminded once again of who I am, and where I need to be going.

The rest of the night is a constant battle between carnal

desire and diligent restraint, but despite Halira's hold on me waning, it never breaks. There's comfort to be found in that, knowing that whatever magic binds us together is too strong for even distance to shatter, even darkness.

By sunrise, the mauve stone crater sinks into view, a colony of churning black cesspits bubbling in the center. The tarry Pits of Bagamore. With the bond between Halira and I stretched to such a thin piece of taught twine, my demon senses are primed and sensitive things. They are nerve endings, frayed along the edges. Every slightest movement of the wind draws my predatorial gaze. Every time I hear claws skittering along the red rocks below, my mouth waters in anticipation of the potentially approaching snack.

But more than anything, the black pool of power summons me. It pulls at something deep beneath my chest. If I hadn't been heading here already, I most assuredly would've veered course, driven by the innate tug that wrenches me forward, beckoning me to the abyss below.

A tantalizing shudder ripples through me when I land. The magic pulsing from the Pits is palpable, intoxicating on every level of my consciousness. It commands my legs to move forward, my thoughts to retreat from my mind until nothing is left but blind obedience. All that matters is diving into the black lagoon and bathing in the corruption I'll find there.

Before I can be robbed of myself completely though, somehow, I manage to cling on to the warmth that Halira has encased my soul in. It keeps me conscious long enough for me to notice the strange system of large, golden tubes and shafts that lead in and out of the Pits. They stretch so far, rising and falling with the natural terrain of the land, that I can't tell where they will end.

But I don't need to. None of that matters to me. Not now.

All I need to remember is who I am as I stare at the tarry pools before me.

There's no denying what I'm being told to do. The Pits of Bagamore want me to give myself to them. But with Halira's tender hold on my heart, it's enough of a filter for me to wade through the alluring call of the Pits to hear the quiet warning being sung inside it.

Power. Magic. Death.

I shouldn't be surprised. Halira said that the Pits of Bagamore were the birthplace of the Primordials, and so it makes sense that they'd behold the same dark magic that Qaeus possesses, that binds her heart in malice and destruction.

Thinking of the Primordial's heart sparks a thought. Halira touched Qaeus' heart and just as Adrien had deduced, the organ had siphoned the Blight from her. Emboldened with hope, I step forward, but my taloned foot halts midair, inches above the rippling blackness. Halira had the breath of life to protect her from being devoured completely. The Elders said it granted life to the wearer in a time when they would've otherwise lost there's, and that touching Qaeus' heart directly—touching the raw black source of magic directly—would kill anyone.

I have no such protection in my possession. And it is likely that touching a Primordial's heart will be nothing like submerging oneself into the tarry origin of its birth. One step inside, and I could be gone forever, in every sense of the word. Not just a mindless demon ravaging the lands. But gone. My bones disintegrating at the bottom of these thick depths until nothing is left of me.

The warm hand around my heart chills, the magic tethering me to Halira fraying and threatening to leave my soul bared for icy darkness to infiltrate it. Rage and uncertainty burst from my clenched teeth in a roar that makes the black lagoon quiver. My options are shit. Return to Halira and forever be nothing that she needs. Stay here and become everything she fears and loathes. Or dive into uncertainty and pray for a miracle.

Only one of those choices ends with any possibility that I might find my way back to my druid body. Halira brought us to Illashore because she believes the answers to defeating Qaeus lie here, as well as the answers to my affliction.

It was always going to come to this.

My clawed foot sinks into the black.

The tarry liquid is surprisingly warm, reminding me of the blood I've thirsted for since becoming a demon. Thick and viscous, its rich scent makes me wonder if I'm not wrong. Temptation burns through me, too demanding to ignore. I spread my lips and lap at the black substance I'm wading through.

Euphoria blinds me, seeping deep into my stomach as pleasure consumes me in waves. I drink and drink until my stomach bulges, a heady bliss making me dive deeper into the shallows. I want more. I *need* more.

It's not until I've drank my fill and then some, that something shatters inside me. My stomach, heavy with a rich pool of dark honey, twists. My gut winds with a sudden burn of sensation, taking everything I am with it. The black venomous fluid gurgles and festers and fear spikes through me.

I chose wrong.

I careen toward the surface but the dark depths reach for me. They claw at my ankles, snakes of black magic coiling up my legs and seeping under my skin by any means necessary. The lagoon bleeds into me. Consuming and devouring, and I scream as I continue to plummet to the bottom.

I can feel the gauntness of my face deepening, my cheeks hollowing as death roils over me. But it's *my* face, I realize. Not that of the shadowcreature I'd become, but me. My fingers search for my mouth and nose, and I gasp when the skin I grasp at is stubbled, not hairy. Is flesh, not fur. Human, not beast.

It's working. Whatever ancient magic the Pits of Bagamore

possess, they have in their power the same ability as the heart of the Primordial. Such a thought should be comforting, but I recall the Elders' warning all too clearly, especially as the demon side of me continues to be leeched.

To touch the heart means death. To bathe in the very lagoon that created such evil, can only mean obliteration.

As I pad along the soft earthen floor, my boots slick with morning dew that they gather from the grass, my ears twitch at the hacking behind me. The coughing has grown worse overnight. No one said anything about it when we first awakened, likely assuming, as I had, that it was from laying so close to the dying flames of the bonfire, or perhaps from the grogginess that comes with sleeping on the cold ground. But as we cleared camp and set out through the woods, as the sun has continued to rise up above, the coughing has worsened. They hunch over themselves when another fit attacks, their lungs thick, their voices hoarse.

Only two of us appear to be breathing fine, which is almost worse than none of us at all.

"It was the both of you," one of the Crusaders accuses, her voice thick and raspy from where she's buckled over. "What kind of magic is this? What did you do to us?"

Alphonse and I exchange a quick glance, but though mine is riddled with worry, his is one of outrage.

"What did *we* do?" he balks, storming to the center of the line to bend down into her face. "Tell me, what possible gain could Halira and I have from poisoning you?"

"So, you admit it?" the Crusader croaks. At his look of confusion she adds, "I never said anything about poisoning."

When she hunches back over her knees, Alphonse throws his hands in the air and twists toward me. "I don't understand. What is happening? You saw nothing of concern during your watch, correct?"

I shake my head.

"Neither did I," he says, even though we both already know that. After Güthric and Eparah's watch, Alphonse and I volunteered to take the second shift, seeing as most of the others were almost even too exhausted to be awoken.

I shuffle closer, cutting the distance between us so that only he will hear me when I whisper. "That's because this didn't happen last night." I can't tell if his scrunched expression is one of confusion or if he didn't hear me over the hacking and gurgling of phlegm. "Igemonar did this. I'm almost sure of it."

The hard line of his brow smooths, rising high up to his scalp. "The smoke."

I nod.

He backs away, a hand rising to his chin and stroking the smooth skin there. "What did he do?"

"I don't know."

"What are *we* going to do?"

"I don't know," I say again, more emphatically this time. "They can't travel like this."

As I gesture to the huddled group, Eparah's bloodshot eyes flick to mine. "That couldn't have been your plan all along. To drag us here just to leave us stranded."

I'm so shocked by her accusation, that my mind goes blank for a moment. "Of course not. We're not leaving anyone."

I glance to the tiny, curled parchment in my fingertips. The landmarks are easy enough to discern, the vastness of the forest crawling over most of the land until it reaches a large citadel in the north. But to the west, a black stain of ink is stark amid the cream, and scrawled above it is the Pits of Bagamore. When we'd left this morning, I'd hoped it would only take a few hours to travel there, but the longer we've trekked, the more I worry that this journey will be longer still. Without being able to see any of the other landmarks Kalli marked—a wide vein of a river that blocks us from the Pits of Bagamore, a set of small mountains with a cave's entrance—it's difficult to tell whether we are hours away or days.

"We have no choice but to stop until they're able to travel again."

Alphonse stares at me like he's not so sure. "Any delay will mean—"

"I know what it means, but we can't just leave them. They are defenseless to magic."

His head dips back, a short, throaty laugh barking out. "I know you think you're Queen of storms these days, but I wouldn't put too much confidence in either of our powers just yet. You've used yours, what, five times? Six? And you spent the better part of yesterday being too drained to even summon a gentle breeze, let alone lightning to strike down any adversaries. I imagine that the few hours of sleep you had before our watch did little to replenish your reserves."

He's not wrong. I've spent the better part of the morning testing my reach, straining for the air and trying to draw in the clouds, but my druid magic continues to rest inside me like a slumbering bear nestled inside a dark cave.

"I've used mine but once, and I'm still unsure of how or what I did. If my magic is tied to water, then I'm afraid this far inland I'll be of little use against the mages."

My fists release, only to throw my hands in the air. "Fine. Neither of us are skilled with magic, but that doesn't make me change my opinion. We are stronger as a unit. For all we know, Igemonar wanted us to abandon the rest of them so he could return to finish the job. Or perhaps he wanted us to head out on our own, and knew we'd become easier targets without our magic."

Alphonse's long dark hair jostles as he shakes his head. "Or, perhaps he's hoping we'll stop moving. He left us on the beach to gather reinforcements, I'm sure of it. If we stop moving now, then he'll return with more mages, and we'll be overrun."

Scowling, I look across the rivulet of bent over heads. Dimitri leans on one hand against a thin tree that is far sturdier than he is. Silver kneels, sitting back on her heels, long gray dress spilling out beneath her as she catches her breath from a brutal bout of coughing that that has made her eyes water. Güthric takes a knee beside her, using the crook of his elbow to muffle his hacking as he rubs Silver's back.

"You want to just leave them here? Like this?" The red of auburn leaves catches the corner of my eye. "What about Fox? If the mages find her while we're away—"

"I've already spoken to Fox, and she agrees." His voice is so low, so stark compared to the bright beams of sunlight that filter through the leaves, making everything around us golden and beautiful, that my breath hitches. What he suggests makes the forest darken. I stare at him like I'm looking into the eyes of an entirely new and terrifying sort of demon. "Of one country, of one blood," he reminds me softly. "Arcathain is what matters now. We came here for answers that we believe to be at the Pits of Bagamore. If we are the only ones able to go on, then we must do so. That is our duty."

A none too pleased laugh hisses from my lips. He sounds like Dimitri, and I wonder if the two of them have had this conversation already as well. My eyes flick to him now, and he stares back at me with unrelenting conviction, as if he can hear us from where he is at the other end of the group, as if he knows exactly what I am wondering. His voice is too hoarse to say anything, to yell his response over the others, so instead, he gives an assured nod.

"They are Crusaders," Alphonse says, bringing my attention back to him. His hazel eyes are impossibly gentle, tucked behind his usually harsh features. "They know what we must do. For Arcathain. For the entire Broken Realm."

I draw my bottom lip between my teeth and suck in a deep breath, but nothing soothes the sharp twisting of my stomach. What Alphonse is suggesting *is* the most logical choice. It's one my sister would've likely surmised hours ago and had no qualms with executing. She'd have left them all at camp, or let them fall behind, one by one, as we traveled.

But we are cut from different cloths, with unique strengths that have guided us this far and will continue to guide us more. I've never made my choices based on logic alone. I follow my heart, my gut, and right now, both are screaming at me that leaving our friends is the last thing we should do. It might be primal self-preservation that's preventing me from accepting any outcome where any of us are put in danger, even if it means putting Arcathainians more at risk, but for whatever reason, I can't bring myself to agree with him.

I open my mouth to say as much, when a thud hits the earth behind us.

Alphonse and I twist, our spines cracking, as we turn to follow the worrying noise.

"Fox!" Alphonse bounds for her, sliding in the dirt as he falls to his knees and takes her head into his lap. He shakes her shoulders. "Fox! Can you hear me?"

But her eyes are glued shut, her long lashes resting over her cheeks almost in a crudely serene fashion.

Another thud. This one far more robust.

Güthric lies slumped in the grass as Silver drowsily pads closer. Her speech is slurred as she calls for him, her movements languid and sticky. But by the time she is hovered over him, she succumbs as well, and crumples over his back like a spineless ragdoll.

One after another, the Crusaders fall where they crouch, kneel, and lean. Leaving Alphonse with Fox, I race over to Dimitri, catching him in my arms just before he can slam face-first into rough tree back. Gently, using the weight of his momentum, I lay him down on his back.

"Dimitri? Dimitri!" There is nothing from him but the slow, wheezing breaths of someone lost in a deep slumber.

My gaze cuts back to Alphonse across the path. But he's no longer watching me, nor is he holding Fox. Alphonse has risen to his feet, his back turned to the group, thin sword drawn as he scans the forest. My own senses flare then. I snatch Dimitri's broadsword and stand over him, pointing the weapon out toward the trees.

"Did you hear something? Is someone out there?" I ask Alphonse, grateful for the steel in my voice. If anyone is watching us, at least they won't know how frightened I am.

"I didn't hear anything, but I'd bet my right hand they're coming. If they aren't here yet, they will be soon."

My muscles ignite against the sword's weight, but I continue scanning left to right and back again, my stance wide over my friend. If they've come for him, they'll have to retrieve him over my dead body.

"That mage wanted to know who our druids were before he attacked us," Alphonse says, his voice sounding louder now. It's not until something bumps into my shoulder and I whirl around, the pointed edge of my sword ready to slice through whatever is at my back, that I realize he's crept his way over to me.

"What do you mean?"

"I don't think he could tell when we arrived. He knew that there were druids because we were able to break through the storm and because of Kalli's raven, but he wasn't sure how many. Whatever spell he used, now he knows that it's just the two of us, hardly enough to be any kind of match against an envoy of mages."

"Imryll said there is a long history of hatred between the mages and druids. It won't be long before Igemonar returns with the Council he spoke of and…Do you think they'll kill us?"

The shrug of his shoulders is almost imperceptible, his focus so fixated on the trees.

"What do we do? We can't just wait here like this, but we can't leave our friends utterly defenseless either."

To my surprise, he sheaths his weapon, a sly grin sneaking up the side of his face. "Well then, it's a good thing I have a plan."

"This is a foolish plan, and it's never going to work," I grumble through my teeth, but even the slight movement causes me to wobble, and I very nearly fall from the tree from where I'm perched. I only barely manage to regain my balance, the tree bark digging into my palm from where I'm gripping it with death-defying strength, as I cast a glare at my cousin on a branch beside me.

His less than apologetic shrug only suggests that I agreed to this madness.

And he's not wrong. I'd opted to reserve my magic for later, for after the mages have arrived to ambush our sleeping companions, and instead chose the more exhausting path of climbing into the trees for a vantage point. Still, it's taken us the better part of the afternoon to climb this high, and we still have no way of knowing whether the mages will be able to detect us once they're nearby. Hopefully, I can trick the winds enough into hiding any scents that might be associated with us —if mages can even scent things in the wind. All of this feels so far out of either of our comfort zones that I'm certain we're in over our heads.

"It's not foolish," Alphonse chides from the ancient pine

next to mine. "You forget, I was the General of the Shadow Crusade for three years before this. I know strategy and how to keep my men alive when we're in enemy territory."

I roll my eyes at the pompous nature of his tone, even though everything he says makes some sort of sense. I *do* forget he was the general, and that at least according to many, he wore the title well enough to protect many of his Crusaders, to inspire the kind of loyalty that had his own unit storming into the Shadowthorn to retrieve his body after his presumed death and then avenge his will to see Qaeus slain. Sometimes, it's still difficult to think of him as anything other than the bully he was when we were children, or the strangely comforting man he's become since we were left for dead in the Shadowthorn.

A silence settles between us, filled only by the chirping and croaking sounds of the forest. We've already been waiting here for a few hours, but my ankles ache from where I'm squatting as if they're about to break at any moment. By willpower alone, I fortify them, cementing myself on the thick branch and peering back down across the way to where our friends are camped. From our vantage point, we've watched them slumber, and not a single one of them has budged since they collapsed. We're too far away to see the rise and fall of their chests, but I can sense their breathes as they mingle with the wind, the air that eases from their lungs and fills the atmosphere with a thrumming sense of life, however faintly.

Two mounds do not breathe.

They are the dummies that Alphonse and I created. Using Fox's shawl and one of the blankets Kalli had packed, we stuffed the items with foliage and padded them into shapes that at least vaguely resembled human bodies. As long as the mages are focused on the many and not the few, it should be convincing enough to buy Alphonse and I time to strike. And if the fake bodies won't do it, Kalli's raven is perched near one of them now, and hopefully that alone will be enough to assure them that even the druids they know to be among our ranks are asleep.

I tilt my head back, trying to see the sky but mostly only finding a thatching of nettles. I remember what the sky had been like earlier though, the clearest of blues.

"This isn't going to work," I say again. "There aren't even any clouds in the sky. There's no storm for me to call upon."

He twists to look at me, one eyebrow springing to his hairline. "You needed no storm to strike me during our duel in the Shadowthorn."

"That was different. I was provoked! You were attacking me. You were…going to kill me, whether you captured me and returned me to your father or just slaughtered me right there in the Shadowthorn."

Some of his bravado is lost, and I see him flinch into himself. His lips part, a remorseful look about him.

But before he can speak, movement catches my eye. He must see my gaze narrow in on the camp, because he whips around without needing any prompting, the two of us settling into the nooks we've found with silent ease.

The man striding into camp blends in with the foliage at first, the green tunic as verdant as the forest around us. But it's his black hair that's drawn my attention. Only at night have I seen that stark shade anywhere in these woods, and even then, I'm not sure any color of darkness has been so bottomless.

Alphonse and I glance at each other when we recognize Igemonar, moving through the camp like he owns the place, like he's not worried in the slightest that we might be up to something. The ruse is working then. Seeing the raven down there with us, and having enough bodies lying around that it appears our numbers are undisturbed, gives him the confidence to march into the camp and do whatever he's come here to do.

A few more people appear behind him, stepping out from

the underbrush, and I can't help but wonder how long they'd been there. Did they slink forward this close without our noticing? Surely, they haven't been there the entire time.

The mages stand over the bodies. They don't inspect any of them, which is a relief, even as Alphonse looks at me with an *I-told-you-so* slant to his eyes. As the mages discuss whatever it is that they're saying, I set into motion Alphonse's plan.

My eyes fall shut. This time, I do not plummet into darkness—the day is too bright to allow such a place to exist behind my gossamer eyelids. But I do drift into the quiet of my mind, to the place where my magic is always staticky and alive. The energy in the air becomes more palpable. Before I could merely detect my friends' breathing into the atmosphere, but now I can *feel* it. Static and heat. The molecules vibrate. They thrum with the liveliness of a thousand buzzing bees, their wings silken soft where they graze me, their stingers sharp.

The clouds shift overhead, slow but gray. A drizzle soon follows, and the rain comes so slowly, that any human would've easily mistaken it for a natural change in the weather, however surprising. But it's not humans I have to convince. Curious to find out, I seize a quick peek, relieved when even the mages don't tilt their heads back.

Alphonse gives me another reassuring jerk of his head and I blink my eyes closed again. The storm clouds are even more charged than the air itself, like a flood gate brimming to the edge and on the verge of bursting. I reach out for it, calling the currents of air around me and channeling them to bend at my will, and my will requires a circle. A forcefield of sorts.

The invisible cyclone begins to spiral downward by my will alone, and I relish the power of it. The release. The innate sense of it and how right it feels to be buzzing, sparking.

"Wait."

Alphonse's whisper is more like a lion's roar, claws scraping against my livened skin.

I manage to open my eyes, but it's disorienting.

"Something isn't right," he mouths but I hear the words nonetheless, carried on the winds I now have tied around my fingers. "They're walking away."

"What?" My senses snap back inside me, the gray clouds staying where I left them as I lean over the branch again.

Gone. The mages are—

Everything goes black. Like the world is a windowless, candlelit room and the flame has just been doused. Being plunged into sudden darkness throws off every one of my senses. My eyes burn in my skull with the effort to see through the nothing. My ears ring, a low-pitched whirling that simultaneously makes me feel like someone is holding their hands just over my ears.

But it's my balance, my sense of direction, that is fractured the most. The moment the light fades, it's like the branch beneath me is no long the thick support beam I chose because of its sturdiness, but rather a precarious board so thin that even stagnant air makes it wobble.

Frantic, I claw for it, needing to hold on to something if I'm ever going to get my bearings again. But nothing's there. The space between my legs is empty. My arms flail, desperately searching for the leaves hanging above me, the solid trunk at my back, but my fingertips graze nothing.

Just as quickly as the darkness blinks around me, light bursts. My eyes scream at the sudden brightness and I crumple to the ground—*to the ground*, I realize with more sickening disorientation. The soft grass is warm beneath my hand, and through the crook of my arm I'm surprised to find that I'm not falling. I've already landed. There's another pair of boots beside mine, ones I think I recognize as belonging to Alphonse, or at least another Crusader.

From behind me, Igemonar's familiar voice slides up my

spine. "Oh, come now. You didn't really think that would work, did you?"

I spring to my feet, Alphonse doing the same, but our battle with sunlight and gravity is still being fought. I sway more than a buoy bobbing in the water, and my body slams into the firm grasp of someone I don't think I recognize. Their fingertips reach up to touch my temples before I can even squirm.

Then, a new darkness settles over us, one where even awareness can't reach me.

THE DEMON INSIDE

PITS OF BAGAMORE, ILLASHORE

Gasping, I breach the black surface and drag my aching, tar-sodden body up onto the rocky mauve terrain that surrounds the Pit. All the while, my eyes remain focused on the blackness that drips from the arms that pull me out of the chilling depths, the arms that I still can barely recognize as my own beneath the sludge caked atop them.

A sudden bite of fear wrenches my chest.

It didn't work. I'm still a demon.

But the more I scrape away the black goop sliding from my face and body, the more I crawl across the earth's surface and let the jagged terrain scrape away every last glob of inky, glistening ink, the more relief settles. It's not the spiny black fur of my shadowcreature limbs that coats my arms, just tar lathered onto my druid flesh. My non-demon skin.

The breaths come easier then, a pressure I hadn't even been aware of slipping off me with the rest of the darkness. When I'm far enough out of the Pits of Bagamore that only rock digs into my toes, I fling myself to my back with a shaking, heaving sigh.

I lay there like that, naked atop the craggy terrain, for what feels like hours, my thoughts churning amid my exhaustion, but always returning to one terrifying conclusion: this shouldn't have worked. The Pits of Bagamore had meant to claim my soul, just as Qaeus' heart would've taken Halira's had she not been protected. This kind of magic is hungry and non-discerning. Without the breath of life to protect me, it should've devoured me whole.

So then why am I still breathing? If Halira needed something to protect her soul when Qaeus absorbed the Blight from her, then what was safeguarding mine? Because something most certainly was, I realize. I've known it for a while. The instant the Blight had finished consuming me, the moment my demon side had won and the darkness coursing through my veins finished corrupting me entirely, I felt it. A cold and chilling snap. My grip on my humanity not just waning but severing completely.

Until Halira.

When we faced each other, woman and beast—woman and monster—there wasn't a single part of me that remembered who she was or what she meant to me. All I knew was she was to be my feast.

But then she commanded me, and her druid magic had been like a warm spool of thread around my shattered being, and I began to feel again. Not much, at first, but enough to remember, to realize what I would've done if it hadn't been for her and her power.

Halira saved me that day.

She saved me again just now.

Her magic had still been inside me when I dove into the Pits of Bagamore. I'd felt the warm light of it beam down on my heart that the demon darkness had been given no choice but to retreat, relinquishing my soul to her as the shadows waited for her brightness to fade. But even as it faded, even as I flew farther and farther from her grasp, a dim candle's glow was always there, just enough to prevent the darkness from seeping back into me and taking me forever. Her magic, that protection, was all that my sanity could cling to. When the monster would prowl toward my heart, when I would cower in the face of evil, it was her light that guarded me. Kept me safe. Allowed me to remain *me*. That very same light must have been strong enough to protect me from obliteration while I swam down into the Pits of Bagamore, as well.

It's not quite dark yet when I finally stir from my resting place, but I can sense the day fading around me. For hours it seems I was drowning in the Pits. For hours the dark, gelatinous sludge ate away at me until there was no longer anything left it recognized, no more demon toxin to siphon from my core, until its cold hand of death had taken everything it could. That is, everything Halira hadn't kept safeguarded.

My thoughts return to her now, the ominous call of danger snapping my eyes wide with the memory of the last time I'd seen her. She'd crossed the Varenholm Ocean. She'd stepped foot on Illashore, a country dominated by tyrannical mages. She'd came face-to-face with one of them, a man who had without a doubt poisoned everyone she'd been traveling with.

Danger. Halira was in danger.

That thought alone drove me to the Pits of Bagamore and now it'll be what drives me away from them. Something lively beats through my veins, a war drum calling me into action, and I peel myself off the crag and back onto my feet. My gaze wanders upward once more, back to the low-hanging sun that seems to be falling from the sky more rapidly now and casts everything in a violet haze. During my flight here, the moon had been chasing me, so now it's time I run from it.

I bolt in the opposite direction, each pounding stride making my weakened joints shriek. But the pain that jolts through me is nothing compared to the agony of everything else I've endured—diving into the dark Pits, becoming a demon, murdering my best friend—and it's even less still than the pain I'd feel if anything were to happen to Halira. She's the reason I'm here and not lost in demonic delirium. She's the reason I held on. And she's the reason I push through every raw stride now, because no matter the burning in my thighs, the throbbing of the soles of my bare feet as they cut through rock and stone, nor the crisp breeze biting against my naked flesh, all that matters is I find her before it's too late.

The Pits of Bagamore are greater than I remember.

Though I run, they seem to go on forever. The pink terrain splotched with black pools of death seem endless, especially as night falls and all I have is the moon's reflection to alert me to the tarry pools surrounding me. I dodge every one of them. There's no telling what would happen if I dove into those dark depths again, and I have no interest in finding out. It would be safer to fly, to transform into an owl and soar far away from this place. But every time I dig for my druid power, I find none of it. I don't know if it's gone forever, if the Blight consumed it or if the Pits of Bagamore did, but I keep trying anyway, every time my foot slips too near the black sludge.

Something glints in the darkness. Something different than the reflected moonlight. It's shinier. Taller than the flat smudge of moonbeams that ripple on the surface of the Pits.

My steady pace falters and I allow myself to veer toward the shine. Even with my druid power gone, or at least buried, I can still sense the magic in this place. There's a static charge to the air that amplifies every time I near one of the pools of inky black and diminishes as I go farther from one.

There's magic in that silver glint too, and it's the only reason I allow my course to stray. Because I'd almost forgotten what the Elders told Halira and I about the Pits of Bagamore. About what powerful weapon resides here.

Jutting from a crack in the earth, a shadowsteel spear stands tall. A strong wind wouldn't have blown it free, but my weary muscles manage to pry it loose with ease, and I begin my journey again back to Halira.

Without a bird's eye view, locating the group is difficult at first. But the longer I'm human, the more my druid senses seem to return. A gust of wind carries with it the familiar scent of people, and considering we're in the middle of a forest, I assume it can only be Halira and her friends and I follow it. Sometimes too boldly. On a number of occasions, I'm so focused on following that scent, that single beacon of hope, that I forget to weave in and out of the trees. My shoulder throbs as I slam into another, the impact so brutal that I'm nearly propelled into another. But the longer I've been human, the more awakened my body has become as well. Strength has returned to me, and with it my reflexes, and I brace myself before launching back into my run.

I'm getting closer now. I can sense it. The wind carries the faintest hint of breaths on every gust, warming the air ever so slightly. The liveliness of the forest shifts as well, becoming still and quiet as the deer and birds have fled the vicinity of the strangers who have stumbled onto their land.

Through a set of clustered trees, I finally see them ahead. A dozen people shrouded in black leathers and cloaks, nestled on the forest floor. Exactly where I'd left them.

My stomach drops and my feet stop. The only thing I want to do is run forward, to burst through the branches and find Halira and make sure she's all right, but something about the very atmosphere here feels wrong. It buzzes with magic, and if

I'm going to run headfirst into a magic-infused trap, I need to assess the area first.

Crouching low to the ground, I slink toward a tree thick enough to offer cover for my broad shoulders, and I listen. Not just to the breathing I can barely make out ahead, but for any rustle of leaves, for sparks of magic igniting the air, or for any other sign that something is amiss. Without the ability to draw on the power that's always been awake and at the ready inside of me, the shadowsteel spear in my hand suddenly feels much more comforting than I imagined it would be on a land void of demons like Illashore.

I hold my position for minutes that feel as heavy and tiring as hours, until my paranoia is finally soothed into submission. The sense of magic I felt here has faded the longer I've waited, telling me that whatever spells the mages might've used—or any druids, for that matter—have long-since passed.

I step out from where I hide, the sun's warm glow casting a net of shadows down upon my skin—creamy and damn near smooth compared to the onyx, jagged clumps of fur that I've grown so accustomed to seeing consuming my arm. It takes me a moment to blink back the surprise, the severely shocking and completely unbelievable revelation that my brash actions somehow worked, but then someone grunts up ahead. A nasally, clogged-throat kind of inhale that sounds more like a bear slumbering in an echoing den than a mere human snore. But as the hours have passed, as my awareness of magic and the elements has deepened, so too has my keen sense of the animals of the forest. There are no bears near here, only the people Halira traveled with, and they are still fast asleep.

As I stride toward the slumbering group, all I can think about is finding her resting among them, sunbeams filtering through the verdant trees and illuminating her cascading, snow-white hair. In our short time together, I've seen her sleeping a handful of times so I know not to expect a peaceful, serene sort of slumber. The life she's led, the life she's chosen to boldly charge into—vowing to defend her country from demon-kind at the risk of her own life, charging into the Shadowthorn just for a chance to live, venturing to the Dark Sea and now to Illashore—Halira does not know peace. At least not yet. But she fights for it, every day, with every breath. Even in her sleep, her brow would always be furrowed, her lips slightly pursed, as if even as she rested her eyes, her mind was still vanquishing evil from the face of the Broken Realms. And perhaps it is a strange thing to look forward to seeing in someone, but as I charge through the density of the forest, the last few yards that keep me from her, all I can think about is laying my eyes on the strength she bears, even in such a vulnerable state such as sleep.

Finally, I breach the clearing. The bodies at my feet are recognizable, even if I don't know or remember their names. But we traveled across the Varenholm Ocean together for weeks, and I'd recognize the fiery red hair of the spirited woman who condemned Halira to her exile anywhere, and the giant lump of muscles resting beside the raven-haired woman who helped Halira to escape execution.

But as I step between the bodies, a stutter catches my heart. As if for the first time, I realize just how high the sun has soared overhead. Noon hasn't come yet, but it's well after any hour that would be typical for people to rise for the day, especially those set on saving the realm. It's then that I begin to notice the skewed placement of their bodies. Sure, they are covered by cloaks and blankets to keep them warm throughout the night, but upon closer inspection it becomes obvious that these people did not simply lay down to rest. They collapsed. Over fallen trees and atop thorny brambles. An older, scrawny fellow lays with his knees buckled beneath him, back arched so that his sleeping face gapes up at the sky. The sun shines perfectly down upon him, bright and blinding enough to arouse even the drunkest man from his sleep. But still, the man rests. They all do. Not even the dirt beneath them appears disturbed, as if the moment they closed their eyes, they never moved again.

I don't even try to avoid disturbing the bodies anymore as I crash through the camp, my gaze whipping from one person to another in search of the familiar form I've come all this way to find.

"Halira!" Her name tears from my lungs like the wild and thrashing claws of a beast frantic to find a meal before starvation claims it. "Halira!"

My second bellow rouses a few of the bodies around me, but I barely notice them as my gaze still cuts from one person to another, returning not once but twice to the people I've already searched in a desperate attempt to even find so much as a glimpse of Halira's silken, white hair, her lush rose petal lips pursed together in that concerned but determined way that follows her even into sleep.

But no matter how many times I search among the people here, I cannot find her.

She is not here.

She is gone.

My thoughts retreat to a dark place, to a dismal, foggy marsh where I often banished myself during the days that followed Ahl'Ro's death. It's here that I am guilty. I am reckless. Worthless. I hesitated too long, giving Ahl'Ro just enough time to betray his innately virtuous nature and kill Halira's parents. And yet again I find that I have reacted too slowly. I did not go to the Pits of Bagamore quickly enough. I did not drag myself from their tarry depths with enough haste. I did not return in time to protect Halira from the mages that were after her.

Suddenly, nothing has ever sounded more desirable than losing myself to the demon that ravaged me. When I sat kneeled in the Shadowthorn forest, there wasn't a piece of me that the Blight hadn't consumed. The good and the bad, gone in an instant. It might've stripped me of my humanity, of my memories and my being, but at least it had also taken with it the heavy burden of pain. The grief of losing my parents too young. The guilt of failing Ahl'Ro in his greatest time of need. And if I was still a demon now, I wouldn't have to suffer the shattering heartbreak of realizing that Halira is gone.

Gone.

But gone doesn't mean dead. For as long as I was in the Pits of Bagamore, I knew she was alive, for it was her druid powers alone that kept me protected. If Halira was alive then, there's still a chance she's breathing now.

So the question I ask myself: where is she?

My shuffling around the impromptu camp and calling out her name has now roused everyone in the group. Most are too bleary-eyed and hazy to do anything more than roll up onto their forearms or resituate their numbed limbs, but a handful have managed to climb to their feet by the time I start to notice them.

One of them, a man clad in black, leather armor with eyes like the lethal quiet of a meadow at dusk, stands before me. A broadsword extends from his arm, the blade steady and sharp where it pokes at my neck.

"Who are you?" the Crusader growls, his voice just as menacing as his piercing sage eyes. "What have you done with her?"

Though we've never been formally introduced, we spent weeks traveling across the Varenholm Ocean together, and I'd recognize Dimitri anywhere. I watched from the distance as he played cards with his friends, eyeing Halira every time she passed by, and stealing precious moments with her whenever he could—moments I'd wished could be mine but feared never would.

The wildness in his eyes is the only indicator I need to

know that he hasn't placed me yet as the demon who traveled with them. From his perspective, one day he fell asleep, and he's awoken now to find the love of his life is missing. He's panicked. Ready to strike down anyone who stands in his way of finding her.

On that, we can relate.

My hand clasps around the gleaming blade. "I believe you called me *demon-guy*."

Recognition blooms in his dark pupils like ink spilling over parchment. The sword falters, but it remains aimed at me until I shove it aside. He allows it to go willingly, though I can tell from his stance and comfort with the weapon that he could've fought me if he wanted to. He might not have the muscle that I do, but there's a precision to his movements, a mastery to his grip and stance that tells me he would be a formidable foe if it came down to it.

"Alphy?" cries a groggy female voice. I turn to find the petite redhead storming among the group, her eyes ablaze as brightly as her fiery hair. "Has anyone seen Alphonse?"

"Halira's missing too," Dimitri answers over his shoulder, but his narrowed eyes never leave mine. His voice draws the attention of everyone, and before they can ask him the obvious, he replies, "This is the demon."

My spine cinches at the way he calls me *the demon*. As if that's my name. As if that's all that I am. It might've been if it hadn't been for *her*.

"Ryven," I say, my voice still a bit low and guttural from weeks of inactivity. "My name is Ryven."

Dimitri's bunched brow twitches, but he nods by way of acknowledgment. "How long have we been out?" he asks.

I shake my head, my hand gliding through my long, umber locks. It stills at the smooth curve on the top of my head. There are no horns for my fingers to catch on now, only hair.

"I...haven't been here long," I say, blinking away the shock and returning my hand to my side.

It's only then, as my fingertips brush over my bulging thigh that I understand the wide-eyed glances the others cast my way.

Clearing my throat, I bring my hands to cover the naked manhood hanging between my legs. "Is there something I can—"

Before I can even finish, Dimitri is unlatching his cape. When he tosses the leathery thing at me, it's the first time he's allowed his gaze to break from mine. "Does anyone remember anything?" he asks the others. "Any ideas as to how long we slept?"

But no one says a thing. I stake the Primordial spear into the ground and make quick work of wrapping myself in the black fabric. It hangs crudely from my waist, a slit hiking up my leg that still leaves the side of my buttocks exposed. But it'll do for now.

Once I'm done tying it in place, I look up to find Dimitri's peculiar gaze fixated on my weapon. The question flares behind his eyes like sunlight flickering between the branches, and it doesn't take him long to deduce what the spear is. After all, there likely aren't many shadowsteel weapons on Illashore, and even if there are, what are the odds that I'd return with one when we are so close to the Pits of Bagamore?

When he meets my eyes again, my head dips by way of answer, and the motion only seems to spark more of his curiosities.

Before he can voice them, the red-haired woman scoffs, derision in her gaze as she looks among them all. "Absolutely useless. Does no one know a thing? Alphonse and Halira are both missing, and we've all been too knocked out to notice!"

"You've been spelled." My lips move too quickly for me to think better of keeping them closed. Every wary eye jumps to attack me, piercing with accusation, dripping with distrust and contempt. Before their twisted imaginations can run too wildly, I add hastily, "Mage magic."

They blink at me. But that's a far cry better than throwing their figurative pitchforks at my head, so I take it as a good sign and continue.

"I don't know how they use their magic, but I know enough about the power that me and my people use to know that sleeping spells like this are possible."

"What do you mean?" Dimitri barks.

Something innately defensive raises my hackles, but I force the words out regardless. "Druids draw from the natural elements: from the earth and air and water. The wind can be manipulated to give a lulling effect; water can flow just as peacefully as it can forcefully; and even some plants and flowers can put people to sleep just with a taste of their leaves or a whiff of their pollen.

"Sleeping spells don't seem too farfetched considering the many ways the elements can inspire drowsiness and serenity. It seems they wanted to immobilize you. Probably so they could take...her."

I don't know why I omit her name. Maybe because of the rage that's simmering just beneath Dimitri's skin, the kind of madness that threatens to eviscerate me if I so much as show an inkling of interest toward her. Like even her name belongs to him.

Catering to the brash defensiveness of the male ego is not normally one of my specialties, but if the mages have Halira, I need these people to trust me. I need them to work with me.

"And Alphonse," the red-haired woman reminds us with a pop of her hip. "We have to find them!"

"We will."

The muscle in my jaw tightens when I hear Dimitri's gravelly tone overlapping mine. Our awkward gazes collide. He stares at me as if he's about to stake his territory, or perhaps even rip out my throat, but it's so obvious to me that we are forever allies. No one could be of more importance to me right now than someone who would do anything to find and save Halira from whatever danger she's found herself in, and I have no doubt the lengths he would go through to do so.

"How are you here?" he snaps, knuckles bone-white where they still clutch his broadsword. "How are you human again?"

A cold, dead hand wraps its icy fingers around my intestines and tugs. One moment I'm standing in the sunlit woodland, surrounded by the familiar faces of the people I've traveled at sea with for weeks, the next I'm plummeting back into the inky darkness of the Pits of Bagamore. The black water bleeds down my throat, tarry and cold, gurgling into my lungs and coating me in a blanket of death.

My skin becomes sheets of ice atop the frozen lake of my body.

My very essence leaks from me, is drained from me, until I am barely alive. Barely anything.

I am drowning.

And drowning.

And just when I fear I've been lost to the darkness forever, there's a spark. A light. Hope.

I've already been here. I've already survived this terrifying abyss and dragged myself from the tarry depths renewed. Cleansed. Purified of the Blight that had stained my soul.

And just like that, the horrific memory begins to fade. As the verdant trees begin to appear, I seek comfort from the reminder that I survived. I am here. I am human.

All notions of comfort dissipate when Dimitri's wrinkled brow appears before me. Concern isn't the word I'd use to describe him. Concern implies care and worry for my own well-being.

But Dimitri? He looks as if he's seconds away from burying

his blade into my belly to protect them all from the danger-ously unpredictable demon-man who can't even answer simple questions like *how are you here* without disappearing back into the darkness.

"I…" My lips part to make way for the words I want to force out, for the words these people deserve to hear. But the more I gape at them, the more my thoughts pile into my throat until there's no room for anything but sounds to squeak by. "I—"

"Piss on a mage…" a familiar voice breathes, the sound rising from the dirt floor as the man behind it finally drags himself up from where he lay. "Ryven, is that you?"

I turn to find a quirk of a smile buried beneath an over-grown patch of facial hair the color of tree bark. Adrien has never been more unkempt, even as a man accustomed to camping in demon-infested woods. Dirt sifts from his hair as he runs a hand through the locks that outline his face, plucking a leaf or two from his wavy tresses.

He barks out a laugh, arms spreading wide. "I thought I smelled self-loathing altruism in the air."

The edges of my lips tick up and suddenly all the shadows of my mind are gone. They scurry back into their respective corners, shirking away from Adrien's light and warmth. The man seems to always have this effect on people, as if his sole purpose in life is to make everyone around him smile, even when they're at their worst and have no interest in doing so.

He reminds me of Ahl'Ro in that way.

With our arms outstretched, the two of us collide.

"Must be difficult to smell anything over the reek of your own arrogance," I retort, clamping his shoulder tight.

He chuckles a moment, but the embrace doesn't last long before he takes a step back. His eyes are luminous as they trail up and down my now-human body. "Astounding," he utters.

The man I recognize as Sai comes to his side. His gaze is less welcoming than Adrien's, but it's still a far cry warmer than Dimitri's was. "*This* is the demon? The one who traveled with us all that time?"

Adrien's grin becomes roguish. "I dare say he cleans up rather nicely."

Sai elbows him in the ribs and Adrien buckles with a breathy air of laughter.

The joy of the reunion is cut short though when another of the Crusaders, a young woman with rich, coppery skin, steps forward.

"This is the demon?" There's a strength behind her tremulous voice, a kind of festering anger that makes her appear larger than her small frame would otherwise suggest. "The one Halira smuggled here?"

Out of the corner of my eye, I see Dimitri nod, almost begrudgingly. If he had his way all those weeks ago, he would've struck me down from the sky and been done with me. It was against his better judgment that I was allowed to live, and he was even less thrilled about me accompanying them overseas.

The woman's sneer inches further up her cheeks, a smoldering fire igniting her brown eyes. "How lucky for you then," she growls, one boot thudding in the dirt as she advances closer to me. She doesn't shirk away from the inches I have on her in both height and breadth. Instead, she stands before me as if we are equals worth fearing. And I find that I do. "We fall under a sleeping spell, and you're magically transformed back into—well, I won't call a thing like *you* human, but—"

Dimitri tugs at her shoulder. "That's enough, Eparah."

She whips around, snagging his hand in her own and ripping it from her body in one clean movement. "Do not touch me again, Crusader. You take orders from me, not the other way around."

He grinds his teeth, but despite whatever impulses he's fighting, he takes a step back, hands splayed at his sides. "Sorry.

I just mean that...Halira trusted him enough to bring him here with us. I know it's not easy to do, believe me, but—" He winces when he swallows, and I know just how difficult it is for him to admit "—maybe we should do the same."

Eparah merely shakes her head, her eyes falling shut in an almost peaceful expression. "Dimitri..." she sighs, rubbing the smooth skin on her forehead. When she looks back at him, all traces of distrust and hatred are gone, the emotions she clearly means to reserve for me. "I know you loved her—we all did, in our own ways. But we have to face the fact that Halira was a traitor to our country. She wasn't who we thought she was. She's a druid! She—we don't know if we can trust her. She fled her capture in Nigh and for all we know she's colluding with the—"

"She didn't flee Nigh because she's colluding with mages!" Dimitri bellows, the force of his words making his pale complexion burst red. "She did it to escape execution! No one would've stay to die if they had the choice."

"You would've," Eparah says, rather pointedly considering how quickly Dimitri's jaw snaps shut. "She unleashed the Primordial upon Arcathain."

"That wasn't her intent," he growls.

I'm about to utter the same, to shed some light on the matter of Halira's allegiance when Eparah continues.

"She lured us to Illashore, to a country full of wicked mages and now she is nowhere to be found. Neither of the druids we traveled with are." Eager to plead her case to the rest of them, Eparah turns to the others now, beseeching them with pleading eyes. "She...she killed Inigo. A Crusader. One of her own—"

My nails bite into the tender flesh of my palms and I can hold my tongue no longer.

"One of her own?" I growl, anger coiling up my spine at the thought of this woman tainting Halira's name anymore. Questioning her loyalty. Her reputation. As if Halira hasn't committed herself full-heartedly to serving and protecting all of humankind from the horrors that would see them devoured. "Inigo was a greater scourge to humanity than the demons of the Shadowthorn."

Adrien chokes on a breath.

A few of the Crusaders gasp, their agreeable nods and gazes tearing from Eparah to me and twisting in shock and horror. But I won't back down. I won't allow these people to speak so ill of the woman who saved my life. The woman who brought them here with the sole purpose of saving *all* of Arcathain, rather than retreating to the Eyve and letting them and their loved ones rot.

"You people abandoned *her*," I remind them. "Not the other way around."

"Is that so?" Eparah snaps, something in her dulcet tone triggering a ripple of caution beneath my chilled skin. "Then where is she now? This *druid* who claims to be on our side. Where is she when we find ourselves lost in enemy territory and attacked by magic? Moreover, why would she send her pet for us now that he's human?"

Unflinching, I meet her distrusting gaze. "I'm not here to harm you."

"Just what a bleeding mage would say." Eparah crosses her arms. "I'm afraid I'm going to need more than that to believe a single word that comes out of your mouth. So tell us, where did you fly off to while the rest of us were unconscious?"

Caution seizes the muscles in my jaw again. Though I spent the majority of our voyage at a safe distance from these people in the sky, I've gleaned enough to know who among them I can trust, and who I cannot. Inigo was a vile man. He made as much clear the day Qaeus was awakened and he felt the need to posture Halira, rather than listening to her advice. I don't know much about this woman, but anyone who would stand by Inigo's side and defend him and his actions over those of

Halira's is someone whose intentions and loyalties I'd be suspicious of at best.

"Tell us," Eparah says again. Commands. Without knowing anything about the Shadow Crusade, she's already made it clear in her reprimand of Dimitri that she holds some kind of rank here and is used to people carrying out her demands. "Where did you go and why have you returned?"

There's no reason to let my distrust of her inhibit my truth though.

"I left to find the Pits of Bagamore. It seemed that if there was hope for me to change back, I'd find it there."

A murmur trickles through the Crusaders.

"The Pits of Bagamore?" Dimitri echoes, stroking the blond growth of fuzz above his upper lip.

Eparah's hand shoots up, her palm as flat as a brick wall to silence him. "Why?"

"I already told you," I say, voice as low as a croak. "To fix myself."

"And it worked?"

It takes an immense amount of restraint not to roll my eyes, but I can't deign the senseless question with a response other than gesturing to my naked *human* torso and the cape draped around my waist.

She nods, a curt, abrupt thing. "And why did you return?"

My teeth grind now with irritation. She's wasting all of our time. There's no telling where Halira is, but the longer we wait to chase after her, the further she'll become and the more danger she'll be in. Still, if I don't answer their pointless questions, I doubt they'll ever bring me with them in their search of her, if they even decide to find her at all.

So I answer plainly, "To find Halira."

One of Eparah's brows arches. "You knew she'd be missing?"

"I knew it wouldn't be long before she stumbled into trouble again," I answer honestly, if not still impatiently.

From around the group, I see that I'm not the only one who understands. A crooked grin sprouts from the red-haired woman's expression as if she's all too familiar with the kind of mischief Halira is known to find. Dimitri sighs, exasperated from a lifetime of helping her out of the trouble she makes for herself. Silver smiles fondly, while Güthric's countenance becomes brutishly proud, like a father watching his child win a fist fight for the first time.

If ever I was going to win these people over, it would be now. But Eparah's mind is quick, her control over the conversation comprehensive.

Her head bobs toward the spear I've left stuck in the dirt. "What about that? I don't recall your demon claws clutching onto a spear while we crossed the Varenholm Ocean. Am I to guess that you found that weapon at the Pits of Bagamore?"

My throat cinches, as if even my body at a cellular level knows not to answer her.

But what choice do I have? To lie now could condemn Halira and I both. Besides, I'm already certain Dimitri has figured that out for himself, and if I were to deny it, he'd be the first to challenge me.

"Yes," I finally answer, the slickness usually found in my throat drying completely.

"It's a Primordial blade," Dimitri says. "Correct?"

I nod. "Not that it matters. They don't slay the Primordials like you were led to believe."

Eparah strides forward, arm outstretched. "I'll decide whether or not such a weapon is of use to us." She waggles her fingers when all I do is stare at her upturned palm.

Begrudgingly, I pluck the spear from the earth and hand it over. Truthfully, I have little use for it anyway. Once my druid powers return, I'll have an arsenal of magic at my disposal, and not even a Primordial weapon could compare. Still, as the pole leaves my fingertips and Eparah's smooth grasp closes around it, dread plummets to the base of my stomach as if I've just made a huge mistake.

The red-haired woman approaches, wonderment etched in her gaze. "When we find Alphonse, he'll know what to do with it."

"Alphonse..." Eparah bites her lip, nodding almost absentmindedly as she stares into the glistening shadowsteel. But with a few blinks of her dull eyes, she manages to pull herself from her daze. As she looks out over the Crusaders under her command, her gaze becomes crisp. "Right, Crusaders. This changes everything. Namely our primary objective."

"What do you mean?" Dimitri asks, his tone wavering.

"I mean," Eparah clarifies, the spear twirling in her grasp. "With a Primordial weapon now in our possession, our new objective must be to return to Arcathain and defend the Capital from Qaeus."

"You can't be serious?" Dimitri growls, his face splotching with heat again.

The red-haired woman's shrill voice follows his. "We can't just leave him. He's—he's your general. We have to go after him."

Eparah's dark eyes cut to hers, her fingers tightening around the pole of the spear. "I am not duty-bound to one man, and neither are you. We came here because we must protect Arcathain from destruction, and this shadowsteel weapon allows us to do that."

"Halira already told you. Those blades don't work on the Primordials like we were told."

Just as Dimitri begins his argument, I let it fade into the backdrop of my thoughts. I already know what he'll say. It's the same case Halira made weeks ago to convince this same group to accompany her abroad. Little did she know, it appears they had an objective of their own: locate the last Primordial weapon and return to the mainland.

"You're wasting your breath," I tell him, cutting Dimitri off before he becomes purple in the face from the fervor he puts into his words. It's admirable, to say the least, how much he's fighting for this. For her. If only he'd have fought like this before, Halira might be in an entirely different situation. "Nothing you can say will change her mind. This has been her intent all along."

The breath all but whooshes from Dimitri's lungs as he watches Eparah. She fidgets beneath his gaze, but holds her head high.

"That's the only reason you came then?" Fox's fragile voice shatters with the chilling realization of betrayal. "To retrieve the weapon and then run?"

"Let her run," I sneer, glancing over my shoulder to the forest around us. None of the trees in this area appear disturbed by any powerful blasts of magic. There are no signs of distress anywhere, as if Halira simply vanished. "Let her and whoever wants to join her race back to the shore. We'll see how far they get before they realize they have no means to cross the Varenholm Ocean again."

Though Eparah is out of my line of sight, I swear I hear her mouth open before snapping shut. The raven Kalli left with her sister ruffles its black feathers, and an idea sparks.

"Or," I say, directing my attention back at the woman in command. "You can join us in finding Halira and her cousin. We can send Kalli's raven back to her, tell her that the two of them have gone missing and to make haste. She believed she could convince your Magistrate to bring the battle to Illashore. Have faith in her and in him and join us in finding our missing allies."

Eparah's gaze drops to the spear in her hand. She turns it over, inspecting the carved wood before admiring its dark steel tip. "We have no weapons against the mages," she mutters, more to herself than anything.

"Don't be such a mage," Fox spits. Reaching for Eparah's

hands, she takes them into her own, spear and all. "You're a Crusader—a Captain, for crying out loud. You've trained to fight the most ferocious beasts to ever walk the Broken Realms. I think you can handle a few pitiful mages." With a clipped, breathy laugh, she adds, "They put us to sleep. Rather than fighting us, they used their magic to make us tired. You know what that tells me?"

An innocent grin brightens Eparah's expression, one that makes her look almost childlike compared to the harshness she's shown thus far. "That they're nothing to be afraid of."

"More than that!" Fox barks. Spinning away from her captain, she addresses the group with the theatric allure of a true leader, and I can't help but think she's channeling Alphonse in his absence. "They're afraid. If their magic was so powerful that we should cower in their presence, why didn't they obliterate us? Why force us into unconsciousness and kidnap two of our own, if they were worthy adversaries?"

"To avoid bloodshed," Dimitri growls, dropping his hand from his chin. "Any opponent knows when to play the offense and when to defend."

Fox rolls her eyes and tosses her short, fiery locks. "Maybe. But there's a reason they fled Arcathain all those years ago. They weren't powerful enough to fight the demons, and so they ran like the cowards they are. Maybe they're no match for us either."

Though Dimitri seems unconvinced, his opinion on the matter is the least of my concern, seeing as I already know what his plans are. He will join me in my hunt for whoever has Halira. It's the others who I glance among to gauge their reactions to Fox's inspiring words. And to my great relief, they appear emboldened.

"I can protect you from magic," I say, cautiously optimistic that my offer will be well-received. "I know you are wary of it, but if it means preventing them from immobilizing you again, if I can give you a leg up in any battle we may encounter, wouldn't it be worth it?"

Eparah's eyes narrow. "You said you didn't know much about mage magic."

"I don't. But the surrounding area is undisturbed. Either they used a spell that reached you through the air, which I can defend against, or it was in the food or water you drank. Considering you brought provisions, I'm guessing it was the former."

Adrien's eyes widen and he snaps his fingers. "The mage at the coast. He disappeared behind a cloud of smoke that left us hacking for hours. None of us recovered from it. Even throughout the night."

"Alphonse didn't fall ill," Fox replies, her eyes now just as wide.

"Neither did Halira," Dimitri admits, stroking his facial hair again.

"A spell that targets humans then," I mutter under my breath. When I notice I've gained an audience despite not meaning to, I elaborate. The last thing I need is to ruin what little trust I've built. "They wanted to know who the druids were among you all. The magic they used targeted those of you without magic and left Halira and Alphonse impervious until they could come for them."

"What would they want with them?" Eparah straightens, fearful eyes darting to the shadows between the trees. "Where would they take them if they're even still—"

"Don't." Fox's warning is like a death sentence, and even Eparah, her commander, heeds it.

The group falls into silent introspection that's difficult to abide. I want to tear into the woods, thrashing and ripping every tree from its roots just to find her. But I know we can't be rash. To carelessly run in any direction could mean running away from Halira and condemning her to whatever fate the mages have planned. No, we have to do this the right way. We have to know where they've gone. There must be clues somewhere—

"You—" Dimitri's low voice makes the hair on the back of my neck rise. He refuses to call me by name, instead letting the hatred in his tone be enough of a name that I know it's me he wants to answer. "You were flying above us for some time. Higher than the canopy. Did you see anything up there? An army of mages nearby? A city where they might congregate? Anything of importance?"

"I…I'm not sure—"

"Think," he growls. "Halira's life may count on it."

He doesn't have to remind me. It's not as if I wasn't planning on exerting every memory and revisiting every minute detail in my mind's eye until we found them. My first response had merely been a knee-jerk reaction. I would never give up so easily.

I close my eyes, remembering the day of our arrival. I'd kept my distance, so I'd been flying higher than ever, just to ensure I wouldn't be spotted. I hadn't wanted her to see me then. I wasn't sure it was in her best interest.

Even the trees themselves looked more like ants from where I glided through the clouds. The entire island was crawling with them. This place reminded me of the Eyve in that way, so lush and verdant, so untouched by the grime of human existence.

In fact, the only place that appeared barren had been the pink terrain speckled in the blackness of death that had been the Pits of Bagamore. There'd been a few villages as I'd made my way there, but nothing that struck me as a place of importance. If anything, they seemed nearly abandoned, as if the people living there had long since migrated elsewhere, away from the ominous magic that radiated from the Pits.

"A targeted attack like that," Dimitri mulls. "One that relied on stealth and precision to identify and extract the only two druids among us, seems militant. Maybe even political." He snaps up from his concentration. "Did you see any government buildings?"

I don't answer him immediately, taking the time instead to let my mind wander over the lay of the land, but truthfully much of it is lost in a daze. When I was a demon, the druid part of me had very little access to the outside world. It was like I'd be buried in mud with a single pinhole to peek through to observe, and another for the faintest access to air. I remember everything, but not as crisply as I would if they were my own memories.

Finally, I shake my head. "I don't know. Not that I remember."

Dimitri resumes stroking his chin again, his brow creased and shadowed as he paces. Suddenly, he looks up. His gaze shoots to a mound of fabric on the ground that I had previously mistaken for a body, but upon closer inspection has become obvious it is nothing more than a crude rendering made from leaves and dirt.

His eyes ignite and, without warning, Dimitri dashes across the clearing. He slides to his knees beside the human-shaped mound and starts tearing it apart.

"What are you doing?" Fox asks him as I jog past her as well, intent on getting a better look at whatever it is that's caught his eye.

"These are Halira's belonging," he grunts, tearing through the strategically placed foliage until it no longer resembles anything. But as leaves and twigs fly about him, as he discards one of the burlap sacks of rice that had been used to form a head, with a wide grin, he finally heaves a satchel into view. "Kalli drew her a map of this place. It was pretty detailed—"

"You're brilliant!" Fox squeals, shoving me aside and

crashing to her knees beside him. She yanks the bag from his grasp and digs into the pocket.

When her hand returns to the light of day, a folded piece of parchment is wedged between her fingers. She rips it open so quickly that I'm almost certain she's torn it to pieces, but when the thing is revealed to completion there are no holes, only fresh creases where Halira has folded the scroll.

A dip forms in Fox's brow. "What am I looking for exactly?"

"Give me that," Dimitri growls, yanking the map from her with such force that once again I'm fearful for the map's safety in their clutches. But yet again, the map remains impervious.

I lean over Dimitri's shoulder as the other Crusaders and Adrien circle around us. Even Eparah tries peering down at the map in search of a potential destination. It's not until I see the spires etched in the northern part of the island that I remember. When we first arrived, there'd been a citadel, not too far from where we came ashore. Halira and the others had almost immediately started traveling southwest, so I put the place out of my mind at the time, but thinking back on it now, I've seen no other place on Illashore that has held such reverence. Where the rest of the island appears underdeveloped, possibly even uncivilized, that city was thriving. Even from the distance, it appeared more advanced than the few towns of Arcathain I've encountered in my time, with spires made of glass or perhaps even ivory instead of the drab shale used to construct most of the buildings in Gravenburg. The city I'd spied in the northern parts of Illashore had been a place of light, almost as if the mages who fled the mainland had made an intentional decision to avoid dark, dismal colors of the towns their human enemies now inhabited.

The drawing on the map isn't quite as intricate as the sparkling city I'd spied in the distance, but even as a one-dimensional drawing, the semblance is clear.

Leaning over Dimitri's shoulder, I press my finger to the

triple-spired citadel marking the map. "There. If they took Halira and Alphonse anywhere, it's there."

He glances up at me a moment, his expression dubious, before folding the map back together and tucking it into a pocket in his tunic. "Then as soon as we send Kalli her raven, that's where we go, as well."

A SUMMONING

UNKNOWN

Shards of ice sting my skin. The cold bites down deep, jerking me from the dark place that had claimed my mind. I don't remember falling asleep, but upon waking, I'm as groggy as I would be the day after an evening spent gambling until the late hours of the morning with Güthric, Sai, and Silver. But the pounding in my head that usually followed those evenings is nothing compared to the shivering cold that's wrapped itself around my bones.

Not even the worst winters in Gravenburg, the ones where we had no means of procuring wool coats and wool socks, were ever this chilling. I can't catch my breath. The icy air burns in my lungs as I blink and gasp, clawing at the cold ground beneath my knees to try to rise and evade the slickness I've been doused in.

But as my fingers clutch the smooth stones, I find them as dry as a hay bale in summer.

Another wave of waterless cold pours over me and I crumple to my face. I choke against the chilling nothingness, the non-liquid that consumes me.

Through blurred vision, I find Alphonse beside me, also gasping for air even though he appears to be surrounded by it.

His wide, bloodshot eyes meet mine and it's only then that the rest of our surroundings collapse into place.

A room appears around us, one spacious and dark, and not too dissimilar to some of the halls I once roamed at the Castle of Nigh. There'd been a permanent, foreboding nature about Nigh though that doesn't exist here, one that trapped darkness in every room and made the shadows appear larger than they should've been. This room breathes life into its grandeur. The ceiling cascades overhead like silver waterfalls frozen in time. The torches hanging from the walls cast golden, glimmering halos across the room, rather than the burnt, dull glow of the candles found in Nigh.

But despite the inviting nature of the room, when I lay eyes on the long, sleek table beyond our feet, and the dozen or so robed figures standing behind it, my stomach clenches.

And suddenly I remember. Crossing the Varenholm Ocean on the Leviathan. Encountering the mage Igemonar. Wandering deep into the forests of Illashore. Our friends falling asleep. Alphonse's and my foolish attempt to save them.

Igemonar finding us, and darkness following soon after.

My head careens, my gaze climbing over the massive table to the indifferent faces on the other side.

And I find the man responsible for it all, the one who immobilized our friends and took us away from them.

Igemonar.

Desperation folds beneath my fury then. I don't know where we are, but I know we've been taken away from our friends, the ones who were left sleeping and vulnerable in the middle of a magical forest with no means to protect themselves.

Our friends might've been defenseless against mage magic, but I am not.

I reach down deep into my core for the spark of magic that's always dwelled there. I call to the brutal storm brewing inside me, the one I know is always just waiting beyond the next cloud to be awakened. But no lightning strikes from above.

Instead, I reach for the wind, for the air circling around us and filling this room with everything we need to survive. I try forcing it into my lungs, try melting into it. But I remain where I am, flailing on the ground for a breath that always seems just out of grasp.

The mage at the head of the table stands. The inky tattoos swirling throughout his face remind me of the blighted blood that had leaked its way up Ryven's neck and sapped the last bit of humanity from him.

There is no reflection of humanity in the eyes of this mage. Time, or perhaps power, have drained him of life until his body has become no more than a flaccid husk of grooves and divots.

His pale eyes bare no pupils from what I can see as he holds his arms up.

The humming in the room stops. I hadn't even noticed it until the room falls silent, but I recognize the absence of magic now that it's released its icy hold on my skin.

Alphonse and I sputter, the air returning to our lungs with a gush. I glance over to him, silently asking if he's all right. The man who stares back at me is hardly my cousin at all. That person, that young man riddled with insecurity and self-loathing is gone, replaced by the brave and tactical general who's led Crusaders to battle for years.

Again, his gaze seems to say, and for once, I obey his command. Once more, my mind calls for the druid power laced throughout my essence. But the place in my core that is usually alive and thrumming with energy, is still. Quiet.

The husk of a mage clears his raspy throat. "You'll find you're unable to tap into the natural world in here. Aeysil Keep was not made from earth or stone, but of magic. *Our* magic. The walls are imbued with it." The black robe drapes from his frail and shaking arms. "Even the air we breathe here is synthetic. So you see, your power is of no use here. If it were me, I'd conserve what little energy I had left."

Grunting with the effort it's taken to dig and search for a power that has seemingly disappeared entirely, I finally collapse onto my palms.

"You have been summoned before the Great Mages. The first druids in centuries to have been invited to do so."

I bristle at his choice of words. If this is what they consider an invitation, I'd hate to know how we'd have been retrieved if we were unwelcomed.

"What do you want with us?" I dare ask.

The mage's thin lips curl into a sickening smile. "To ask some questions." He holds his hand out, and Igemonar steps forth. "You may begin."

In the company of so much grandeur, Igemonar appears smaller than I remember as he stands. His perfectly manicured and slicked-back hair makes him seem smarmy amid the company of so many with an air of greatness about them.

He dips his head in a dramatic fashion that somehow doesn't jostle his slicked-back hair. "Thank you, Your Eminence." As Igemonar adjusts the round buttons of his meadow-green tunic, Alphonse and I help each other to our feet. "Now," the mage says, clapping his hands. "Shall we begin?"

"What is it you'd like to know?" Alphonse asks, his tone diplomatic. He's had years to practice such an inflection in the company of his father and all the other political figureheads he's endured conversations with.

"Let's begin with something simple. I believe we've already introduced ourselves, Halira Devonshire—"At the sight of fear sparking in my bulging eyes, he smirks. "I'm afraid I never forget a name. But yours—" he says, turning to my cousin "—I'm afraid I haven't the pleasure yet."

Alphonse inclines his own head, a curtain of dark hair cascading past his shoulder. "Forgive me. We are civilized men, and as such, names are a must." Clasping his hands behind his back, Alphonse bows deeply at the waist. "General Alphonse Reid Graham. It's a pleasure."

"A general?" the head mage cuts in, one bushy brow trying to hike up his wrinkled forehead. "Does that mean you have come to declare war? The two of you?"

"On the contrary," Alphonse replies, a little more hastily than I would've liked. "We've come to prevent one."

"Hmm." He glances among his peers. At the indifferent shrugs, his drowsy eyes return to ours. "You must be mistaken. Our people are not at war."

"No, but ours are. They've been fighting the same war for centuries, defending the country from the Primordial Qaeus and the extinction her unchecked power would mean for mankind."

The decrepit mage watches the two of us for a long moment, stroking the tufts of hair that have sprouted as singular streams from his cheeks, leaving most of his chin bare. His silence is so profoundly worrying, my knees actually begin to quake. These mages could kill us. Alphonse and I have no defenses against them. We have no idea where we are in relation to where our friends are, nor do we know how to escape. If they wanted us dead, they could have their wish.

But we didn't come all this way to be slaughtered. If anyone knows how to contain or stop the Primordial, I believe it's the mages, and though the circumstances in which we were brought here were unpleasant at best, I couldn't have asked for a timelier encounter. They've saved us the trouble of finding them.

Now for the difficult part: getting them to share what they know.

Finally, and with great pains to do so, the head mage eases

himself back into his chair. "I see," he groans, his voice as ancient as the discarded bones of the demons the Crusaders have let to rot in the Shadowthorn after every expedition. But despite the weariness weighing down his words, there's a commanding power to them too. "And what has led you to the belief that the answer to preventing your war can be found on Illashore?"

"Your Eminence?" Igemonar leans over the oak table, peering down the vast, smooth surface to the head mage at the end.

The old man waves him off. "They have been brought here for questioning and they will answer my questions. What has brought you to Illashore?"

"We already told you. We came to stop a war—" As an afterthought, I add "—Your Eminence."

The mage swats at the air again, his irritation rising. "Bah. There is no respect between the two of us, Halira Devonshire of the druids. Do not insult me with such a careless and impertinent use of title. Calling me by name will suffice for the purposes of our conversation."

My cheeks heat. "Okay. Then what—"

"Varyn," he croaks, and reaches for a glass of water on the table. He swallows a gulp with a loud smack of his lips. "Varyn Brenthan Ephemeris, should you feel the need to use my surnames."

It feels like the respectful thing to do, so I dip my head.

"Very well," Alphonse says. "What is the purpose of this conversation, Varyn?"

"Why, to determine your intent here, of course."

Igemonar clears his throat then. "Yes, I'm afraid you still haven't spoken as to why you've come here. You mentioned a war, but as you've already pointed out, your people have been battling the Primordial for centuries. Your people have never come to us for aid before. Why now?"

Alphonse and I exchange a worried look.

This is what we came here for. Holding back now would be foolish, even if I'm still unsure we can trust these people. But Alphonse nods his silent approval, and I relish the confidence he gives that such a small gesture provides.

"We believe you may offer some much needed insight," I say shakily.

The robed figures glance among themselves, but only a few moments pass before the room erupts with boisterous laughter.

"What makes you believe we'd help the likes of you?" Varyn chuckles, the hair coating his jowls jiggling with glee. "Surely, you're aware of the history between our peoples. We fled your country because we have no interest in dying at the hands of the Primordial."

The worried look Alphonse shoots my way mirrors my own concern: they are just as terrified of the Primordial as all of Arcathain. And I suppose we should've known. Why else would they have fled, putting as much distance between them and the ancient being as they possible could?

They don't know how to get rid of the Primordial.

Fortunately, that's not our only option. In fact, it's not even my preferred choice.

"We do know the history of our peoples. Yours used a spell to contain Qaeus beyond a barrier. It withstood for decades and kept Arcathainians safe. But now that it's fallen—"

The lighthearted chuckles are snuffed as the mages around the table gasp.

"What does she mean it's fallen?" a woman demands, leaning over the table where she sits to stare down at Varyn.

A man opposite her does the same and wrenches forward, but he addresses them all. "Don't you see? This makes perfect sense. We've suspected magic is weakening for years, and this is the confirmation we've sought. If we don't do something soon—"

"Silence!"

Varyn's fists bang against the solid oak with room-shattering force. He pushes out of his chair, his breathing ragged with rage. His simmering glare finds each and every one of them, the mages hanging their heads like scolding children and inching back into their seats.

When he has finally made each and every one of them cower, he returns his attention to Alphonse and I, muttering to himself, "To speak so freely in the company of strangers, you'd think they'd call us the Foolish Mages, not the Great. Now," he says, shifting gears so abruptly that I almost don't even realize he's not speaking to us. "Leave from my sight before someone else slips privileged information."

With a careless wave, he dismisses the mages who have congregated, and they turn from the table without hesitation and vacate the large room. All but Igemonar.

He steps out from the table, his striking, sunken eyes pinned on the two of us.

That bottomless gaze pulls me down with it, a brick of dread settling in the pit of my stomach and unraveling all of my thoughts as it plummets.

"Why were we brought here?" Even though I doubt I'll receive an answer, I still ask the dark question my mind turns to. "You could've asked us these questions when we had first arrived. But you didn't. Instead you spelled our friends, kidnapped the two of us, and brought us here. Why?"

Beside me, from the corner of my eye, I see the ball of Alphonse's neck bob. He's figuring it out too. This doesn't bode well for us, invitation or not.

To my surprise, and the sickening swell of dread twisting within me, Varyn answers.

"Well," he croaks, his voice like the crackling embers of a

dying fire. "It's been decades, perhaps centuries since strangers have landed on our shores. When we first absconded the mainland all those years ago, we never dreamed Arcathainians would follow us. They are a suspicious lot, and the dangers of the Varenholm Ocean were known, even back then.

"But some came. They believed it to be their duty, and when they landed on our coastline, we were waiting for them. Those were unpleasant deaths, overwrought with magic and anger. But eventually we developed our border, and no others have crossed since. Until you."

His bushy, wiry brows lift as his attention cuts to Alphonse and I.

"The first outsiders to ever successfully traverse the spell that guarded us. Not just traverse it, but dismantle it. Druids, Igemonar told us. And given what we knew happened to those people, given that we believed them to be trapped behind a spelled wall with that gods-awful Primordial, we had to meet you. But first, we needed to know how many of you there were."

A wicked grin coils his thin lips. Beneath his robes, his footsteps are silent, but the dragging fabric along the smooth, marble floor sounds like death approaching.

"It seemed unlikely that it was just the two of you, but we confirmed it. Two single travelers and a gaggle of magicless humans. We were tempted to leave you to your devices, but you see, such immense power like that of which you've shown is rare anymore. And we couldn't exactly let you walk away.

"Like you believed we possessed something you want, we believe the same of you."

Cold iron burns in my gut, my watery insides turning solid as I meet his dead gaze, those pale eyes that seem emptier than the moon itself. He wants our magic. Rather, he wants Alphonse's. And the moment he discovers it was Alphonse's power alone that destroyed their barrier, they will have no more use of me.

I swallow the stony lumps of fear stacking in my throat and his grin widens.

"But that's for another time." Varyn leans back, straightening his hunched back as much as he can before signaling to Igemonar. "Take them to the dungeons. Make sure they're kept separated. We begin the tests tomorrow."

THE STIFLING DARKNESS

THE DUNGEONS, AEYSIL KEEP, ILLASHORE

*O*ur knees crash against solid stone as the metal door clanks shut behind us. Darkness bleeds throughout the room like a ghost of death.

I glance beside me, curious to see how Alphonse is holding up or what he's thinking of our current predicament, but I can't see him. His elbow is touching mine where we are both crouched and bent, but as far as my eyes can discern, I'm utterly alone.

"Well," he remarks his boots scuffing against the ground as he shifts. I can hear him pat dirt from the sleeves of his tunic. "That was unnecessary force. It's not like we were struggling."

Biting my lower lip, I, too, shift positions. "Maybe we should've. Once we were awake, we could've fought."

I can sense his gaping expression snap to mine. "And what would we have done? Fought an entire Council of mages who are apparently so skilled at what they do that they're deemed the Great Mages? We wouldn't have stood a chance." As if he can read the rebuttal in my mind, he adds with sharpness, "Even if you did find your magic."

My hands fold into my lap and my head drops. Even now,

the absence of my magic is palpable, a hollow ache swallowing my core.

"I don't understand what happened," I admit, voice near quivering. "Where did it go? How can they just make it disappear like that?" My gaze slides over to where I can feel him squatting at my side. "Is that a mage thing, or are druids capable of it too?"

He snorts, slumping to the stone ground with a firm thwack. "You're asking the wrong person."

As I listen to him getting comfortable, I'm tempted to do the same. We have no reason to believe that we have any chance of getting out of here. They possess the kind of power that can stifle other magic. Surely their dungeons are secured with spells to prevent their prisoners from escaping.

But the absence of magic crawling beneath my prickling skin refuses to let me sit idly. I jump to my feet and begin pacing.

"What are you doing?" he sighs. "You can't see anything. You're just going to get yourself injured."

"I know how to be careful," I say, throwing my arms out in front of me to act as a buffer should I encounter a wall.

"This place could be booby-trapped."

The laugh that cuts from my lungs is void of amusement. "What's the worst that could happen? They already have us imprisoned."

"Oh, I don't know. Death?"

My footsteps falter and I curse myself under my breath for feeling even the slightest ounce of hope that we might still make it out of this alive.

"Alphonse," I snap, spinning around to scold him. But my gusto is lost when all I find is pitch black. "If we stay here, we're as good as dead. The mages have no reason to keep us alive. They're toying with us."

There's a long pause before he finally groans. Rustling

fabric fills the darkness, as does shuffling feet. Fine. But I highly doubt we'll find anything of use." He meets me where I stand halfway across the room, apparently having a keener sense in the dark than I have. "What are we looking for?"

"I don't know," I admit, my boots scuffing on the stone floor as I start tiptoeing around the room again. My hands are splayed out before me, but only darkness sifts between my fingers. "Anything, really. A door. A window. Something that can be used as a weapon."

A derisive chuckle bubbles up from him. "Sure. Because when they built this dungeon, they believed it wise to give their prisoners ample opportunity to fight back and escape. I have no doubt I'll find my very own shadowsteel sword down here."

I shoot him a caustic glare over my shoulder, even though he can't see it. "Are you always so negative?"

"Only when I have reason to be."

Rolling my eyes, I turn away, and the two of us continue meandering around the dungeon in near silence. The space is small, larger than a single cell, but still nothing like the great hall we'd been standing in just moments before. There's something about the air down here that feels suffocating, like it's not even air at all, but rather the ancient, infinitesimal particles of dust that had been trapped down here during the construction of this place.

The air is just as suffocating as the darkness itself.

As we peruse the wide, open space, neither of us have much luck in finding anything useful. I manage to step my foot into a bucket that I believe is meant to be our latrine—and thankfully, empty—while Alphonse strides atop a bed of straw that we decide must be here for when we're ready to sleep. Aside from that, the room is sparse. It turns out there are no windows. No weapons of any kind. And the only door, the one they slammed behind us after tossing us inside, is flush. There is no handle to jiggle, no lock to try picking—not that I have the skills for that anyway.

We are trapped.

Eventually, Alphonse slams his body against the wall, the fabric of his clothes catching and tearing on the jagged walls the only sign I have to know he's sliding down to the cold floor. Exasperation eases from his lungs.

My skin still pricks with incessant urgency though, so I remain on my feet. I pace the room, less worried now about colliding with anything painful. Nine. It only takes me nine strides to get from one side of this cold, oppressive room to the other.

Everything is so quiet, like the room itself mutes any noise that would even dare try echoing off these barren walls. It's more unsettling than I'd like to admit. A room like this, built of stone with nary more than a bucket to occupy its spaciousness, should reverberate every single exhalation that passes my lips, every thud of my frantic steps.

The silence anchors itself to me, dragging me down to a place where I almost forget that Alphonse is even in the room with me until he speaks.

"Honestly, what good can come of all this pacing?" he snaps, and I can practically see him rolling his eyes the theatrical way he does. "Sit. There's no use in exerting what little energy you have left. We may need it."

The cleverness edged in his tone makes me stop abruptly. "What do you mean *we may need it*? What are you planning?"

Another sigh. "I'd hardly call it planning. It's more like… assessing our dire circumstances and knowing when the cards are stacked against us."

"Like you know anything about stacked cards," I grumble. "Unless they're in your favor."

"Oh, Halira. You still think so little of me that you believe me capable of cheating at cards? What did weeks at sea teach you if not that I'm simply naturally talented at everything I do?"

At the hint of amusement that lifts his voice, my itching panic burns hot and I whirl around. "How can you be so calm about this!? We have been captured by the mages. We're being held against our will and who knows how long they'll keep us here! Who knows how long it'll be before they kill us. And our friends? Last we saw of them they were utterly incapacitated and vulnerable. When they wake up—if they wake up—what happens then? What will they think about us and where we've gone? How are you not reeling right now and doing everything in your power to get us out of here?"

Heaving, the last words leave my lips, but not even they reach the walls to echo back at me. It's like the darkness devours them the moment they're breathed, and Alphonse doesn't respond for so long that I fear I am too far from him to be heard. That maybe he's not even there at all anymore. Maybe the darkness has consumed him too.

My heart jolts when I hear his low voice.

"We must conserve our efforts. You can fret about all of those things, but don't let them destroy what few opportunities we are granted—and there *will* be some. There always are. I don't care if they possess magic so strong that they zapped yours away. I don't care how thick these stone walls are. Mistakes are always made. There will be oversights. Maybe it's when they bring us our meals, or empty out our bucket, or do whatever it is they have planned for us—but it's in those moments that we must be ready. It's in those moments that we will make them rue the day they ever crossed the likes of us."

LEVELS OF ALONE

THE DUNGEONS, AEYSIL KEEP, ILLASHORE

"They're never coming!" My thrashing boot kicks through the straw. But the swift motion, after days of no food or water, makes my head spin, and I stumble forward, the wall bracing my falling shoulder with an audible thud. Gritting my teeth, I lean my forehead on the warm stone and close my eyes. "They've left us down here to rot and there's nothing we can do."

"They'll come," Alphonse insists. He's been insisting for days now. But I think even he's starting to doubt whether or not he's right. Every time he suggests it, he gets more and more elaborate with his reasonings, as if he's trying to convince himself. "This is strategy. They starve us first, make us so desperate for a single drop of even the most stagnant water, and once they think we're finally at our wits end, they'll come for us."

If I had the energy, I'd argue the matter further. His entire theory revolves around the idea that we have anything to give the mages, let alone something they want. As far as they're concerned, we are trespassers. We are the offspring of the enemies they fought so long ago that we've likely become the villains in their story, the ones responsible for them living on this small island while we live lavishly on the main continent.

There is no reason for them to speak to us, to feed us, to check in and make sure we're still breathing despite there being barely enough oxygen down here to fill a single lung, let alone both of ours. That's why they haven't returned. They will leave us down here to die. We will be forgotten, and it could be years or even decades before one of them remembers that they had placed two prisoners down here.

It's moments like these that my thoughts drift back to the others. To Dimitri and the Crusaders. I wonder if they're still resting peacefully on the woodland ground or if monsters have found them yet. I wonder if they ever woke to find us missing, if they are still pursuing a way to defeat Qaeus or if since Alphonse and I are missing, if they've abandoned the cause and returned to Arcathain.

I think about my sister and whether anyone has thought to inform her that I'm missing. I wonder if the Magistrate's ships have embarked for Illashore yet, or if Kalli and the armada are still on land. I wonder if it's only a matter of time before they go to war with the mages. Perhaps Alphonse and I will be freed then.

But mostly, my cyclonic thoughts return to Ryven, to the man I swore to protect and save whom I don't even know where he is, let alone if he's still alive.

Before the very idea can mangle itself into a dark claw that's scraping its way up and out of my throat on a raging scream, I begin my pacing again. I ignore the exasperated sigh that whispers in the darkness, and the soft thud of Alphonse plopping backward onto the straw as I march to the end of the room. Nine strides and my breath bounces off the wall in front of me to caress my face with damp heat. Pivoting, I cross to the next corner. My fingers trace along the rough cracks in the wall, the fissures reminding me of the lines of demon toxin snaking up Ryven's arm and across his chest in those final moments before the Blight had claimed him completely.

My eyelids press shut, a desperate and foolish attempt to shake away the unwanted image, but the darkness behind my eyes is the same as the one around me, and so the memories remain.

I jerk my hand to my side and rub away the sensation on my thigh until I reach the next corner. This time, when my breath reverberates from the wall, it's mixed with a subtle chill. I've paced this room enough to know that this corner is simply like that. The air swirls here as if an enormous vulture is perched somewhere overhead, wafting its wings every time I draw near.

A chill skitters down my spine. I twist, intent on hurrying from this corner to stride to the other side of the room, when a thought reverberates through me like the toll of a brass bell.

My lips split open in a gasp.

"What is it?" Alphonse asks. Judging from the scuffling of straw, he scrambles to sit upright. "Did you find something?"

The eagerness in his tone confirms my suspicions. I'm not the only one who has begun to lose hope. If I'm right about this though, we might stand a chance at freedom after all.

"The wards they have on this place that block out druid magic, surely they can't reach everywhere. Maybe there's somewhere where the mage's influence over our powers is weakened."

"What do you mean?" he asks warily.

"I mean that maybe there are pockets where we can feel our magic again."

"Where *you* can feel *your* magic," he corrects. "I feel exactly as I always have."

Ignoring him, I stomp back across the room to where the gentle breeze swirls in the corner and hold my hand into the zephyr. "Places like this. Why can I feel wind here when I'm not even sure natural air has reached this place in centuries?"

"What are you talking about?" Alphonse meets me in the darkness. His leather tunic squeaks as he raises his arm to feel what I'm feeling. And with an ear-splitting thud, his arm slams back against his body. "Dungeons are always drafty. It's nothing more."

"You can't be serious?" I shout after his retreating steps.

My jaw hangs loosely, unable to utter a word of outrage until he plops back onto the straw. For days he's done nothing but lay there while I've searched this place, bottom to top, for any sign of hope. He tells me to conserve my energy, but I can't help but feel like conserving energy looks an awful lot like giving up. Especially since no one has come for us to be able to launch into our surprise attack or make a break for it.

"I am being serious," he answers, and judging from the way his voice lifts up to the ceiling, I can all but imagine the way he's leaned back, his arms folded behind his head, eyes closing as if he's ready to drift off to a blissful sleep. But the words that leave his throat next are anything but dreamy. "How many dungeons and prisons have you frequented? How many times have you walked through the buried corridors to check on the prisoners being held in those cells?"

He doesn't wait for my response. Maybe because he already knows it. The only two dungeons I've been in are the one he threw me in at the Castle of Nigh, and the one in the Eyve where he was held until my aunt could vouch for his release.

"You are not as familiar with places like these as I am. Yes, I was the General of the Shadow Crusade and I oversaw the imprisonment and sentencing of those we held captive at Nigh. But I was also accustomed to the dungeons of the Capital. When I lived there with my father, he made sure I spent ample time down there. Character-building, he called it, for a young man like me to spend hours with nothing but the stench of piss and vomit in my nose, the hollering and screaming of outraged men who were slowly going mad.

"Tell me how you're more versed than I am in places such as these."

My teeth are firmly clamped shut. I know he's not wrong. I only spent a matter of hours in my cell at Nigh before my aunt freed my sister and I, and my visit to Alphonse in his own cell hardly lasted longer than a few minutes.

My experience on the matter of drafty dungeons is undoubtedly limited. But it doesn't mean that my idea is invalid.

I open my mouth to insist as much, when the rusty hinges of the door beside us screech, and the door swings wide.

After days of nothing but darkness, of no sounds but the muffled, inaudible padding of our feet on the muted stones, the sudden clash of our existence inside this dungeon colliding with that of the outside world is like a razor blade to a taut harp string. Both of us recoil from the sudden burst of brightness emitting from the torches lining the hallway outside. We stagger backward, our hands clawing to rid our eardrums of the booming thuds of footsteps that enter the room. The sudden gust of fresh air let in by the open door makes my skin pinprick with frigidity and I want nothing more than to curl up in the hay for warmth.

Once the shock that ripples through my senses has had a moment to calm, once I remember where I am—trapped against my will on Illashore, imprisoned by the mages—I force myself to stand tall, force my eyes to strain through the blinding lights.

Alphonse's shoulder bangs into mine and he shouts, "Let go of me! Where are you taking me?"

Tears sting my eyes like molten metal, but I keep blinking, keep trying to see through the blurred haze of shadows and light. I try making sense of the masses. Of the blurs that are moving away from me. Bodies, I know. But how many? And which of them is Alphonse?

The vague shapes stride farther away, deeper into the light spilling into the room, and panic finally yanks on my chest. It doesn't matter which one is my cousin; I reach for anyone.

"Stop!" I shout, my voice grating against my throat like it's made of rusty blades. "What are you doing? W-when will we be released? Let us speak to someone. Anyone! This isn't fair. You can't just—"

But my cries are silenced by the sudden, flinching bang of the door as it's slammed shut. The light blinks out once more. I shuffle backward, away from the door and farther into the black behind me as if here is where I belong.

In the darkness.

In the silence.

In the nothing.

"Walk quieter," I growl at the thunderous footsteps over my shoulder, back to the uncoordinated Crusaders thrashing through the overgrown forest like dawdling children. "We don't know these woods, nor what dangers that lurk inside them."

"It's been days," Sai groans, hefting his stout sword carelessly through a bushel of leaves. "Surely any dangers that might've been here would've shown themselves by now."

Some of the others grunt their agreement, and it takes every ounce of my willpower to continue forth instead of chastising them. You'd think I was leading a gaggle of geese to a pond for a nice soak, rather than a unit of trained warriors to a keep of deadly, duplicitous mages.

Pushing farther ahead, I mutter under my breath. "Is stealth and sure-footing not among the skills they teach you at the academy?"

"Academy?" Fox appears beside me almost silently, her mouth quirked in a playful way. "You make the Castle of Nigh sound so prestigious."

I glance at her sidelong. "Isn't it?"

A bubble of laughter spurts from her nose. "If you consider

the dank underside of a warthog's belly to be a respectable place to hang out, then sure. It was the most prestigious place in Arcathain there ever was. Drafty corridors. Stiff cots that whenever you laid on them you felt like your back was breaking. Grueling days—Oh! And don't forget that half of the castle was in ruins because the Shadowthorn had already crept up to it." Dreamy-eyed, her hands float behind her head. "Ah, those sleepless nights, wondering if demons would cross the barrier, silently slaughter the Crusaders standing on guard, and kill us in our sleep before we were any the wiser. I do miss those."

The undergrowth thickens. The tree trunks, as thick as they are ancient, have been thinning for miles, leaving plenty of fresh soil for wild flora and plants to thrive. I've been surprised by how many of them I recognize. Being this far away from home, from the Eyve, it's easy to forget that Illashore was once part of Arcathain, and therefore closely connected to my own homeland and the greenery that lives there. Every time we pass a pale yellow bushel of lady's mantle I feel a little less lost and removed from my home. The lanky stalks of yarrow sway in the gentle breeze, as the air becomes seductive with the scent of nightshade and henbane, and I'm reminded of the days when I'd traipse through the poppy fields along the Ushines with Ahl'Ro and Ceph, two friends that had become more like brothers.

Reaching another wall of vines of ivy draped between the trees, I use the tip of the Primordial spear to shove them up and out of the way.

As Fox dips beneath them, I force the bittersweet memories out of my mind. "I thought you enjoyed your stay at Nigh," I say at last. "Maybe not initially. Halira told me you were brought there against your will, but I was under the impression that—"

"Did she now?"

I swallow the abrupt dryness in my throat, and attempt to

assuage the sudden feeling that I've just offended her. The last thing I want is to make things more difficult between Fox and Halira, whenever we find her. And we *will* find her.

"She did," I admit. "She said you, and many people like you, weren't given much of a choice. Imprisonment or battle. Death by hanging, or death by Shadowthorn."

She scoffs, but doesn't deny me, so I keep going. If I'm to work alongside these people, I need to understand them. I need to be able to trust them. And she's still someone I'm not sure I can.

"What changed then?"

With one brow raised, she glances over her shoulder. "What do you mean?"

"What made you change your mind and decide you wanted to stay in that drafty, decrepit place?"

She holds my gaze as she stomps through a tall patch of hyssop. "Didn't she tell you?"

I think for a moment about whether I have any reason to lie to her, only to find that I do not. I am well aware of the betrayal between Fox and Halira. After spending a week or more in the Shadowthorn with the two cousins, I've heard Halira and Alphonse talk about it at great length, Alphonse always defending the fiery-haired woman before me, no matter how many times Halira protested her actions were anything but forgivable. But I also watched them on their journey here, saw the gains and strides they made toward repairing their friendship. If I am to be supportive of it, at least in any way that wouldn't require fake smiles or wary eyes, then I'd like to hear Fox's side of the story.

"She did," I say honestly, again. "But I'd prefer to hear how you would tell it."

It's with a heavy sigh that she finally averts her attention to the ground, just in time to step over a fallen sapling. "Comfort? Safety? Love? Take your pick. I never had a home or a family growing up. I never knew what it was like to live behind walls for weeks at a time, to have warm meals put on the table without having to risk getting your own hand chopped off to steal them. And I'd never..."

It all sounds like excuses to me. "Been with a man?"

She snorts again, an incredulous sound that makes her mouth unhinge. Without warning, she slaps me in the shoulder, a friendly, jovial gesture that gives me some insight into the charms she uses on people.

"Hey!" I bark, glaring with bewilderment.

"Hey, yourself," she says, the crooked smile she flashes at me confusing me all the more. "I had been with men before. I'm not some prude. Need I remind you how desperate a life I lived? Believe me, I learned young how to get what I wanted from men." Her expression sobers. "But that's just it. Though I'd been with plenty of ale-soused apple John's that called themselves men, I'd never really *been* with a man. Not the way I was with Alphonse. With him—he wasn't some fop to con. I wasn't trying to play him for a meal or a quick coin. I wasn't even trying to steal any of his fancy statuettes or clothes to pawn off anywhere. He was just... He was a distraction. At first, anyway. He was fun. And then...then he became—"

"Something more."

I startle myself by answering for her. But hearing her talk about him is more relatable than I'd anticipated. I'd been so alone when Halira's and my path's first crossed, so entrenched in my grief and self-loathing. I'd told myself the only way to repent was to protect her because I thought I owed it to her. I believed that was the payment I needed to give to make amends to Ahl'Ro. But truthfully, doing so was the only thing that kept my mind from my darkest thoughts. I told myself I was protecting her—saving her—but really it had been the other way around.

"Oh?" Fox says, eyeing me with a smirk. "I see I'm not the only one who's been beguiled by one of the Graham's."

The name takes me aback. "Graham?" I ask, skirting around a particularly beautiful patch of flowers with petals so crimson and bright that they almost don't look real.

Every Crusader in my wake promptly tramples over them without a care.

"Well—" Fox shrugs "—Graham was the family name. Apparently all the brothers—Alphonse's dad and Halira's—shared it. It should've been passed on to Halira and her siblings, but her family took her mother's name instead." A startled laugh escapes her. "I guess it makes sense now why. Her mother being a druid with different customs, and all that."

I run my hand through my dark hair, trying to rid myself of the ill-will I'm currently wishing on the men behind us. "N-not exactly," I say, attempting to bring my focus back on the mission ahead. "Upon marriage, most druids take the paternal surname. The only ones who don't are—"

My feet stop moving, heels planting firmly in the lush, overgrown grass. The Crusaders behind me, the ones who bump against me, and the ones who bump into them, cast every curse my way that they can conjure.

It's their outrage that draws Fox's attention. She twists around to investigate, and when she finds me frozen, she stops as well.

But it's only out of the corner of my eye that I see her approaching, for I'm too enthralled by the innerworkings of my mind, and the mysteries I'm piecing together.

"What is it?" she asks, her previously light tone cracking with concern. Her eyes flit to the tree line and I hear a number of weapons drawn. "Are they here? Have we found them?"

I attempt to shake my head, but I'm not sure it moves. I'm not sure *I* can move.

"Then what is it?" she asks.

"What's going on?" Dimitri strides forward, his presence like a cinder block dropped from a tower.

I blink, my head shaking with more vigor as I look between the two of them.

Fox's eyes narrow on my gaping expression as she turns to Dimitri. "We were talking about surnames and how Halira's family chose to keep her mother's, when—"

"The only druids who passed on maternal surnames were the Elders," I breathe, and no lighter nor heavier words have ever been spoken from my lips. They leave me dizzy. They leave me anchored. Confused and simultaneously comforted. For as long as there have been druids, Elders have been among them, a select few whose connections to the elements ran more fiercely than all the others. And we chose them as our leaders. Them and their daughters, and their daughters' daughters. "She's an Elder."

"What's that mean?" Dimitri growls, his patience wearing thin like the rest of the nervously agitated party. "Who's an Elder?"

"Halira," I answer, and already the realization is becoming easier to accept. More obvious.

The way Halira has wielded the wind—the way she can become it herself—the way she was able to tame me when I was a demon, goes far beyond the usual capabilities of a normal druid. I should've known. I wonder if Halira even knows.

Or the mages, for that matter.

A wave of icy dread ripples through me and my eyes meet Dimitri's. "We have to find her."

"Who?" he asks again, throwing his arms out at his sides.

"Halira!"

Fox takes a timid step forward, her hand patting my shoulder. "Uh, I hate to break it to you, but that's what we've been doing. Searching for her. And Alphonse."

I jerk away. "You don't understand. This changes everything."

"Then enlighten us." Dimitri leaps before me, grabbing me by the frayed tunic I'd donned at the first abandoned village we passed through. "Quit being vague, and just tell us!"

Glaring down at my shoulder, to the white knuckles clutching the worn cotton, I suppress an urge to shove him off me. Time is too precious now. Even more than it had been. Besides, Halira cares for this man, regardless of whether he deserves it or not.

Slowly, I reach up for his hand and gently pry it away. He steps back willingly, and only once I've composed myself, do I finally answer him. "Halira is a descendent of an Elder. Her magic is stronger than most druids. It's likely why she can summon storms without ever having training."

"Or disappear on the wind in the blink of an eye," Fox adds, a little uneasily.

"Yes."

Dimitri and Fox fall silent, as do the others as they huddle nearer, ears straining to overhear what's made us stop. When neither of Halira's betrayers speak, I clear my throat and elaborate.

"And the mages now have her." My gaze is the cold, unflinching strength of glaciers as it meets Dimitri's. "Think of what they could do with that kind of access to power. Access to her. Think of the war that could ensue if the druids discovered one of our Elders was taken hostage."

"Whatever wars you people fight have no impact on us," he replies, but there's no resolve in his tone. He's fishing. Or at least, he's setting me up to explain how dire the circumstances are to the others so that they might believe it. Only I have this kind of information. Not him. Not anyone else who didn't grow up in the Eyve.

My voice is deeper, more resonate when I speak again. "By

now, we should all know just how untrue that is. The humans and mages and Primordials and druids have been at war with each other for generations. Your people condemn their people who condemn ours, and the cycle continues. The very land we shared was ripped in two during the last war, a wall erected to sequester another section of the country before that.

"If the druids discover that one of their own—someone hailing from one of our most powerful bloodlines—has been kidnapped by the mages, there will be a war unlike anything else you've ever seen."

Sai snickers as he steps forward from the crowd. "Not to make you look the fool but, you do remember that all of us trained as Crusaders, right? We were taught how to defend the Shadowthorn border, to eviscerate demons. I don't think there's much we haven't seen, nor couldn't handle. Not that I'm arguing that we shouldn't do what we can to stop another war, but—"

"A war fueled by magic." I look him dead in the eyes, my voice a low roll of thunder that makes him shrink back. "A battleground of lightning and fire and earthquakes. My people would part the Varenholm Ocean just to cross the seafloor. And what do you think would happen to all that water we pushed aside? Where would that tidal wave go? Surely they couldn't aim for Illashore if that was where their rescue mission was headed."

Letting the severity of the statement settle, the cataclysmic picture I'm painting take root in the minds of the already disenfranchised and frightened Crusaders, I walk among them. A chill slithers down my spine as I realize that the picture I'm painting isn't one purely sculpted from fear. My people may be peaceful, but even in our own history, we've known war, and after being sequestered from the rest of the Broken Realms for so long and now finally having our freedom back, there is unrest. There is rage. Rightfully so. Even without the knowledge that the mages have stolen one of their own, I'm not convinced that druidkind is ready to live peacefully with the rest of the world just yet.

"They'd drag the earth with them," I continue, swallowing the stony lump in my throat. "They'd command all of your livestock to rally by their sides. They'd deplete your forests of all that is green, and ride to Illashore with a tumbling waterfall of vines and florae, leaving nothing in Arcathain.

"Your country would be left in ruin, even if the fight was taken abroad—and I'm not sure it would be.

"How many of you have actually seen war?" I ask the group of young faces. Few of them hardly have more than a wrinkle of worry etched into their skin. "How many of you know that even when the fighting occurs elsewhere, really it's the people who suffer? The famine. The grief and loss. The trauma."

"Spoken like a battle-hardened warrior," Dimitri says, eyeing me skeptically as he folds his arms. "You already convinced them to search for Halira. You don't have to keep warning them. They know what's at stake."

"No," I utter, twisting around so my dark eyes meet his. "No, they don't. It's not just the people of Arcathain at stake now. Nor is it just the druids. The mages can't be trusted with Halira in their grasp. But more than that, our entire realm is in danger if my people retaliate.

"We have to find Halira. For the sake of *all* existence."

COUNCIL

THE DUNGEONS, AEYSIL KEEP, ILLASHORE

can't take it anymore. If I have to spend another moment down here, I just might die of…

I'm not even sure what to call it. It's not boredom. Far from it. A person cannot feel bored while fearing that the blackness surrounding them could be encroaching with suffocating alacrity. Most days, I swear the darkness reaches for me like it possesses the hands of monsters, ready to bury me in nothingness so that when someone does finally return for me, I will already be gone.

More times than I can count, I struggle for air. My throat feels like it's closing, my chest collapsing. I gasp. I claw at my neck. And then I believe I lose consciousness, only to awaken to the same fears again.

In all the nights I spent inside the Shadowthorn, none of them were as suffocating and terrifying as the moments I spend here.

There's no telling how long Alphonse has been away. I only know that my lips have not yet quite cracked from dehydration, nor my ribs begun to protrude from my belly. I would guess he's only been gone for a few hours, though time has cascaded like an avalanche, seconds piling atop me like smothering snowballs.

At some point, I timidly make my way toward the metal door and press my ear upon it, but I hear nothing coming from outside. It is yet another terrifying reminder of my isolation, my burial here—wherever *here* may be—and again, I succumb to the cinching of my throat and chest until my eyes flutter shut.

The next time I come to, it's with a painful gasp. I shove myself off the stones, my straw-strewn hair falling around my face, and try desperately to get my bearings. As always any time I have awaken here, it takes me a moment to remember that my eyes will do no adjusting, and it's at that moment that the events of the earlier—I can't call it day or afternoon or evening since I have no concept of time—begin to unravel me anew.

Desperate not to lose the one sense I still have down here— my awareness, my consciousness—I press my palms against my eyes and begin to rock. The motion is jerking at first. It makes my head swim just about as much as it does to try to stand in utter blackness, the ground seemingly shifting beneath my feet and wrecking any chance I have at understanding up from down. But after a few moments, the rhythm of my swaying becomes soothing. My breathing settles back into my lungs. I stop feeling the darkness leaning in on me like heavy arms draped over my shoulders, and instead feel the air on my skin.

Not that I can call it air, I remind myself as I finally raise my head from my hands and dare to open my eyes. Air is something that's light and rejuvenating. The stuff trapped down here with me is anything but. My thoughts drift then to the crisp, winter mornings in Gravenburg, and how my breaths would fog from my lips even while I was still inside our cottage. What I wouldn't give to breathe in my mother's melting beeswax one last time, or the wooden, freshly polished scent of my father's arrows.

When the pang in my chest becomes too unbearable to endure, I force the hopeful meanderings of my mind away from the dead parents whom I will never encounter again, and instead to things that are actually attainable.

Breathing in the scent of burning wood as my friends and I sit around a bonfire and recount whatever memories occur to us.

A bottle of Sai's amber ale shoved under my nose and simultaneously tantalizing and repulsing me.

The saltwater of the Varenholm Ocean as I return to Arcathain on the Leviathan's back.

The verdant, aromatic trees of the vivacious Eyve.

Dare I say, I'd even look forward to breathing in the scent of sweat and blood as I buried my face in Dimitri's shoulder after battle.

And then, I think of Ryven.

Above all else, his is a scent I miss most. When the Blight finished off his humanity, it took with it the familiar, soothing aroma I'd grown to associate with him. The nights I'd spent with him on the Leviathan, trying to talk to him, to reassure him that everything was going to be alright, all I could smell was the sea around us, and the leathery scent of his wings. I've lost count of how many times I've thought about wrapping my arms around him—my hands grazing, not demon, but *human* flesh—and inhale him and the cedar forest in moonlight that he always smells of, that I've grown so accustomed to having by my side.

But that won't happen as long as he remains as he is.

And it certainly won't happen as long as I remain trapped here.

I can't allow it. I can't allow my last memories of him to be ones as devastating as watching him trapped in the body of a beast, tearing off into the night sky. I can't abide the thought of breaking my promise to find a way to return him to his human flesh.

A spark of determination ignites inside me. Alphonse might have been right before. We should conserve our energy and wait for the opportune moment to strike. But it doesn't mean we should just sit here and do nothing. In order to seize those opportunities with any chance of success, it'll be important to know every advantage we have on our side.

For the first time since the mages came and grabbed my cousin, I remember what Alphonse and I had been doing just before their interruption.

Scattering straw across the clammy, stone floor, I race to the edge of the dungeon. My hand reaches up toward the rafters or whatever lays above me there, and I only stop moving once the gentle waft of cool air caresses my fingertips again.

"Where are you coming from?" I whisper into the expansive nothingness, fingers coiling and sifting through the breeze as if it were a tangible thing, a string to be pulled on to unleash all of my greatest hopes.

Stretching to the tips of my toes, I reach higher into the black, the air getting cooler, crisper, the farther up my fingers stretch. I inhale the scent, a freshness imbued in the air pocket so profoundly that it makes my eyes tear. It becomes all too easy to imagine myself in the outside world again, racing through verdant forests, sailing the seas, soaring through the clouds with Ryven.

Fortified with hope, I rest on the balls of my feet once more, and grin. The smug mages might've said that this place was shut off to druid magic, but our magic is tied to the natural world. They can imprison us behind dead stones and stifling cement, they can shut off our senses to the animal kingdom, to the nurturing light of the sun, to the vivacity of the thriving forests, but not even the Great Mages of Illashore can silence all sources of nature. Not even they are powerful enough to inhibit the flow of elements as vital as air.

My hands float to my belly, to the core of my being and where I've always felt my magic most resides. Through my nose, I inhale the sweetly cool air, letting it fill my lungs, letting it anchor me to what I know to be true:

Air is vital.

Air is life and breath.

Air is magic.

My magic.

When I exhale, I imagine the breath coursing through my veins. It bursts from my belly down through my legs and up my arms. My skin tingles with anticipation of the power building beneath my skin—

But it doesn't build.

There is no magic. No static tickling my skin. No electric force of life bubbling inside of me to hurl out into the world.

The air I filled my lungs with is just as dead as the rest of the dusty atmosphere in this place. What I had felt was nothing more than false hope.

My eyes flick open to inky black. This can't be right. How is it that the mages could suffocate our power so thoroughly? Not just *our* power, but the natural world's. Nature is…it's everything. It's everywhere. Nothing should be able to exist without it.

What have I been breathing these past few days if not air—if not nature's breath of life?

Maybe this is why they never gave Alphonse or I food or water, to continue cutting us off from every part of nature. Perhaps there are druids that could use the fluid found in food to aid in their escape. I won't pretend to be imaginative enough to think of how exactly water could ever be used as a key or something, but I've seen the way my aunt can manipulate vines to create impenetrable structures that kept out behemoth demons from dusk until dawn. Druid magic is powerful. But the magic of the mages goes beyond my comprehension.

With nothing left to hope for, I meander back to my mound of straw, and wait for Alphonse to return.

The hours bulge and wither until the time I've spent confined in this musty dungeon feels infinite compared to any other portion of my life. It feels like I've been here longer than I was traveling through the Shadowthorn in search of a cure for being blighted. Longer than the months I spent training at Nigh. Longer than I've known Dimitri. Longer than my family had lived in Gravenburg.

It can't have been more than a day though, maybe two. Any longer and my body would've wasted away more. I reach my hand up the bottom of my bodice now to trace my fingers over my abdomen and see how much more of myself I've lost since the last time I checked. My skin feels heavy over my bones, like it's too big for my body. My ribs protrude far more than I ever remember them jutting from my body, even during the worst winters.

Before I can imagine myself as a shriveled up shell, I withdraw my hand and lean my head back against the stone wall.

I rest there for a long while, or maybe it's no time at all. Thinking and not thinking. Drifting in and out of consciousness.

In my moments of awareness, there are times when I forget that I ever knew what the sky looked like. Or the slightly wet sensation of dewy grass beneath my feet as Dimitri and I traipsed through the forest when we were children. Or that I used to be able to tell the difference from one of my mother's hives from another, purely based on how loud the bees inside would hum to each other.

On occasion, I'd even forgotten the way I'd imagined the leathery scent of Ryven if he ever would've enveloped me in his wings during the many nights we spent on the Leviathan.

Every time my thoughts snag on Ryven, I jolt upright. I convince myself to pace again, always, inevitably ending up back in the corner with the gentle, misleading breeze. As I stare up into the darkness, the breeze wafting the fine hairs across my forehead and around my neck, I think about how pathetic I must be. I could be dwelling on a number of things, thinking about any number of people—of family, friends, or the numerous innocents in Arcathain who need my help in stopping Qaeus—but it's always only Ryven who sparks me into action. Only my promise to him invigorates my conviction.

I reach back up into the blackness, but at the same moment, the metal door swings open.

I'm blinded once more by the harsh light, but this time my eyes don't have time to adjust before hands wrap around my forearms and begin pulling me forward.

"Hey!" I protest, my feet stumbling along, uncoordinated from my lack of sight as much as hunger. "What's happening? Where are you taking me?"

They drag me out of the dungeon where I'm met by a welcomed rush of warmth. I hadn't realized just how cold I'd become these past few days in the darkness, but the hallway they drag me through is well-heated and well-lit, thanks to the many torches I'm able to discern on the walls the more rapidly I blink and strain my sight.

I struggle to keep up with the pace my captors set, my feet stumbling over every bump in the stones and tripping over themselves at every sharp turn, but the mages keep their grasps firm as they lead me through the twisting hallways. Once my eyesight has cleared, I try focusing on getting my bearings. I keep a mental tally of how many corners we turn down, how many cell doors we pass, which ones are open and which ones appear to be filled, and anything else of note. It's not long before it becomes too much though. My head is too foggy from dehydration and hunger, my heart thumping too rapidly in my chest for me to be able to focus on anything but the swell of panic taking over me. I ask the mages on either side of me every question that comes to mind—where they're taking me, what will happen once I arrive, whether I can have food or water, who they are, what they want with me—but they provide no answers to anything.

Eventually, I stop asking. Even if they wanted to, I doubt they'd have answers to give me. Judging from their simple robes and the iron keys that jingle from one of their hips, it's obvious that they are of no great stature. Taking a page from Alphonse's playbook, I clamp my lips tight and decide to conserve my energy instead for whatever is to come.

Once we reach a flight of stone steps, they put a bag over my head. Or at least, that's the sensation that folds over me, a blanket of black dropping down before my eyes and shadowing the world back into darkness. But in reality, I feel no bag over my head, and I saw out of the corner of my eye one of the mages flick their hands in my direction.

I'm blindfolded by magic.

As they shove me up the stairs, I wonder how long a spell like this will last, and I hope to the gods that it's not permanent. Although, I suppose if I'll be trapped down in that void of a cell, what use would my sight be to me anyway?

They herd me along like a lost sheep for quite some time, guiding me through long corridors and vast rooms that echo with each of our footsteps, past ambling bystanders who mutter and whisper in our wake, until the arms latched to mine abruptly tug and I am pulled to a stop. Our final destination.

Relief floods through me when the veil of black falls, and

my sight returns to me as if it had never been taken. But dread is quick to twist back into my belly when I find myself amid the familiar surroundings of the great hall.

Most of the chairs seated around the long table are without occupants. The empty back supports seeming even taller without anyone to fill the space, the table appearing even longer, endless, like a hopeless, never-ending desert of polished oak and cutlery. But there is one mage left in the room as the guards toss me to my knees and leave.

My eyes trail down the smooth surface to the end of the table to find the Head Mage Varyn slouched in his chair at the end. His bottomless eyes are soul-piercing as they watch me. I can neither look away, nor do I want to. I don't want him to know how hopeless I already am, how broken the time in the dungeon has made me.

I set my jaw to a hard line and fight through the burning of my dry throat to demand, "Where is Alphonse?"

In silence, Varyn watches me, his eyes narrowed in the way that powerful men often do to intimidate those beneath them. It's how Alphonse would address his Crusaders before our thrice daily training sessions. It's the same way my uncle Esmond would look down upon my father, as if not even his own brother deserved to be in the same room as him.

I feel myself shrinking further. I tell myself it's just from the glaring light that beams in through the stained-glass windows, but even I can admit that I'm no longer squinting from such subtle lighting. My thoughts are a cyclone of everything I've feared over the last few hours—the last few days—and they tear into me until I'm near oblivion. Alphonse must be dead. They tormented him and toyed with him, like demented cats playing with their food until he had nothing left to give, and now I've been brought up for their entertainment. The only good thing that will come of my death is that I won't have to be the one to break the news to Fox, to Eparah, and to any other of Alphonse's loyal Crusaders.

But just as tears begin to sting my eyes, I realize there is no audience for my suffering. It is only Varyn. He could've left either of us in that dungeon to rot. He could've executed us on the spot when we'd first arrived. But instead, he had his scout, the mage Igemonar, bring us here.

It is all the reassurance I need that we have yet to outgrow our usefulness.

My back straightens and I bite down on the searing lump of hot coal in my throat. "What did you do with Alphonse?" I ask again, my voice steeling to stone. "Tell me, or—or I'll say nothing more."

Varyn leans forward, fingers steepling atop the table. His bushy eyebrows make him appear wild. Feral. "Bold statement for someone in your predicament. What makes you assume I require anything from you but silence?"

My fists tighten, nails digging deep into my palms. "If you needed my silence, you would've left me in that cell. Instead, you brought me here, didn't you?"

"Yes," he says after a long pause. Something dark crosses his features, but it's gone before I can put my finger on it. The sinister nature of it, however, remains in his tone. "*I* did."

Ice crystallizes in my veins. I stagger backward.

"Just as *I* summoned your friend," Varyn continues. "You'll soon learn that what I decide, what I declare, is revered as law. If your presence were to suddenly prove useless, if your existence became impractical to the way I conduct my affairs, rest assured that being kept in your cell would be the least of your concerns."

"Okay," I say warily, swallowing the scalding coal that's lodged in the back up my throat. "That settles it then: I do not want to die, for obvious reasons, and therefore I do not wish to prove myself useless. You need me for…something. Just tell me what it is you need from us."

"*Us.*" His thick brow arches, the word spoken more as a statement than anything. "I'm afraid it's only you I'm interested in now." As if he can read my thoughts through the worrying wrinkles in my brow, he answers my unspoken question. "Alphonse provided me with what I required of him already. Or at least, a version of it. Now I need yours."

I hardly hear everything he says. I'm too focused on the first part. *Alphonse gave me what I needed,* as in he's already spent his worth. Varyn has already made it clear what happens to those who prove they're no longer of use to him. Suddenly my concerns about Alphonse grip me with renewed force.

"Where is my cousin?" I splutter, only faintly aware that I've just given him personal information that could be used against either of us. But I don't care. All that matters is finding Alphonse so that the two of us can get out of here. "What have you done with him?"

"Only the same treatment I have in store for you, Crusader Devonshire."

I should be focusing on the ominous tone of his threat, but instead my nose scrunches, his use of my former title catching me off guard. "I-I'm no Crusader. Not anymore."

One of his hands lifts, gesturing up and down my body. "My memory of Arcathainian garb might be outdated, but are you not donned in the necro-ink-black Crusader uniform?"

Glancing down at myself, the dark leathers I received during my first night at Nigh glare up at me. They are a reminder of everything I fought for, everything I lost, and the life I'm still fighting for, even though it can no longer be mine. They are long overdue for a good wash after the Blight I've put them through, but on most days, I hardly notice them. This uniform has become a part of me, even after I was shunned by my own country. Or perhaps it's just a part of me that I still have yet to be able to let go of. Sure, the journey here has been long and arduous, and I've hardly had a chance to catch my breath between battling demons, escaping Primordials, and beckoning a Leviathan to take me to a foreign place full of terrifying magic that fueled my childhood nightmares, but surely, I had at least a few moments where I could've discarded these leathers in exchange for something else. Why am I still wearing the uniform of a Crusader if I truly believe I no longer am one?

"I completed the training, but when our people discovered I had magic—that I was a druid—they exiled me." The truth escapes my lips before I can think better of it or decide whether I want to share it.

Varyn keeps his steady, scrutinizing gaze on mine as he inches back into his chair. "But the people remain unaware of druids, even now. Correct?"

Eagerly, I nod. But then I realize I'm giving away too much, too freely. My expression hardens. "Why are you so interested in what the Arcathainians do or do not know about us?"

"I'm interested in many things," he drawls. "Like how it is that two druids and a dozen Crusaders found themselves on the shores of *my* land, a country protected by magic so raw and powerful that it was meant to be impenetrable?" At the mention of our lost friends, panic tears through me anew and my jaw snaps open, but he silences me with his glazed, soul-piercing eyes. "I would advise you suffuse your tongue with truth, and truth alone in my presence."

With my mouth still hanging wide, I consider the options. Truth or not, I need his focus to remain on me, not the others. Until now, the mages have only appeared to be interested in Alphonse and I anyway. I need it to stay that way. I need to bide my friends time to find the answers they seek, or at least to flee the island before the mages return for them next.

"They were also exiles," I lie. "They were strangers, sailors familiar with the Varenholm Ocean who offered to guide us here. Nothing more."

Without warning, a bolt of pain spears through me. As if I've been speared through the back, the sheer force of it throws me forward, my elbows and wrists the only things even remotely quick enough to catch my fall.

My teeth clamp tight as the raw agony bursts through me like wildfire. The blaze burns away all of my senses, until all I have left is the smoky haze of my own suffering to occupy me. My screams don't sound like they belong to me at first, but to the people I witnessed dying in Gravenburg the night of the demon scourge. My tears are just as hot as the lancing pain.

And then, abruptly, it stops.

In its absence, I'm not even sure what is left of me. I am nothing but hollow and raw, my insides still simmering from the pain that had blazed through them.

My cheek, wet from tears and sweat, is pressed to the ground, the granite floor soothingly cold beneath me. I don't bother moving. I'd rather lie here for hours, letting my body— my very soul—piece itself back together while the rest of the world goes on without me.

But across the room, a chair scrapes against the granite, drawing my attention away from my misery as Varyn rises.

"Perhaps the next time you are given a warning, you will heed it."

At his condescending tone and cold address of me, my temper flares. I reach for the simmering fire that had just moments earlier been blazing inside me, my shaking fingers curling around its fiery neck. Claiming it. Taming the flames to be used at my own bidding.

"There was no ship," he says abruptly, states it so plainly that my roiling anger settles. "Seasoned sailors—a crew of them—would have a ship. And yet, none was found where you landed. How were you transported here?"

Wiping the wetness from my face, I stand. My legs threaten to give out beneath me, but by fortified resolve alone I force them to remain in place. "Magic," I sneer. Then, remembering the flare of pain that lashed out at me the last time I lied to him, I add hastily, "Or something like it."

Varyn runs a hand down the wiry patch of hair dangling from his chin. "Yes. Something like it."

He draws nearer, the hem of his robes heavy as it drags across the granite until he stops just before me. For someone so old, he still stands taller than I'd expect, and up this close, I can just barely make out gray designs swirling throughout his sallow skin. The longer I stare, the more I can swear that they're moving, pulsing as if they are nearly translucent veins. As curious as I am about them, what purpose they serve and how he got them, I can't bring myself to ask.

Varyn reaches with one withered hand and, before I can jerk away, he takes mine into his own.

"Let us try this again," he begins, his tone just as chilling as the finger he strokes on the back of my hand. "You did not come here by ship. Nor are your people—let alone just the two of you—capable of traveling across the Varenholm Ocean by magic."

"Your people did it," I snap, jerking my hand away. The history of the Broken Realms and the destruction of Arcathain —of my homeland—screams in my mind. "You used your magic to cross the Varenholm, dragging an entirely new continent in your wake. Why couldn't the druids do the same?"

His nose twitches, a flicker of distaste souring his expression as he folds his arms back against his stomach. "For a prisoner, you sure demand a lot without offering anything in return."

An incredulous breath escapes me. "Why would I offer you anything? You've already taken more than your fair share. You kidnapped me and my cousin. You've stolen our freedom.

You've done nothing to prove that you mean us anything but harm, nor have you given us any reason to believe that cooperating with you will benefit us in any way."

Without realizing I've done it, I've cut across what little space remained between us. The tips of my boots step atop the bundle of robes that have pooled at his feet. The proximity between us forces our gazes to meet like swords clashing in the Shadowthorn, and I swear I see surprise flash behind his dulled, lifeless eyes ever so slightly. How rare it must be for someone of my lowly status to stand tall before him. But I refuse to cower in his presence.

"Your people—the mages," I continue, my blood hot beneath my skin. "They have done nothing but take from us for years. For decades! You stole my father's homeland. The Great Rift cost my father and countless others their parents, their children, their wives, and brothers, and so much more. And the mages just fled with Arcathainian livelihoods across the ocean as if they belonged to you. As if you hadn't just wrecked hundreds of lives and condemned generations to poverty and struggle and fear.

"So, you're right, Head Mage Varyn Ephemeris. I do demand a lot, and I give even less because my people have given you enough already, and now it's our turn to receive something from you in return. Tell us how to defeat the Primordial, and we will go."

The room falls silent aside from my heaving breaths. Varyn does not speak. He hardly blinks or breathes as his cold, unrelenting gaze pierces mine. But I refuse to show my discomfort. I remain firm in my stance, my spine ramrod straight, and my gaze never once drifting away from his. Not until he gives me the answers I've come here to find. Not before he rights the wrongs that his people have done to mine.

Finally, he moves, tugging at his robes and yanking them from under my boots. Caught off guard by his bluster, I stumble backward. Once again, I'm surprised by how much this show of strength contradicts the image of the frail, ancient man before me. I'm quickly learning that Head Mage Varyn is not someone to underestimate. There is power inside him, a dark kind that channels through him and makes him capable of things that no man his age should be capable of.

"I will ask you again, as I asked your cousin," Varyn says softly, turning away from me and starting back for his chair. "How is it that two mere druids were able to break through our barrier? According to our scout, neither of you show much skill with your magic. You're novices. Do you deny it?"

My nostrils flare with the urge to tell him he's wrong. But my insides are still tender enough from the jolt of magic at my last lie, that I refrain. I shake my head at him and the corners of his mouth twitch upward.

"Very good. So tell me: how?"

Biting down on my strangled groan, I realize I just want this nightmare to end. I want to return to my friends in the forest. I want to find Ryven and help return him to his true form. I want to return to my homeland—whether that be Arcathain or the Eyve—and find it in a time of peace instead of unrest.

It's apparent that my show of bravado hasn't granted me any stride with Varyn. He is just as stubborn as Kalli when she's on the hunt for information. Cooperating with the Head Mage just might be my only way forward. With a man like him, I should've known it from the beginning. I've dealt with his kind before.

Dipping my head in a show of submission, I channel the small and frightened child I used to be. The one who was always too afraid to stand up to Alphonse and instead wanted to appease him, even at the cost of my own self-worth. The child who would stammer and say "yes sir" any time my uncle Esmond appeared in a room, menacing cloak billowing behind him. The child who meekly accepted any scolding Dimitri ever gave me whenever I'd sneak away from my duties at home or utter a disrespectful sneer toward anyone who had authority over us.

For a brief moment, I allow myself to forget the resilient, determined woman I've become who has learned never to back down from her bullies, whether they be human or demon. I take solace in the knowledge that that woman will still be waiting for me once I make it out of this. But for once, I have to think like my sister. I have to treat this predicament like a strategic game of chess. And so, for now, that means I have a role to play.

Clearing my throat, I begin to tell the Head Mage Varyn just about everything that happened during our journey across the Varenholm Ocean.

Everything except the demon-man who traveled with us. Everything except Ryven.

"We're getting close," I say to Dimitri, peeking over his shoulder at the worn map that's splayed open in his rough hands. Reaching across him, I jab a finger at one of the scribbled lines. "That stream is just on the other side of this field. We must be getting close because the gnats and mosquitos are getting worse."

He jerks the parchment away, quickly folding it before shoving it back into the pocket on the breast of his black tunic, right beneath his white phoenix sigil. "I know how to read a map. And I know what gnats and mosquitos mean about our proximity to water." Dimitri clears his throat before addressing the rest of the group who are spread out behind us. "We should find a place to rest for now, and plan to travel throughout the night. It's less than a half day's journey from here, and we'll be harder to detect under the cover of darkness."

A gush of air breezes past Fox's lips and tussles the shortened, garnet locks dangling over her eyes from where she's bent, relacing her boots. She looks up, a mocking glint edging her expression. "I hate to break it to you, Dimitri, but this field you have us traipsing through isn't exactly the ideal spot for staying out of sight. If you had just listened to me and kept along the tree line—"

"Then we would've wound up hiking through mountains, taking us who knows how much longer to reach Halira. Alphonse too," he adds quietly, undoubtedly as a second thought. A vein bulges, slithering down his throat, another coiling tightly around his temple and threatening to spring and attack should anyone argue against him. "And I'm sure I don't need to remind you what could happen the longer it takes us to find them. Every second they spend imprisoned by the mages—"

"Is a second they will survive," Fox growls, finishing with her laces and whipping up to face him. Her pale skin is as bright as blooming poppies in spring, both beautiful and deadly. Even I recoil from the venomous glare she casts him. "Alphonse is strong. So is Halira—maybe even more than our general. They are druids, Dimitri. They have magic to protect them from whatever horrors the mages might possess. They know how to—how to survive." Her eyes flutter then, her lips drawing into a thin line, as she repeats to herself, "I'm sure they will survive…" It takes her a moment to return to us, to flee the dark *what ifs* that have infested her mind, as well as Dimitri's and mine. Those *what ifs* have cost each of us many nights of sleep, wondering the suffering our loved ones might be enduring.

When Fox finally returns to reality, she stands tall, wincing only slightly at a discomfort in her boot. After weeks at sea, where everyone's shoes spent at least a few nights water-logged and full of sand, and then trekking through woods and across country, her shoes aren't the only ones in need of repair.

"They have magic," she continues, resituating her balance to her other hip. "Which is more than we can say for ourselves. If we're found by the mages, we're as good as dead. Worse, we'll be of no use to Alphonse and Halira. The cover of the forest would've protected us—"

"Like it protected us then?"

Fox is stunned into abashed silence for only a moment. "At least now we know what we're up against. The mountains would've offered us shelter and, at times, advantage points. We might as well be lambs bleating inside a wolf den by wandering these fields—"

"It doesn't matter now," I cut in, exasperated by their bickering.

It's been like this with them for days. Weeks, if I include the voyage across the Varenholm Ocean. If the two of them fall within two feet of each other, it's like they can't help but glare, and taunt, and ridicule, and push one another to the brink of wanting to throttle each other's throats. And I get the distinct impression that they've been like this for months even before I met them.

But arguing serves us no purpose. Not here, and not now.

"We already skirted the mountain range, and we're here now. We make do with the coverage we can find."

Inhaling the tall, dry reeds, I steel myself to the onslaught of disagreement that I'm sure will follow. If Dimitri and Fox bicker every chance they get, the Crusaders I'm traveling with are ten times worse.

However, no protest comes. Perhaps it's because they're exhausted too. Or frightened. Or maybe, just maybe, I'm beginning to earn their trust, and the future that Ahl'Ro and I set out to create is unfolding before me without me even realizing it.

After an uncomfortably long pause, with every eye still trained on me, I glance out over the field. It's a large, open space, brimming with wheat tall enough to crouch behind while remaining unseen. But the thing about grass like this is it's often brittle. A deer trots a lush meadow, and the path it takes is visible for a few hours by the matted grass, but eventually the verdant blades perk back up. To amble through a dry area like this, the weak stems would break from every reed we passed. Our path would be a flattened beacon behind us, and if the mages have any aerial view at all, they'll be able to spot exactly where we were by following where we've been.

As I look across the flaxen field, I spy a few areas that might be able to conceal us. A hundred-year-old willow tree. A large and grassy rock. And even the beach itself isn't too far from us now, the tumbling waves peeking into view just where the field meets the sandy shore.

With the slow return of my magic, I know I can't summon a weave of wheat to conceal us while we rest here, nor constantly beckon the winds to shield our scent, but I think I might be able to muster enough power to revitalize the paths we take to reach our more secured locations.

"It might be best to separate into smaller groups," I tell them at last. "So as not to draw attention to a larger camp."

The accusations I evaded earlier come pouring from their lips like blood sprayed on the battlefield. Most of them, I expected. Hatred is ingrained in a bloodline, and Arcathainians were raised to believe that all mages are evil, all demons are too, and I represent both to them, regardless that I am neither.

Shocking me, however, is the distrustful spew from Dimitri.

"No way are we splitting up. We've traveled this far together, and we will continue to do so."

I shouldn't be surprised by him, then again, I'm not sure that's the thing that's caught me off guard. There has been tension between us from the start, sure. But the moment Halira's life was in danger, and the moment we both agreed to save her, there's been an unspoken truce between us. Dimitri doesn't have to trust *me*, but he's always backed my decisions to keep the group safe because I think he realizes just how much his sway over the others means.

Perhaps this suggestion pushed his comfort too far. If I

were in his shoes, with a former demon suggesting we break the already disadvantaged group into smaller, more disadvantaged groups, I guess I'd be hesitant too. I am. I awaken every night, trembling from a nightmare that felt all too real, my hands grasping at my shoulder blades and my head for any signs of the demon I still fear is inside me. It takes me hours to convince myself that the wings are gone, so are the horns, and so is the blighted blood that contorted me into the creature I became.

But even my reassurances aren't enough. The only thought that gets me through those moments is the idea that I will see Halira again.

It's all that gets me through these moments, as well.

Taking a shaky breath, I remind myself that, despite my frustration with his ill-timed bravado, Dimitri is still the key to saving Halira, because he is the key to convincing the group to oblige me.

"I am not suggesting that we travel separately from here out, nor that anyone stray too far from one another. If any of us were spotted and attacked, we would want those remaining to be close enough to come to our aid, should we need it. But it would be foolish to rest as a large group in this field. We would be easily noticeable, and my magic cannot conceal us."

Dimitri's mouth twists open in a sneer, but Fox smacks his chest with the back of her hand.

"Let the man speak, already," she grumbles. "It doesn't hurt to hear all of our options."

Dimitri flicks her hand away. "Fine. What is it you're suggesting?"

"That we break into smaller groups," I answer swiftly, leaving no room for someone else to interject. "There are a few places that could be safe enough for three or four of us to rest, no more. The willow tree over there," I say, pointing across the swaying blades of flaxen grass to the first landmark. "That boulder." Once they've seen both, finally, I swing east. "And another group to head to the beach. All of us will be within earshot—"

Güthric's groan is raspy, not unlike usual. Of all those around me though, I expected protest from him the least. He has always seemed indifferent about me and my kind, and I know he is loyal to Halira. Not to mention, in the short time I've known him, I've learned that he is a man of few words.

But for that reason, the few words he wants to speak will hold weight.

"What is it?" Dimitri asks him, the eagerness of his tone infuriating. He'd like nothing more than to see everyone here turn against me. Perhaps then he'd feel less inferior about Halira's refusal of him.

"Sea, loud," Güthric replies with the voice of a slumbering bear. "Not hear others."

Adrien's expression is one of dawning worry. "He's right. Anyone sent to the shore won't be able to hear much of anything beyond the roaring ocean, and maybe the odd seagull squawk, or two."

"They could risk being ambushed themselves," Sai offers, just as frantic.

When we'd first brought Sai back to the camp, I was certain he would suffer the same fate as Ahl'Ro and I. *Tossed like a drunken wench around the bar,* was how he'd described his encounter with the behemoth creature in Ashenvale. *"Only much more painful, and not nearly enough grog to make it any fun."* But when we'd checked the Crusader for wounds—serrated teeth marks and flesh-tearing scratches—the entire encampment was surprised to hear that we'd found none. Utterly unscathed—aside from a minor concussion.

Without blighted blood coursing through him, Sai had been yet another of the numerous folk who were unable to understand me. And yet, I always felt a certain kind of unspoken connection between the two of us. It might've been because we were both considered new to the Wardens, I only having arrived a few months prior. Or maybe there was a sort of loyalty that developed because I was the one who carried him all the way from Ashenvale to the Warden's camp. Or, I suspect, it has simply always been that we remind each other of ourselves, that we see the grief of losing a brother reflected in one another's shadowed eyes, and with only a silent nod, can express more to each other than anyone ever could with the use of their tongue.

As our gazes cross now, I feel as if I'm looking upon a stranger. Nothing but fear stares back at me from his hollowed-out eyes, a distrust that never even existed back when we were living in the Shadowthorn.

"That's probably what he wants," Eparah sneers. "To get us alone."

I'm eager to turn my attention away from the burning ache in my chest at the suspected loss of yet another friendship to her. Until, that is, that I notice her twitchy, defensive stance. One of her hands rests atop a sheathed sword at her waist, her coppery skin pale on every clenched knuckle.

"We'll be easier to pick off that way," she explains, and my blood runs hot.

Like a weakened gazelle gazing in the grass, I sense the predators circling around me.

Half of the group jeers their agreement, and this time, Dimitri doesn't stand up for me. His gaze is wary as it flicks to mine, as if he's seeing me in a new light—rather, as if he's finally allowing himself to behave the way he's always wanted to toward me. In his eyes, I have always been a monster capable of slaughtering them, and he is a monster slayer.

The hairs on the back of my neck rise, and I stagger a step backward. The pack of Crusaders glide forward in time with me—all but Silver who's back is turned to us as she crouches down and disappears beneath the reeds. I don't have the time to wonder what she's doing or what's caught her attention, because the deranged eyes fixed on me have my blood pumping. It's the kind of mania I'd only associate with murderers and demons, and despite having known the hatred and distrust these people have held in their hearts for me, never before has it been quite this...palpable.

I know something isn't right, but the doubt that's always waiting, heavy in the back of my skull, drags its black talons across my thoughts. Dimitri is right to fear me. Maybe they all are. With Halira, the Blight had been different. She was cured before it submerged her completely into darkness. But me? That wicked corruption pierced my very heart, slamming me into oblivion while it ravaged my body—my very being—and unleashed me upon the world as one of the creatures who haunts fairytales.

It didn't just tuck me away; it consumed me. It *was* me.

Maybe the demon inside me still exists, only now it's wrapped in a pretty fleshy box tied with a bow. I can't say for certain that it's gone. For all I know, the monster inside me is so cunning that even I am not aware of it, and as soon as it gets the chance, it will want to taste blood again, the way it had wanted to when it had seen Inigo's corpse drifting out at sea—when *I* had seen Inigo's corpse.

They would be fools to trust me.

I would be a fool to trust myself.

I should run.

I should run before they can free their blades, or better yet, before my claws grow back—

"It's the mayhem weeds," comes a soft, lilting voice from behind the mob. We all twist to find Silver emerging from the tall grass, her onyx hair stark against the pale straw color surrounding her.

It takes me a moment to register her words, but even then, the meaning eludes me. "What about the weeds?"

"Piss on a mage!" Fox grumbles, head thrown back. "I hate this crafty place. Of course there's mayhem weed here, and of course we stumbled upon it."

"What's mayhem weed?" I ask again, though, judging from the name and the way things have been the last few minutes, I have a few suspicions.

"A plant that causes paranoia," Silver answers helpfully. Still facing away from us, she points back the way we came, along the now-trampled path of golden grass. Something like shimmering dust settles over the flattened blades that lie there. "We stormed through an entire patch of it and have been inhaling the spores ever since."

It takes me a moment to rid my face of the look of shock that smacks against it. Knowledge of plants is an area I pride myself on, and it's very rare I learn of one that I don't already know about, let alone from an Arcathainian. I suppose there's an entire continent of herbs and medicinal plants and trees and nature for me to uncover now though, now that the Shadowthorn has dissipated.

With the new information, even the Crusaders consider her. I'm further surprised by the lack of confusion or argument, as if they were all aware of such a weed. Perhaps they'd been taught about mayhem weeds as they trained alongside other Crusaders, or maybe the plant is so common that's it's well-known among the populace.

However, still gripped by paranoia, it seems difficult for them to reassess their stance on how our group should proceed.

Surprising me, yet again, Dimitri is the first to show any successful signs of shifting away from negativity.

"That's why we've been arguing instead of working together," he says, voice low and with more than a modicum of regret.

Hopefully he's realizing just how much time we've wasted standing here. He's quick to steel himself with his usual sense of duty and dignity. "We can't stay in the field. The beach is our only option."

"You can't be serious—" Eparah begins, but she is swiftly silenced by Dimitri's fierce and hardened gaze.

"We can't trust anyone's judgment as long as we're in the vicinity of the mayhem weed. We have to leave, now. We can discuss our options later."

There's no arguing with the man, nor his valid reasoning. And so, Dimitri leads us east with his nose crammed into the crook of his arm as he trudges through the last stretch of the unkempt field. We follow the gentle roar of the unresting sea until the crunch of the dry grass beneath our feet gives way to a soft padding of sand. The field around us shortens, wildflowers ruling this particular edge of the coastline and making it difficult for the grass to grow with such fullness.

Just as we crest over the meadow and the ocean begins to peek into view, my attention is drawn to the large, black bird soaring in the distance. It's too far away to discern it, but my first thought is of Kalli. Days ago, we sent her raven back to her, and we've been eyeing the sky ever since, wondering if and when the creature would reach her.

When I spy the ships, I know my answer.

An impressive fleet—at least fifty, maybe sixty ships that glisten like pearls—drift in from the sea. Most keep their distance, anchoring a safe way off the shoreline to allow rowboats of men to descend upon Illashore. Towering high above each of the vessels, a single banner whips about, the varying colors likely noting which city or general the ships belong to. But they all bear the same crest: a white bird of fire. Every single one of them is an Arcathainian ship.

Growing up in the Eyve, and largely unfamiliar with the politics of the mainland, I never knew that Arcathain had such a massive fleet. It's hard to fathom what it's even for. There's rumors that there once was a time when there was more to the world than the small continents of the Broken Realms, but I've heard none of the Crusaders I've encountered speak of other countries.

It's possible the Arcathainian armada was built solely for this moment, for the day they finally infiltrated Illashore.

The Crusaders around me breathe a collective sigh of relief. Just seeing their banners must be like feeling like they're back at home, safely reunited with their people.

But my stomach lurches. While everyone else marvels and grins at the fleet before us, my eyes fix on the raven circling above, and the ship with a golden banner beneath it.

Before anyone else can charge forth, I grab our Dimitri's tunic and jerk him backward, taking us both down to the ground with a grunt, and startling the others enough that they pause and crouch with us. The effects of the mayhem weed are already wearing off.

"What is wrong with you?" Dimitri growls, twisting and scrambling to pull himself out of my grasp.

But I hold firm, my bicep bulging as I jerk him nearer. "Is it really wise of us to charge ahead so hastily?"

"They're Arcathainians!" he balks. "They're our allies!"

"They *were* your allies," I retort, and seeing the look of confusion twist into his anger, I finally release the collar of his tunic. "You entered the Shadowthorn to retrieve your Magistrate's son, but then you never returned. They'll label you a deserter, at best." Glancing to the sky, I nod at the black bird that's still gliding around and around the one boat, noticing—not for the first time—how much distance it's keeping from the ship and how it has still never dived down or landed. "Kalli must be with them, but we don't know how it went when she delivered the message. Once they discovered you were traveling among fugitives on a rogue mission to infiltrate Illashore, they might've deemed you enemies like the mages."

Whispers of concern ripple behind me, but Dimitri's scowl is set.

"Of one country, of one blood," he growls, glancing to the rest of the group with contempt. "Our brothers and sisters have not abandoned us, nor would the Magistrate. He will hear us, and we will explain the circumstances that lead us here."

My eyes all but roll to the back of my skull. Frustration simmers in my throat like a low growl, but the sensation is so animalistic, so terrifyingly close to the wicked gurgles of the demon I had become, that I blink away all traces of annoyance. Dimitri simply believes in his country. That is no crime, nor is it worth me losing control and giving these people any more reason to distrust me. I cannot afford to let my emotions rule me. Such primal, human reactions are too risky.

With a subtle inhale and exhale, I clear away the tension in my shoulders, and try again. "You know your people and your country better than I ever will. So I can understand your reluctance to trust me on this. But I have a bad feeling." A sound of impatience skirts past Dimitri's lips, but I dig deeper. I have to make him understand. "Kalli's raven," I say plainly.

The sage hue of his eyes sparks like wildfire as his gaze snaps to mine. "What about her raven?"

"When did you ever see her without it?"

His forehead crinkles, but when he can't make out where I'm taking this, reluctantly he answers, "Only when she'd send it off with a message. Why?"

From where we're crouched, one of my arms now propped on my knee, I flick my finger up to where Kalli's black raven still circles the clouds. "Because her bird has not landed once since we've been here. It hasn't left with a message and it's not returning with one."

His frown deepens as he and the rest of our group watches

the bird in silence, the churning waves ahead of us almost deafening now.

"We should watch them," I say, breaking the silence at last. "See if Kalli's raven ever goes down to her, or if we can overhear anything suspicious."

"Kalli sent for them," Dimitri says, but rather than his usual argumentative tone, he sounds more like he's rationalizing, trying to better understand.

"I know. But for all we know, they've received Kalli's intel and the only reason they're here isn't to negotiate, but to strike."

He considers what I've said for a moment, gaze flicking between the tall wildflowers to the ships we can barely glimpse beyond. It's not long before he's shaking his head.

"No. We don't have the luxury of waiting." Dimitri springs to his feet before I have the chance to stop him. "Halira is in danger. You might be willing to postpone her rescue, but I, for one, am not."

A bluster of bravado, Dimitri charges forth, a cordial welcome carrying through the air as he waves to the soldiers awaiting him. Without much hesitation, most of the others follow suit, Eparah casting a glare my way as she passes. Few remain squatting though. Güthric. Silver. Adrien. Sai.

Even Fox stays where she's crouched, though judging from the way she's biting the inside of her lip, I'm not sure how long we can rely on her.

"I didn't know Kalli well," Fox says, but then cuts herself off with a snort. "Okay, I didn't know her at all. But Halira spoke of her often, and about that blighted bird that seemed to follow her as if it were part of her shadow. If what you're saying is true—" Another guttural sound climbs up her throat as she clutches her forehead and shakes her head. "Piss on a mage! Gods know I want to help Alphonse and Halira, and if the Magistrate and his army are here, they might be able to aid in their rescue. But if Dimitri is wrong...I—We can't risk it."

I dip my head to try to see the eyes she's still shielding. "What are you saying?"

Her hand falls and Fox looses a huff of air at the hair cropped around her face. "I'm saying that I'd like to stay behind and observe. I think it's the right thing to do."

I nod to her before twisting around to address the others. No sooner than I'm focused on them, does Adrien speak.

"I believe we're all here for the same reason. We can't all walk into the belly of the beast." With a wink, he adds, "Especially not those of us who are known fugitives, and well, I'd say that's just about all of us present."

My head bobs again, but it's not the only appreciation I can give them. "Thank you. Both for your allegiance, your faith in me, and for doing what's best for Halira. If the Magistrate and his fleet are friendly, I will return to you in the hour."

A crack forms in Silver's usually emotionless expression. "You plan to go with them?"

"It was your idea!" Fox protests.

"It was. And if the others had listened, I would've stayed here with you. It's the wiser option than charging in headfirst without any intel. But if Kalli told your people anything, then she likely would've mentioned what happened to Halira and possibly me. They will expect to see the demon-druid, or at least the man who had been one."

No one tries convincing me otherwise. By now, I think we all know human nature better than we would like to.

"So," I continue, glancing through the tall grass. The others are finally free of the meadow, a small crew of Crusaders, or some other kind of soldier, charging toward them dutifully. "I will join Dimitri and the others while you stay here. Keep a close watch. Remain hidden. And I will return once I know their intentions."

I start to move forward, but a firm hand lands on my shoulder. Adrien holds me back.

"Be careful," he warns. "You are right to doubt the intentions of my brother. He is motivated by his own personal gain. Nothing more. If you are not part of his solution, you are the problem. And with you having magic—"

"I know." My hand claps on top of his and my thoughts briefly flick to Ahl'Ro. "But my people have lived in the shadows long enough. Today your Magistrate will meet the monster he's been told to fear. Hopefully he'll discover that I'm no different from any man."

THE ARCATHAINIAN ARMADA

UNKNOWN BEACH, ILLASHORE

My heart thuds against my ribcage like a riled and rioting ram as I emerge from the tall grass and stand in view of the Magistrate's fleet. At first, they don't notice me, too distracted by Dimitri's and the rest of our group's sudden arrival, and confused to recognize the black leathers and—in some cases—the renowned sigils that mark the soldiers of the Shadow Crusade so far from their homeland.

With his hands still held high, Dimitri looks over his shoulder, drawing the attention of the Magistrate's men upon me. The swords and lances they'd let sink in the air amid the confusion, straighten until their aimed for my chest. Four break away from the rest, flanking me, two on either side.

"He's with us," Dimitri growls, a warning edging his tone.

But they heed him none. Halira and Dimitri only joined the Shadow Crusade a few months ago, which means there's no way he holds rank.

Instead, he shoots a glare at Eparah, who has been largely ignored thanks to the sigil on her chest that notes her high rank. As the warriors close in on me, begrudgingly, she rolls her eyes.

"Lower your weapons," she says with a sigh, one hand tossing the dark, thick locks away from her shoulder.

The soldiers hesitate though. Anyone would. For the first time since the Great Rift, they are stepping foot on soil that had belonged to their ancestors, a part of their country and heritage that the mages stole from them long ago. The overwhelming sense of fear and adrenaline that must be pumping through them is exactly how I felt when I first left the Eyve. Our homeland had been surrounded by the Shadowthorn and the demons that prowled it for decades, we'd heard nightmarish stories of the seething hatred Arcathainians held for *all* magic-users, and neither Ahl'Ro, nor I, knew where we were going, only that whatever laid ahead was something that would be written in history.

One of the soldiers drags his distrusting gaze up and down the length of me, his eyes snagging on the strange, burlap clothes we snagged.

He turns a dubious expression back at Eparah. "I-I'm sorry, Captain. I'm afraid we can't lower our weapons. Our orders are to capture any locals we encounter, so that they can be taken to the Magistrate and—"

"He's no local," Eparah snaps, glaring at the man so fiercely that he's forced to look away. She gestures to me. "He's with us. Why else would he be here?"

"Y-you could be under a spell that's forced you to say as such. But he didn't arrive with you. He just emerged from the bushes, long after the rest of you." This warrants another glare from Dimitri, as if to scold me for not following sooner. "His clothes aren't even…they're not Arcathainian."

Dimitri's hands fall down from the sky to his sides with a resounding clap. "That's because we were attacked shortly after we landed, and this man's clothes were destroyed. We did our best to find him new ones—" he leans over, pretending to whisper to one of the guards, though we can all still hear him as clear as the blue sky above "—believe me, you don't want to be caught wandering around this place naked and completely vulnerable—but all we could find were some scraps from a village we found, just a few days back." With a casual bounce in his stride, Dimitri continues to stroll forward until he's reached the soldier whose weapon is still drawn on me. Gesturing with one arm to the meadow behind me, he clasps the man's shoulder with his other hand and gives him a disarming smile. "Feel free to go check. We hide nothing from you. We would've stayed hidden if we feared you were our enemies. But we saw your banners."

"This one here stayed hidden," the soldier argues.

Dimitri's fingers dig deeper before giving a little pat. "This here is Ryven. He was the sailor we hired to cross the Varenholm Ocean. He's from Drayfil Shore, so, you know how distrusting that lot can be. He insisted on hiding in the bushes while we greeted you. After everything we've seen from the mages since coming here, I'm sure you can understand—"

The soldier's spear drops so suddenly it almost slices through the itchy fabric draped over my chest. "You've seen them then? The mages? They're really here?"

Softening, Dimitri inclines his head.

It's all the confirmation the man needs. His wide eyes find his comrades' and seeing the fear reflected in each other's gazes makes them finally lower their weapons the rest of the way.

I doubt any of them thought this day would come, when Arcathainians would venture across the ocean in search of their stolen land, seeking retribution from the mages who wronged them. Or at the very least, I doubt that they thought they'd be around when that day came.

Shoulders drawn as if to ensure the soldiers will see the status of her sigil, Eparah clears her throat. "We'd like to request an audience with the Magistrate and share with him what we've learned about the mages since our arrival."

It takes a little more convincing before they send word for the Magistrate, and the entire afternoon before we're granted access to him and find ourselves aboard his magnificent ship.

I suppose I don't have much else to compare it to than the dilapidated vessel that was cemented by mollusks on the Leviathan's back, but it is nothing like the grimy, water-logged ship I would've imagined. The Magistrate's vessel is new and freshly lacquered. Despite the arduous journey they made across the ocean, the entire deck is spotless thanks to the small crew working tirelessly at keeping the floorboards scrubbed and the seawater off the main deck. The crew on board is just as pristine and tidy. They appear more as doctors or students than soldiers or sailors, seeming as if they'd squirm inside a dusty library, let alone at sea for weeks.

We're greeted with salutes and respectful nods by almost everyone. Some of them even utter the familiar adage that the others have used from time to time:

"Of one country, of one blood."

Hearing it puts even me at ease, despite the phrase holding no meaning for me. But I recognize it as one of respect and loyalty, and if that's the way we're viewed, then perhaps I have nothing to worry about.

A crewman who wears the same sigil as Alphonse—the white phoenix atop a black backdrop with a purple X struck through it—leads us across the main deck into the cabin on the other side.

The door creaks open on salted hinges, the only sign that this vessel has seen any wear and tear, and we enter. At the far end of the room, a man stands over a desk, his back to us where he's hunched. The door alerts him of our presence, but he doesn't so much as twitch, either too consumed by the parchments he's examining beneath him, or because he knows that nothing can harm him here.

"Sir," the general says, standing at attention. "May I present to you Senator Devonshire's associates." He doesn't wait for any acknowledgement before bowing at the waist and fleeing the room.

The door squeaks to a close behind us, entombing us in an uncomfortable silence.

The reassuring welcome we received from the others is nulled by the Magistrate's intense presence. Every instinct that had flared at the sight of Kalli's raven is triggered again as my senses heighten. I search the cabin for everything and anything. What kind of person is this man? What can his belongings tell us about what he intends for us?

But before I get far in my assessment of his sparse, but tidied belongings, his head lifts, black, slightly greased hair stopping at his shoulders.

When he turns to face us, his stubbled smile is cold and brittle, so weak that it doesn't even come close to penetrating his eyes. But the others with me either don't see it, or don't care. They dip in a bow of a respect, and I follow suit so as to keep up the appearance that I am like them.

"Welcome," he says with a voice as irritable and cunning as a badger. "I believe we have much to discuss."

THE MAGISTRATE

VARENHOLM OCEAN

"Let me see if I understand you correctly."

The Magistrate twirls the amber liquid in his glass before taking another sip and setting it on the desk behind him. When he laces his hands behind his back, the resemblance between he and his bastard son is comically uncanny.

They are both men of harsher, sharper features. They bear the same angular eyebrows that make them look as if they're permanently scowling, and the same sharp nose that they enjoy sticking up in the air whenever they're talking to those of lesser status. Though his hair is streaked silver, underneath it's just as dark as Alphonse's, and nearly the exact same cut and length.

It's difficult to tell how much of their similarities are familial traits, or just how much Alphonse strived to walk in his father's footprints.

The Magistrate begins a slow, meandering pace, walking across from his desk from one side of the room to the next.

"General Alphonse Reid Graham lives," he says without a trace of credulity. "He was there the day the Primordial awakened and the Shadowthorn fell. And he led you here, to

Illashore, to seek the *wisdom* of the mages, our natural-sworn enemies." The creases around his dark eyes deepen. "Forgive me, but you'll understand my reluctance to believe such inventive notions as you've described them."

"Of course, sir," Eparah says, dipping her head. "We had a difficult time adjusting to it ourselves. But much has changed since the day the general was attacked in the Shadowthorn. The stories he has to tell are—"

"Are the same ones he's always told." The Magistrate gives a bored flick of his wrist. "He is a general of the Shadow Crusade, after all. He's seen more days inside the Shadowthorn than most rookies see in their first year combined."

Dimitri strides forward. "This was different. What happened to Alphonse changed him. It changed us all. If you had been there when Qaeus rose, if you had seen the way Halira—blighted with demon venom—entered the black zone surrounding the Primordial's heart only to return moments later fully healed, it might not be such a farfetched notion to grasp."

The Magistrate's dark eyebrows tick up a notch. "I believe that's General Alphonse Reid Graham to you, Crusader."

As if realizing his boldness for the first time, Dimitri slinks back in line. "Yes, sir."

Not many people have that effect on him, but oddly it's not as satisfying as I might've imagined it would be to see him put in his place. Mostly because what he's saying is true, and yet, it doesn't appear that the Magistrate believes a single word of it, let alone that he has any intentions of helping us end the Primordial's reign of terror on the people of the Broken Realms.

I need to get back to the beach and warn the others who are waiting for me. Already they've been left there too long. It had been hours since I left them in the meadow. But now that we're here on the Magistrate's ship, all I can do is hope that the conversation will end soon, and we'll be brought back to shore with the others when they finally dock.

But for some reason, seeing this man's impact on everyone he encounters is something I cannot oblige.

"When was the last time you were in the Shadowthorn?" I ask him, and then add sardonically, "Sir."

His gaze snaps to mine, a mixture of mild irritation and amusement roiling inside it. "I wouldn't know. My place is at the Senate, running the country and preventing further famine, rebellion, and otherwise ensuring the peoples' safety and well-being."

"Then how long has it been since you last saw a demon? In the flesh."

"Ryven," Dimitri growls, his fists clenched.

"It's an honest question," I reply, throwing him a glare of my own before returning to the Magistrate. "I mean no offense, I'm merely trying to understand your experience on the field."

If I'm getting to the Magistrate at all, he doesn't show it. "There are units of Crusaders designated with the task of capturing demons and bringing them to the Senate to be studied. I oversee those experiments, but if you're asking when the last time was that I was at the Shadowthorn border or inside it, my best guess would be a decade or more."

He doesn't so much as flinch as he admits it, as if he truly believes he's better than the rest of the population who has been facing down that horrific border for years. But I can't dwell on shaming him for that yet.

"Then you'll forgive me for saying this, but I believe your expertise is limited on this matter, just as ours would be limited on the ways of the Senate." Eparah, Dimitri, and the other handful of Crusaders standing beside me stiffen.

Before I can continue, a wicked grin curves the Magistrate's thin lips. "Oh, how embarrassing for me. I had no idea I was in the presence of an expert on the Shadowthorn." His lips smack open in a feigned expression of dawning. "I do recall a certain group of fugitives that had been reported to live inside the Blighted zone—a wretched place to call home, if you ask me. But I suppose when you've raped and murdered your way through the country—"

"They're not rapists and murderers!" I hear myself shouting, long before my common sense catches up to me.

His smile becomes an even crueler thing, a coiling snake that's reading to pounce. "The Wardens of Qaeus," he says before addressing Eparah, "Is this the company you choose to keep now?"

"No!" she replies frantically. "It's not what—We didn't have a—I was only following your son's—I mean, General Alphonse's orders."

"And when his orders lead you to fraternize with a known group of ruffians and thieves, did you not think to yourself that perhaps your general had abandoned you, as well as his country?"

"I—I—"

But it's all Eparah can manage as she searches her hands for the answers that won't come.

Beside me, Dimitri pinches the brim of his broad nose and sighs. "Yes."

The room turns toward him.

I watch with my heart climbing up my throat, unsure of whether I should interject or let him continue. But I don't know what I could possibly say that would improve the situation. Maybe Dimitri does.

"Yes?" the Magistrate echoes, taking a step closer. "Explain."

The ball of Dimitri's neck bobs before he meets the Magistrate's gaze. "Yes, when we first found him, we wondered whether Alphonse—whether *General* Alphonse—was still loyal to Arcathain and therefore worthy of following. The group was very divisive about it. We have been much of the time."

"Then what led you here? Against explicit orders to return to the Capital."

Out of the corner of his eye, Dimitri looks over at me. I think the edge of his mouth ticks up with a sad sort of grin. "It's as Ryven said. As Crusaders, we know the demons of the Shadowthorn. We know how they move, how they travel in packs or alone, how they feast, how they survive, and how they die."

Pointedly, he turns his attention back to the Magistrate. "The thing that awakened in the Shadowthorn was no mere demon. It was the Primordial, and it was more volatile than any creature we've ever heard of. Arcathain is not prepared for its wrath. Even if General Alphonse wasn't worthy of being followed, we knew that Arcathain was doomed if we didn't do something. It was a risk. We put our lives in danger, forfeited our reputations, all for the small chance that what we were doing—coming to Illashore to find a way to defeat the Primordial for good—was right, and would benefit the people."

When Dimitri finishes, no one speaks. No one so much as breathes. The Magistrates returns to his desk, grabbing his glass and finishing the amber contents in one great swig.

"For a long time, I have believed the same as you all. That the mages hold the key, or some secret to defeating the monsters that they left us with. It's why I rallied the Crusaders and took them to the Capital. The time has come for us to confront the mages. We tried, of course, in the past, but their dark magic kept us away from Illashore. Any idea what happened to it?"

The group glances nervously among themselves.

"It disappeared as we came through," Eparah answers. "But we don't know why or how."

With a thoughtful expression, Dimitri says, "There was a mage waiting for us when we arrived. I've wondered if it was intentional. If they cleared the barrier because they wanted us to land here."

The Magistrate runs a hand over his five o'clock shadow. "Perhaps. Or maybe there is one among you who possesses magic that was capable of breaking it. A mage. Dare I say a spy." With his hands clutched behind his back, he begins his pacing again, glancing among us like he's selecting a prized cow to be sent to the slaughter. Those dark eyes fix on mine. "You. It's not uncommon that mages congregate with my brother's roguish band of misfits. Tell me, did the Wardens send you here specifically, or was your mission something grander?"

"I am no Warden."

The words come out quiet but firm. Rather than trying to convince him, a man who seems just as likely to disregard us as heed us, for me it's more about being true to whom I am. The truth is, the Wardens of Qaeus were never my home. Though Adrien was kind enough to shelter me during my time of need, that place, nor those people, were nothing more to me than strangers in a strange land.

For periods of my life, even the Eyve didn't feel like it was meant to be my place in the world. It had the familiar comforts of being the one and only place I'd ever lived, and of course it was where Ahl'Ro and I grew up with his family. But even though we were both content there for a time, our destinies drove us out of the Forgotten Forest and out to explore the rest of the Broken Realms.

But it wasn't until I met Halira—the day she fled the Wardens in a delirious and reckless search for her sister and aunt—that I finally found my place in the world. My home.

She taught me about strength in the face of adversity. About fighting for others when you've lost everything. About never giving up on a brighter future, even if it's just a future that will be enjoyed by others.

Dimitri clears his throat, drawing my attention back to the

room and away from the silver-haired heroine who stole my heart.

"He's from Drayfil Shore. Not the Warden's, or whatever you called them in the Shadowthorn. But I won't lie. We did cross paths with them, as you already know. When we went in search of General Alphonse's body, it was at their camp that we found the map that lead us to the Primordial."

The Magistrate's penetrating eyes never break away from mine, as if he's watching for a crack in the façade Dimitri has constructed. Part of me wants to rip off the mask now, to show myself as the druid I am, and welcome whatever is to come. This was the moment Ahl'Ro and I had looked forward to, a chance to speak before the leader of Arcathain and show them who we were and how invested we were in a shared future.

But my dreams and ideals are meaningless until we find Halira. And if Dimitri believes that my ability to use magic will ruin our chances at securing the Magistrate's aid in finding her, then I'll pretend to be Arcathainian for as long as I am able.

Finally, the Magistrate's calculating brow relaxes. "I am pleased to hear it. I feared I would have yet another heathen in our barracks to feed."

Somewhere outside, high above the swaying ship, a raven screeches.

My gaze cuts to Dimitri's at the same time his eyes lock with mine. He may have little to no experience with druid magic, and even less so with the intimate bonds between familiars and their human companions, but his understanding is clear as day in those wide, sage eyes.

Kalli is in trouble.

"So where is Alphonse?" the Magistrate asks, returning to his desk. He empties the decanter as he pours himself another drink, the stringent scent churning with the sea air. "Where is my bastard son? I assumed he'd be first in line of your little greeting brigade. But I suppose he wanted to wait for me on shore, wanted me to see him standing on the stolen island before I was ever able to set foot upon it. Is that it?"

Everyone shifts uncomfortably. I had wondered why we hadn't opened with this bit of information, but now I understand. No one wants to be the one to break the news. But I don't understand why. From everything Alphonse has shared about his father and upbringing, it seems like the Magistrate hardly ever showed any affection toward him, and often outright denied any love he might've had for a bastard son.

The Magistrate turns around, but he doesn't even get the chance to bring his glass to his lips before sensing the unease in the room.

"What?" he says, more of a demand than a question. "What are you not saying?"

Eparah lowers her head. "I'm afraid he's been captured."

"Captured?" The glass thuds where he slams it on the desk.

"Yes, sir. By the mages." She tests a glance up at him, but swiftly re-averts her attention back to the ground at the sight of his growing frustration, his concern and fear and every other emotion that would be bubbling up inside a parent right now. "They took him in the middle of the night."

The Magistrates bounds off the table, cool exterior all but obliterated as he addresses us all. "And you just let them? You are his Crusaders. His defenders! You are meant to lay your life on the line in order to protect him!"

"We were indisposed," Dimitri informs him, shoulders shrinking.

The Magistrate's red-hot glare beams down upon him for a long moment before he whips around. He strides behind his desk, reaches for a frayed rope dangling from the roof at the back of the room, and tugs.

"When?"

"A-about a week ago?" Dimitri answers. "As far as we can tell. We don't know how long we were left there after they—"

The door swings open behind us and collectively we jump.

"Sir?" the man barreling into the room asks. "You rang?"

The Magistrate knocks back one final swig before slamming the empty glass back on the table. "Bring me my armor. Give the command to prepare to disembark."

"S-sir?" the man in the doorway stammers. "Our scouts haven't yet returned with enough intel—"

"I don't care about the blighted scouts!" the Magistrate bellows, the ship practically rocking with the sheer force of his wrath. "We came here for war. So let it begin."

WHERE LOYALTIES LIE

MAGISTRATE'S CABIN, VARENHOLM OCEAN

It takes the man in the doorway a moment to snap his gob-smacked jaw shut before he bows and flees the room to deliver the message to the rest of the crew.

The Magistrate wastes not a second. His fingers hastily work at the clips securing his tight-fitting, perfectly unwrinkled jacket as he prepares to be fitted with his armor.

"Thank you for the intel you've provided," he says to all of us, not glancing away from his task. "You may leave now. Explore the ship, if you like. But when we dock, I'll ask that you remain nearby. No wandering inland. Preferably sticking to my ship, and mine alone, in case we need any of you for further questioning."

He doesn't even attempt to conceal his distrust with a careless wave of his hand or a friendly smile. He wants us to know we're on a short leash. He revels in it.

"Sir," Dimitri says, standing at attention. "If I may—"

But the Magistrate will hear none of it. "You may not, Crusader. You aided a known mage in her escape from Nigh, you either failed or absconded from your mission to rescue my son—and I'm not entirely sure which is worse—and rather than returning to your post, to protect our people from the

Primordial you unleashed upon them, you wandered to the land of the mages, and in doing so, ensured my bastard son's capture into enemy hands.

"If you know what's good for you, Crusader, you will learn to obey an order when you are given one. Now go."

Dimitri blinks, stunned into silence.

But I'm half-cocked and ready to protest, or at least to insist that he tell us the plan of extraction if he won't allow us to be involved in rescuing Alphonse and Halira. But just as I open my mouth, a flurry of soldiers barrels into the room. We're shuffled out of the cabin so quickly, I barely have time to register that the lumps of welded metal and intricately designed leathers are varying options for armor that will be presented to him.

Then, the door slams at our backs.

"Well, that could've gone worse," Eparah says, a light and fluttery sigh in her throat.

"Worse?" Dimitri flexes and closes his fingers at his sides. I feel like doing much the same. "We've been sidelined! While the Magistrate charges the Keep with his army, we'll be stuck here like prisoners."

Eparah shrugs. "You can't blame him. We've been gone for who knows how long. We're lucky they didn't just throw us to the sharks and call us fish food."

Dimitri growls, tossing his hands in the air and storming off a short distance away, creating much needed space to fume silently in.

I can understand his frustration. All the time we've spent waiting for this moment, hoping for this rendezvous, and it wasn't anything like I had hoped it would be.

At my wits end, I drag a hand through my hair. "What does this mean then? For Alphonse? For Halira? For the mages?"

Shaking his head, Dimitri stares off into the distance, to the coastline that already appears to be rapidly approaching. "It means the Magistrate intends on launching an attack against the mages. Whether he'll attempt to rescue Alphonse first is anyone's guess."

A breathy laugh escapes Eparah. "My guess is not."

"And Halira?" I ask.

Dimitri flinches. It takes me a moment to realize the reason he won't meet my gaze is because he's ashamed. "We never mentioned her capture."

As quickly as he utters the words, I spin back around poised for the door, the handle practically within my grasp. "We have to tell him. He has to—"

But Dimitri and Eparah grab my shoulders and jerk me backward. When I spin around, I watch them with incredulous fury. Eparah's hesitation, I can understand. She's been skeptical of this plan from the start. But Dimitri? Where's his sense of loyalty? Where's his sense of duty now that his lifelong friend —the woman he's supposed to love—is stranded in the middle of a soon-to-be battlefield and doesn't even know it?

Dimitri's jaw is set as he glances at Eparah. "We've been given our orders. We stay put."

She nods her agreement, placated by his show of submission. But what she fails to see when she allows her attention to be drawn by the vivacity of the ship and its crew is the concerned look Dimitri casts my way.

There's something he's not telling me—something he can't tell me in her presence. As my anger simmers, I realize how right he is to be cautious. We are aboard the Magistrate's ship, the very man who sentenced Halira to her execution when it was discovered she had magic, the same man who—if I'm not mistaken—has imprisoned her sister, Kalli, likely for the same reason. What good would it cause Halira to inform the Magistrate that she was taken by the mages as well? As far as he's concerned, they'd be doing him a favor in ridding her from his land.

My head tilts back, my gaze sweeping across the sky to the black dot of feathers circling above.

For now, we wait.

For them, we wait.

It takes no more than a couple of hours for the ships to anchor on the coast and the army to descend upon Illashore. They slink along the coastline. They seep in through the meadow. Hundreds upon hundreds of battle-ready warriors eager to unleash generations of fear and hatred and revenge upon any living soul they encountered.

To my surprise, the Magistrate leads at the helm, clad in shining, shimmering gold-plated armor from head to toe; he is like a shooting star flying across the darkening realm as the sun begins to set.

Dimitri, Eparah, and I, and the handful of Crusaders who traveled with us, are among the few who stay behind. Deck-hands and steward's assistants who continue to man the sails and swab the main deck. Cooks and chefs with little skill on the battlefield. Gunners awaiting orders to ignite the cannons, should things go south.

"Well," Eparah says at last, breaking the eon of silence that's stretched over us like a thin veil ever since we left the Magistrate's cabin. "I'm starved. Who's up for a meal if they'll feed us?"

The other Crusaders we came with agree, but Dimitri shakes his head.

"Can't eat. Not until I know she's safe."

The carefree and excitable manner in which Eparah had

held herself just moments before softens. She gives Dimitri a gentle pat on his shoulder. "You might not be eating for a while then."

When he shrugs his shoulders, I feel the tangled heap of dread and despair in my own stomach lurch.

"Suit yourself," she says. As she turns to join the others, she looks at me only briefly, but I receive no special invitation. If anything, her glare is one to put me in my place. "Be sure to keep an eye on him, yeah?"

Dimitri nods. "Of course."

I wait until she's out of earshot to launch into the vortex of concerns that have been on my mind. "What are we going to do?"

"I don't know," he says, leaning over the banister on the boat's edge and rubbing his chin.

"The Magistrate will kill her."

"I know."

"Or find Alphonse, save him, and leave her to die."

His eyes squint a little, as if he'd like to disagree with me about part of that statement, but all he says again is, "I know."

Blinking, I throw out my arms. "Then what are we going to do?" But my emotions get the better of me and I ask more loudly than I intend, drawing the suspicious glances of the busy crew around us. I come in closer and whisper again, "What are we going to do?"

"I don't know." He enunciates every syllable as if they're each a slice of his sword. With his hands pressed to the railing, his knuckles burn white. "They have Kalli. When they find Halira—if they find her—she'll be brought back to meet the same fate they mean to give her sister."

"Then we stop them."

"I can't!" His fists slam against the railing. His nostrils flare with the restraint it takes to steady his breathes before he shoves himself away, those light green eyes still cemented to mine. "Don't you understand? I can't do anything! I have to stay here!"

Before I know what I'm doing, I grab his collar and yank him closer. "You make your own choices. You decide your life —" and when I hear the faint whisper of their beloved motto chanting in my own skull, I add "—mottos be blighted. *You* do what you believe to be right. That's the only way to live."

Instead of pulling back, his jaw clenches and he seems to bore into my hold, as if it's the only thing tethering him to what he holds dear. "This is my chance. My *only* chance. If they label me a deserter—or worse, a mage-sympathizer—I'm as good as dead."

I finally release his leather armor, an incredulous smile forcing its way out of me. "You really believe that after all of this, life as you knew it will return to the way it was? Arcathainians have breached Illashore for the first time since the Great Rift. There are druids here as well, and soon the rest of Arcathain will know about them too. Do you really believe that being a member of the Shadow Crusade is the only option left for you?"

"Yes."

He answers so swiftly, that any further argument is swallowed up in my throat.

"Let's be honest," he adds, his somber gaze drifting to the dark waters tumbling over the edge of the ship. "Before the Shadow Crusade, I had nothing but a home stained in blood, and a friend I wanted more with. When I became a Crusader, I never dreamed of anything grand. I figured I'd serve my duty to my country, and maybe die a hero by defeating the Primordial. I never dreamed Halira would…"

Our bodies must be in sync because the moment my heart twists into a burning knot, Dimitri stops talking. He takes a deep, painful inhale before beginning again.

"The honest truth is she didn't choose me. Her family died

and I was leaving Gravenburg—leaving *her*—and she clung on to me because I was familiar. I was the only family she had left. I'd hoped it was more than that, but…it wasn't." He meets my gaze, gesturing to the ship around us with wide, sweeping arms. "*This* is all I have. If I can't have her, then what point is there in risking the only security and comfort I'll ever know?"

At that, my blood boils. I'd actually felt sorry for the man until now.

"Simply because she doesn't love you, you won't fight for her? You'll let her die, all because your ego is too fragile?" Red clouds my vision. Rage pumps through my veins and I suddenly feel no different than the demon I'd been a few days prior. I'm not even sure I care. I'm ready to unleash the monster and kill them all. "She deserves better!"

"No! I know!" His eyes go wide and he throws his hands in the air. "I'm not saying that I won't help her. I will. But I have to be smart. I can't jeopardize everything. I will help, but only in the ways that I can, that will still keep my life intact."

My expression becomes dubious. "What are you saying?"

"I can't leave. I can't help you—not directly, anyway. But I know these boats. Silver and Güthric spoke about them often while you were…flying with us." He clears his throat and juts his chin toward a grate on the other end of the deck. "You see that, there?"

I nod.

"That's the brig. If they have Kalli—"

"They do."

"I know. That's not what I meant—" He shakes his head, a shaggy mess of golden-brown hair shuffling over his conflicted eyes. "That's where they'll be holding her. The brig. And *you* have to break her out."

I'm so stunned by his suggestion that I almost just repeat it back to him. But I knew this was coming. I knew that me or him or both of us would need to orchestrate her release. I guess at this point I just didn't think I'd have his support on the matter.

But he's still leaving something unsaid.

"You said you couldn't help directly, but you still want to help," I say. "What will you be doing?"

A smile breaks loose then, one I saw many times aboard the Leviathan, the inviting, confident kind that won so many of his friends' hearts. But it's different now. There's a sadness weighing it down, a slight tilt that prevents it from hiking up as high on his cheeks as it used to climb.

"I've spent enough time on a ship to know how to entertain bored and stir-crazy people," he says with a shrug. "I'll just channel Sai and invite everyone to gamble."

A smirk tugs at my cheeks. Most of the time, I think I have Dimitri pegged, but then he goes and surprises me.

"Are you sure?" I ask him, my tone sobering. "Your Magistrate, I don't trust him. More important, he doesn't trust you."

Thinking, Dimitri nods. "Maybe not. But I can earn that trust back in time."

My eyes narrow on him. "It might be difficult to earn back that trust if on the first night of your return, I go missing alongside one of their prized prisoners." Voicing it out loud actually makes me more nervous for him, and I fold my arms protectively over my chest. "You shouldn't stay here. You should leave the ship, take the others with you if they'll come, and meet us somewhere. We can do this together. Just like we have been."

Something like surprise and gratitude rises in his expression before the war of duty wins. "I have my orders. I will remain here while you go after Halira."

Laughter erupts from the deck above, my cue that Dimitri's ploy has worked and that it's finally safe to step out from my hiding place. I peek around the cargo boxes, just to be safe, but no one is anywhere to be seen. I'd taken some convincing when he told me that people stuck out at sea could never resist a good round of Primero or other card game. I should've known better after watching Halira and the others play almost nightly during their trip on the Leviathan.

Making my way back to the main deck, I'm careful to check around every corner, to heed every sound, so as not to risk being spotted. Dimitri had been accepted as one of them because of the black leathers they associate with the Shadow Crusade. Me, on the other hand, I don't have that luxury. There are plenty on this ship who likely didn't see me when I boarded, and to encounter any of them while I'm sneaking around will look suspicious to say the least.

Fortunately, Dimitri played his part well. I don't run into a single soul as I make my way back to the main deck, and the boisterous waves of laughter soon become drowned out by the crashing waves as I emerge above.

He can't keep them there forever though. Soon, the men will grow tired, or in need of food and drink, or some may be compelled to return to their watch of the shore. We don't have much time and so I make good use of it and rush to the grate in the floor.

Hovering over it, I peer down below and spy a familiar head of silver, ropey hair.

"Kalli?" I whisper.

Her head lolls back. Two gray eyes, dulled and heavy-lidded, blink up at me, but they might as well be staring right through me. "You..." Her gaze flickers then, catching on something behind me and my stomach lurches thinking I've been caught, until I hear her breathe the words, "My raven..."

Surely, I look up, and her blighted bird is still relentlessly, dutifully flying overhead. The poor thing has to be exhausted. I have some experience with flying for hours at a time, with nowhere safe to land, while the person you care most for is somewhere below, out of sight, and possibly in danger.

Breaking my gaze away from the loyal bird drifting through the stars, I turn my attention to the grate.

"I'm here to break you free."

"Can't," she says weakly, and I'm struck again by how delirious she seems. Could they have drugged her? Will she be able to run once I get her out? "Can't...change."

It takes me a moment to realize what she means, but even when I think I do, I have to ask her, "What do you mean? You can't shift?"

"No," she croaks, voice dry. "Nothing."

In stunned silence, I stand there gaping for a moment. If I hadn't just lost use of my own magic temporarily, and spent the months prior without it as well, I might've discredited her. Before being blighted, there had been no recordings of druids losing touch with their powers. Our magic comes from the land and from the living, and therefore as long as we have contact with one or the other, we should be able to call to the elements.

But when I was blighted, I'd been cut off. When I emerged from the Pits of Bagamore, it had been much the same.

Though Kalli can breathe the ocean air, and though I can see the dampness from a few sea storms glistening beneath her feet, for whatever reason she can't access her power. If she had been able to, I have no doubt that she would've shifted, taken the form of a bird and flown through the large gaps of her prison door and joined her raven in triumphant and glorious freedom.

Something is holding her back. She's not blighted. She's not freshly emerged from the Pits of Bagamore. But something is cutting off her connection to the natural world.

"I'm getting you out of here," I reassure her. Circling the iron door, I pull a crowbar from my belt. "I can. And I will. You will know freedom again, Kalli. And then we're going to find and save your sister."

A whimper leaks past the stronghold of her lips, but not a word more. Without wasting another second, I shove the edge of the crowbar between the seal, just as Dimitri had instructed. How a priggish man such as him knows the intricacies of breaking free a captive from a ship is beyond me, but he's surprised me on more than one occasion, so I didn't question him now.

I apply pressure and the grate creaks, a gods-awful screech of rusted metal grinding on rusted metal. But the corner I'm working on pops open, and so I move to the other side. I peer down through the lattice ironwork and find Kalli slumped back against the wall.

"Kalli," I hiss, placing the crowbar underneath the next edge. "Can you stand?"

There is no response, she simply obliges, swaying dazedly in time with the ocean waves. The second corner screeches as it pops free.

"Hold this side up while I get the others."

Feebly, she stretches. Her fingertips barely reach the rusted grid of plated bars, but behind those glazed eyes, determination billows like the stoked flames of a rekindled fire. How long she must've fought to have become so exhausted. The journey from the Claimed Coast to Illashore was long, but there's no telling how long it was for Kalli. I'm unfamiliar with the western side of Arcathain—my knowledge of the country doesn't extend much past Gravenburg and Nigh—but whenever someone made reference to the Capital, they said it was northern. How far north, I'm not sure, but Kalli could've been trapped in this cell for weeks.

I make my way to the third corner and pry it open with a hearty shove. With each corner I work free, Kalli resumes a little more of her fierceness, the life returning ever so slowly to her glazed eyes. My inquiring mind is once again drawing the question of *why* and *how* she's come to be this way, but I force those wonderings aside as I make my way to the final corner, wedge the crowbar between the grate and the floor, and heave.

Hoisting the grate ajar is the loudest noise of the evening, even in contest with the roaring ocean and the unruly laughter. I flinch for only a moment, my ears trained on the otherwise silence around me, before lugging the grate aside and reaching down for her.

Kalli does what she can to help, but it's clear whatever they've done to her has her weakened. She gasps when I yank her from below, the crisp night air filling her lungs. Unsteady on her feet, I set her in front of me and let her cling to my shoulders.

My heart shatters when her eyes meet mine. They're not the same chrome-silver as Halira's, eyes that catch even the stray beams of moonlight on the darkest nights. But they're similar enough that for a moment it almost feels as if she were here in my arms and not her sister. This is the closest I've felt to Halira in weeks. And judging from the way Kalli stares up at me, I get the impression that the feeling is mutual.

I'm about to gently release her arms so that she can try standing on her own, when a honeyed, familiar voice calls from behind me.

"And just where do you think you're going?"

On instinct, I spin around, pivoting my body between Eparah's voice and Kalli to ensure I keep her guarded while this ambush is in progress. I should've known to expect it. We had been able to convince Eparah to work with us periodically, but she could never overcome the distrust in her heart.

She's not alone, I realize. Two others have joined her, both of whom I recognize as the Crusader lackeys that traveled with us and who also never could trust working alongside a druid.

Thrusting an arm out behind me, I hold Kalli back. "We are leaving."

The man on Eparah's left sneers a contemptuous grin at his friend on Eparah's right who just shakes her head as if to tell me I'm wrong.

"You know we can't let you," Eparah says, taking a step forward and out of the shadows of the cabin walls. I wonder how long they'd been standing there. If they didn't come from below deck, then they must've been waiting for this. Maybe they wanted to face us both—the demon-boy and the druid-captive. "If we let you leave, the Magistrate would think we helped you escape with a prisoner, and we'd be tried as traitors."

My head hangs low, my eyes pressed shut. I told Dimitri much the same, but he either underestimated the Magistrate's cunning ire, or he didn't want to worry me.

I can't think about him now. Only one person matters.

"Let us go in peace," I beseech her. "All we want is to find and rescue Halira."

Eparah draws her blades first, the other Crusaders not far behind her.

A snarl tears from my lips. My stance widens and I sink into the heels of my feet, ready to fight to the death if I must. I call to the elements around me, but the plants that are my specialty are distant, and with my power still recovering, they'd be difficult to summon.

"Finally," the Crusader man snarls, his grip tight around the hilt of his broadsword. "Inigo gets his revenge by your death."

An ear-splitting screech cuts through the night sky, terrifying us all. A gust of wind blusters past me, a blur of white carrying forth in its wake. I crouch to the floor and shield my head, unsure of what's attacking but certain that there's magic around. When Eparah and the Crusaders begin to scream, their swords and daggers flailing to no avail as they bolt every which way across the deck, I finally glance up.

A snow owl dives down for them, two black ravens flanking her on either side. Kalli. Her raven. And—I'm shocked to even think it—but I believe it's their aunt, Imryll.

Suddenly realizing that I'm a fairly capable and strong young man crouched on the ground while three birds are fighting off our attackers, I jump into action. I draw the Primordial spear from my back, grip it in both hands, and run toward Eparah, the closest Crusader to me. She's clutching one of her eyes and swinging one of her twin short swords violently at the attacking raven. I don't want to hurt this woman. Though she's made our travels difficult, she's never been outwardly cruel. She's shown poor judgment, sure, but that hardly means she should die.

Behind me, I hear a heavy splash as one of the Crusaders jumps overboard.

Kalli—still in her owl form—screeches as she dives for another Crusader, their guttural cries the only indication I have of their slow and agonizing death.

It's just Eparah. She can either die here or—

On her next frantic rotation of slicing and stabbing, when her back is facing me, I take the butt end of my spear, and whack her over the head. She crumples to the ground, utterly motionless.

The three birds drift to the banister beside me. Before the owl lands, her wings shift into arms, her claws to feet, and soon, Kalli stands before me, wild and naked and covered in a splattering of blood.

"Where is my sister?" she demands, bending to retrieve the pile of clothes she left behind from her transformation. She doesn't put them on though. She pauses, waiting for my answer as if she already knows there will be more travel ahead. "Where is Halira?"

"The mages have her," I tell her, the muscles in my jaw recoiling against the words.

"Where?" she growls.

I throw my arm out, deftly aware of the shouting in the decks below us. The soldiers are rallying. We don't have much time.

"At the Keep," I say. "It's less than a day's walk from here."

She drops her clothes where she stands. "Then let's not walk."

In the blink of an eye, she is nothing but white feathers again. She and the two ravens take to the sky.

A stampede rumbles beneath me as the sailors and chefs race to the main deck to see what caused the commotion. I won't be here when they arrive though.

I shift, summoning the spirit of a vulture so that I will be large enough to carry the Primordial spear. Before I join Kalli and the others, I veer to the coastline, to a small patch in the meadow where I left all of Halira's and my friends. Even if we won't slow ourselves down so that they can keep our pace, they at least deserve to know that we're on the move, and we're heading to the Keep, straight into the impending war with the mages.

THE SILENCE OF SHADOWS

THE DUNGEONS, AEYSIL KEEP, ILLASHORE

*D*ays have stretched into a terrifying increment of time that no longer holds any meaning. I try to hold on. I don't want to give up. But never before have I known such darkness. Such isolation. Such cold unfeeling nothingness.

I thought confessing to Varyn what little I knew might've earned me my freedom, or at least a reprieve from the dark solitude. I should've known better though—I *did* know better. Men like him don't believe in reciprocity. But what other choice did I have? Telling him nothing would've earned me the same result, if not worse. It's an intuition I cling to during my darkest and doubting days.

It's been...a long while since I last saw the sun that had filtered in through the stained-glass windows of the great hall. Or felt the warmth of the torchlight's glow as the guards dragged me back through the dungeon halls and threw me into this hole. It's been even longer still since I saw Alphonse. I don't know where they took him, what they've done to him or are continuing to do. I've had to stop asking myself. Those questions only inspire mania.

At least they provide me with a small glass of water and a few modest bites of stale bread every so often. That alone is a worthy improvement. It's enough to keep me going. Keep me alive. Which is all I can ask for now.

When I'd been in the great hall with Varyn, I'd felt the absence of my power, could sense the way the magic-infused stones had snuffed out that surge of energy that had always been humming just beneath my skin. It was the same way one could tell when their garments were not situated correctly on their body, leaving a small gap for air to touch, taunting and provoking the most attuned of senses. Something had been missing, that much I'd been vaguely aware of by the chill. But the absence felt then is nothing compared to the taut stiffness in my skin now.

The pitch-blackness of the dungeon amplifies the nothingness.

Without even the slightest ray of light, without the sounds of any other living being to fill my ears, I'm left with only my sense of touch, the awareness of my own flesh and the hollowness festering inside where my druid power had once been.

Varyn said this place was made of—not stone and earth, but —magic. However, I'm not so certain. Magic has always had a vitality to it. A hum. A vibration.

These walls emit nothing. They stifle even the sounds of my own screams as I call out to anyone and no one, until sometimes I wonder if my mouth is even open at all.

I weep, but my tears never splash on the stone floor.

I pace, but there is no pitter-patter of my cold, raw feet to echo off the sepulchral walls.

There is no wind. There's hardly any air.

And there is certainly no lightning.

I've stopped trying to summon my power, just like I stopped trying to search for any signs of my cousin. Stopped hoping that Dimitri and the Crusaders might find me and break me out of here. How long before they presume me dead and send word to Kalli?

My eyes snap open. Suddenly, it strikes me; I've called out for everyone, but one. In the first nights upon arriving, Dimitri's, Kalli's, and Ryven's names flooded this room with a melancholic hum too great for even the magic-infused stones to stifle. I cried out for Alphonse, for Silver and Güthric, for Adrien, for Sai. Once or twice, even Fox's name circled my thoughts, if not my lips.

But there's been one person I haven't called to. Someone who's association with my life I'm still growing accustomed to, so, admittedly, I had honestly forgotten about her existence. But more importantly, someone who actually might be able to help.

Remembering the dull shadows pooling in my mother's eyes as she took her dying breath, I utter the same word that had breached her bloodied lips and filled my mind with doubt:

"Imryll."

My ears sting, straining for the slightest hint of sound, my eyes almost bleeding as they search for any amount of subtle movement or fluctuation in the darkness.

But I hear nothing.

I see nothing.

I feel nothing but the blackness pressing against me like the stone walls caving in to bury me alive.

Foolish. I am so foolish to continue trying. To bother hoping that there might be some way out of this horrible place when I know that there's not—

The dungeon door creaks open, light bursting into the room and burning my eyes. I shield my face in the crook of my elbow, but not even that's enough. Tears pour from my eyes and I blink, furiously, trying desperately to peer up at the figures advancing toward me.

"Where's Alphonse?" I manage, my throat dry and scratchy.

Someone grabs me, either arm being lifted until I'm forced to my feet.

Through the blinding sheet of light, another shadow steps into the room, someone thin, their clothes seeming perfectly tailored judging by how snugly they clung to their form.

The person stops before me. It's not until they grab my chin and lean in close that I'm able to register their sunken eyes.

"Well, well, well," Igemonar croons. "If it isn't Ms. Devonshire."

I'm too starved, exhausted, and wary to muster the strength to ask him what he wants. My head just lolls in his grasp, my eyelids fluttering.

He takes in the sight of me, tutting about his disapproval. "No bruises. No lesions. No signs of torture anywhere. No wonder you've been so tight-lipped." When he nods to the guards beside me, they tighten their holds. His expression sours with feigned sympathy. "I'm afraid that ends today."

The blood in my veins becomes a thin stream of ice. My sluggish thoughts bristle and awaken, fear blasting me back to the painful moments I'd spent in the great hall with Varyn. I had no doubt that the magic that pierced through me whenever I'd lied will be nothing like the torture Igemonar promises now.

A sharp, chilling force of power traces down my spine as he straightens, eyes fixed on mine. "You have one—and only one— chance to answer me correctly. Fail to do so, you'll regret it. Pretend that your memory is more impaired than it should be, you'll regret it. Lie, and you'll regret it."

Without realizing I'm doing it, I shake my head. I just want this nightmare to end. We came here for answers to save our people, not to be held against our wills and tortured for eternity.

"Anything," I rasp, my throat practically ripping open with the effort it takes to utter sound. "I'll tell you anything."

His blooming smile is like a spreading puddle of oil. "Good. I'm glad you're feeling cooperative today. But just in case—"

With a snap of his fingers, two others filter into the room. "I've brought you some incentive."

Gagged and bound, Alphonse's battered face meets mine as he's dragged into the room. The entire left side of his face is purple and black, layers of dirt and grime matted into the lesions and blending in with his bruises. Blood has soaked through the gag in his mouth. I try not to flinch from the breeze that wafts into the room, carrying with it a pungent and fetid stench.

"Blech," Igemonar complains, his nose instantly pinched in his hand. "Did he shit himself again, or was it vomit this time?"

"Both," the guard holding him says, the two of them grinning.

Alphonse looks as if he would whimper if he could, but the fabric tied over his mouth is too tight. His eyes press tight though as he averts his gaze away from mine.

The sight of him, so broken and beaten, sends a pulse of hatred through me. Shame follows close behind, putting out the flames that had only just started to rekindle. Why him? Why did they treat him so poorly and leave me alone? What information were they hoping to get from him, and was he ever able to provide it?

Igemonar steps between us, forcing my gaze upon him. "The Head Mage suggested that I show him to you. He said you might be more cooperative knowing not only that he lives, but that his continued breathing is entirely up to you."

I lunge for him, but the guards gripping me are far stronger than I am in my emaciated state.

Igemonar jerks back, startled by my outburst, but he's quick to recover. He tsks, waggling his finger. "Ah-ah. What did I just say?"

Before I even have time to realize what I've done, Alphonse jerks forward, agony tearing through him. His screams are so powerful they break through the gag and echo all around me.

Despite the walls having always silenced sound before, now they mock me. Taunt me. Shame me.

I crumple to my knees—as much as the guards will allow me while maintaining their brutish grip—and try blocking out the sound.

"Stop!" I shout. "Make it stop!"

The torchlight from the outside hall flickers and Alphonse's pain ends. Igemonar glances briefly over his shoulder toward the doorway, but then straightens the golden buttons of his green tunic as he returns his attention to me.

"You're ready to cooperate then?"

"Yes," I say through gritted teeth.

"Let's get to the point then, shall we? It's clear by the armada on our border that you and your cousin are far better liars than we credited you of being."

"Armada?" My brow twitches, hope sparking in my chest when I realize who he's talking about. "They came?"

I can't believe it. Kalli actually managed to convince the Magistrate to join us.

"Indeed." He eyes me with a look of poisonous contempt. "Now, what I need to hear from you is how many druids are among them."

None, I almost utter, but then my thoughts race. I don't know how much Kalli told the Magistrate, but if she managed to convince him to come to Illashore, she must've told him about the druids. Otherwise, she'd still be tried for treason as a mage, and I doubt he would've trusted her instructions to come to Illashore if he believed she was one. He would've seen her cajoling as a trap, and steered clear of this place.

But even if she told him about the druids, he wouldn't have trusted any to sail with him. I'm not even sure there's an army in the Eyve who would've been ready to join them. Which means he and his soldiers have just arrived to a war where one side has unfathomable magic, and the other has none.

They'll be slaughtered, if they're lucky. If they're less than lucky, they'll be treated as I have and imprisoned for no reason other than a slow and torturous climb toward death. Perhaps they'll even be tortured as Alphonse was, beaten into providing them answers to whatever secrets Arcathain still possesses.

"An entire fleet," I finally say, cruel satisfaction curling my lips. "The most powerful druids we could find. Far more powerful than the likes of us."

The brief moment of gratification for concocting such a clever ruse is cut short when Alphonse hangs his head. I've answered incorrectly. I hadn't even thought there could be a wrong response, but I'd found it.

Worry twists into me like a knife as Igemonar's expression turns to one of disappointment. "It's as I feared then," he says. "Either one of you is lying or neither of you know the truth. Of course, we'll never know because I have to treat this situation as if you are lying. And I already told you what would happen if you lied."

Desperation claws through me like a rabid demon bounding across the Shadowthorn. I should've told the truth. Instead of trying to save the Arcathainian army, I should've focused on the present and saving Alphonse and I from our fates. I should've told the truth; I'd learned that lesson already, had I not?

But I'd also learned to trust my intuition. For whatever reason, in this moment, it was telling me to buy the Arcathainian army as much time as I could. If the mages were assured that there were no druids among their ships, they'd be quick to slaughter them. I know they have their ways of finding out—they'd used at least one of their methods on Dimitri and the others—but that would take them time. For now, that was what the Magistrate and his army needed, I was sure of it.

Even if it means Alphonse and I will suffer longer, the only thing important now is that the Magistrate and his army are able to do what they need to do to protect Arcathain.

The screams that burst from Alphonse's lungs burn my flesh. I flinch from the guilt that sears into me, the heartbreak that will leave me branded. I can do better. I can still buy the Arcathainian army time while not subjecting my cousin to unending pain.

"Stop," I plead, my lips quivering. "I was lying."

Igemonar holds up his prim hand and Alphonse immediately deflates, his breaths ragged.

I force myself to continue. "You were right. I was lying. I don't know how many druids will be with them."

Igemonar takes an eager step closer. "But there *are* druids with them? That's what you're saying?"

Biting the inside of my lip, I consider my options, but ultimately, only one seems truthful enough not to cost us suffering, but vague enough that I've told him nothing. "Alphonse and I are druids. We grew up in Arcathain. It's likely that others did too, perhaps even some who joined the Magistrate's army."

After holding me in a long, calculating stare, he finally leans back on his heels and averts his gaze to the ceiling as he considers. I take the opportunity to sneak a glance at Alphonse. He's recovered, if only enough to bring his eyes to mine. In them, I'm shocked to find nothing but understanding. None of the hatred I knew from him growing up. None of the self-importance or superiority complex. None of the selfishness. Just as I would do anything for the well-being of innocents, Alphonse would give his life for his country.

Of one country, of one blood.

Thinking the Shadow Crusade mantra sends a profound chill of pride through me, as if my entire unit were standing here beside me, ready to stand up to the mages, once and for all. If I listen hard enough, I swear I can almost hear them chanting it, over and over, in the gentle, dank breeze.

Alphonse's eyes widen, a question burgeoning. As if he can hear them too, he looks around the room then back at me.

That can't be possible. Igemonar might've told us that the Magistrate arrived with his ships, but I would never have expected that meant they were already *here*. Even if they were, there's no way Alphonse and I would hear their battle cries from the dungeons. I'm not sure how many levels below ground we are buried, but there were at least three flights of stairs between my cell and the great hall, one of which wound down and down for multiple stories, it seemed. The ground level would have to be at least five, six—maybe as close to seven stories above us.

I don't care how loud the people were screaming, or how brutal the fighting became, it would be impossible for anything to reach us down here. My own sobs were barely even audible at times.

Another breeze wafts through the open dungeon door, and the chanting grows louder. It's almost as if the soldiers are whispering in my ear, breathing along my neck as the breeze whips around my hair, white strands flying behind me into the darkness.

My eyes catch on the flickering torchlights.

My thoughts buzz with everything we were told about this place and the stone here.

But my mind also settles on a memory, one of watching the dark, magical barrier between us and Illashore dissolve when Alphonse knew Fox was in danger.

It's been so long since I've felt my druid powers. So long since my skin has tingled with the thrum of everything alive in the natural world. But I dare let myself listen for it now. I dare hope beyond hope that there is a reason a breeze has made its way down into this darkness.

I close my eyes and burrow inward, to the place in my

center where the magic has always lived, to my core that had become so hollow the moment we awoke in this place.

The hollowness is gone.

My eyes snap wide. A cunning smile is just beginning to spread across Igemonar's smug face, but the vivacity of renewed life must be visible in my gaze because the color from his face pales.

His mouth stretches open, a warning and command a mere fraction of a second away from bulging from his throat.

But I'm quicker.

I may not be able to see the sky, nor feel the clouds that give me most of my power, but air is enough. Air is everything.

As if the air in the room had a tether, I grab for it and tug. The two mages at my sides, the two holding Alphonse, Igemonar—they all gasp. The life that they had tried to withhold from us is no longer theirs to claim. I rip it away from them, imagining their lungs flattening from its absence like my core had felt in the wake of my snuffed power.

In seconds, they're on their knees. They claw at their throats and reach for me, but there's nothing they can do now. Not as long as I have Alphonse by my side.

It's not until every one of the mages is dead that I allow myself to wonder why it hadn't worked before, why when we were in the mage hall, Alphonse and I standing side-by-side that my magic had evaded me. But even if I asked him, I'm not sure he'd know. I'm not sure he could answer, given the state of him.

When the mages had released his arms in favor of clutching their own throats, trying to suck in any ounce of air they could muster, Alphonse collapsed to his face on the floor. He remains there still, steadily breathing, his torso rising and falling where he lies.

I race to his side. "Alphonse?"

Hearing my voice causes him to startle and he looks up at

me, feebly shoving himself onto his knees. "Is it—is it done?" He glances around the room, to the bodies scattered all over the floor and sighs.

The moment he does, the tingling of my skin stops, my power cut off again.

My hand floats to my chest. "What just—"

"I was holding on as long as I could," he tells me. "As long as you needed. But it-it's too much." He smiles weakly, but it falters when he almost loses his balance.

I catch him, wedging myself under his shoulder. "What did you do? How did you figure out how to use your power?" And then with a disbelieving laugh, I add, "I'm still not even sure what your power is."

"I'm an inhibitor," he whispers, every word coming with great effort, and yet he still forces himself to use large ones like *inhibitor*. "At least, that's what I've gathered. My power nullified their barrier. They told us that this place was built with stones that negated druid magic, but druid magic is the natural elements, and every now and then, I'd feel them. Mostly drafts, but sometimes the air would be damp with signs of moisture. When they'd come for me with their torches, I could, on occasion, feel the warmth of the fire's glow on my skin.

"Mostly though, I didn't know what I was until just now. Their voices—"

"On the wind?" I say hastily. "I heard them too. It sounded like Crusaders."

"I know." He shakes his head with disbelief. "And when it happened, when I heard them and saw you were hearing them as well, I knew it was the wind, and I knew it was because of me." Closing his eyes, he takes a shaky inhale. "Before it happened, I was thinking no matter what happens to me, we have to protect the people. The same thing happened on the Leviathan with Foxlynn. I didn't care about me, only that I do whatever was in my power to save her. Maybe that's my trigger?"

A faint smile tugs up one side of my face. I don't think I've ever been more proud of him.

But as I gaze upon my battered cousin, I'm reminded of the gloomy room we kneel in and I tug him up.

"Come on," I urge him. "It's time we get out of this place."

A RAVEN, AN OWL, A BAT

AEYSIL KEEP, ILLASHORE

As the Arcathainians surround the Keep, and the mages prepare their magical strikes, no one glances twice up at the three creatures flying overhead. If they had, they might've realized how strange it is for a raven, an owl, and a bat to be traveling so tightly together. Especially for one of them to be holding a spear.

There's a small, sardonic part of me that hopes when they write about this day in the history books, somehow that detail will make its way onto the pages.

We made better time than I'd hoped, thanks to the wind Imryll mustered for us. It's a good thing too because once the battle begins, I wouldn't want to be anywhere out past the Keep; the Arcathainians have no idea the obliteration they're about to walk into.

Down below, at the base of one of the sleek, pristine towers, I spy an open door, our way into the Keep. We begin our descent, three thrashing predators with claws and beaks hungry for blood.

The poor mages don't know what to expect, presuming that the laws of nature had gone haywire today of all days as the three of us screech and dive for them. It's not until the surviving stragglers see that we've either blinded or sliced the jugular of everyone on this side of the promenade that they begin to doubt that we are ordinary animals. Our attacks were too precise. Too lethal. Too vengeful.

Their realization comes too late though, and between the three of us, we make quick, bloodied messes of the dozen of mages stationed here before finally turning back into our human forms.

Below us, back on the battlefield, the generals chant their invigorating speeches, the ones meant to soothe the men's fears and reassure them that they are the heroes of tomorrow, that their names will be remembered in infamy among those who were there the day the evil mages were defeated.

They are empty promises that I can't bear listening to, and so I turn my attention to finding clothes. I'm not sure what we'll come up against once we're inside. It's entirely possible that it'll be wiser for us to stay in our animal forms, making it easier to remain unseen as we lurch in the shadows as mice and snakes. But until we're inside and until we know which animals will be most advantageous, wearing clothes might help us be a little more inconspicuous. Especially now that we have access to tunics and robes that the mages wear themselves.

It takes Kalli and Imryll no time at all to find an outfit that fits them. They're both of average size, a little on the slender side, and so fitting into the button-up, tailored jackets of the mage defense team is easy. All they have to do is find an average sized man or woman.

Me, on the other hand? Of the dead mages scattered about, none of them quite have my same physique. With Halira just beyond these doors, it's not a task I care to waste much time on. I settle for undressing the largest man I can find, but even his crimson jacket is too tight in the chest and arms, the black buttons threatening to pop open when I fasten the last one.

With the Primordial spear in hand, I wave to Kalli and

Imryll to follow. "Keep your guard up, and your power ready. There is no telling what we'll find once we're inside."

Neither of them respond, but behind me I sense a buzz in the air as Imryll calls to the druid magic around her, readying to strike.

Inhaling a breath of courage to settle my stampeding heart, I barrel through the intricately carved, marble door, and cross the threshold into the Keep.

Instantly, a silence washes over us. Not a silence of sound since the battle-cries of the soldiers charging their enemies outside roar through the decorated walls without effort, but rather a silence of sensation. A snuffing of power. A blazing fire that's been doused by a lake.

Twisting around, I search Imryll's expression to find she's noticed the same.

"What is that?" Kalli asks. Her hands paw at her stomach and chest. "I don't...I don't *feel* it anymore."

I try shifting back into the bat I flew in as, a form I've become rather familiar with over the past few weeks, but nothing happens.

Imryll sticks her hand back outside, rotating it at the wrist. Wind swirls in her fingertips. "It's some kind of spell. I don't think we'll be using our magic in here."

"How is that possible?" Kalli demands, and I see in her the curiosity and need for problem-solving that Halira always articulated so fondly. But thinking of her and her capture, her imprisonment, brings a sourness to my tongue.

"It doesn't matter," I say, resituating my grip on the spear. "At least we know we can't rely on our power here. Hopefully the mages can't either."

A scoff blows through Kalli's lips. "I highly doubt that."

Striding forward, I lead Imryll and Kalli through the quiet halls of this foreign place, increasingly more aware that I am no warrior. I never trained for battle. It wasn't something we did in the Eyve. Though our home was surrounded by a wall of darkness teeming with demons who terrorized our borders at night, our people knew we were safe. We never intended on going to war. Not with the Arcathainians and certainly not with the mages.

What little knowledge of fighting I've gained has been learned over the course of the past few months, struggling to survive in the Shadowthorn as a human, protecting Halira and the others as a demon, and making my way across Illashore.

But there are some things about fighting that come natural to me. We might not have trained with swords and shields, but in school we practiced our magic proficiencies daily, and there are some lessons that I think apply to both. Afterall, the natural laws of life apply to humans. If you want to see a weed thrive, give it water, nutrients, and love. If you want to watch it wither, cut off its access to all essential resources.

As we tiptoe through the halls, the vaulted ceilings stretching so high overhead that I almost can't see where they end in the shadows above, I prepare myself for what I will have to do if we come across anyone.

Humans need air in their lungs, so I will block off their access to it with my bare hands.

Humans need the blood in their bodies to remain inside them, so I will slice and gouge until their bodies spew fountains and streams of red.

Humans need safety and peace, so I will make them quake with fear when they see me and the beast I can become.

For Halira, I will stain these halls scarlet, and my hands along with them.

For Halira, I will fight.

When I return from peering around a corner, nodding that the coast is clear, Kalli pulls ahead.

"This place is structured much the same as the Capital building. We already passed the servant quarters, the great hall.

The dungeon will be in the lower levels. If we could just find some—" Her confidence increases as she moves, her strides lengthening and quickening, Imryll and I struggling to keep up behind her. She turns another corner. "There," she says, pointing all the way to the other end of the long corridor. "Stairs."

Without her to point them out, from this distance I wouldn't have seen them. The long hallway gives a tunneling effect that makes my head swim and the walls ripple. I've only ever been in a place this grand before on one other occasion, and that was when the demons infiltrated the catacombs at Nigh and I went inside one of the neighboring buildings to guard Halira.

But that was the catacombs. A dingy, dark tomb full of dust and death. It was nothing like the grandeur of this place. I'm distracted by every doorframe we pass, each one carved with intricate, blockish designs and polished so that it shines like silver.

I'm so distracted by the strangeness of this place, that I almost miss the white head of hair emerging from the stairs Kalli's staring at.

If I had missed the sight of Halira climbing up the stairs with a bloodied Alphonse slung over her shoulder though, the sharp inhale Kalli takes would've alerted me to it, and to the mage who steps out from a room ahead of us, and spies Halira almost instantly.

He thrusts his arms back, hands gyrating against each other until a ball of dark, electric magic pulses between his flexed fingers.

Halira's life flashes before my eyes and I'm frozen by the fear of losing her.

But her sister? Kalli lunges into action.

And I watch with horrified hope that she can stop him in time.

A SHATTERING REUNION

AEYSIL KEEP, ILLASHORE

Too many steps. We've climbed too many steps and are both too weakened to climb any longer. And yet, we still have higher to climb.

A full rotation of steps below, Alphonse stopped aiding me in the hike up. His head has become a hefty bag of flour dangling from his shoulders and swaying with every effort I make to hoist us up one more step.

The moment he succumbed to unconsciousness, access to my druid powers was suppressed again by these oppressive stone walls. Fortunately, we haven't needed it. But the higher up we climb, the more we dig ourselves out of the bottomless trench that had been our impending tomb, the more ominous the air becomes. War is in the air. And my senses are on high alert as we crest another level of stairs and come to—

Something is wrong on this floor. Before I've even reached the top step, I feel the danger here. Then I see him. A man, clad in drab mage robes, alit with a dark purple hue. That purple light grows beside him until I realize what it is: magic. A ball of blazing electricity that he intends to send hurdling toward us.

I reach ahead, attempting to siphon the air from the flames

and squelch them in his palms. But without Alphonse, there's nothing to grasp. It's as if there is no air in the room.

The ball of fire builds and builds. The flames roil and coalesce until they become so great that they must be scorching his hands.

His eyes are set. He means for us to die. And without access to my power, or any means of defending ourselves, we will.

But out of nowhere, the mage collapses forward, the fireball disintegrating to smoke as he plummets to the ground, face-first.

A woman collapses with him, thick locks of white tumbling over her shoulders as she lands atop him.

"Kalli?" I breathe, drawing my sister's frightened and frightening gaze toward mine.

It rouses Alphonse too and we both gaze upon my sister. She is pure adrenaline. Pure savagery. She is a cougar defending her cubs by barreling into a bear and taking him over the edge of the cliff with her.

But her sacrifice is for naught. The mage beneath her is unfazed as he lands and quick to launch a new attack. With his hands pinned between the two of them, he summons another fireball effortlessly. A purple glow emits from the space between their stomachs, and it's not until the light flashes and Kalli screams that we both realize what he's done.

I stare in disbelief as my sister collapses beside the mage. Kalli came for me. She's here.

But she's not moving. Not breathing as far as I can tell. In my head, I tell her to get up, but she doesn't. She's stronger than this. I know she is. She is the strongest person I know. She has to get up.

"Get up!" I scream, and the tears slicing down my cheeks are iron-hot.

But she doesn't move, and my voice only draws the attention of the mage who's pulled himself back to his feet and is squaring off with me as if he hasn't done enough already.

I practically throw Alphonse to the ground when I feel the pulse of life buzzing around me again. His consciousness, his awareness of the circumstances, has dropped whatever barrier the mages have on this place, and I won't waste this opportunity for vengeance. I've lost too much. My brother Tor. My parents. And now my only sister.

Piss on a mage if I'll let him live.

As the fire grows between the mage's hands again, I summon the sky above. Now that we're not ten levels below the ground, I can actually scent the fresh air, practically see the dark storm clouds roiling up above.

I sink my vengeful claws into them and tug them down upon us.

Lightning spews from the ceiling. Jagged and hot, it lances down from above like the gods themselves are spewing their wrath. The mage is lit up like the sun. He doesn't stand a chance. The first lightning bolt strikes him clean through the skull. The rest are just for my own assurance. Pure satisfaction.

Only, as his body crumbles to the floor in a heap of ash beside Kalli's lifeless form, there is no more satisfaction to be had. Kalli is still gone. It doesn't matter if the mage is too. My sister is dead.

My knees are weak, my legs barely cooperating as I race across the room and slam into my sister's side. My sobs rock me. I brush the ropes of hair away from her face and gaze through tear-filled eyes upon her paling flesh. Her stomach is a charred hole, glistening with so much blood that I have to look away. A wound like that is too fatal.

She can't be dead. I can't lose her too.

Cradled in my arms, I shake my sister's still form, screaming her name, her head heavy where it hangs behind her, but I keep shaking and trembling and screaming. I can't stop. I want her to open her eyes. For her lips to curve into a grimace as she glowers at her obnoxious sister for rousing her from a peaceful slumber and nothing more. She can't be dead. She has to—

A hand appears on my shoulder, a comforting warmth bleeding into me. I'm not even sure how long it's been there but I manage to pull my gaze away from Kalli long enough to glance up to Alphonse, only to find it's not my cousin at all.

Ryven kneels behind me. Not a horrifying, wicked demon plucked from the discarded nightmares of children. But Ryven himself.

My mouth plummets open, a tremble catching the single, pathetic syllable that manages to escape my lips. Nothing is real. Kalli is dead and Ryven is healed and none of it feels real.

Before I can make sense of any of it, I realize he's shoving me aside. Something primal inside me bristles. No one will take me away from my sister. She's not dead. I won't leave her here like this!

Just as I'm about to scramble forward and assert my position at her side, I notice his splayed hands hovering over Kalli's abdomen. My heart leaps into my throat on a flurry of hope. Druids have healing powers. I'd almost forgotten. I hadn't even thought to try it myself. It's not like I've had any experience with it personally, but I've seen my aunt use it on Silver when we'd first fled from Nigh, and Kalli accessed the healing power in the Shadowthorn before I woke Qaeus.

Magic flows from his hands like spun gold.

I hold my breath for fear that one wrong move, one distraction, could ruin everything.

I glance over my shoulder and find Alphonse crouched on the floor, his brow etched in hard creases and deep shadows. He's the only reason Ryven can do this. Without Alphonse, we very well might all be dead.

I am so grateful for them both that an unbearable heat

builds in my throat again, one I can't swallow.

Instead, I choke on it as a gasp bursts from Kalli's lungs and she catapults upright. Ryven staggers back, his work done and likely trying to give her space to breathe, but I fling myself forward and envelop my sister.

"You're alive!" I cry into her shoulder. "You're here and you're alive!"

Her arms wrap around my back, and she gives an ever so gentle but reassuring squeeze. "Of course, I am," she simply says.

Blinking back the tears, I notice Imryll racing toward us from down the hall. I might've been startled by her presence, if I hadn't just watched my sister brought back from the dead and seen Ryven—

Now that Kalli is safe and breathing, I'm able to peel myself away from her and twist around to face the man beside me.

Our gazes catch, pain and fear and doubt colliding as we assess one another in disbelief. A hundred questions fly through my mind. I want to know everything. How he became human again. How he wound up here. How he found me.

But for some gods-awful reason, the only one that makes it past my lips is, "Where did you find that outfit?"

We've only known each other a short while, but I honestly don't think I've ever seen him without his chest bared. The crimson suits him, even if the tunic itself is a tad small for his broad shoulders and corded arms.

A crooked smile kicks up one side of his face and, as my hungry eyes rove over him, over the body and face I feared I'd never see again after the Blight took hold of him, I lose it. I throw myself into the black abyss of his eyes. I tear away everything that has ever held me back. The uncertainty of what we might mean to each other. The worry of not being able to save him from the Blight. The guilt and shame of having mistakenly giving my heart to another before. The fear that this, too, will be temporary, and what it would do to me if it were to end. I release it all and fling myself into him.

Our bodies crash and even though it's unfamiliar and new and desperate, nothing has ever felt more right. My arms squeeze until there is no space between us, until my curves fit against his like the way the ocean's tide fits with the shore. And to my great relief, he squeezes me back. His hands and arms wrap around me, a blanket of security and comfort and reassurance. He holds us steady. Strong. Keeping us together. Refusing to let anything, even air, come between us again.

We pull our heads back at the same moment to gaze again into each other's eyes, and this time the fear and pain is gone. Only joy remains. Only hope.

I can't wait any longer. I've waited too long already.

I press my lips against his and drink in the ecstasy of his touch. Sparks skitter over my skin as his hand finds the base of my neck and drags me in tighter, deepening our kiss.

A moan escapes me, one I regret, if only because it causes my sister to sigh and brings my attention away from Ryven and this moment and back to reality. We just narrowly escaped death but we're still sitting inside a mage stronghold. Danger still looms about. It's obvious from Imryll's face as she finally arrives, nearly panting.

"There are more behind us. We have to move."

Ryven helps me to my feet.

"Where will we go?" Kalli asks, wincing and clutching her stomach. Whatever magic Ryven used on her wasn't enough to heal her fully. He tries offering her his hand, but she smacks it away, rising to her feet on her own. "If the way we came is blocked—"

"We'll find another way," Ryven assures her. "But you're still healing. If you insist on walking on your own, you'll slow us down."

I know my sister well enough to decipher the rage

simmering in her gray eyes for what it really is: embarrassment, her shattering pride. But for what it's worth, she manages to bite back her usual retort.

"And what are you proposing then?" my sister snaps.

Ryven glances down at me, to where our hands are interlocked. Regret suffuses his expression and a moment later he releases me. In his abrupt absence, the hollowness threatens to return, but I tell myself he isn't *gone*-gone, not like before. He is still here, and we will leave this place together. Stronger than ever.

He takes a step back and without warning his sun-kissed skin sprouts with fur the color of cedar. His bones crack and shift, his face disappearing as the head of a bear replaces it.

My stomach plummets at the sight of him as something other than himself again. A creature. A bear. An animal that, at times, can be vicious and wild and terrifying. I've waited so long for him to be human again and already—

A hand squeezes mine, my sister hobbling beside me. She watches me as if she can read my darkest thoughts, as if she has any way of understanding my panic and fear of losing him again.

My attention is drawn back to the bear—to Ryven—as his large, soft head bumps into my shoulder and a gentle, sad moan escapes his lips.

"It's different this time," my aunt says, a warmth about her that isn't usually there. "He chose this form. He can change back when he is ready."

I nod my understanding, shaking the forming tears from my eyes.

Down the hall behind her, footsteps approach. Sparks flicker, reflected in the pristinely polished walls, and alerting us to the magic heading our way.

"Get Kalli and Alphonse on his back," my aunt says. "We need to move."

WHAT WAS FORGOTTEN

AEYSIL KEEP, ILLASHORE

After what feels like hours of running, I think it's finally safe to say that we're lost.

The Keep is far grander than any of us had imagined, even Imryll who has done her best to guide us around based on her understanding of the view she's had from the outside. Every now and then, Kalli shares her opinion as well, but she's so focused on holding onto Ryven's bouncing back, and clutching onto our periodically unconscious cousin, to be able to give her undivided attention to it.

What's worse is every time we think we're getting close to an exit, the mage population thickens. Imryll and I can't fight them on our own, especially not with Alphonse's nullifying effect on the Keep waxing and waning sporadically.

And so, we run.

We keep running.

We keep twisting and turning, bounding down any hallway we come across, through any and every open door that doesn't promise the threat of mage magic on the other side. The metallic stench of blood grows heavier. For a while now, the charged pulse of magic has echoed around us; somewhere in the distance Arcathainians are facing off with the mages for the first time in ages. But for the most part, we've evaded any of the action.

Until Imryll stops mid-stride in a doorway. Wedged between her and Ryven, I slam into her stiff back, and the bear lumbers into me. Despite his size and the sheer force of him, his fur is still soft where it presses in on my skin and I find myself leaning back into him, relishing the nearness of him, of his touch, even if it's not the way I'd wanted it. I've spent so long away from him, I just want to be near him, and his heavy fur coat brings me the comfort I need to peer past Imryll's shoulders.

Bodies.

Dozens of them are strewn about the once-alabaster floor, it's shiny lacquer now coated in red glistening pools of blood that creep across the room. Imryll tiptoes ahead, making sure to avoid dipping her toes into the expanding puddles that fill the room with the saccharine, coppery stench of death.

When she's finally far enough away from me that I have a clearer view, I gasp. Some of the men and women who died here are dressed in black, phoenix sigils resting atop their unmoving breasts.

I don't know why I'm so stunned to see them, nor why their presence has cracked my chest open and filled the gaping wound with a red-hot iron poker. This is what happens in war. People die. Innocents. Friends. Loved ones.

By now, I should be all too familiar with the aftermath. My people have been at war with the demons of the Shadowthorn for decades. I've watched neighbors be torn from their homes in the dead of night. I've lost my brother—a soldier, a Crusader —beyond enemy lines, never to have the closure of laying his corpse to rest. I watched my parents die at the hands of a demon. I, myself, was almost torn to shreds by one in the heat of a battle and nearly died—I *should've* died.

When I joined the Shadow Crusade, I knew that everyone I

knew who was still alive would likely die a horrible death soon. I steeled my heart to that knowledge. Or at least, I'd tried to.

But seeing the bloodied bodies of my comrades here, a hot fist clenches my gut and twists.

The only Crusaders I know who were here were the ones I hold dearest.

Silver.

Güthric.

Fox.

Dimitri.

I don't want to look down at my feet as I walk into the room, but I have to. I have to know if it's any of them.

Behind me, a sorrowful sound moans into the palm of my hand as Ryven nudges me. If I had any reserves left, if Alphonse was conscious and able to counter whatever magic the mages have set on this place, I might be able to hear his exact words. But his meaning still finds a way to me, through his dark, russet eyes that have always been able to communicate with me.

I have nothing to worry about because Dimitri and the others aren't here.

My chest eases. I suppose I should've known. They would've been with him when he found Alphonse and me.

However, the relief is short-lived.

Because if Dimitri and the others aren't here, then where are they? Are they still slumbering in the forest, forever trapped in the sleeping spell that the mage Igemonar unleashed upon them? Were they killed the same day Alphonse and I were taken? Or were they left for the animals to ravage?

As Ryven nudges me forward, I try ignoring every dark possibility that my mind conjures and focus on our present circumstances. We need to find a way out, while simultaneously avoiding stumbling into an open war.

"We might be near an exit," Kalli hisses through her teeth.

Jumping around to rush to her aid, I realize she's not further injured, merely struggling with Alphonse's unconscious weight.

"What do you mean?" I ask, shoving our cousin to the center of Ryven's back.

Exhausted by the effort, Kalli heaves herself over Alphonse's back and shoulders, using her weight to hold him in place as Ryven and I begin maneuvering through the room again.

"This early in the battle," she begins. "If our army has breached the Keep walls, I doubt they've made it far. In fact, I'm surprised they're even inside at all. The mages, their magic—I don't know how well the Magistrate's men will do against them."

As Kalli talks, I do my best to follow the path Imryll laid out, but the puddles of blood continue to expand beneath the bodies so rapidly that not far into the room, I eventually have to find my own way ahead. Ryven is equally unlucky. His giant bear claws make it impossible to move without stepping in the sticky fluids, and he gives up trying to avoid them almost the moment we entered the now tomb-like space.

Kalli continues talking, her voice low as if the dead might rise if they hear us. "This is a small unit of men here. I don't think they were part of the main rank."

My eyes squint. "Like…spies?"

"Something like that. Or at least a special unit meant to find a more discreet way in." She's quiet for a moment and I finally reach Imryll who's waiting beside another door at the opposite end of the room. "They were sent to find Alphonse."

My head whips around just as Ryven hops over the last pile of dead, jostling Kalli where she's hunched over Alphonse. She glowers down at the bear. His ear twitches as if he can feel her ire searing into him.

"Are you sure?" I ask. "Uncle Esmond—the Magistrate—he's

never been exactly affectionate toward Alphonse. I know he's his son, but…"

"The night your—" Her squinted eyes flit down to Ryven again, something like repulsion or confusion swirling behind her dark lashes. "The night your *friend* freed me—"

"Freed you?" My voice becomes shrill. "What do you mean *freed you*? I thought you came here with the Magistrate?"

"I did, but not willingly. Or at least, not in the end." She shakes her head. "None of that matters right now. Before we fled, I heard the men talking while we were sailing to shore. That hadn't been part of the plan. They had sent a few ships inland to scout the lands and locate where the most mages congregated, return to the armada, and then they were going to strike from the sea. But that all changed when the Magistrate learned that the mages had taken Alphonse. He commanded the entire armada inland, aside from a few men who would stay behind to guard the boats and keep them ready. That's how Ryven was able to get me out. The crews had mostly left the ships, heading off to the battle that would happen here."

Biting my lip, I consider her words. "So you think these people here found a secret way inside?"

Kalli nods, her silver, unruly braids falling over her shoulder and slapping Alphonse's face.

He jolts awake and they both nearly fall over.

Imryll whips around and hisses at the both of them, "Will you two be quiet? There are people ahead."

The conversation dies, as does the groaning and bickering that had only just begun. The others strain to listen for the voices Imryll alluded to hearing, or for any other indication that we might soon be discovered, but I'm more interested in learning where this secret passage is. So far, it is our best chance at getting out of here alive, and one of the only ways we're likely to leave here without having to fight our way through the entire Illashore line of mages, and then the entire Arcathainian legion.

But four separate doors led into the room we stand in, and as I glance beyond Imryll, I notice the hallway leads in at least two directions with who knows how many doors and rooms to enter at each end. We need to know which direction to go before we head anywhere, otherwise we could be walking away from our best chance at salvation.

An idea strikes then.

"Alphonse?" I ask, my cousin's wide eyes snapping to mine. "I need to use my power."

No further instruction is necessary. He closes his eyes and a moment later, power sparks beneath my skin. I inhale a deep breath. At first, it almost makes me vomit, the stench of blood so thick in the air it almost feels like I'm snorting it in through my nostrils. But I keep inhaling, keep pulling on the air and reaching for the freshness that I know is somewhere beyond these walls.

In no time at all, a breeze creeps up behind us. My inhale deepens and I devour the aroma of fresh cut grass that fills the room, the blooming daisies, the clear blue sky. I follow it without question, without any word to the others, but fortunately they come without command or request.

After meandering through another room, into another corridor, the breeze guides us into—

A library. One of great magnificence, even if I only have the library of Nigh to compare it to. But those shelves had been old and rickety, dust coating thousands of the tomes kept there because few ever visited the library and, when they did, they so rarely needed anything but the few books we were assigned for our studies.

Like the rest of the Keep, this place is in pristine condition. The bookshelves are neatly stacked, the books lined perfectly with each other so that large books are on the bottom rungs and the smallest on the higher ones. What this library lacks in height compared to the one in Nigh, it seems to make up for in horizontal expanse. Hundreds of rows of shelves stretch out before us in either direction. And no matter how far they go, some unknown source of light seems to illuminate every corner, ridding every shadow from ever touching the well-cared for tomes here.

At a desk just ahead, a woman dressed in long, gray robes fusses with the unruly books atop her table. Their pages flip angrily about, as if they're sentient beings with their own free will. And though she's collapsed over them, arms splayed atop as many as she can reach, she still can't hold them all down.

Abashedly, I release my hold on the wind and the books still.

The woman freezes too, before abruptly standing to glare down at the table with a look of distrust as if she's not sure if she believes the pages are done.

I don't know what overcomes me—perhaps it's just the familiarity of being back inside a library—but I call to her, "Excuse me?"

The woman jerks, clutching her chest with one hand and her mouth with the other. A faint smile appears as she adjusts her glasses. "Goodness. You gave me a fright—" Terror rips through her at the sight of us. "Y-you're druids," she breathes, her voice as soft as whisper. Louder, she cries, "D-druids! They're here!"

Ryven charges forward, almost dumping Kalli and Alphonse from his back as he snarls and bares his teeth.

The woman, a frightened mess of bones, staggers backward and falls to the floor.

"We mean you no harm," I say over Ryven's menacing growl.

He stops lumbering toward her and looks at me, giving me time to inch forward. I hold my hand out to the woman, but she doesn't take it. She's too busy pointing up at us, her bottom lip quivering.

"How are you—D-druid magic d-doesn't work here." Understanding flickers behind her gaze. "That gust of wind? That was y-you?"

Tucking my arm back at my side, I nod. "We aren't here to hurt you. We're just looking for a way out that won't lead us directly onto the battlefield. Do you know where it is?"

Slowly, she blinks up at me. "Where what is?"

Kalli scoffs and slides off Ryven's back. "This is a waste of time. Just call the wind again and we'll find the door soon enough." She charges forward without even waiting for me, as if she already knows which way to go.

I spare a final glance at the middle-aged woman cowering on the ground before going after my sister. Imryll and Ryven follow close behind me, Alphonse alert enough to hold himself on the bear's back. We don't make it two steps before I hear the woman scramble to her feet.

My blood flows hot and I spin around ready to attack her before she can strike us. Never again will I allow a mage to attempt to harm my family.

But to my surprise, there is no fireball in her shaking hands, only the ropes that tie her pale robes together.

"Y-you're really leaving?"

Relaxing a little, I nod. And there's something about her, something so unthreatening and meek, that I find myself explaining more than I should to a stranger deep in enemy territory. "We were brought here against our wills. The only reason we came to Illashore was to ask the mages—to ask your people—if they knew how to defeat Qaeus."

"The Primordial?" she balks, a hand drifting protectively to her chest and cinching her robes tighter. Her thin lips purse and she averts her eyes for a moment as she considers something. "We're not *all* mages, you know?"

Doubt pulses through me. "What do you mean?"

She aims a sad smile at her feet. "It's true then. They really did make you forget." A soft, humorless laugh brushes past her lips. "It's no wonder no one came."

I glance over my shoulder to the others hoping to find some understanding, especially from Kalli who is usually so adept at solving riddles and puzzles. But she seems even more confused than I am.

I return my attention to the woman. "What do you mean? Who made me forget?"

"Not *you*. Your ancestors. All of them."

Ice seeps into my veins until I am brimming with chilling understanding. She's talking about the druids and the reason why no one knows they exist anymore. No one in Arcathain, that is.

Suddenly, Imryll appears at my side, a curious tilt to her chin and a dubious glint in her eyes. "Explain. What exactly did they make our ancestors forget?"

The woman bites her lip to keep it from trembling. She glances between the two of us, the magnitude of what she's about to say nearly consuming her before she can find the courage to say it. But eventually she does. Eventually, she convinces herself that, despite not wanting to be the messenger, we still deserve the message.

"Everything," she says plainly, her breath catching. "They made you forget everything."

A HISTORY UNKNOWN

AEYSIL KEEP LIBRARY, ILLASHORE

After a little more coaxing and reassurance, as well as a promise to keep the bear well out of reach *and* sight, eventually we convince the woman—the librarian of Aeysil Keep, we soon learn—to lead us to the information she is alluding to. At first, we'd demanded she simply tell us, but she insisted that we'd want the full story, and that she wasn't equipped to provide it on her own.

So despite the war raging just outside these book-lined walls, we follow her to the back of the library.

There, we gape in stunned silence at the woven tapestry that engulfs the entire two-story wall from ceiling to floor, from one end of the nook to the other.

"What is this?" Imryll breathes, her fingers trailing over the dark threads.

The deep shades of red. The shadowy hues of black. The midnight blues and dusky evergreens.

The scene before us is one of carnage painted beneath the moon's bright halo. Human bodies litter the dark field, a thick layer of blood drowning the grass beneath them where they lie. And in the background, cresting the hills and darkness seeping from each steep, four large beings rise.

The Primordials.

I glance down to the panels beside it, the colors becoming more vibrant the farther I look, the story's beginning seemingly brighter than its grim end.

The librarian swallows a lump in her throat before speaking. "This tapestry was dyed and woven by some of the greatest artisans of their time. It's an homage to the accomplishments of the mages, leading all the way up until the Great Rift."

My gaze continues to wander down the other end, and I see it now. A depiction of the ground cracking, the continents splitting apart. In the foreground, the screaming people of Arcathain are blurred, their misery and woes ignored by the triumphant mages who have just escaped the tyranny of the Primordials.

The librarian takes a timid step forward, her brunette bun, dulled by the onset of aging, bunching at the base of her neck as she looks up the length of the artwork.

"Long ago, there were only humans and druids," she says, jutting her chin to the scenes farther down to our left. We follow her as she makes her way down to the first tapestry. "The druids were special people. They had access to something that was so unimaginable to the humans that it seemed like magic, far long before there were ever mages. The druids knew and felt things that no human ever could. They were connected to the land and wind and sea in indescribable ways. But there were four in particular who carried the most power."

Imryll sucks in a sharp breath as we reach the first tapestry. "The original Elders."

Four women stand, their heads lifted to the sky and their fingers interlaced. The elements dance around them: one shrouded in vines and flowers; one wind-blown with lightning striking down from above her; one with a fox resting beside her ankles, a snake wrapped around her thigh, and birds singing by her ears; and the fourth standing in a fountain of ocean spray, a dolphin peering up from the water behind her with love and loyalty in its eyes.

"Some of the humans coveted the druids for their power," the librarian continues, ambling to the next scene. "It was a long time before they knew what to do with that jealousy—or how they call it: ambition—but it also gave them enough time for it to fester. The more that the druids aided with the woes of the humans, creating the most bountiful harvests that would be impossible to attain on their own without the manipulation of the winds and rains, or taming horses and mules with a mere whisper in their ear so that transportation between the cities became more accessible to the populace. No matter the druids merits or good intentions, some of the humans felt it was wrong that they—and they alone—possessed so much power."

She stops before another tapestry, this one of a pink, rocky land and a crystal blue lake. It's an unnatural color, the blue as bright as a clear sky but dazzling as if the stars could be seen from within it during the day.

Something about it looks familiar...but different. It almost reminds me of the depictions of the Pits of Bagamore that I'd found on the wall surrounding the Eyve.

"At the time," the woman continues. "It was well-known that the lakes of Bagamore were a great source of power to the druids. I wouldn't know why, but they kept them connected to the elements of the realms, and so they were a sacred place. The druids would visit them frequently, so the story goes, to realign themselves to their guiding element, to bathe and cleanse in the restorative waters, to honor the land and give offerings to the creatures that dwelled there."

Kalli's neck snaps so fast I'm afraid she almost breaks it. "The Primordials?"

The librarian flashes a sympathetic smile. "No. Not yet. The Primordials have not always been in the realm. They were born."

We're guided to the next tapestry, an image of four nearly-shriveled women standing inside the lakes of Bagamore, back when they still glittered and glistened like blue liquid diamonds.

She sucks in a breath. "When the Elders neared the end of their lives, the druids took them to Bagamore to be laid to rest. They believed that this would return the Elders' magic to the land and, in turn, strengthen their connection to it. Depending on the storyteller, some might say they demanded to be brought there because they wanted to be immortalized. But I believe that what came next was purely accidental.

"The Elders were submerged in a separate lake each. They were held under as they took their last, dying breaths. And no one knows how much longer it took—for the druids remained at Bagamore for weeks in a constant mourning and celebration of the loss of the lives of the great Elders—but what we do know is that eventually, four Primordials arose from the lakes."

Everyone halts where they stand. Imryll, Kalli, and I twist to glance among ourselves. Judging from Imryll's horrified expression, this was unknown information, part of the story kept hidden by the mages' memory spell.

I don't know why this knowledge is making my knees buckle. I didn't know the great Elders. I barely even know the druids as they are today. But my heart twists regardless. Perhaps because, despite not knowing them personally, I feel a connection to them. Call it a druid's curse, or maybe it has more to do with the fact that I now know my mother was destined to become an Elder, which means I am a direct descendant of them.

I wonder if the one I faced, if Qaeus, is distantly part of my lineage. Maybe that's why she was able to speak to me.

"The poor Elders," I say at last, breaking the silence. "They wanted to give their magic to the land and instead they were turned into monsters."

"No." The librarian's hands shoot up. "They weren't. Not at first." She scurries to the next panel and gestures up to the four beings. Their bodies are as bright as the lakes of Bagamore. "The Primordials were docile and benevolent. For a long time. They watched over the people and seemed to create a balance in the realms. Whereas before, some sides of the continents faced drought and others monsoons, when the Primordials rose, the environments balanced. The people, for the most part, rejoiced. Even the animals adapted and seemed more content."

"Then what happened?" I ask, unable to tear my gaze away from their beauty. "What made them what they became?"

"Jealous humans," Kalli sneers, hatred seething from her darkened eyes. "The mages."

The librarian nods. "It is true. Once they saw the Primordials rise, they wondered if the benefits of the lakes of Bagamore could be shared. Up until then, they were mostly governed by the druids who saw no need in allowing humans near them. They were sacred, remember? But one human—the first mage, Head Mage Varyn Brenthan Ephemeris—he snuck into Bagamore, and through alchemy, perfected a method to bestow humans with magic, thus creating the mages.

"When the druids found out, they were conflicted, but Head Mage Varyn berated them as selfish, power-hungry mongrels until they finally allowed him and others like him access to Bagamore. With the aid of their newfound magic, the mages developed an intricate pipe system that extracted some of the lake water and transferred it to Aeysil Keep to be alchemized and prepared for doses to create more mages, and eventually to re-dose, as they soon discovered the effects of the magic were not permanent, no matter what they tried."

"Because it's unnatural," Imryll scoffs, shaking her head up at the rejoicing mages and their pipes. The lakes are still as lush as ever in this tapestry, but I have to wonder if the adverse implications weren't already in effect. Especially when we arrive to the next scene.

The pools are now black. The water no longer looks like something that would be refreshing to dip into, but a heavy substance that could drag someone down to their deaths.

"The druids eventually came to understand that by taking magic from the land without replenishing it at the same rate, the wells were soon tainting. Not only the wells, but also the Primordials.

"They became the wicked creatures you know today. Everywhere they roamed, they wreaked havoc on the people. The druids wanted to help them and stop the madness, they wanted to right the balance that had been broken. But the mages needed the magic. They didn't want to give it up. They couldn't."

Finally, we reach the tapestry we'd seen first, the one of the battle with the Primordials standing victorious in the background.

"The Primordials largely left the druids alone, unless otherwise provoked. But the humans had been attacked and slaughtered by the thousands. Even the mages who possessed magic from the Pits themselves, didn't possess enough to go unscathed by the Primordials' wraths. Or perhaps they possessed too much. So, they banded together, human and mage, and created the Primordial weapons that would be used against the creatures. By using their own bones, it seemed they could capture the Primordials' souls—the Elders' souls as well as their magic—and return them to what became known as the Pits of Bagamore. They succeeded with two of them. Khaymus and Qhistus were killed by Primordial weapons and the weapons discarded to Bagamore."

Not my axe though, I realize, noticing its depiction now in the tapestry. According to the history book I gleaned in Nigh, the Crusader who wielded it died during the fight, and the axe was swallowed up with the remaining shadowsteel weapons.

"Khunas was slain, but the axe that claimed her soul never reached the Pits of Bagamore," the librarian says, confirming my suspicions. "And once Khunas fell, the Primordial Qaeus entered a chrysalis state, almost as if she knew that humanity was coming for her. The Shadowthorn was born from her final resting place and demons leapt from her dark shadows to keep her guarded. The mages knew they wouldn't be able to reach her, and even if they could, the people were growing weary of battle and suspicious of the mages' intentions.

"In order to prevent everyone from blaming them for the Primordials' tyranny and the Shadowthorn's development, and to avoid having to give up their newfound power, they cast a forgetting spell across the continent while simultaneously trapping Qaeus on the other side of the Wall." She stops strolling in front of another scene woven in thread, a progression of angered faces becoming serene and docile, folks scratching their heads and continuing about their days as if they had nothing to worry about. The images are so realistic it's like being there when it all happened. "It took every single mage to make the spell successful, and it was the first time they truly understood the power they now had at their disposal. The druids forgot they birthed the Primordials, the humans forgot about the druids, and most importantly to the mages, everyone forgot they had once been human."

Nearing the end of the tapestry, we stop. Slowly, she turns around to face us. "And that's the history that none of your people knows."

I'm too stunned to speak. I grew up believing the mages were powerful enough to sever a continent in two and drift away with a chunk of it, but there's something far more frightening about them being able to alter the memories of every living human and druid.

"It's your fault then." Kalli strides forward, exuding an unruly kind of anger that makes me recoil. It makes the librarian recoil, as well. "The Primordials are vile, evil things now because your people leeched their magic and spoiled the well. All you have to do is stop taking magic away from the land and everyone would stop suffering, but you're too selfish!"

"Not all of us are mages," the librarian snaps, and I realize it's not the first time she's said it. She drops her gaze to her knotted fingers and my heart pinches at the emotions warring in her expression. "There were humans on the west side of the continent when it was torn away. My family among them." Her gaze lifts, her eyes as fierce as they've been since we stormed into the place. "I am no mage. But, thanks to the mages, I am also not Arcathainian."

And suddenly it hits me. A shame so intense that my entire body might as well have burst into flames. I wasn't around during the Great Rift, but from everything I've heard about the time before, the humans and mages were mostly intermingled about the continent. So why had it never occurred to me that humans had been caught on the wrong side, forced away from the mainland? From their homes. Their families.

Looking at her now I realize she can't be much older than my own father, Oddo, who also survived the Great Rift. He lost his parents that day. He nearly lost his brother Adrien as well if he hadn't run into their collapsed home that had been on the edge of the crack and rescued him from falling.

I can't even imagine what it must've been like for her and people like her, to have lived through it and remember everything since—

Then it dawns on me. "Why do you remember?" I ask her. "The mages cast the memory spell before the Great Rift, right? Shouldn't you be as clueless as the rest of us?"

Her head bows but she holds a hand up to the draped wall. "I didn't for most of my life. But when I was old enough to be employed, I found a job here. You can learn a lot from history books that were reserved for the mage classes, and I had access to them all. Including this rather graphic tapestry." She clears her throat as if the memories are still too painful to face. She wasn't alive for all of them, but the ones she did endure are bad enough. I know as much because of the way my father would speak of the Great Rift, distantly and like it was a pain he carried with him everywhere, every day.

"To answer your question," she says softly. "The mages cannot stop. They will die without the magic now. Truly. They tried, long ago. Long before the Great Rift. But once they began infusing themselves with the concentrated magic from they gathered from Bagamore, it seeped into them; it became an inseverable part of them."

Behind us, Ryven appears, a nearly imperceptible growl rumbling in his chest. I'm the only one who appears to notice him, everyone else enraptured by the forgotten history of our people—of the entire Broken Realms. But I sensed the warning before Ryven even appeared, and I know he wouldn't have broken our vow to the librarian to keep him away from her if it wasn't for a reason. Fortunately, she doesn't seem to notice him either, and he disappears back around the corner before she can.

I understand him well enough. The war is encroaching farther into the Keep and we don't have much more time.

"To stop siphoning that power," the librarian continues. "It would mean the genocide of an entire race. And they feared that's what the Arcathainians would demand of them, to give up their magic, and their lives in turn. So they fled."

"You say that as if they were justified," Kalli spits, her tongue a painful whip that the librarian hadn't been expecting across her bared flesh. "Why did you act like you were afraid of us when we entered your precious library? If you knew the history of the rest of the realm, and you knew what the mages had done, why are you afraid of the druids? They're the victims in all of this."

The woman shrinks into herself all the more, but she doesn't back down. Her voice may be timid, but it's steeled with a lifetime of being surrounded by the enemy and forgotten from her people.

"No one is the victim in this story. Everyone made choices and each of those choices had consequences." Her hands stop wringing the ropes around her waist. "I was afraid because I assumed you were here for vengeance for what they did to you. People who rally around vengeance rarely think before they attack. They do not care about the innocents who are hurt along the way. They just kill."

"We're not the ones killing," Kalli snaps, one hand still pressed to her side.

I reach for her shoulder and spin her back. "Stop. We don't have time for this. We need to leave. There is still a war raging outside."

The hard set of her eyes softens and she nods.

Beside us, one of the tapestries is tugged aside, a door revealed behind the heavy, dyed fabric.

"The exit you're seeking is here," the librarian says. "You should go while you are still able. They sound close now."

For the first time since being brought here, I hear the battles raging outside. Glancing over my shoulder, I spy Ryven stepping into view again, Alphonse still draped over his back, barely seeming to hold onto consciousness to allow Ryven to remain as he is.

Kalli swings the secret door ajar and indicates inside. My aunt goes first, desperate to rid herself of this place that she never even wanted to set foot in. Reluctantly, Ryven bounds inside too.

I stay behind. "Come with us," I say to the librarian. "You don't have to die here."

She shrugs, a sad and defeated look suffused in her expression. "This is my home. I do not belong wherever it is you are going. Besides, I might not be a mage, but they are not cruel for no reason. They will not harm me, only your people will. As long as the mages are able to hold them off, I will be fine."

I'm about to argue with her when the library door bursts open. Her eyes bulge, as do mine as they lock on hers. But the moment passes and I dive into the corridor, fairly certain that when the door shuts, I sense no presence of another behind me.

THE ONE MISSING

UNKNOWN MEADOW, ILLASHORE

"Where are we going?" I ask, fingers wrapped tightly in Ryven's thick fur as he bounds through the tall field of grass. But my question goes unanswered. Now that we're out of the Keep, Imryll has taken to the skies. Kalli has as well. And if Ryven tries answering me through the mental connection druids can develop between animals, I'm too exhausted or distracted to notice.

My mind races with the information we've just uncovered. The facts tumble about like boulders in my skull, crashing and slamming into me with alarming and disorienting force.

The Primordials were created by druids.

The mages were created from sacred waters.

As long as the mages exist, the Primordial Qaeus will forever be tainted. But we can't kill her because the shadow-steel axe didn't work on her. It made her stronger.

There's a solution here, to *everyone's* problems, but I'm too delirious and drained to be able to figure it out. I need water, a meal that is more than crumbs, and perhaps a long nap.

We've been traveling for half a day, presumably to put as much distance between us and the battle at the Keep. I refused to glance back once we were free. I couldn't stomach the thought of seeing all that killing. I may have joined the Shadow Crusade to fight demons, but people fighting people is different. Especially after everything we've learned...

Mages and Arcathainians were once the same. Cousins could be fighting cousins right now. Great grandchildren eviscerating great grandparents.

Perhaps I'll skip a meal, with the way my stomach still churns at the thought. We have to do something to stop this. But what?

Through a clearing ahead, I finally make out what I expect is our destination. Relief tugs at me, settling my stomach, as I lay eyes on some of the familiar faces I missed so much during my imprisonment.

With a log held against her chest, Fox makes her way to the simmering embers of the fire. But the wood never makes it. She spots us the moment I see them and the log falls from her grasp as she bolts into a run.

"Alphy!" she screams, tall blades of grass whipping across her face. "Alphy!"

He'd been unconscious since our escape, since he was finally able to relinquish his grasp on his power without fear of any of us losing ours. But he stirs now. Hunched in front of me and cradling the bear's broad neck and shoulders, Alphonse's head lifts. Even though I can't see their faces, I can tell the moment his eyes snag on hers by the way his spine lengthens, his shoulders square, and in an instant, it's like he's all but forgotten about the beating he took in the Keep because he flings himself over the side of Ryven.

Ryven's quick and steady gait prevents me from watching Alphonse and Fox slam into each other, but Fox's shrieks and expletives carry across the field loud enough for us to hear the concern in her tone, and to discern the moment Alphonse crushes her head into his shoulder.

We slow as we approach the fire, our friends gathering

around with broad grins and relief flickering behind wet eyes. I slide down Ryven's back to be engulfed in a hug from my uncle Adrien. Next in line, Sai gives my shoulder a hearty pat. I continue down the line, giving Silver a hug and nearly losing consciousness when Güthric wraps his thick arms around me, but then there is no one left. It's just the four of them.

All this time, the entire way here, I told myself not to worry. I reassured myself that if something happened to Dimitri, someone surely would've told me by now, instead of making me wait with hope in my heart all this time, until this moment.

Staggering back, I search my friend's faces.

"What is it?" Silver asks. "Are you hungry? We prepared food."

One of Güthric's arms thrusts out, something charred on the end of a stick in his hand. "Fish."

Slowly, my head begins to shake. They think I'm declining the offer, but more than anything, it's an argument with myself. He can't be gone. I don't want to ask them where he is because I can't hear the words that Dimitri has died.

There are others missing from our ranks too though, a realization that only serves to confirm my fears and reinforce every narrative I've begun concocting in my head: they were ambushed by the mages and Dimitri was slaughtered; so was Eparah and some of the others, apparently.

From behind us, Alphonse and Fox casually stroll to the circle we've formed. His arm is slung over her shoulders as she guides him to Ryven, handing him off so that he's leaning on the bear's shoulder.

When he's stable, the silence draws her attention. She looks at me, then to the others, before turning to me again.

"Piss on a mage," she mutters, striding forward and taking my hands into her own. "Dimitri's alive. These halfwits should've said as much the moment they saw you."

Behind her, everyone looks mortified by their carelessness,

but I couldn't care more. The relief that floods through me could practically levitate me into the night sky.

Dimitri is alive.

"Where is he?" I ask, eagerly looking about their makeshift camp.

It's not much. It's not anything, actually. Just a log atop some burning embers, a few knapsacks spread out like they were used as pillows and beds, and a pile of fish bones. But I'm searching for only one thing, any sign of my friend. His broadsword. A shaggy head of golden-brown hair nestled in one of the bed rolls. But I find nothing, no trace of Dimitri.

Fox worries at her lip with one sharp canine. "Sorry. He isn't here. He is alive though, but, he just didn't come."

Like she has just sank her hand into my chest and begun twisting my heart, something sharp and molten aches inside me. What does she mean he *didn't come*? As if he had a choice and decided that finding me—or at the bare minimum, being here when I was rescued—wasn't on his list of priorities for the evening.

Before I can ask her to elaborate and help me decide whether or not I am painfully worried or irritatingly offended by his absence, a commotion happens behind us. Something like large branches snap, followed not long after by Alphonse's retching. I twist around to find Ryven shifting out of his bear form, his arms and legs snapping into human limbs as his pelt of fur retreats deep below his flesh. My eyes betray me as they veer farther and farther down, confirming that he is stark naked.

"He's on the Magistrate's ship," Ryven says, startling me with the answer to my previously unspoken question, and making me rip my gaze away the moment I realize it. "He believed staying behind was the best way to save you since he wasn't sure of the Magistrate's intentions if they found you."

He's talking about Dimitri, I realize. A man I'd once shared a bed with. A man I once believed I loved. And I'm standing here, ogling at Ryven's impressive length and tantalizing physique.

Ashamedly, I tear my gaze away. It's just as well because now that he's drawn my attention back to Dimitri's absence, my stomach sours. I look out toward the sea, an endless black that whispers of danger and demise.

Part of me wants to go to him, to tell Dimitri that I'm all right and that he doesn't have to stay there now that I'm here. But I've known Dimitri all his life, and I know I'm not the only reason he remained behind while the others came looking for me. He is bound by his duty to his country, and perhaps always will be.

Besides, I can't return to the Magistrate. If anything, Dimitri was right to worry about the Magistrate's intentions for me. He's already imprisoned me once. My sister twice now, it would seem. Showing my face there would just mean I'd be thrown into another dungeon, another cell.

Never again.

Ryven turns his attention to my uncle. "Did you get what I asked for?"

Adrien's mouth slants with a mischievous grin as he retrieves a pile of folded clothes from the ground nearby. "It wasn't easy, you know? Stealing from the Arcathainian army."

Sai folds his arms. "I don't know. It didn't seem too difficult. Those men seemed awfully eager to undress for you. Same with the women."

Adrien's smile broadens and he gives a sheepish shrug. "It is a curse to be this enchanting."

Sai just shakes his head, seeming mostly amused as Adrien drapes his arm over Sai's shoulders.

My uncle juts his chin to the shadow by his feet where he pulled Ryven's outfit from. "I grabbed the ladies some clothes as well. I hope they suffice."

My aunt and Kalli dive for the clothes and gather them quickly as if they'd been eagerly perched, just awaiting the invitation. They disappear into the darkness for privacy, but the brightness of the moon tonight catches on Kalli's silver hair when she shifts, even if the tall grass covers the rest of her.

Ryven is quick to climb into the provided garments as well, a pair of black leather trousers and a black plated tunic, just like the ones worn in the Shadow Crusade. It's strange to see him dressed as such. Stranger still to watch his bare chest disappear. It leaves me feeling disappointed, but perhaps now I'll be better able to focus on what we need to do next.

The Arcathainians have brought war to the mages' front doorstep, but they're fighting because of history that they know nothing about. I can't say for certain that the knowledge we gleaned would change anything, but what if it could? What if there's a way for both sides to work together to save Qaeus from the monster she's become?

While I'm busy mulling over our options and their possible outcomes, Kalli finishes dressing. At the sight of her, I forget everything I was trying to do. I'd expected more Crusader garb, even though in hindsight, I should've known that most of the warriors under the Magistrate's command are not of the Shadow Crusade. But since I've grown so accustomed to being surrounded by black uniforms so dark that not even demon blood can stain them, I nearly gasp to see someone dressed in a cream-colored palette of padded cottons and flowing chiffons. She glows like the sun against the backdrop of night and I can do nothing but gape at her beauty.

Adrien didn't just snag a warrior's attire for my sister. For her, he grabbed something more suiting.

The imperial outfit almost looks like something that could've been taken straight from Kalli's own wardrobe in the Capital. It's not something she would've worn often, but something dawned for special ceremonies or events, meant to make her seem elegant and prestigious, while simultaneously being light enough for her to engage in battle if need be.

The intricate golden stitching that blooms in floral patterns around her shoulders and trickles inward at the waist, accentuating her hips, gives her a sort of high-ranking status that is not common among warriors.

As she emerges in the moonlight, her expression is so serene and calm that it's as if she's just returned home after a long, wearisome journey.

Adrien dips his head. "I present to you, the new Advisor of —what did she say she advised?" he asks, glancing sideways at Sai who merely shrugs. "Well, Advisor of this little squad, at the very least."

Dangling from one shoulder is a long, ivory stream of sheer fabric that billows as she ambles forth, hobbling with impressive grace and authority or someone still clutching their healing side.

When she finally clears the tall grass, she tosses the scarf over the other shoulder, her raven landing to perch atop it not a moment later.

Already close behind, Imryll steps out from the darkness as well, only her outfit appears...less suiting. She looks like a common sailor, one who might've gutted a few fish and used her own tattered shirt to wipe away their guts from her knife when she was finished.

Poorly, Adrien attempts to cover a snicker inside his hand. "I believe this just belonged to one of the prisoners they had on board who escaped the night you broke Kalli free." He glances to Ryven, who sheepishly ducks his head.

"I hope he wasn't being held for anything serious."

"Nonsense," Adrien says, blowing through his lips and smacking the air. "My brother locked up any poor soul who so much as dared look at him wrong. I'm sure the man was a fine one."

Even in the near darkness, I can see the distinct arch of Kalli's rolling eyes as they trace along the top of her eye sockets. "If by *fine one*, you mean a criminal, a thief, a treasonous lecher, and someone with a mouth so foul that he made even the crewmen blush, then yes. I'm sure he was a great asset to society."

"Sounds like my kind of company," Adrien whispers, throwing an elbow into her side.

The small jab makes her double over, nearly falling to the ground on her knees.

Fortunately, Imryll is there to catch her. "We need to finish healing you. You should've never taken the form of an animal until you were fully healed."

Kalli grimaces, shoving my aunt away. "I'm fine."

But she staggers back, my aunt catching her elbow. They glare at one another, the intensity between the two proud women awkward to behold. Finally, Kalli lets out a sigh, surprising me thoroughly, and allows my aunt to lead her to lay in one of the bedrolls.

"I'll just stay here and wait my turn then." Alphonse waves at them as they walk by, his smile tight and mocking.

I'm not sure who to feel sorrier for, my sister who was almost incinerated by a ball of magical fire, or Alphonse whose face is covered in dried blood and patchy, purple bruises.

"Waiting won't be necessary." In an instant, Ryven is beside Alphonse. His knees bend slightly, his arms aimed to support my cousin's back and legs.

"What are you—"

But Alphonse doesn't have time to finish the rest of his question because Ryven swoops him into his arms as if he weighs no more than a small child. My cousin shrieks at the sudden and unexpected change in positioning, humiliation settling in a moment later as Ryven proceeds to carry him to another mat by the fire.

"Put me down! I am quite capable of walking on my own," is the last thing I hear from them before Fox appears at my side, startling me from watching them.

"Come on," she says, and I sense the effort it takes for her to drag her own gaze away from them. "You look like you could use some food."

With her arm looped in mine, she guides me to a makeshift table where Güthric had been working when we'd first arrived. Atop the bound logs and sticks lay a half dozen gutted fish, the creatures fileted, deboned, and charred to a crisp. The sight of them reminds me of Kalli's engulfed stomach, and the black flesh I'd spied beneath her singed clothes, and my appetite becomes quickly entangled in nausea.

My face must turn as green as the seaweed that's drifted up on the coast because Fox shoos me to sit by the fire and returns a few moments later with a freshly plucked banana instead.

"There. Is that better?"

I nod, snatching the deliciously, yellow fruit from her hands without another thought and cramming it into my mouth.

"Go slowly," she warns. "If you haven't been eating the past couple of weeks, then your stomach is going to need to get used to food again."

When I take another one-two-three wolfing bites, she reaches across me and gingerly takes the remaining bit of the banana from me. I turn feral eyes on her. I'm ready to snap my jaws around her wrist and gnaw the banana clean from her grasp when I catch the gentle understanding in her expression. It reminds me of her own past, and the hunger she used to endure that led her to understand such things as how to ease one's stomach back into eating.

The realization sobers me and I manage to bite my lip instead of her hand.

When Güthric, Silver, Adrien, and Sai join us, no one brings food with them, despite it obviously being their dinnertime. I don't know if she asked them not to while I was busy trying to curb the nausea, or if they're all too relieved to see me alive, or what, but it doesn't matter. All that matters is that we are together again. Friends who have become more like family, and family who is finally living up to the role now that they're not exiled in forbidden sections of the Broken Realms.

For a moment, I worry where the conversation will go. It's too soon, yet, for me to talk about what happened at Aeysil Keep. I fear that so much as thinking about that black dungeon will somehow cause it to reappear around me, and I'll find myself trapped and alone all over again.

But to my great relief, no one asks me to tell them about it. Instead, they share their own stories. Of traipsing through the unknown forests of Illashore. Of who snored the loudest during their journey, how many bug bites they endured, who's boots became soaked when they tried crossing over a stream.

The conversation is so easy and lighthearted, it almost hurts. Because I know it can't be like this forever. Soon, we will have to face the darkness ahead of us, as well as the shadows of our past.

But as we laugh and bicker, as we poke fun at each other like we did during our training days in Nigh and during our journey across the Varenholm Ocean, I realize that moment will come, but it isn't now.

Tonight, we simply enjoy all that we have.

Tonight, we are grateful that we still have each other.

Well into the night, long after Imryll and Ryven finished healing my sister and cousin and they all joined us to eat around the fire, long after the moon began its descent across the sky, the conversation finally starts to lull. Silver and Güthric are first to excuse themselves, curling up together on a conjoined mat just behind where we're gathered in a circle around the fire. Imryll slips off next, though instead of finding a place to sleep, she wanders into the field, presumably to keep watch for a time. Kalli follows her lead but veers in the opposite direction, her watchful eyes turned to the ocean and to where some of the Arcathainian army lingers on the coast. Shortly after their departure, Fox tugs a drowsy Alphonse away. Despite being healed, the beating the mages gave him, followed by him having to exert his power constantly as we made our escape from the Keep, has sapped all of his reserves.

When it's just the four of us left by the fire, the dull glow of the dying embers barely flickering strong enough to emit any heat, Adrien whispers something to Sai, who stands to retrieve a log.

"Would you mind walking with me?" Ryven asks, startling

my attention away from everyone else and to him where he sits beside me. His voice is a quiet rumble that almost gets carried away in the roar of the sea.

Looking into his dark, russet eyes and seeing the simmering, orange embers reflected there, I forget how to speak. For weeks, going on months, all I've wanted was this moment with him. To be together, in our own flesh, as we had been back in the Eyve during the night we'd spent at the Ushines. Alone together with only the stars to keep us company and douse us in their silvery glow.

When my tongue fails to communicate any of that, I settle for merely nodding. Gently, Ryven takes my hand into his and we rise together, as one, our gazes locked onto each other's and nothing else. We don't so much as spare a second glance back at the camp as we leave, and no one dares calls after us, not even my uncle who I'm sure is watching us as we head off into the darkness on our own. Perhaps they realize that nothing that awaits us out here will be anywhere near as terrifying as the monsters we've faced already.

Our fingers intertwine together in a perfect lacing, as if this was how they were always meant to be. But there's a jittering skitter to my heart that reminds me that whatever *this* is, isn't solidified. The last we spoke to each other about anything, he was seconds away from turning into a demon. Weeks later, he saw Dimitri kissing me, and before I had the chance to explain myself, Ryven fled to the sky and disappeared.

The kiss we shared in the Keep was one of urgency, but it alone can't be the basis for which we define our relationship.

I tell myself to let go of his hand and to simply follow at his side, but I can't bring my fingers to give him up. And until he pushes me away, I don't think I will. Whatever conversations we need to have, we will have them while embracing one another.

"Ryven?" My fingers tighten around his and I tug his arm

until he stops. We turn to face each other, but once again breath abandons my lungs. I want to tell him everything, but I'm too scared that I'll say the wrong thing and he'll run like Dimitri did upon learning of my druid powers—like he, himself, already has. "I-I'm sorry for—"

The words shock him so thoroughly that he drops my hand for a moment, only to collect it and the other up a split second later. He brings them into his chest, warmth exuding from him, even through the Crusader leathers.

"Sorry?" he says, his tender voice like a caress to every vertebra of my spine. "Halira, you have nothing to be apologizing for. You saved my life. I begged you to—" His throat seems to close around the painful words, the ones that would've meant his premature death in the former Shadowthorn by my hands.

He shakes his head as if to clear away the thing lodged inside him, and I squeeze his hands tighter.

"I know." Blinking back tears, I gaze up into his eyes, hoping that I might be able to express everything I need to say with just a look. That I am so very grateful he's still here. So thankful that I didn't cave into his request despite all the odds stacked against us that told me I should've.

His dark eyes lower. "If it wasn't for you, I wouldn't be here right now. In more ways than one."

My brow crinkles. "What do you mean?"

With a deep, ragged sigh, Ryven begins telling me about how he became human again. He tells me about the moment he realized we were in danger and the arduous flight north. He tells me about the Pits of Bagamore, and how the black, viscous depths drowned him in an abyss that sounds far too similar to the horrifying darkness of my own dungeon cell.

"I should've died that day," he continues, eyes lifting to the sky. They glisten like the stars themselves in the reflection of the moon and I find myself longing to just stare at them until the end of time. Unfortunately, he blinks, looking down at me in seriousness. "The Pits of Bagamore aren't meant for the living to bathe in anymore. They devour everything. They would've devoured me, if not for you."

"Me?" I'm so stunned by the insinuation that my mouth falls open. "What did I do? I was trapped in Aeysil Keep by then."

In a quick, jerking motion, he shakes his head. "The hold you placed on me when I became a demon, it lasted. Despite whatever wretched wards the mages had on that place, it didn't stop your magic from holding onto me. It was like—it was like an orb of light hovering around my core. The blighted shadows that threatened to consume me could never penetrate through its brightness. And neither could the Pits of Bagamore. When they swallowed me up, they tried. The demented, twisted magic inside those sludge-pools clawed at me and scratched; they ripped and they pulled, but they could never crack through the shield your power threw over me."

At a complete loss for words, I find myself gaping again. I still don't quite understand what I did. Even after learning that the original Elders became the Primordials, and therefore the demons of the Shadowthorn stemmed from them—druids—it doesn't explain why I could protect what fraction of Ryven's humanity that I was able to reach. According to Imryll, no other druid has ever done that. The only answer that I can think of that might explain it is that no other druid had been blighted before and survived.

Except us.

"You saved me again," he says at last.

The warmth in my cheeks surges to full-blown dancing flames. "I didn't know..." I say meekly, but my thoughts trail back to the reason I started this conversation. Back to Dimitri, and the night he kissed me. It wasn't what I wanted, and I know I shouldn't feel guilty about it, but I do. I could've been firmer with Dimitri. I could've made my change of heart more blatantly obvious rather than just avoiding the topic so that I wouldn't have to hurt his feelings. I lower my gaze, hoping Ryven won't see my embarrassment. "What you saw—the night you found Dimitri and I on the main deck—it wasn't what you think—"

"I know."

It's a simple, succinct response. But for such small words, they're able to lift such a heavy burden.

"You know?"

His head thoughtfully tilts to one side. "Or at least, I think I've come to understand." Taking another step, Ryven closes what little space had been left between us until I feel his body pressed against mine, our arms pinned between us as our hands are still clutching onto each other. "I never wanted to stand in the way of your happiness, Halira. Your happiness— making sure you were all right and cared for in this world— that's how this all began. I wanted to ensure that after every- thing Ahl'Ro did—everything I let him do because I couldn't stop him in time—I wanted to make sure you were still able to live a long, and happy life."

A smirk ticks up the side of his face. "Then you joined the Shadow Crusade, essentially making my mission impossible. But even then, I saw you grow during your time there. I saw you find friendship, and family, and love. Or at least, I told myself you had. But…that's not the whole truth, is it?"

Something cracks my chest open, turning my heart into a burning, throbbing thing that oozes something molten inside me. I can't tell if this is an old wound re-splintering, the reminder of the life I'd mistaken at Nigh that turned out to be a lie still too painful to reminisce about. Or if this burning sensa- tion is a matter of new wounds forming at the realization that Ryven still doesn't think he's worthy enough. He thinks he's pieced it together, but he's still uncertain. Still doubts himself and whether someone like him could have earned my affections.

A freshly plucked ember from a blazing fire lodges itself in the back of my throat, making it nearly impossible to speak. But somehow, I force myself through it. For Ryven. For me.

"Of all of the people I met at the Castle of Nigh," I say to him, the stars seeming to dazzle around us like a hailstorm of glitter. "Of all the friendships forged and re-forged, none of them mean more to me than you."

He stiffens, bristling as I relax, the weight of the confession crumbling from my shoulders. I lower my gaze to my hands entangled in his upon his chest. For a moment, I imagine him as he usually is, shirtless, his broad shoulders and bulging pectorals making my knees weak at the thought of nothing but his flesh beneath my fingertips.

"You know," I start, my voice cracking. "Before we met, I thought I knew the happiness you speak of. I had no real complaints. I had parents whom I loved. I had a friend whose company I enjoyed. A job to keep me fed. A sister who was... well, a sister. I'd lost my brother to the very demons that were encroaching upon our village, but I had been content. Or at least, I thought I was.

"Looking back now, I realize just how empty my life had been. I never actually *felt* anything. Not true joy. Not excitement. And certainly not fulfillment. The only thing I can really remember ever feeling was longing. I never wanted to be a beekeeper, let alone a candlemaker. I didn't want to spend my days fearful of the Shadowthorn and what else it might take from me while I helplessly watched from the false safety of our hovel. I-I wanted to fight back, just as Tor and I had dreamt about when we were younger, but circumstances prevented me from doing so. *I* prevented me from doing so."

Ryven's hand untangles from mine, and I think I might break in two at the sudden absence. I fear it's happening again.

The minute I try to open up to someone and let them truly see me, I'm too much for them to handle.

But just before I can stagger backward with the shattered remnants of my heart bleeding in my hands, his careful fingers caress my chin. He dips my head back. Our gazes don't just meet, they collide. The world bursts around us like blurred stars as if we'd been carrying the weight of the world in tow behind us and it crashed at the same moment we did.

I wet my lips, my eyes drifting agonizingly to his lush mouth, wondering if I might ever get to taste him again. But there's still more to be said.

I swallow my desire, for now, and finish what I've wanted to tell him for weeks but never had the chance, or maybe the courage.

I lean into his touch. "It wasn't until I left Gravenburg that I started feeling alive. Like myself. But even then, something was still missing. There was a part of me I never knew. Magic I'd run from long ago. I'd buried it so deeply, that I barely even knew it was there. I never wanted to face it because I knew that the few people I had in my life who mattered to me wouldn't be able to accept it.

"But *you* helped me embrace who I am. More than just my druid self, it would turn out. You see, it wasn't just my magic I fled from, it was everything about myself. I let my family and friends dictate the person I was. I let their perceptions of me become how I saw myself. My whole life, I was told that I made careless, rash decisions and that I was wrong for doing so. But you helped me to see that my fearlessness wasn't a weakness, but a strength. My family judged me for not being more dedicated to my work. They made me think I was someone who lacked commitment, but you helped me to understand that I wasn't uncommitted, I was just waiting for a worthy cause to fight for. You helped me understand and embrace all of the parts of me that I thought were wrong—that I'd been led to believe were wrong.

"It has only been since I met you that I've known true happiness. You showed me that."

Finally, the mountains of self-loathing and torture, the monumental weight of insecurities and uncertainty, cracks, and it all comes tumbling down, finally freeing Ryven's stiff shoulders. He sucks in a sharp, ragged breath, and I let him have it. I let him take that one gulp of air, let it fill his lungs and cleanse away the darkness, because I know it'll be a long while before his mouth is free of mine again.

Once the air has eased from his lungs, a flicker of mutual understand crosses our gazes, and we dive for each other.

His lips are mine and mine are his. Our bodies collide into each other, our hands desperate and tearing. My skin sings to be closer to him. To feel him all over me. To engulf him in my everything as he has engulfed me.

Our mouths are still locked when he leans or falls back to the ground—I can't tell. I'm too dizzy from inhaling the cedar scent of him. I'm too drunk from drinking in the sweet, unyielding taste of him, my lip quivering every time he dares break away to aim for my mouth at a different angle.

My legs slide into place around him, and even though they've only been there one other time before, I realize that's exactly what it feels like. Like they're sliding into place; like they belong here; like we belong together. He is the grounding roots and trunk of my ever-reaching branches. He is the calming rhythm to my otherwise tumultuous ocean waves. He is the peace I find in darkness, and I'm the light he finds in his.

The kiss deepens, both of us unhinging for each other at the same time as if we can read each other's minds. As if we are both at our breaking point and can't bear to wait any longer.

My fingers fumble with the latches of his Crusader armor,

but fortunately they've already been well-trained. They know which buttons stick more than the others, and which ones can be torn apart without fear of ripping. Once they're all free, once his bare chest is peeking through the front of his leather, I pause.

His hands have already found their way beneath my garments, one hand gripping my back and the other latched onto my hip.

"Wait," I groan, the word coming out as a pained whisper. My eyes peel open and gaze upon his concerned expression.

"What? What is it?" His hands snap away from me so fast that it almost sucks the breath right out of me.

"No," I say, grabbing for his hands and shoving them back. "I don't want you to stop. I just—" Glancing around the meadow, I can barely see over the field line, the top of my head peeking up just past the tall grass from where I'm perched atop him. "My sister and aunt are out here somewhere. I don't want them to—"

With a breathy half-laugh, he takes my chin into his hand. "Would it help if I could conceal us?"

I squint down at him, though my curiosity is quite piqued. "Conceal us how?"

With his lashes still lowered, his gaze fixed steadily on the shape of my lips, he raises one hand over us. But he doesn't just lift it and hold it high, he drags his arm in a sweeping motion, out from my hip, arching with my shoulder, and curving over my back, his fingers stretching and pointing back down to the earth on the other side of us. It's not until the moon's glow begins to fade that I realize something is blocking it, something he put there.

My neck snaps and I'm awestruck by the tall blades of grass that stretch around us, cocooning us in a peaceful dome. There are just enough slits between some of the strands for the moonlight to seep through, casting him in a silvery glow that makes my heart race. He is dazzling in all his perfect imperfection. He is everything.

And despite knowing that this blanket of weeds draped over us will do nothing to contain the sounds that might erupt from within, I give myself over to him entirely because we've earned it.

We deserve happiness.

We deserve each other.

RISE

UNKNOWN MEADOW, ILLASHORE

The following morning, when my eyes drift open, it's to the sun's gentle, early-morning kiss upon my flesh. My cheek, warm where it rests upon Ryven's chest, rises and falls with the relaxing rhythm of his expanding and collapsing chest.

I tilt my head back to see if he's awake.

"Good morning," he says, voice warmed like a jar of honey that's been sitting in the sun beside us.

I want to drink it up—drink *him* up like I did last night. But unconcerned grogginess and a catlike desire to continue lounging prevents me from being as ravenous as I was the night before.

I yawn into his chest. "How long have you been awake?"

"Only an hour."

My eyes bulge at the sight of us, naked as the day we were born, curled up in the middle of a field and visible to everyone and anyone who might've come across us.

"An hour?" My voice reaches that squeaky octave that would stop even a demon in its tracks. My knee hikes up protectively to cover as much of myself and him as I can. "And

419

you just let us lay here, utterly naked and exposed to the world?"

He smirks, a low laughter rumbling in his chest. "If anyone came, I would've sheltered you."

An ache builds in my chest, hungry once again for his touch. Though I had him for hours last night, wrapped up in his arms, filled with every long and shuddering inch of him, it suddenly feels like it's been years. Too long.

My body craves the feel of him. It wants all of him, all around me, inside of me. My stomach dips in the same thrilling way it did last night as his hands explored every inch of my bare skin, and as easy as that, a dampness begins to build between my legs.

He must sense it too because out of the corner of my eye, I see the length of him grow. His engorged salute undoes me.

I kick my leg over him, straddling his lap as I perch atop him. The open field around us hardly even exists as I press my hips into his, grinding my slick wetness upon him.

He moans, his hands grasping tightly against my hips and rocking them with me. All the inhibitions I had last night are nowhere to be found when I reach down for him, my fingers wrapping around his girth and stroking. I need this. I need him more than I need self-control or modesty. Last night has come and went, and the day has arrived far sooner than I would've liked, a day that will surely prove to be more challenging than any of the others before it. Today we will need to stop a war.

But not right now.

Right now, I want to evoke one. A war between our bodies, both carnal and brutal.

With a breathy gasp, I plunge him inside me. A wave of heat rolls over me like a tidal wave and I ride it like the goddess of a wild and churning ocean. Each thrust submerges him deeper, the length of him delicious and scalding as it reaches farther and farther for my core.

Drowning.

I am drowning in euphoria.

Every place our bodies touch is like liquid fire. Scorching me. Devouring me.

I dive forward, his hips grinding in time with mine as our mouths crash into each other's. My arm loops behind his neck and I pull him closer. Dragging him against me. Deeper into me. But somehow there's still too much space between us, and I can't bear it.

Neither can he because he bucks, flipping me onto my back. The weight of his body presses over me, enveloping me like a blanket and I moan my satisfaction. My approval. My elation.

He draws back. Too far. Far enough to create a crevice of distance between us that feels more like a chasm. But then his hungry eyes rove over me and my entirety like I'm a feast he can't wait to devour, and the distance no longer feels hollow and empty, but full. Bursting with anticipation of every possible glance or caress or nibble.

Finally, his gaze finds its way back to mine, the swelled girth of him throbbing with restraint as he holds himself steady, slowly lowering himself back into me until I, too, am filled to the brim.

"Ahem."

I gasp, my attention jolting from Ryven's luscious russet eyes to the impatient sound somewhere above my head in the clearing. Ryven's quick to reach for the cape from his new Crusader uniform, tossing it over me perfectly while he grabs for the Primordial spear. He's on his feet before I can scramble upright to my knees, the weapon aimed at a woman dressed in a pearly white uniform.

"If you two are quite finished." Kalli's jaw is tight as she speaks, her gaze fixed stiffly on the horizon above the ocean. "We need to go speak with the others, tell them what we discovered, and form a plan of action." She starts to turn to head back to the camp, but stops before her back is fully turned toward us, allowing me to glimpse her exaggerated eye roll. "I suggest you get dressed and join us."

I roll my eyes back at her. Not that she notices, but it feels good to do something so mundane as being frustrated with my disapproving sister. Just like old times.

Hastily, Ryven and I get dressed. Not because Kalli told us, nor because either of us are in any rush to leave behind this field and the deliciously wicked acts we'd planned on carrying out here, but mostly because we want this war to end before it can go any further.

Ryven squeezes into black leather pants that cling to him in ways that make me have to swallow the burning desire in my belly. He throws on the black silk undershirt, the fabric rippling and shining as he tucks it into his trousers. If we weren't so close to a war, I imagine he'd just wear this—leaving the leather chest piece, bracers, and tassets where they lay in an effort to be more casual and comfortable. Each piece of armor he cinches into place seems far too constricting compared to the airy bared-chest he's used to.

Tightening his belt—the final piece of his uniform—into place, he catches me staring. "What?"

"N-nothing," I stammer, hastily clasping the last few notches of my own armor in place. "I was just—"

"You were staring." One of his eyebrows arches in an expression a little too shameless for simple amusement. "Does seeing me in Crusader uniform please you?"

I can think of around a hundred things about him that pleases me, half of which we tried last night. But before my cheeks can burst with the redness of freshly bloomed roses, I hold my chin up high.

"No. I was just thinking I preferred the crimson outfit you were wearing before. It suited your eyes."

Those same dark, alluring eyes capture mine now no matter

how hard I try not to look at them. "Then I'll just have to find another crimson tunic to wear when we get back to the Eyve."

Before I can act on my impulse to tear all of his clothes right off him again, I spin on my heels and follow after my sister. It's time we discussed our plan of action.

"Well, it's simple then. Isn't it?" Sai says, hands extending over the dying embers from last night's fire. "We let the mages destroy the Arcathainian army, and we lay low, find some place remote and quiet far on the other side of Illashore, and we live out the rest of our lives in peace."

"Saimenimus!" my uncle gasps, the back of his hand thudding against Sai's chest.

"What? I'm just saying what we all know is the inevitable choice."

Silver stands abruptly, her fists clenched at her side. Her lips are drawn in the thinnest of lines, seeming more like a crack in her porcelain skin that is about to shatter completely. "It is a coward's *choice* to leave our country to die." She spits the word out like it's laced with poison. "I, for one, will not stand idle while our people continue to suffer. You said the mages caused this. They stole magic from the Pits of Bagamore and now the Primordials have darkened. I say we go to the source. Cut off their supply."

Beside her, Güthric rises with a menacing expression, clamping a fist in the palm of his hand.

Adrien sighs. He rubs at the tension between his temples. "And how do you suppose that will go? Hmm? We race back to the Pits of Bagamore, and by some stroke of luck are able to break through the many pipelines Ryven saw there. Then what? Do you think the mages won't come to investigate? Do you think they won't rebuild their systems as quickly as possible and slaughter anyone who stands in their way?"

"We fight." Güthric's voice is a throaty rumble.

Silver nods at him.

But Adrien grows exasperated. "We can't fight an entire army of magic-wielding mages! They barely made it out alive and they are three druids!"

His gesturing to Ryven and I causes the entire group to look our way. After recounting the story that the librarian shared with us about the origin of the Primordials and the truth of what happened between the humans, mages, and druids all those years ago, we've mostly been silent. Observing. Pondering. Listening.

At this point in time, our options are limited, and all of them seem less than fruitful.

What Sai is suggesting is true. The people on Illashore appear to be safe from the Primordial's reach, and if we can't stop Qaeus, then there is nothing for us on the mainland anyway. The country and its people will fall. We could, in theory, try to ferry everyone across the Varenholm Ocean, but given the animosity between Illashore and Arcathain, I doubt many but the druids would come, and once they discovered the truth of their isolation, we'd just have another war on our hands here.

The other option, as Silver pointed out, is trying to prevent the mages from siphoning magic from the Pits of Bagamore. But I'm not even sure we have that kind of power. Even if we did, it would mean killing an entire race, people who were once Arcathainians.

Neither option is something I can proudly stand by.

Besides, I can't help but shake the feeling that the third, unspoken option, albeit seemingly impossible, might actually be the answer we've been searching for.

As the others continue to argue, I glance to Ryven at my side. My heart skips at the way he's watching me. Like he's been waiting for this the entire time. As if he had no doubt that I, and I alone, would come up with a third idea. There is no doubt in his eyes. No judgment or apprehension for whatever rash thing might come out of my mouth next. He trusts me and my choices in ways that no one else ever has, and I am emboldened by his unwavering belief.

I squeeze his hand in mine, still astonished that he has a hand for me to grasp and not some demon-claws.

"There is one other way," I say, cleaving the heated conversation before us.

The others turn to listen, waiting with bated breaths.

Fox, however, from beneath Alphonse's arm, cocks an eyebrow. "Oh? I am going to love this. What dangerous but miraculously useful solution have you conjured for us?"

From her lips, I believe it's meant as a compliment. But the accusation still stings, as it always has. But with Ryven's hand wrapped tightly around mine and the reassurance I feel when I look in his eyes, the blow doesn't reach as deep as usual.

"If the Primordials rose from the Pits of Bagamore, I think they can be returned. Just like how I was able to go into the heart of the Shadowthorn when I was blighted and have all the toxin leeched from me."

Adrien watches me with a worried expression. "You do remember almost dying in the process? Don't you?"

Appearing on my left, opposite from where Ryven is still standing firmly, united at my side, my sister taps her chin thoughtfully. "Only this time, it wouldn't be Halira whose life was in danger. It would be the Primordial's."

Leaning over to whisper in Adrien's ear, Sai is anything but discreet when he says, "And anyone unlucky or dumb enough to be in the area."

It earns him a smirk from Fox, and a few considering nods

from the others. Everyone, that is, except Kalli and Ryven. My sister seems to be piecing everything together now, but I'm familiar enough with her process to know it'll be a little while longer before she's worked it all out.

I turn to Ryven, his thumb drawing circles on the back of my hand. My words aren't meant solely for him, but his proximity, the intimacy of his touch, makes me speak as if they are, my voice becoming barely more than a rasp. "If we can lure Qaeus to the Pits of Bagamore, no one else needs to die. The mages can keep their magic, as far as we know. And Arcathain can rebuild. The druids—our people can reemerge from their seclusion, if they so desire."

"It could work," he says simply, as if no other truth could even be fathomable. When this is all said and done, I remind myself to kiss him, hard, for believing in me so fervently.

"We won't know until we try," I respond.

"Excuse my interruption" —when I twist my attention back to the group, I find Fox's hand raised— "But, pray tell, how will we lure the Primordial to the Pits of Bagamore? Last I checked, the mages retreated across open water because presumably the Primordials can't cross it."

The smile that breaks across my face is an unruly, giddy, and wholly manic thing that I expect will only serve to fan the worry of the others. But I can't help it. This idea is so reckless and wild, and in my experience, those are precisely the plans that work.

"Well, friends, that's where you all come in," I say, meeting the group's uneasy gazes with unyielding audacity. "I think it's time we return to Aeysil Keep and stop this war."

HUMANS, DRUIDS, MAGES

OUTSIDE AEYSIL KEEP, ILLASHORE

The coppery stench of blood weighs heavy in the air as we approach the Keep, and it's not long until I realize it's more than a mere stench. Blood mists against the shield of air I've constructed around us, the ruby droplets dribbling down the clear walls to the corpse-covered ground beneath our feet. It takes everything inside me not to fall to my knees beside every one of the fallen we pass—the Crusaders, the warriors, even the mages, not to mention the handful of civilians we find coughing up blood from shadowsteel wounds or scorched by magic.

I see the librarian who helped us escape in every face among the sea of dead. I tell myself I owe it to her to try to help as many of them as I can, many of whom are still breathing, still clutching onto life while fear ravages them. But my resolve never wavers. My gaze, no matter how much the carnage demands to be seen, remains focused on the pristine, sleek towers before us.

I can't stop now. Not even to save the few who are here, no matter how much it breaks my heart every time one of their agonizing cries ceases.

The war between humans and mages has lasted long enough. It stops now.

Wedged between Kalli and her resolve of steel, and Ryven who has taken the form of the largest, most ferocious-looking bear he could conjure, my own focus doesn't waver.

We march forward, across the carnage and bloodshed. The battlefield is quieter than I imagined it would be, making my heart sink deep into the pit of my belly where it twists with the rest of my insides.

"It's likely they retreated," Alphonse whispers from behind me, either afraid he'll draw the attention of any nearby mages, or that his voice could disturb the dead around us.

Panic rises in my throat. "We need the humans here though. Or at least some representative. The plan won't work if no one is here to hear us tell them the truth."

"They wouldn't have gone far." He attempts to reassure me with a pat to my shoulder, but the motion is so stiff that it's anything but. "But they would've put enough distance between them and the Keep to regroup. They're likely tending to the wounded while they plan their next attack."

Without warning, a screech pierces the silence. I whip back around toward the Keep just as a golden burst of flames ignites from the battlements. It hurtles toward us with such celerity that I don't even have time to register it until it explodes against my magic. The air surrounding us warms as my hold struggles against the force of the fireball. But every time I use my power, I learn more about its limitless potential. As long as there is air around me, I can draw upon it.

Behind me, Alphonse makes a sound that's somewhere between a gasp and a sigh of relief. "Well done!" he says, patting my shoulder harder. Then he turns to my sister. "A wise suggestion."

Her face remains nearly expressionless, aside from the faintest proud tick of the corner of her mouth. "I'm not sure I'd call it wisdom to suggest that we don't wander defenseless into an active battlefield. Instructing Halira to use her magic was more of a given than a strategic play."

Fox snorts. "Some might say anything that prevents us from dying could be considered a wise strategy."

Before my sister can retort, another blaze erupts before us, the explosion causing everyone to jump. This time, the heat seeps into the sanctuary I've created for us. Not enough to burn or scald, but enough to remind us that the only thing standing between us and the flames is magically-infused air.

Tightening my grip on the invisible force, I shove my magic outward. The barrier expands, giving us more room and providing what I hope is a deeper sense of security for us all. But I know it is only temporary, both the sense of security as well as the shield. Just because the elements themselves are nearly limitless doesn't mean my power is. Already, my hold isn't as strong as it was. My arms quake where they're outstretched from my body.

"I think it might be time for our next show of strength," I say over my shoulder through gritted teeth. "Imryll? Are you ready?"

She strides forth, without a word, giving her hair a careless toss over her shoulder once she's in front. Then, she begins.

Her fingers twitch in calculated and precise movements that seem to orchestrate a symphony of chaos around us. The grass that had blanketed the courtyard peels back in sheets, bodies tumbling and being swept up into the fold as it rolls the bloodied earth out of our way. With another flick of her arm, she sends the lush trees that had offered shade along the main path scurrying away, charging the Keep as if they were a small militia sent to aid in our bidding. Imryll beseeches the roots to spear up from the dirt like demon claws tearing through flesh.

If our presence had been unknown before, we are impossible to ignore now.

Dozens of mages pour onto the battlements. At first, I recognize none of them. I don't know why I'd expect to, but I was almost looking forward to seeing my cell guards among them, maybe flinging them from the wall with a vengeful gust of wind. But as we descend upon the Keep, the fresh earth beneath our feet blood-soaked despite Imryll's removal of the bed of grass, I catch sight of Igemonar's vibrant green tunic.

And standing beside him, his wrinkled hand resting upon a gnarled, wooden staff, is the Head Mage himself, Varyn Brenthan Ephemeris.

When we're close enough to the Keep's walls that the only thing preventing us from speaking with him is the towering height of the stones, I nod to my aunt. Her fingers twirl at her sides like they're pulling on strings, and within moments two birch trees have joined us. As if they are living, sentient beings, they reach for each of us, their branches cradling under our arms and around our waists just long enough to rise us up to a canopy made of sticks and leaves and tree bark.

A canopy that is at eye-level with the Council of Mages.

"You have returned." Varyn's voice is an ancient, hollowed-out thing, but it still carries enough power to command the silence of the mages around him. "It seems an odd decision for a prisoner to make."

Penetrated by his dead gaze, my flesh runs as cold as ice, and I shatter into a thousand splinters from the brutal blow of his reminder. Every blink sends me back into that horrible cell. I can practically feel the darkness closing in around me, until Kalli's shoulder brushes against mine.

"Former prisoner," she corrects him, her eyes flicking momentarily to me before cutting back across the chasm to him. "Perhaps we realized there was no real threat here to fear anymore. Not now that we know your blockades against druids are worthless."

Now it's Varyn who feels just how sharply words can cut.

The heavy sack beneath his right eye twitches. But as someone who has lived as long as he has, he knows how to recover quickly and pretend as if being publicly humiliated has no effect on him. His gaze drifts to the coast as if he's already grown bored of us.

Only, it's not boredom that holds his attention there. Annoyance, maybe even a sense of concern, wrinkles his forehead.

Glancing over my shoulder, past Ryven's furry and hulking form, I see the Arcathainian army marching toward us. I let my magic float into the coastal winds whipping around them and pull it closer. Their hushed whispers carry. They heard the commotion and were both hopeful and fearful of what might be transpiring. When they lay eyes upon us, their unease grows stronger. They freeze. The foot soldiers. The generals. Even the Magistrate himself who leads in the vanguard.

Before they can flee again, I send a gust of wind back to them, suffusing it with my own voice.

"Stay. Hear what we have to say. For Arcathain."

We wait for the winds to reach them, their billowing flags the only indication we receive because they do not move. They stand, ready, waiting. And now, the real work begins.

"Our people have fought each other for decades. Perhaps longer. Since the dawn of time, for all we know. We know what we can accomplish when our forces are pitted against each other. Betrayal. Bloodshed."

I have to pause to catch my breath. This constant use of my power, of me maintaining the shield around us while also projecting my voice in the air to the Arcathainians in the distance, is depleting me more rapidly than I expected. Then again, I should've expected it. I'm still recovering from the starvation and thirst I endured the entire time I was here, in this place before me.

Ryven's thick, brown coat of lush fur leans into me and I

relish the support even if I know how weak it makes me look. Leaning on friends—on the people we love—isn't weakness though. It is together that we are strong. All of us.

"We could keep fighting each other," I continue, running my fingers through Ryven's soft fur. "We could kill each other until no one else is standing, and then let the Primordial turn Arcathain into a dismal tomb of death and destruction. Or we could choose to work together."

The wind can hardly keep up with the outraged cries that pour from the Arcathainians. The mages, too, grow agitated on the balustrade. Our people have been enemies for so long that suggesting an alliance is like suggesting fire befriend water. Mages hold the advantage of magic over humans that makes them wary, but what humans don't know is that they hold just as much power. If they knew the mages secret, if they understood that wiping out the mage race would be as simple as disrupting their intake of the sludge at the Pits of Bagamore, they'd understand why the mages fled and took part of their country with them, why mages continue to separate themselves from Arcathainians.

Beseeching the humans first, I hold up my hands. I've thought a lot about what to tell them, what they deserve to know. The truth is, they should know it all. If the mages hadn't cast a memory spell upon our people all those years ago, they would already know. We would've grown up with stories of the druids who created the Primordials and whose magic turned the Broken Realms prosperous. We would've also known about the humans who tampered with druid magic, who imbued their own bodies with the concentrated source, and turned the Primordials into the evil creatures they became.

They deserve to know the truth. But that piece of history will only fuel the inferno that's built between these two races. And now is not the time to give Arcathainians any more reasons to hate magic, nor is it the time to give mages any more reason to fear humans.

The truth will have to come later.

Now is the time to unite us.

Facing the Arcathainian army—a once powerful force that already seems so much smaller, so much more broken and fragile than the last time I saw them—I fortify myself, digging deep and holding tight to all that makes me strong. My heart for humankind. My fierceness for doing what's right by the people I love; by all the people of Arcathain, and more.

"Ask yourselves: what it is you truly want. Revenge or peace? What will improve the lives of your loved ones? Initiating a war with the mages where half of you will die, or banding together to end the reign of the Primordial, the creature that started this whole thing?"

My voice blusters around them like the unforgiving winds of a deep-sea storm. Their capes whip about them in time with the flags they hold, the ones that declare their allegiance to a country that is, as we speak, facing an unforeseen terror. The flag that represents their heart and their commitment.

It's silent, and so I do not get to glean their thoughts from the winds on mutterings to one another, but I can almost see the thoughts knocking about in their minds.

Of one country, of one blood.

We were once one continent. Can we be united again?

"And you?" I say, turning on the mages. Varyn stands tall, recoiled in a way that suggests he's not sure what to expect but patient enough to hear it. This time, my voice doesn't carry across the hundreds gathered today. My words are meant only to reach him. "Your magic on the people worked. They remember nothing. They have no knowledge of you tampering with the Pits of Bagamore and what that did to the Primordials, so you have nothing to fear from them if they don't know your weakness."

His thick eyebrow raises. "And what weakness is that?"

"The knowledge that your lives are connected to the Pits of Bagamore now."

A murmur ripples across the balustrade.

Varyn shifts on his feet. When Igemonar leans across him to whisper something in his ear, Varyn waves him off quicker than I can summon the wind to tell me what he's saying.

"Then what do you suggest, Halira Devonshire?"

It dawns on me that no one is attacking. The mages haven't launched a single fireball and the humans are standing ready, but not charging into battle. I have their attention, and they are at least mildly invested in what I have to say.

I fill my lungs with enough air to carry across the land. "We reunite the land. Return Illashore to the mainland. And lure Qaeus back to the Pits of Bagamore, back to where she came."

My uncle Esmond guffaws, readjusting his freshly polished armor that dazzles in the morning sun like jewels. "You expect us to live in harmony with these heathens? The very monsters responsible for fracturing our country and costing families untold grief and sorrow?"

"Harmony is not what I'm suggesting," I clarify. "Not yet anyway. Right now, the mages are not a threat to you, nor you to them. The only threat facing our countries is the Primordial—"

"And you?" the Magistrate says, cutting me off. His vitriolic gaze pins onto someone behind me and without even having to look I know Alphonse is aware of it too. "What are your thoughts on the matter? Have you abandoned your country as well?"

I can feel him stiffen behind me like he's been turned to stone. If anyone has ever intimidated my cousin, it's been his own father. But Alphonse has grown immensely since the last time he faced his harsh father. He's endured the Shadowthorn. He's survived attacks with behemoth demons, discovered an entire new race of people, learned about his own druid magic, uncovered the Primordial. He has come into himself over the past few months in ways he never would've if he had remained in Arcathain. So I'm not surprised when his rigid posture becomes less about fear and more about confidence.

"In fact, the opposite, Father." Watching the Magistrate recoil at the title only serves to invigorate Alphonse. "I stand here today because I want what's best for Arcathain. We cannot survive the Primordial now that she has awakened. We have to destroy her, and you do not know how. For years, you've told our people that shadowsteel is the answer, but I can assure you and your army that it is not." He pauses long enough to glance my way, as if to ask me if his message is reaching them. I nod and he continues. "We tried. Kalli told you as much, but you either refused to listen or—well, no. That's exactly what you did. You let your bigotry blind you. Your hatred for magic has clouded your judgment. All of you. So set that anger aside and listen to us now."

When he stops speaking, the attention shifts back to me and I fill the silence. "We know how to rid the land of the Primordial. But we can only do that with the help of the mages."

"What? With magic?" the Magistrate spits, his boot slamming into the dirt and causing the man beside him to jolt. "You would doubt all of these good men and women so easily?"

"I do not," I say firmer, resolute. "It's the opposite. I believe in them and their ability to adapt. They're experts in changing to survive. When the mages stole part of the country, Arcathainians banded together to rebuild the shoreline and shelter those who were displaced. As the Shadowthorn grew, it was Arcathainians who housed those who'd fled the demon-ravaged villages and gave them a safe haven to turn to, food, protection. Arcathainians built the Shadow Crusade, studied the demons of the Blight, and learned how to kill them.

"I think adapting is in Arcathainian blood. So is loyalty to the people."

The Magistrate's grimace deepens, but the people around him, his loyal subjects, their demeanor shifts. The weapons that had been readied since their arrival seem to wilt in their hands. They watch me eagerly, hanging on every word, and I know, if I can convince them, the Magistrate will have no choice but to agree.

"So I'll ask you again: if there was a way—a *real* way—to stop the Primordial for good, would it be worth working together at least temporarily?"

"Speak. Tell us what you request."

"It's simple, really. Use your magic to move Illashore back to the mainland—" I pause, shifting my attention back to the humans. "From there, we will lure the Primordial to the Pits of Bagamore, where she will be laid to rest and no longer able to terrorize Arcathain."

Varyn shifts, his stiff robes creaking and drawing my attention back to him. My hackles raise. My hold on the shield around us deepens, the air around us tensing and fortifying while I prepare for a powerful blow. But none comes.

"What makes you believe that's all it will take?" he asks. I'd almost forgotten that they didn't know. It's why they fled with the land instead.

"Because it's what worked with me when I was blighted. I touched Qaeus' heart and it leeched the darkness from me. Ryven experienced it as well. The Blight is drawn to itself. If we can get the Primordial back to the Pits of Bagamore, the waters there will pull her under."

For the humans, I leave out the part where it might even cleanse her, and allow her to walk the lands once more as our protector. They'd find no reassurance from that thought, not in the way that I or the other druids might. But I glare across the gap between the canopy I stand on and the balustrade; I stare into Varyn's cold eyes and know that he is thinking the same thing.

"It's the only way you and your people keep their magic. Their lives." I whisper so softly that I'm not even sure Ryven or Kalli could hear me from where they stand so closely, but I send the information across on a pointed breeze, one that barely wafts the long, white hair over Varyn's ears.

He considers for a moment. "Very well. The mages of Illashore will reunite our lands, if the humans agree to stand down."

I'm so surprised that I almost forget to send a tempestuous gale out across the battlefield. Arcathainians have to hear it for themselves that the mages are willing to cooperate, to return what they so long ago stole. They will help us end the dark reign of the Primordial.

All it will cost them is to lay down their vengeful prides.

The Magistrate holds up his hand, silencing the conversation that has awakened around him. Frozen in anticipation, everyone watches him.

"Nothing matters more than the demise of the Primordial." His words are calm, reasonable even. But the tightness in his jaw and the way his teeth stay glued together as he speaks gives his true feelings away. "And the reunification of *our* land." He pauses. Too long. Like he wants the Head Mage to correct him and for the hatred between them to bubble over. But to Varyn's credit, he does nothing of the sort and begrudgingly Esmond continues. "Before we hastily jam the two lands together, we will need time to prepare the coastal towns so that people are not killed again as they were during the Great Rift."

"How long?" I ask him, and the question has more than one meaning.

How long will it take to prepare the coast?

How long will we leave Arcathain to suffer under the Primordial's wrath?

How long will humanity have to survive?

"Two months," is his response. "One for traveling back to Arcathain, and another to make the proper preparations. Perhaps we could be finished sooner, in which case I believe it best for one of the mages to return with us, to act as liaisons between our people to report on our progress. They will be well-provided for; I can assure you."

The suggestions catches me off guard. It does Kalli and Alphonse as well, both of who practically lunge forward as if they're prepared to jump right off the platform of greenery we stand atop, and march all the way to him on a tirade.

I catch their wrists, stilling them both with a single look of warning. This is progress. This is compromise. It's what we came here for.

"We accept," Varyn rasps, and Kalli's and Alphonse's expressions turn to ones of shock.

Mine likely would too, if I wasn't so wary of what is transpiring. It seems too easy. Too perfect. But perhaps everyone is simply tired of fighting. Of just surviving. Maybe they're ready to put our differences aside and finally live?

"I will send one of my most trusted advisors with you."

When Igemonar steps forth, I have to stop myself from openly snarling. He's the reason Alphonse and I were captured. He's the reason we were starved, interrogated, and—in Alphonse's case—tortured.

But I remind myself I'm not the only one with a grudge against a mage, and if the rest of Arcathain can set aside their grievances, so can I. For now.

"Then it's settled," the Magistrate says. "We will give your advisor a day to pack and meet us on the shore. Please, take your time. I still have some traitors to contend with back on my ship." Something cold and sharp spears through my ribs, piercing my stomach and making my pulse quicken. His dark gaze cuts to mine. "And should anyone try to intervene, it will be seen as a breach in the truce, and an act of war." Nothing but threat burns in his words.

He spins on his heels, leaving me gutted and gaping, as he and the Arcathainian army retreats back to the shore to deal with the traitors on his ship. To deal with Dimitri.

TRAITOR

VARENHOLM OCEAN

The magic-infused treetops and branches untangle themselves too slowly.

We descend from our pedestal at the pace of a sickly snail.

But once we're finally on the ground again, once my boots sink back into the blood-soaked earth, the act of patience evades me. I avoid Ryven's dark, russet gaze as I storm across the battlefield. My legs have never worked harder. Every muscle in my body is as rigid as the bones beneath my skin. The squelch of my boots sends a slippery chill down my spine, but I press on harder, unflinchingly.

"Halira," someone implores behind me.

They mean to stop me, but all they do is assure me that they —and likely the rest of our party—are following. Which is all the reassurance I need, really. The sooner we're out of the mages' sights, the sooner my friends don't need me to spell the air around them for protection. I won't have to hold myself back any longer.

My pace hastens.

Over my shoulder, I watch the Arcathainian legion head east while we move south, toward the place where we left the

Leviathan. But it's the wrong direction. For we aren't marching toward the Magistrate's ships. We're not heading for Dimitri.

Someone has to warn him. Someone has to save him from his imminent demise.

"Halira, slow down."

This time, I recognize Kalli's commanding voice. But the power she once held over me, the power anyone once had over my actions, is so far gone from this moment, I don't even miss a step.

I no longer doubt my impulses.

I obey them.

When we are finally far enough away that I'm confident the mages won't be able to reach us, and that the Arcathainian legion can no longer see us, I take a deep breath and summon my power.

Ryven's sorrowful, beseeching gaze is the last thing I glimpse before I become weightless. Before I become as light as air.

I let the wind carry me away. Before, when I'd faced the Primordial and let myself dissipate into the strange, buoyant state, it had been like flying. It had reminded me of the moments I'd been wrapped in Ryven's arms as he'd vaulted us into the sky, or dove down from the Eyve's canopy toward the forest floor.

There had been a rush. An anticipation.

It's not like flying now.

I am merely existing.

Being.

Faster than I can fathom, I slip over the continent and through the air as if I am merely stretching my arms out and reaching. It's like I am already in every place I touch, like I am anywhere and everywhere the air touches.

As far as I can tell, I reach the coast in a matter of seconds.

The legion of soldiers is somewhere far behind me, as are my friends, but at least no one is here to stop me from doing what needs to be done.

But staring out across the armada, my legs lose the ability to move. My feet sink into the dry sand the same way my heart sinks into my belly. It's a rough, salty feeling that leaves my gut in knots.

Esmond had made it clear what it would mean to intervene with his prisoners. Treason. Treachery. The grounds war.

The weight of the sand around my ankles becomes heavier, fortifying with the sickening realization that I shouldn't be here, no matter how badly I want to.

I don't know how much time passes, only that I've lost count of how many times I've gone back and forth in my head about whether to charge forth or not, and that the sun that had been high overhead when we first addressed the mages has long since started its arch down toward the horizon. My eyes are raw from how much I've had to rub away my stubborn, conflicted tears. My knees are weak from how many times I'm *almost* lifted a foot, only to stop myself.

The bushes behind me rustle and the ground quakes. I don't need to turn around to see what's bounding toward me. Or who.

Ryven staggers out from the meadow, his legs still shifting, making him unsteady and clumsy as he approaches me. The satchel in his hand is the same one we draped over his shoulder this morning with his clothes inside. He doesn't waste a second getting dressed though, leaving the satchel untouched.

With dire intent in his dark, bottomless eyes, he strides forward.

"If you've come to stop me from going," I say, my voice shaking as I turn to him with tear-filled eyes, "You can hold your breath."

Without losing momentum, he barrels into me, enveloping

me in a warm embrace that smells of cedar and darkness and home.

"I'm not here to stop you," he says into my unkempt hair. I can't remember the last time I bathed, other than rinsing off a bit last night while we camped by the beach. But he doesn't seem to mind, inhaling the scent of me as deeply as I inhale him. "I'm here to be with you. Whatever you decide. Whatever happens."

A shattered, broken thing squeaks in my throat, but before it can manifest into the heart wrenching sob it threatens becoming, someone else comes storming through the meadow.

Unlike Ryven, who didn't pause to redress, Kalli arrives completely clothed, though it's clear from her panting that she likely flew just as hard as Ryven ran.

"Well, if he won't stop you, then hopefully I can help you see reason." Kalli's shoulders are pulled back, taut. The outfit Uncle Adrien procured for her is in miraculous condition, not a single clasp unhooked or bracer missing, despite having just put everything back on herself moments ago. Yet the wild fury simmering in her eyes is anything but her usual collected exterior. "You can't risk humanity for the butcher's boy—"

Ryven's neck whips around so quickly, it startles her from advancing farther. Before he can speak on my behalf, I put their minds at ease.

"I know." The words are stubborn. They bulge and expand as I force them up my throat to the point where I fear I might choke on them. "I know."

The hardened gaze my sister had fixed on me softens. She glances around us as if she's noticing for the first time where we are, or perhaps who isn't here beside me.

"You waited."

Because the guilt and shame are too much to bear, I merely nod.

She swallows. "I imagine that was a difficult choice to make. But I assure you, Halira, it was the right one. The selfless one."

"It's not your fault," Ryven offers, spinning back into me and stroking the back of my head. "He was given an option. He chose to stay. Even if you had gone out there to break him free or convince him to run—"

"I know."

It's all I appear to be able to say. Perhaps it's because it's the only words that seem to make the aching hole in my chest feel a little less torturous. Like those two little words are enough to convince me that there was only one choice, an obvious choice, and I've made it.

But inside, I'm in turmoil. I know what's right for the people of Arcathain. They deserve to know true peace. They deserve to raise their children in a country where they don't have to fear being eaten by demons. Or trampled by a Primordial. Or incinerated by mages. They deserve to have their country back—wholly. The way it used to be. And that's only possible if the Magistrate maintains the truce.

But sitting back and doing nothing when my friend faces danger goes against every natural instinct of my bones. I've thought through a million and one scenarios, trying to find a single solution that would gain Dimitri his freedom without me having to break the truce, but no matter what scheme I conjure, nothing works. I can't blast Dimitri's ship away on a mighty gust of wind because the Magistrate would blame either me or the mages for tampering with his ship. I can't try to convince Dimitri in secret to leave because no matter what, his disappearance would be linked back to us, regardless if we played a role or not.

The only option that seems even remotely feasible is one that is also the most impossible.

"The only way Dimitri is leaving that ship alive is if we can convince the Magistrate he isn't a traitor."

Ryven pulls back just enough to glance down at me and cup my cheek into his hand. "Do you really think you could? I don't know him well, but he doesn't seem like the kind of man to listen."

Kalli scoffs. "I'm sorry. Is there a reason you're still standing around naked?"

Sheepishly, Ryven clears his throat. As he steps away from me, he draws the satchel in closer, using it to do what it can to cover his impressive length as he saunters back into the field to change.

"Besides," Kalli says when only his dark head of hair peeks over the reeds. "I'm not sure we'll get the time to convince him."

Spinning my gaze away from Ryven, I whip around, my feet kicking up sand as I scramble to get a better view. Kalli's right. The Magistrate has reached the shoreline and is boarding one of the small boats that will take him to his ship.

Which means there's still time.

"I have to go after him—" I start, magic simmering beneath my flesh and just waiting to be pulled so that I can launch myself across the beach and onto his vessel.

"I wouldn't do that if I were you." Igemonar's grating voice is like the sharp, chilling tip of a blade scraping down my spine. "In fact, I've been sent here to make sure you do nothing of the sort. Punishable by a fiery death, if you choose to tempt me."

Instinctively, my hand drifts to that vacant spot on my thigh where Tor's dagger belongs but is missing. It's been so long since I've held it in my possession. It's been weeks since we communed with the sirens of the Dark Sea, so long that I've mostly grown accustomed to its absence.

Until moments like these when I truly need it.

The dagger isn't my only weapon now.

My fingers splay as I prepare the cyclone I plan to blast him with.

But his fingers twitch too, a ball swirling with golden flames forming at his fingertips.

"You can blow me away with your wind," he says, lips cracking into a snarl. "But can you do it before I release my fire upon your beloved sister? She was already burned once, so I'm told. Nearly died from the wound. I can promise, my blaze would leave her no chance of survival. So, what will it be? Whose life is of more value to you? The man on the boat, or—"

The raging winds I'd summoned around me fade, whispering around us and returning to the sky from where they were drawn.

"Very good. Then, might I suggest" —his shoulder brushes mine when he passes me, taking a seat on a boulder overlooking the ocean— "Let us sit back and enjoy the show."

I inch forward like a numb, mindless sapling being blown in the wind. There's no enjoyment in this. There's no place in the realms I want to be less than right here, in this moment, stuck on this beach and helpless to the immediate future.

But...

There is no other choice...

The hours it takes for Esmond's boat to row across the open sea to his ship are agonizing. My fingers lose their feeling where they're clasped in Ryven's steadying hand.

When the Magistrate finally boards, Dimitri is brought to him swiftly. His arms are bound behind his back, despite my sister and Ryven speaking about how he'd been left behind as a free man. I suppose that all changed the minute the Magistrate was forced into this truce. It likely had been his plan from the start, considering how he'd treated Kalli on their voyage.

Still, seeing Dimitri like this, watching the way the guardsmen jerk him, Eparah and the others around, it's a new aching level of sorrow that dizzies my skull and wrenches at the cold, watery thing beating in my chest.

"Dimitri," I utter, not meaning for it to be anything more than that. But the wind catches my voice, whether by accident or my own intrinsic need, and carries his name across the sea.

They are so far away—*we* are so far away—that I can't make out his sage eyes, but there's a noticeable twitch of his head, a stillness that occupies his body as he gazes back to shore.

"Halira?" he asks, the air whispering his voice—a voice I haven't heard in weeks but grew up hearing every day—into my ear.

Slowly, Igemonar rises. "What did I say about interfering?"

An orange light reflects off him, but I don't dare tear my eyes away to see the fireball he's summoned.

Ryven's hand slips out of mine. "She's not interfering with anything. She's saying her farewells, and you will let her."

My awareness of them weakens as the truth of what Ryven said tumbles over me like the ocean's powerful waves.

My lips part, something burning deep inside my chest and fissuring. "Dimitri, I'm so sorry. I—I tried..."

"Don't—"

The guardsmen behind him kicks the back of knees, jarring the rest of Dimitri's words from his lips as he falls.

A woman gasps behind me, followed by a man bellowing, and I don't have to look to know the others have arrived. Grunting and begging, Adrien and Sai struggle to hold Güthric back as he tries rampaging forward. Ryven does what he can to warn them all of the threat that Igemonar poses should we prove uncooperative, but the large, bellowing man can't seem to hear him.

I don't blame him.

Neither can I.

My ears are flooded. No sound can permeate them except the thudding of the Magistrate's boots as he crosses the main deck. The metallic ring of Dimitri's broadsword when Esmond pulls it from its sheath. And Dimitri's final, heartbreaking farewell, the words that are uttered for my ears, and mine alone, "I should've listened to you."

Mistaking the comment for himself, the Magistrate pauses, considering. "Indeed, you should've."

"I'm sorry I let you down. I'm sorry I failed you when you needed me."

The Magistrate doesn't move for a long moment, but not long enough. Eventually, he raises the broadsword overhead and the guards shove Dimitri's head down, baring the back of his neck.

"Yes, well," Esmond begins. "I'm afraid we're well-past apologies. Desertion of the Shadow Crusade is a crime punishable by death. Any last words?"

A choked cry warbles in Dimitri's throat, but he fights to maintain his control on it. "Halira, I will always love—"

A flash of silver.

A spray of red.

A shriek, both piercing and dull. Distant and near.

The ground bucks as if the sand is possessed by the ocean. As if the world is flipping itself upside down and inside out in outrage to have lost such a fine and promising and loyal young man.

Dimitri.

My best friend.

My first love.

Gone.

The air has left my lungs. Left me entirely. No magic pulses because there is no life in this moment. Not for me. I only sense the end. Death. One after another as the Magistrate goes down the line beheading Eparah and the rest of the traitors who traveled here with us.

And all of them, all of their blood, is on my hands.

I brought them here.

I forced the truce upon the Magistrate.

And I stood by and simply watched as he executed them all.

Bleary-eyed, I press my face into Ryven's chest. But the black leather armor is foreign between us, catapulting me into a barrage of painful memories of nights spent with my fingers tracing up Dimitri's chest once he'd redressed after our tumble in the sheets. Of me asking him if he's sure he has to go, and his response always being one of responsibility, rule-following, and just a hint of remorse that we'd chosen this life. And then I'm thinking of our conversation in the forest, just before the sleeping spell had taken its effect, and wondering if the life Dimitri had planned for himself—for us—could've ever existed.

I pull away from the man I will love for the rest of my life, spinning to face the man I grew up loving.

The Magistrate stands over the limp, bloody forms with his hands clasped behind his back. Two guards, one on either side, take Dimitri's arms and lug him across the deck to the balustrade. It's a ghastly, unnatural sight, to see his headless body dragging, but I don't gasp. I don't allow myself to look away or shed a single tear as they hoist him over the rail, and his lifeless body splashes into the sea.

A numbness washes over me. My fingers tingle in the cold loss of sensation, my spine becoming so brittle it feels as if it could crack.

Another splash distorts my vision, and another, as body after body are tossed overboard.

When I finally manage to yank my tearful gaze away from the churning ocean and the bodies sinking beneath it, I don't know where to look. My eyes wander, drifting aimlessly up the ship's rounded belly, back to the balustrade, to the deck.

They settle on Esmond. From this distance, it's hard to

discern his expression, but on a gust of wind, I hear his pleased snarl, and my mind can all but conjure the smug grin he's casting across the sea.

Two months.

He has two months before I'll have my vengeance.

THE LABYRINTH

A thorn tears through my chemise as I walk the wide halls that are narrowed by overgrowth. It pricks my skin, a line of blood forming on my forearm.

Sheepishly, I glance over my shoulder.

Alphonse notes the cut and rolls his eyes.

Fox merely shrugs. "Well, look at it this way… Now we'll know sooner whether the behemoths are still here."

Ryven steps around them and grasps my arm. He holds it close, dabbing at it with a cloth he pulled from his belt that not only looks as if it has never been washed, but also appears to have been dragged through an entire continent of dirt and saltwater and tar, even though I know it hasn't.

Yanking my arm out of his grasp, I scowl. "I'm fine. Let's just get this over with."

He holds my gaze, but he doesn't reach for me again. "I think we already know what we came here for. The behemoths are gone. They haven't been at the Eyve's border for a week now."

I worry my bottom lip between my teeth. "But where did they go? And why?"

A curt, squeak of a laugh bursts from Fox's lips as she folds her arms. "Yes, why ever would anyone leave this place?"

Alphonse nods. "With the Shadowthorn down, what reason would they have to stay?"

The wrinkles in my forehead deepen, the suggestion rational but never leaving me fully satisfied. It's a likely reason, it really is. The druids who had been caught in the Shadowthorn and turned into the behemoth monsters who made this place their home are gone. With the border down, most of the demons have fled the barren lands. They scour the country, terrorizing every village they come upon.

The only good news is that now that they aren't bound by the border, their numbers aren't as overwhelming. The Magistrate has been able to place small militias in every major town to aid in its defense.

But there's been no sighting of the behemoths. No mention of them in any village or town.

I half expected missing druids to start appearing at random all over the Broken Realms, with macabre stories of losing their humanity, becoming trapped beneath a demon's flesh, the atrocities they inflicted, the years they lost.

But that hasn't occurred either.

"But where did they all go?" I ask again, and it's at least the dozenth time they've heard it from me. "Creatures like that don't just disappear."

"Maybe so," Ryven says softly. He grasps my shoulders in a tender gesture. "But I think we have more important matters to deal with now. The two months is up, and it won't be long now before the Magistrate—"

"Esmond," I correct. "And I know. Don't you think I know?"

The moment the words leave my lips, I regret them. Ryven doesn't deserve my wrath, but hearing Esmond's title awakens a fire inside me so wild and scorching that I lose control for a moment, forgetting who exactly my hatred is targeted at.

"I'm sorry," I mumble, averting my simmering gaze away from him and down the vacant Labyrinth corridor. I imagine a horrifying monster—like the hydra, or a shadowhound, or even any of the fiends that would skip along these walls with impish delight—charging around the corner and giving me an outlet for my rage.

But, as these halls have been for a week now, the place remains silent. Utterly abandoned.

"The Rejoining will happen any day now," Alphonse says.

The scowl I flash him is one that I hope will remind him that he doesn't need to tell me such blatantly obvious things. I'm well-aware of the schedule we've been on and how far along in the process we are. For two months now we've prepped the country. With Imryll's help, we convinced the druids to help soften the coastal towns with lush, ample greenery so that the collision can be as smooth as possible. Kalli and other shapeshifting druids, and those capable of communing with animals, took to the sky or sent their birds and horses to the coastal towns to encourage them to evacuate. Ryven and other plant-based magic users, ensured that the crops of every large village and kingdom harboring refugees would have a plentiful harvest to be able to feed everyone. Some druids, myself included, even did what we could to keep Qaeus tame and away from the masses. She still rampages from time to time, occasionally regressing back into a vengeful, dark place, but we've done what we can to prevent her from harming anyone.

The demons, however, have been left to the people. But at least no new ones appear to be spawning, and the Shadowthorn is still a thing of the past.

But my hard expression dissipates before the message can reach Alphonse. Instead of finding him staring at me in that condescending, arrogant way that he does, I find his attention is elsewhere entirely.

With Fox under one of his arms, his free hand entangled with hers, he gazes upon her as if no one else in the world matters.

Ruefully, I glance to Ryven, to the man I traveled across the entire continent, an ocean, and another island just to save. The slight bob of his shoulders sends a flutter of wings to my stomach. He can't read my thoughts, but somehow, he can discern my meaning, just by looking at me.

I haven't been good to him weeks. My misery, my grief, my anger—they've consumed me. To the point where some days I don't even recognize myself.

And somehow, throughout all this, he still seems to.

I want to curl up in his arms and rest my head upon his shoulder, but every time I do, I watch Dimitri's death play out all over again. The metallic whoosh of the sword slicing through the air. The thud of his head hitting the deck. The splash of the waves as his body went over.

I want the comfort I know is awaiting me in Ryven's arms, but I've scarcely been able to allow myself to enjoy it. I'm not sure I can until justice is served.

Once again, as if Ryven can hear my every thought, he reaches a hand for me. Not an arm. Not an embrace. Just a hand.

This time—after weeks of distance and sorrow and frustration and loneliness and numbness—I finally take it.

Warmth floods the hollow ache where my heart used to be. It stings and burns. But despite the pain, despite my every instinct telling me to fight against it, I don't. Because I know the difference between bad pain and good. Deep down, I know that the hurt I'm feeling now is one with the power to heal the shredded remnants of my soul.

Watching Dimitri's death gutted me. It left me broken and lost. But Ryven's steady hold on my hand now, his constant presence and commitment no matter how many times I've lashed out on him these past few weeks, or suddenly broken down in tears, it fortifies me.

My breath hitches at the reassuring smile he flashes me, as if to tell me that we will get through this. I hope we will. I know we will.

Alphonse plants a kiss atop Fox's forehead before continuing. "When the realm is restored, it won't be long before the Magistra—before my father sends for the Primordial. If we don't leave soon, we will miss the event."

There's a thud as Fox's hand smacks him in the chest. "Don't talk about it as if it's the social gathering of the century."

"But isn't it?" he balks. "It's not every day an entire island rejoins to the mainland, and mages and humans are forced to set aside their differences for the common good."

She rolls her eyes before settling back under his arm and diverting her attention to me. "You know, if all of this is about you not wanting to attend, then no one is forcing you. You've done more than enough for—for everyone."

My fingers tighten, Ryven's poor hand caught up in the middle. Fortunately, his grip is just as strong, and he squeezes back, a comforting and supportive gesture that reminds me to breathe.

"No," I say sharply, trying hard to ease the tension in my clenched jaw. "I'll be there. I'm seeing this to the very end."

When the continents merge, everything goes as planned. The druids are even praised, by some, for the way they aided in minimizing the potential destruction. Thanks to the efforts of our people and our magic, we are able to keep the oceans tame and avert any tidal waves that would've enveloped the coastal towns. We keep the earth calm, preventing the jostling impact of the two continents colliding from spreading into a devastating earthquake that might've otherwise split the continent anew.

The day we reach the former coastal region of Arcathain and step across into mage territory is so surreal and so terrifying, I actually hesitate. My leg all but refuses to step foot on Illashore ground until I glance to my sister and Ryven. In their determined, proud eyes, I'm reminded that this is what we need. It's what our people—or rather, my *former* countrymen—have been fighting for all these decades, and it was always going to come to this. Or at least, we'd hoped it would.

Adrien and Sai leave us, my uncle's childhood home in Drayfil Shore summoning him on an adventure all of their own. Perhaps one day I'll have the chance to visit as well, to see the cozy region in its entirety like my father used to describe. But today is not that day.

Kalli, Ryven, and I press on, with Fox, Alphonse, and Imryll following close behind. There are others, too, who make the journey. People from all over Arcathain form a thick trail as we trek across Illashore. Druids join us, having ventured out of the comfort of the Eyve to witness the event they've been promised, the event we're all looking forward to:

The end of the Primordial's reign.

Knowing what I know now about the first druid Elders, part of me is saddened by the thought. But without forcing the mages to stop using the Pits of Bagamore for their magic and thereby forcing them to kill themselves, I see no other option. The Primordial has lived a long life. I'd like to believe that even she is ready to rest.

By the time we arrive to the site, the Pits of Bagamore are shrouded behind a sea of thousands of people, flocked from all over the Broken-now-United Realms.

Though I've refused to communicate with the Magistrate, Kalli has remained in contact with his advisor, and therefore leads us through the masses.

"Come," she says. With my hand in hers, she pulls my arm taut. "He wants us there. I told him you were able to speak with Qaeus, however briefly, before. Now he wants you present. In case she needs to be…reasoned with."

I scoff, Ryven jerking forward with me as Kalli drags us along. Since the day in the Labyrinth, I've hardly let go of him once. Today more than anything I need him by my side, and I won't let anything take him away.

We make it through the crowd of humans and mages so hastily that I barely have time to be in awe. But as we emerge on the other side, the black, bubbling pits steaming before us, the momentous, historic moment finally hits me. Today will go down in history, the day when humans and druids and mages came together, set aside their grievances, and ignored centuries of betrayal and war and bloodshed, and banded together to vanquish a common enemy.

My chest actually feels restored for a moment, the dark cavity inside me finally full of warmth again.

But the sensation is quick to fade when I see the robed figures standing across from us.

Head Mage Varyn Brenthan Ephemeris and the rest of his council. All except Igemonar. His notable absence causes me to realize that another prominent figure is missing from this momentous occasion.

"Where is Esmond?" I blurt, asking no one in particular. But I scan those gathered around this particular black pool, searching for my uncle, his advisors, or any members of his Senate.

"We were hoping you'd know," Varyn rasps, one eyebrow inching up in a distrusting way. "We have followed through on our end of the bargain, and yet we see no signs of the Primordial, nor your ruler—"

"He's not my ruler." My teeth ache as if they're clamping down on stones.

A hand grasps my shoulder. I spin to find Ryven's dark, pleading eyes burrowing into me. They seem to say, if he were able, he would reach deep inside my chest, take my heart into his hands, and smooth away every painful wound and scar.

I force my head to bob in the slightest of gestures, trying to assure him that I'm all right and can remain calm, but his expression only becomes more sorrowful and dubious. His thumb rubs my forearm before sliding down to my hand and releasing me.

"Halira speaks the truth." The baritone of Ryven's rich voice sends a chill down my spine and causes the mages to jump. "He is but one ruler of the realms. One of the druid Elders will be arriving shortly, I can assure you."

"Your assurances mean very little. If there is no Primordial, and no leaders present, what reason do we have to be here? Our people were safe and prosperous where we were—"

A condescending voice cuts across the field of people. "Yes, but for how much longer?"

On horseback, steeds as white and shining as the ships in Arcathain's armada, Esmond and his entourage come galloping into the center. My sister nods at a few of the men and women. Judging from their capes and sigils, I'd say they are members of the Senate, though not all are present. Like many, some have chosen not to be here for this moment, fearful of what may happen, or perhaps incapable of making the long journey.

I can't even fathom not being here. At the very least to make sure the Primordial is treated with the dignity she deserves. No one but us understands who she really is: one of the original Elders, and quite possibly the Elder of my own lineage.

Esmond swings his leg over his steed to dismount, coming

so close to kicking Alphonse in the head that he has to duck. Fox cradles him protectively in her arms, the glower she burns into the back of Esmond's head as blazing as the sun.

"Hello, Father," Alphonse says once he's finally collected himself, and I swear I catch the faintest signs of a smirk touching the edges of his lips.

If he is meaning to get under Esmond's skin, it has the desired effect. My uncle's shoulders hitch, becoming as rigid as the pipeline behind him.

"It is the Magistrate to you, boy. Always and forever, now."

The caustic lance is more effective than Alphonse's, tears visibly brimming his eyes. With a shrug, and a quick, clipped laugh, he wipes them away. "It's just as well. Turns out I do much better when I'm not beneath your micromanagement."

One of Esmond's razor-sharp eyebrows raises as he looks from Alphonse, to Fox, to me. "I strongly disagree. But the people you foolishly choose to surround yourself with is hardly the reason we've convened here today."

"Indeed," agrees Varyn.

Esmond turns a cloying smile on him and bows. "Apologies for my delay. Apparently, it is far more challenging to lure a Primordial than I initially believed it to be."

Varyn folds his arms into his baggy sleeves. "So where is the creature? We've been rejoined with your land for days now, and still have seen no signs. However, we've had to dispose of one or two of your demons."

There's accusation in his tone, but Esmond's smile doesn't falter.

"Why," he says, looping an arm behind him. "My men are bringing the Primordial here as we speak. In fact, should you listen closely—"

Instead of finishing his statement, Esmond brings his hand up to his ear. I can't help but notice that it's the same hand he used to pull Dimitri's sword from its sheath. In my mind, it's still splattered with his blood, and Eparah's. My vision blackens until only a pinprick remains and all I can see are his deadly fingers, that cruel palm, and a wrist that deserves to be hacked clean off.

Just before my vision can flash red and I can lunge for the nearest armed soldier, a ripple spreads across the tarry pool. Then another. Each one that follows becomes bigger, the wave reaching farther and farther until the black, viscous fluid is lapping at the shore.

Collectively, we take a step back. Some of us, like Ryven, even leaping. It makes me realize just how much he has been grieving and hurting as well. In the weeks that followed our return from Illashore, I was too wrapped up in my own trauma to even think to ask him about what his experience as a demon had been like, what it was like to jump into the Pits of Bagamore and climb back out renewed. He's spoken about it only a few times, and each time he hasn't gone into much detail. I always assumed it was because there wasn't much to tell, but maybe there was too much. Or maybe he just didn't want to unload that weight upon me when it was obvious that I already had enough on my shoulders.

Snatching his hand into mine now, I pull him closer. The way his wide eyes soften suggest he understands my belated apology, but I still intend to give him one later. For now, this is the best I can do.

The obsidian lakes all throughout the Pits of Bagamore ripple, the earth quaking with each of the Primordial's hastened steps. A hush blankets the crowd, the people still like frightened deer in a clearing before a hunter.

It's not long before Qaeus' head pops over the dunes.

She snarls at the small unit of Shadow Crusaders egging her forward. Her long, heavy arms swipe and claw at everything in her way. The ground thunders. It trembles beneath her mighty strides.

The people caught between us and the dunes begin to grow anxious. It starts as nervous shifting, people slowly scuffling backward as their brains catch up to their instincts. But once they do, they are livened with the impulse to flee. It's what Arcathainians have been bred for and mastered ever since the Shadowthorn first appeared and demons began prowling the border towns and villages.

The druids take a moment longer to register that they're in danger. For decades, they lived in harmony with the Primordial on the other side of their border, unharmed and unafraid because—little did they know—they were connected to her, and therefore she would not harm them, unless otherwise provoked.

Now, however, it's impossible for them to ignore the fear of the humans around them. They join them as they scramble and scream, shoving their way to the west side of the Pits, and clearing a path for the Primordial.

Kalli leans over to shout in my ear so that I might hear her over their shrieks of terror. "I believe this is where you come in, Sister."

Blinking, I nod and take a step forward, away from my friends, and toward...something.

Everything feels like it's been leading up to this moment. My parents' deaths. Dimitri and I joining the Shadow Crusade. My discovery of my magic and fleeing into the Shadowthorn, only to instantly become blighted. It's like I have been hiking a steady climb toward the summit of something great, something meaningful.

My strides become more certain, my head held higher, as I approach what I believe to be my destiny.

"Sh-she's grown since our last encounter," one of the mages stammers behind me. It's easy to forget that some of them were alive when the war on the Primordials was in full motion.

I glance over my shoulder, prepared to remind them that Qaeus is no longer simply one Primordial, but two, when Ryven catches my eye. For a moment, the chaos around us fades away until it's just me and him. As he promised me in that clearing all those weeks ago, he's made a point to wear every shade of red he can get his hands on, but it's this one in particular that is my favorite. The maroon tunic compliments his bronzed complexion, his dark russet eyes. It's a lighter fabric than anyone else present here today, other than the cowering civilians, but he and I both agreed that armor wouldn't be necessary. Today is about peace and good faith.

But truth be told, if things go south, I'm not sure any amount of armor would protect us anyway. It's why he and my sister have been practicing their transformations though, ensuring that they can take the form of any animal necessary to bring us to safety should war break out again.

For my part, there's always the wind to guard me.

Once my mind can move past how handsome he looks in his loose-fitting tunic, my gaze catches on the Primordial spear. He's jammed the butt-end into the craggy terrain and is leaning on it as he would on anything.

Today the spear, as well as the Primordial, will be returned to the Pits of Bagamore. The Elders will be laid to rest for the first time in centuries.

Just as I'm about to tell him to dispose of it now, something grates against the inside of my skull. I taste dust. I smell old leather. But the Primordial's ancient voice is the thing that snaps my attention back to the dunes behind me.

"You again..." she says, languid and curious.

My jaw hangs open. "I—you can speak."

She's crossed enough distance between when I turned my back and now that her shadow encompasses me. I'm not sure where the Crusaders are. I didn't see them run by me, but it's likely they resumed rank somewhere nearby, just in case this goes awry.

"I can," is her reply. *"For those who will listen."*

"I want nothing but to listen to you, to all you have to share. You must possess a limitless supply of fascinating stories."

The black mass before me tilts her head. I swallow the lump in my throat.

"But first, we—I have a request." When she doesn't respond, I pray to the gods that it's an indicator that I should continue. "Will you step into the pool behind me?"

The tranquility that had exuded from her flees on a mighty gust. *"Why?"*

But no amount of wind that she could cast would scare me. I close my eyes as air threads through every strand of my hair. I breathe it in, through my lungs and my skin. It is intoxicating. Rejuvenating. It is pure magic because it is pure life.

I think about our last encounter, how it had taken all but a moment for something evil to take hold of her, and I wonder what amount of restraint she's using now to be present, here, with me. There had been fear in her eyes that day. She didn't want to hurt anyone.

"Because we believe it could help you. I know you haven't meant to cause anyone harm, but...something is wrong. It's time to return from where you came. To heal. To cleanse in the lakes of Bagamore like our people once did long ago."

With bated breath, I await her reply. The silence charges the area, making the hairs on my arms stand on end and my heart leap into my throat.

Finally, her old, tender voice caresses my mind. *"A cleansing sounds nice."*

When she raises her foot to step forward, the masses gasp.

"It's all right!" I shout to them. "It's okay! She's going into the pool."

Their fear either doesn't faze her, or she can't hear them over the rumble of the earth as she places her foot as gently as she can into the tar. Her foot is too massive, however, her leg the girth of three large cedar trees squeezed together, for the black fluid to go undisturbed.

It splashes on impact. Most of the people surrounding the area are able to jump back in time. There are those who are less fortunate though, the poor souls who were under a trajectory impossible to avoid.

Humans, druids, and mages scream and writhe. They flail their arms as the dark goop seeps into their skin like coals burning through flesh. Their agonizing cries vibrate the air, their torment a song that shreds my eardrums and imbeds itself into memory, as the black substance pierces their very souls and begins darkening their lifeforces.

The moment brandishes us all in terror.

It takes me a moment to realize what's happening. Merely touching demons was never the cause of death; it wasn't until their toxic venom entered the bloodstream—via fang or claw—

that humans died, and druids disfigured into behemoths. But perhaps the gunk here is more potent than the darkness that creates the demons. And these pits are ravenous.

It takes me a moment longer to realize that there might be a way to stop it.

Once my blighted body was near the heart, nothing could stop that darkness from leeching everything from me. Nothing except the breath of life.

Or, at least, that's what we believed until Ryven came here. He told me that my powers were what saved him from dying completely when he submerged himself in the dark pits here. The way he describes it, it was like having a part of me with him, keeping the core of humanity safe from the Blight that wanted to ravage him.

I was a shield.

I was a light to keep the darkness at bay.

Without waiting a moment longer, I reach out to the nearest person, a member of the mage council, judging from his robes. The fabric is matted to his skin from the tar, and he claws at it like it is acid. I propel my magic inside him, envisioning it as the brightest light imaginable. I let it coat his heart, let it fold over him so that no amount of darkness can reside amid the light, hot and blinding. Even when it feels charged to its maximum potential, even after I'm sure I could burn brighter if I tried, I force more and more power into him, my hold on his soul tightening, my arms and legs quaking.

Until finally, at last, his screams stop.

Wide-eyed and sputtering, they paw at their chests. Disbelieving smiles flutter across their frightened faces, and I'm smiling too. My druid magic never ceases to amaze me, and I can never tell if it's a normal kind of power. If it's because I was once among the blighted and so I have a different relationship with the darkness than others. Or maybe it's because of my druid heritage and the fact that I am connected to one of the original Elders. Or it very well could be a combination of everything. Regardless, whatever the reasons, I'm just relieved I could help.

But the relief fades in an instant.

The mage closest to me twirls her fingers through the air, the corners of her lips tugging downward. "I—I don't understand. Where's my magic?"

Before anyone can really grasp what's just happened, an animalistic growl bellows from Esmond's throat.

"It didn't work!" he roars, dark creases cutting into his flesh around his eyes and lips. "The Primordial still lives! Soldiers! Crusaders! Ready your weapons!"

Everything moves too fast then. The citizens running become blurs. The soldiers and Crusaders flood Qaeus' feet like a noxious wave of fog. The screams and stampeding and roaring and everything becomes one raucous mess of horrific panic.

Esmond appears beside Ryven as quick as a bolt of lightning flashing across the sky. Instead of drawing the sword at his waist, he yanks the spear from Ryven's grasp, and though memories of Dimitri's unjust and cruel death threaten to shove me into an oblivion of panic and terror, Esmond spins away from him quicker than my mind can plummet into those dark possibilities.

Relief floods through me, light and airy.

But even that is fleeting.

For when Esmond is finally armed with what he assumes to be a normal shadowsteel weapon, his arm cocks back.

"No!"

The Primordial spear whizzes through the air, whistling as it tears its way across the ether and lands its mark. It pierces Qaeus' shoulder, but considering her gargantuan size, the pathetic weapon likely feels more like an annoying sliver than something meant to kill her. If it had just been a normal shadowsteel blade, it would've done nothing but prove to be a mild irritation. She's too large now for any of the shadowsteel weapons in Arcathain's possession to harm her. Still, if it had been a regular, harmless spear, we might've been able to apologize on Esmond's behalf for his rash stupidity and continued trying to work with her. She can be reasonable when she wants to be. When she is unprovoked. When an influx of more power does not leave her unhinged.

But this is not a regular shadowsteel weapon.

The essence of the third Primordial, Khaymus, surges into her like shimmering flashes of light made of gold and honey. Qaeus throws her head back. A mighty bellow spews from her lips like a volcanic eruption into the clouds.

The people are unable to contain their terror now. They run. Some, back toward the lands they had once felt remotely safe in. Others in any direction that's not here. They trample each other. Humans use their shoulders to knock druids over. Druids use the power of the elements, of the earth and air, to set themselves ahead, while burying the humans in dirt or blasting them with powerful gusts of wind.

They scramble south, deeper into the unknown forests of Illashore.

They flee north, toward Aeysil Keep and the mages who may still be hostile.

They clamber west, racing toward the ocean as if they plan to swim to whatever lay beyond the Varenholm Ocean now that the continents are reunited.

But Qaeus isn't the only monster among us today. With chaos descending, other creatures emerge from all around, as if they'd been waiting for this moment. Demons and fiends alike, tear and claw into the people, leaving a trail of bloodied ribbons as they thrash through the terrified crowd.

Behemoths join them. I spy the hydra and a shadowhound,

but I hear so many others. Snarling and howling. Hungry for blood.

We weren't prepared for this. We couldn't have been. But now it makes sense why I couldn't find any of the behemoths in the Labyrinth. Whether intentionally or not, Qaeus brought her own army today, almost like she knew the people would turn on her, just like they have done for years.

Aware of the anxious, fearful, aggravated soldiers circling her, the Primordial does what any beast would when they are threatened. She becomes the deadliest form of herself. She becomes our most fearsome predator and a threat to every person here.

With a single sweep of her heavy, black arm, she knocks thirty or more Arcathainian soldiers away. Their bodies are nothing more than flailing, broken limbs as they're catapulted across the Pits of Bagamore in every direction but east. Before they've even made their landings, before the sounds of crunching skulls and shattering bones can crackle over the wasteland like wood popping in fire, her other leg lifts.

She bellows as she begins her aimless, menacing chase after the frightened people. Some are smashed beneath her strides. Others grasped and flung.

My pleading cries hit an obsidian shield around her mind. No matter how loudly I scream for her to stop, no matter how much I bang on those heavy, fortified walls, she doesn't listen. She can't. With the second soul of a Primordial coalesced with her own, the darkness has been almost too much for her to control. She had flashes of serenity and her former self, but the battle was lost every time a druid like me wasn't near to help her. Now that she has a third, I fear there is no hope of saving her.

Even if there was, I'm not sure I know how. The plan should've worked. When she stepped into the Pits of Bagamore, the darkness should've been leeched from her body.

It might've killed her in the process, that much I was prepared for, but at a bare minimum, it should've taken away the Blight that's infested her and these waters the same way it cured Ryven.

"Why didn't it work?" The words drift from my lips like smoke, harsh and yet faint. I'm not speaking to anyone in particular. There is too much pandemonium around me for anyone to hear me anyway. And yet, someone must.

"We have to get out of here." Ryven's hand clutches my own. I don't know how he found me amid the panicked crowd of people, but I'm so grateful he has.

I tighten my fingers around his, but my stomach churns as I play our escape plan through my head. "We can't just leave. The people need us."

Anyone else might've argued against my judgment. Perhaps one of these days it will stop surprising me that he doesn't.

"Okay. What do you have planned?"

"No," my sister replies harshly, appearing behind him like a ghost rising from the earth. Her dreads are already splattered and caked with dirt and blood. I fix my expression with concern, trying to ask her without words what happened, but she's undeterred. "We have a plan, Halira. If the truce was broken, or matters between the humans and mages proved disingenuous, we were to return to the Eyve with haste, where we will be safe."

"No one is safe!" I shout, my voice barely loud enough to carry over the turmoil surrounding us. "Don't you see that?"

"It's alright to be afraid," Ryven says to her, every bit the image of brave calm. "But Halira is right. That was no plan. This situation needs to be contained." He turns those dark eyes on me then and my stomach twists. "What did you have in mind?"

A curt, humorless laugh breezes past my lips. "I don't have anything in mind other than saving these people. Or at least as many of them as we can." My eyes drift back to Qaeus as she drops to her hands and knees, the earth rumbling with her hefty weight and nearly knocking us to the ground. I try not thinking about the people flattened beneath her. "I can use a blast of air to hold her back while you and Kalli clear as many of the citizens out of here as possible."

Ryven's nod tussles his already unkempt dark locks. "We can direct them back to safety, try to keep them organized. The ones who have been injured, we can transport ourselves. We've been practicing taking the forms of larger animals like horses. But once we do, no one will be able to understand us."

"Oh, my. This is no good. No good at all."

A frightened cackle rises from the chaos. An old woman with a mess of flaxen hair hobbles into view. Her presence here is so unexpected, seeing as she is on the wrong end of the continent, that it's not until I notice the birds fluttering in the nest weaved atop her head that I realize who she is.

"Elder Nebadri." Ryven bows. "We're so grateful you made it."

She flinches when two people collide behind her, and resumes twirling a strand of tattered hair in one hand, while chewing the nails on the other. "Mmm. Yes. Well, no. I can't say the same."

Her chuckle is humored, but her expression is anything but. The way she squints her eyes almost makes her look as if she's in pain, and I suppose in many ways she likely is. She was fairly skittish the last time I met her, and I'd imagine all this commotion is very off-putting and terrifying for her.

"But I was sent here by my sisters to be part of the event and to witness the coming together of all the races and so here I am—even if it's not where I or my pets want to be, or where we think we should be—here we are." She's trembling so hard that she struggles to even gulp.

Ryven strides forward, taking her wrinkled hands into his.

"Well, I for one believe you are exactly where you are needed. I was just telling Halira that I could use someone who can speak with animals so that once I shift, humans can still understand me."

She stops worrying with her hair for a moment, considering. "Hmm. Yes. Humans cannot understand the wisdom of animals no matter how much they chirp and mewl and whinny —they understand growls though; they've learned about those —but a horse speaking is not something they are prepared to hear. Not without help, no. Not without help."

"Exactly," he tells her. "You'll make an excellent translator. But first, we need to start guiding folks back to the mainland, to their homes."

He ushers her along, glancing back at me more than once as if to ask if this is really what needs to be done, for us to separate. I don't like it any more than he does, but I fear it is our only choice.

My sister has been quiet the entire time, arms folded over her chest as she considers. Finally, a low groan escapes her, one that I know means although she doesn't want to agree with me, for once she knows I'm right and is willing to cooperate.

"What about the mages?" she asks. "Their magic might be useful in a moment like this."

Stupefied that I hadn't thought of it sooner, I blink at her. "You're right."

Throughout all the pandemonium, I haven't seen a single fireball scorch through the sky, and now that I've realized it, my skin becomes as cold and slick as ice. Glancing west, I see the crowd dashing toward the coast that's just barely visible beyond the desert crag in the distant. But among those who are fueled by pure adrenaline and fear, the humans and druids bolting without a single care for how many of the black pools they stride through or who they knock into along the way, are a small handful of robed figures ambling away from us.

"Where are they going?" she snaps, her voice a raw, venomous thing that could bite. "And why aren't they running? If they're not afraid, why aren't they here helping us?"

"I don't know," I answer honestly, shaking my head. I fix my attention back to Qaeus. "But right now, I don't care. Are you ready?"

She recovers in an instant, nodding to me before racing off to the north, opposite from where Ryven and Elder Nebadri went. Together they'll bring some organization and direction, some semblance of leadership to the poor, frightened people of the United Realms.

And while they take their places and offer the people the guidance they so deserve, it'll be up to me to keep the Primordial at bay.

Wind, please don't fail me now.

WIND & STEEL

PITS OF BAGAMORE, THE UNITED REALM

It's not the first time I've dashed over a field of dead bodies. With any luck, it will be the last. I try not looking down at them, the lumpy, bloodied masses that jostle beneath my feet. I try not thinking about who they were, if they were in agony when they died, and whether they had family left behind. Or worse, if their family had been here with them.

All I focus on is the colossal, rampaging form of Qaeus ahead.

The closer I advance, the more I feel like an ant by comparison. A small, infinitesimal thing that could be squashed by her mighty feet, just like the dead beneath mine.

But even ants have their strengths. Even they can endure more than they look like they should be able to.

With Qaeus' back toward me, she can't see me coming, and I hope to keep it that way for as long as possible. I might be a druid, a descendent from one of the original Elders, but she *is* an original Elder, and a gargantuan Primordial on top of that. There's no doubt in my mind that having surprise on my side will prove gravely useful in whatever is to come. I suppose I should've thought about it more, analyzed every possibility and their potential for success or failure, and determined which of my options of occupying Qaeus would be wisest and least likely to result in my imminent death.

But there'd been no time. People were dying. Action needed to be taken. And regardless of how this ends for me, no matter what action I take now, I know that lives will be saved.

Hyper-focused on the Primordial, I don't notice the crook of someone's elbow protruding from the ground. It catches my foot and threatens to send me tumbling, but I manage to summon a gust of wind strong enough to counter my fall.

I'm grateful not to have landed face-first into a pile of death and carnage, but it has cost me the element of surprise.

The Primordial spins around, the rage in her red eyes replaced by a hint of curiosity but mostly suspicion.

I wanted to wait until I was closer. I wanted to make sure no one was standing between me and her. I have no choice now.

A cyclone of air swirls between my outstretched hands like a powerful geyser. It cuts across the barren desert, knocking down everyone in its path. *They'll thank me later*, I assure myself. Scraped knees and bruised foreheads are better than thousands of people dying. The Primordial has slaughtered too many of them already, both today and over the years. She has to be stopped.

But for now, she just needs to be contained.

The torrential twister pummels into her shoulder. The blast spins her around, knocking her onto her back, the wind so wild and powerful that it holds her down, preventing her from getting back up. She strains and strains, but the wind holds her.

My muscles ache and burn the quicker I dash toward her. The closer I can get, the less of an obstacle I pose for the people, and the easier it'll be for them to escape. The easier it'll be for me to keep her contained.

Or at least, that's what I had hoped.

With a deafening bellow that makes my stomach curdle, the Primordial lifts her fists, shaking, and slams them into the earth. Fissures crawl across the bone-dry crag like the way the Blight crept through Ryven's veins. The ground splits apart like broken shards of glass, dozens of people getting caught in between the shifting earth.

The rumbling, jagged cracks rupture beneath me, the ground splitting right out from under me as I bound across the desert. My toes catch on one of the rough edges, my body jolting forward before slamming into the ground.

My torrent of wind promptly ceases.

Distantly, I hear someone cry my name and know that Ryven is watching.

The Primordial rises like a deadly, bleak smog. Her shadow rushes over me like a bucket of frigid mountain water as she stands. I try pushing myself up, but my hands are wedged between dead bodies and the broken earth, my fingers scraping against the abyss of whatever lays beneath us. Panicked breaths hitch in my throat at the same time my neighbors start their screaming.

None of them rise, I realize. None of them are fleeing this doomed place as if we are all stuck here. As if Qaeus wills it.

I launch my pleading cries back against the obsidian walls erected around Qaeus' mind. But this time, one of them slips through, like cracking the realm's surface has also fissured a part of herself.

"Don't do this," I beg her, a sudden image flashing in my mind, one of clear blue lakes and joyous people in celebration. I recognize the Lakes of Bagamore from the tapestries in the Keep, and though I can't tell if it's a memory conjured from her mind, or one from mine, I draw from the emotion of it regardless. "This place was once sacred to you, to our people. I believe it still is. Our magic comes from these waters, and they've been tainted. You're connected to them too, and it's why you can't control the darkness inside you."

The creature holds still. Even as she has me pinned down at her feet—the world scrambling in terror—she doesn't strike a killing blow. She pauses.

It's the boost of confidence I need to continue.

"Because it's not just *your* darkness. You know that; I know you do. You remember a time when you weren't this monster that Arcathain believes you to be. You were peaceful. Benevolent. Loved."

Her head tilts, ever so slightly. It's really working. After everything, she really is still inside there, somewhere.

Or at least, that's what I foolishly allow myself to think until her passivity ends. The dark, vague shape of Qaeus' face does something akin to snarling before scanning the area. She gazes across us all—and lumbers away with a chilling look in her eyes that makes me fear for all of mankind. She is out for blood.

I tug and yank on my arms like a bound, thrashing demon, until my skin is bleeding. A heaviness builds in my chest. Time is dwindling and the pressure to act, and fast, threatens to cave in on me.

Suddenly, I stop straining against the jagged terrain. I don't need my hands to do magic in the same way that mages seem to.

Instead, I reach deep inside my core for the thrumming, electric star of power that crackles inside me. I focus every ounce of energy I have on it, every bit of attention, every one of my emotions. My fear. My desperation. My determination. My loyalty to the innocent people caught up in the mess our ancestors left for us.

I channel it all into my roiling center, and release it in an exhale.

The world drowns out around me until nothing is left of the screams of terror and pain. Soon, I can't even see the people struggling on the ground beside me, all around me. Everything turns to darkness. My other senses, too, fade. No longer does the acrid stench of death churn my stomach and prick my tongue with every breath.

Nothing exists. Except me and my power. The power passed down to me by my druid mother, and her mother, and all the mothers before her. The power that very well might've been given to me and my family by the Primordial before me.

A twinge of guilt twists its way into my chest, but I try ignoring it. I try reminding myself that this is as much for her as it is for everyone. She didn't deserve this wretched life. And now, her time has come.

My eyes flutter open and the world returns around me in slow motion. Dark clouds roll in overhead, casting the earth in a fittingly dismal shadow. But where there is darkness, there is opportunity for light to prevail.

A spark ignites in the sky. A flash of light illuminates our dreary faces with hope.

As I inhale, I fortify myself with the strength of everyone's sacrifice before us. When I breathe in, I think about all the people who were forced out of their homes to escape the Shadowthorn and its demons. I think about all the lives lost that are soon to be avenged. I think about my brother Tor. My parents. Ahl'Ro.

Lightning crackles above, a storm brewing and building as I draw from the strength of the people—of their need for justice —until finally the entire sky is alight. It's only then that I scream, commanding the mighty bolt to rain down from the heavens.

But just before the lightning is cast, I notice what Qaeus is headed toward.

I should've known. I felt myself reaching her. I felt her making a connection.

It's not people she's after.

She's heading for the pipeline.

PITS OF BAGAMORE, THE UNITED REALM

The people are terrified when they see me shift into a horse. The ones I had been shepherding back toward their eastern homes now race away in greater fear. I forget that though they've grown up aware of mage magic, most of them never knew about druids until a couple months ago, and even then, they've still never seen what we can do with our powers.

Fortunately, they're running in the correct direction, and so, instead of chasing after them and trying to explain that I mean them no harm—nor do any of the druids—I let them run. I turn my efforts back on the rest of the scattering masses.

With Elder Nebadri's help, our task proves easier than anticipated. I don't know how many creatures she is connected to, but judging from how many she summons to aid us, I imagine it may be all of them.

Hundreds of birds flock to the skies from the west and south. The beasts of the forests come too. Dozens of deer, warthogs, and foxes, interspersed by the hundred or more squirrels who follow, emerge from the tree-line and scurry along the craggy earth.

The poor humans become even more frightened, but at

least the animals provide a funnel, and force them back toward the safety of their homeland. The druids among them catch on fairly quickly, realizing that the only way animals congregate like this is because they've been summoned by a druid—and not just any druid, but the Elder Nebadri herself. Some of them do what they can to soothe the terrified people of Arcathain, offering brief explanations and assurances of help as they dash together for the east.

It warms my heart to see the two peoples working together to flee this nightmare. It almost feels as if Ahl'Ro were here today with us, and I guess in some ways he is, for I carry his spirit with me always.

As the people clear the Pits of Bagamore, I trot back to where it all began, where Qaeus entered the tarry pool and remained unchanged, and where the Magistrate of Arcathain provoked her. I start my search for wounded survivors. Nebadri joins me, aiding the hobbling people or commanding the animals in the area to.

When suddenly, the air hisses.

My gaze is drawn to the place I've been dutifully trying to ignore, to the northern edge of Bagamore where Halira faces the Primordial. I haven't wanted to look; I haven't dared. Because I knew seeing her take on such a monumental feat would give me no choice but to join her, despite having no usefulness up there. It's already been proven that she is far more powerful of a druid than I ever have been, or ever will be. The Elders' magic runs through her blood. I would be nothing more than a distraction. An obstacle. Another person that she would feel the need to save if I was put in harm's way.

Looking at her now, a vortex of wind blasting across the open land and knocking the Primordial down to her back, I know I'm right. Halira is formidable, and I'm still not sure she realizes just how strong she can be, in so many ways.

She has this handled. I need to remain focused on the task at hand—

The Primordial's fists lift and slam into the ground. The earth shakes with tremendous force, and I'm reminded of what it was like flying through the sea storms just to keep up with the Leviathan. Even from this distance, the force thrashes through me, and everyone around me. I manage to stay on my feet, perhaps solely because my time as a flying demon has given me a better sense of balance over these past few months.

But from where I stand, feet wide and riding the rolling waves of the earth, I watch Halira fall.

"Halira!" I shout, but all that comes out is a horrendous whinny. Her head twitches, and I am reminded that even though her natural inclination toward the elements is air, she could also communicate with the Leviathan, with me as a demon, and even me as a horse.

I expect her to move. To shove herself off from the ground and send another cyclone of power hurdling toward Qaeus before she can stand, but she doesn't. She can't. Halira jerks and writhes, but something is pinning her in place. Everyone, from the looks of it.

She could've done this on her own; I know that much. But she doesn't have to.

Kneeling the front of my equestrian form down, I look to Nebadri. As her connection with animals is strong, she can already read my thoughts, and reaches for the wounded man atop my back without my asking.

Once he's safe, once they've both cleared my path, I bolt into a gallop and head for the woman I love.

To my relief, as I'm charging forward and leaping over the black cesspits and the dead bodies that my path crosses, the Primordial turns away. She leaves Halira where she lies, even though she could demolish her with one mighty stomp of her obsidian foot. Qaeus trudges away, but my pace hastens. Halira is still trapped, her arms—from the looks of it—wedged into crevices.

As I reach her, I release my hold on the power keeping me in the form of a horse. The transition is always jarring when one is mid-run, and I stagger toward her, sliding on my knees as I reach her side.

"Ryven!" she gasps. "What are you—"

My hands are already prying at the fissures in the ground. "We have to get you out of here. Before she comes back for you. We can regroup and try again. Your wind was working." I tilt my head back to the flashes still illuminating the dark sky. "Your lightning will come in handy soon, but please wait."

Underneath my mighty grip, the ledge of the crevice begins to crumble. I continue digging and hitting the earth around her arms until one of them is free. Then both.

I take her arms into mine and we rise together.

"I don't think we have to worry," she says, sparks of lightning reflecting in her gray eyes and giving them an electric charge that is only present when she's using her power.

It's both terrifying and alarmingly alluring. I have to stop myself from gripping the back of her neck and tugging her close against my naked body. I want to kiss her. I always want to be kissing her. But now seems like an inappropriately dangerous moment.

"What do you mean?" I ask, eyeing the Primordial who is a safer distance away. But Qaeus has stopped shuffling, and that makes my muscles taut with anticipation. "Are you ready to attack again?"

Halira shakes her head, more incessantly this time. "I don't think I need to. Look at where she's gone."

I follow the line of Halira's outstretched arm to the tangle of golden pipes that lead out of the black pools scattered across the Pits of Bagamore. And suddenly, it starts to make sense.

I turn back to Halira, to her dazzling, now-silver eyes. "She's only here to destroy them."

The smile that crests her face is dubious. "Well, not at first. She doesn't always have control. The darkness inside her is the dominant force most of the time. But she's in control now. And all she cares about, I think, is restoring this sacred place—restoring herself and druidkind—to what they once were."

I'm not sure I understand what she means by restoring druidkind. As far as I'm aware, the druids were uninhibited by the tainting of the Pits of Bagamore. But then again, I can't converse with Primordials, and it's possible Halira knows something I don't.

What I do know, is she's right. Qaeus has stopped above one of the largest pipes. She gazes down upon it, her chest heaving with the weight of a hundred years of regrets and wrongdoings.

And then, she raises her foot, and slams it down into the pipe. The metal flattens where she lands her blow, but on either side of her foot, the tube buckles up. Bolts fly from where the pipeline becomes unhinged. The black goop that had been inside sprays like a fountain up and around her.

Fortunately, none of the mages are nearby to be harmed. Although, come to think of it, I haven't seen any mages since the start of all of this chaos…

"Look!" Halira exclaims, her hand drifting down to point at the black pool.

The dark waters are fading. The murky black ripples, the shadowy fluid turning an iridescent gray before fading still into a white that's creamy and opalescent. In a matter of seconds, the entire pool is utterly clear.

The Primordial lumbers over to the next pipe, storming right through it and tearing the thing clean out of the sludge. Like the pool before it, tainted darkness seeps out of it like someone's sucking it away with a straw, leaving nothing behind but water so clear, that even from this distance I can still make out that there are rocks and pebbles and greenery—actual living plants—beneath the surface.

One by one, Qaeus makes her way across the Pits of Bagamore, destroying the mages' pipeline and restoring health to the once-sacred lakes. Halira and I watch, awestruck by the transformation happening before our eyes. As Halira releases the lightning, letting it return to wherever she had pulled it from, the color of the sky shifts just as rapidly as the dark waters, until there is nothing but a bright blue expanse above us. The pools reflect it, and suddenly this place starts to feel even more magical.

The first time I came here, I could feel its allure. The dark, seemingly-bottomless pools beckoned me forward like I had a chain around my neck that would drag me into their depths. That sensation is different now. The doom and gloom that had been attached to that feeling is gone. Now, I feel connected to the land, not because it wants to drain me of my life and power, but because it wants to restore them.

The more of the pipes that the Primordial destroys, the lighter and brighter she becomes as well. No longer does she look like a monster rampaging the lands, but a protector of them. The way she and the other Elders had been before.

I'm beaming like a foolish boy when I turn to Halira, only to find something sinister reflected in her expression.

"What is it?"

She doesn't answer me for a moment, glancing up at me from the corner of her eye as if she's afraid to say it. "I know this is a victory," she finally utters. "But it will cost the mages their lives. And who's to stop them from building those pipes again?"

Her mention of the mages snaps me back to something I

noticed earlier. "Where are the mages, anyway? I haven't seen them since Qaeus started attacking everyone."

Understanding flickers behind her calculating eyes, but before she can answer, someone bellows in the distance. "No!"

We turn and start running. We don't even know toward who or what, but it's obvious that whoever is screaming is in need of help.

"No! No! No! You can't!"

We find the Magistrate holding his ground and blocking the Primordial's path to the final pipe.

"You destroyed the others," he snarls, spit flying from his peeled-back lips. "I won't let you take this one too!"

Qaeus starts to swing her leg at him, apparently deeming his death a necessary evil in her process to restore our land. But suddenly the Primordial stops. I'm the only one who seems to notice Halira's intent gaze upon her, and the slight movement of her lips.

When the Primordial places her foot back on the dehydrated earth and steps back, Halira approaches her uncle.

"I don't understand. Why would you want to preserve the pipeline?" She runs her slender fingers—covered in dirt and blood from where they were wedge in the ground—through her white hair. "And what happened to the mages? What did you do, Esmond?"

He all but hisses. "I am no mere civilian, niece. And you will show me the proper respect I deserve." His hand raises as if he's going to swing at her.

But Halira is swifter. Stronger than this pathetic man could ever hope to be. She calls up to the sky and the dark clouds are quick to respond. They sizzle as the electricity builds until a single bolt pierces the ground at his feet.

"Do. Not."

It's the only warning she gives. It's the only warning he appears to need as his hand retreats to his side.

"I'll ask you again, what did you do, *Esmond*?"

His teeth grind behind his pursed lips. "I did what needed to be done. I rid Arcathain of our enemies. I vanquished the mages. At least all the ones that I could."

Halira blinks back at me, stunned and horrified into silence.

"How?" I demand, taking one powerful step closer.

I don't trust this man, uncle or not. He's already proven to be sneakier than we anticipated, and even with Halira's power, they're still standing close enough to the last black pool that I am uneasy. The sludge might not have done anything to normal druids, but Halira and I were once blighted, and I've been in those dark depths. I know what they want. They would devour her.

The Magistrate looks every inch the embodiment of smugness when he shrugs. "Why, I promised their other enemies prosperity, should they slay the council. The rest of the mages I will deal with myself once I have the power." His gaze drifts to the bubbling waters.

With a sickening twist of my gut, I make the same realization Halira does.

She all but recoils. "You planned on giving yourself magic? After everything? All those years of hatred and vengeance. You would make yourself one of them?"

"I will never be one of them!" he barks, a vein throbbing down the side of his throat. "I will be better than any of them ever were. I would fight for Arcathain, not against her. I would be a powerful force that no druid would dare challenge. I would—"

"You will do nothing."

Halira strides forward, hair blustering behind her, and not entirely of natural causes. Wind wafts from her so innately that I'm not even sure she's aware it's happening. She's getting stronger. Or perhaps it's being in this place that has grounded her even closer to her nature.

Standing about a foot shorter than her lanky uncle, she doesn't let his height force her to appear small. She reaches up for the curved ridge of his chest armor and yanks him down to her level. For a moment, I think he might fight against it, but it's not just wind wafting in her hair; it's lightning. It flickers over every inch of her skin. It sparks from her fingertips. It threatens him into silence, and he obeys.

"No human will be allowed near the Pits of Bagamore ever again. Not without an invitation from a druid Elder, which you will never have."

With a disdainful glare and a mighty thrust, Halira launches her uncle to the side. As he slams into sand as hard as rock, the Primordial returns to her mission and removes the final pipe from the waters. I wonder if she refrained from breaking this one for fear of harming us because when she lowers the golden tube, I swear she seems to nod at us as if to say "you're welcome."

I'm still staring at the shifting waters and marveling at the brightness Qaeus exudes the moment the pipe is out of the lake, when Halira speaks.

"You said you sent their other enemies after the council. Who did you send and where did you take them?"

The Magistrate groans, pushing himself up to his knees before patting the rocks off his palms. Another cry bellows from his lungs as the last of the black waters become clear. But once the initial belting of air is out of him, once he's expended every last reserve of energy, he's bent back over with his forehead on the ground. His grunts and growls turn vicious and cackling, making the hair all over my naked flesh stand on end.

When he finally looks up at her to answer, it's with the crazed vengeance of a madman reflected in his eyes. "You can't save them now. You can't be the hero you wanted to be."

"Where are they!" I yell, intervening before he can say anything more that would make her doubt herself. Her family has spent a lifetime doing that already and I won't stand for it any longer.

The Magistrate doesn't answer immediately. His malicious laughter prevents him. But finally, he manages to pull himself together long enough for his lips to curve into a wicked grin as he says, "Go to the beach and see for yourselves."

We drag my uncle with us, hands bound by a leather belt pulled off one of the dead, and keep him surrounded by two bears and a half-dozen elk who await Elder Nebadri's command to attack him should he step out of line.

As we're leaving the Pits of Bagamore and the glowing Primordial behind, I scan the grounds for any signs of life. Most of the people have fled, hopefully toward safety thanks to my sister and Ryven, but we run into Alphonse and Fox. I'm not sure how they did it, seeing as they were right next to us when Qaeus was provoked into a rampage, but somehow, they managed to survive with hardly a scratch on them.

My sister joins us as we venture toward the coast, seeming as if she has nothing better to do now that most of the civilians have been cleared and Qaeus is docile. But I know the truth. The way her gaze keeps snagging on Esmond as we reach the meadow and wade through the tall grass, I can tell she doesn't believe him. She has every right not to. This was the man whom she served for years, only to then be imprisoned when she returned to him with news of how to stop Qaeus and eliminate the threat to Arcathain. No doubt, she believes he's sending us into a trap. But I am fairly certain the trap has already sprung.

When we finally reach the coastline, I'm proven right.

All of the mages—every single one who had been present today, and who I had watched earlier meandering away from the chaos—they're all dead.

Not just dead. They are nothing but bloody heaps of sharp bones now. Flesh was torn clean off their bodies as if sucked away with the tide. The few chunks that remain are serrated and ragged, torn away by something that had to have been sharp and jagged, the likes of which I can imagine in an instant because I've stared something like that down before.

"The…sirens?" I say, disbelieving. "But how? No one even knows about them. No human, that is."

Behind us, Esmond's cackle is a grating, mocking thing that crawls up my spine.

I spin to chastise him some more, to demand he tell us what happened here, and why. But I catch sight of Kalli, her hand gliding up to cover her slowly-parting lips.

"I did this," she says, her words barely more than gentle breaths. "When I sought him out. Before he imprisoned me. I told him about our encounter with the sirens."

"You did," Esmond agrees. "But surely, you can't blame yourself for being so trusting with information you had no idea would prove so powerful."

My brow furrows, but no matter how I look at it, I can't make the pieces fit. "It doesn't make sense. The sirens were in hiding. They were tired of being hunted. Why would they do this for you?"

"Ah," he says, his head bobbing back as an arrogant smile exudes off him. "You were unaware of the reasons they were hunted. And dare I venture a guess that you were also unaware of who was their most formidable predators?"

"The mages?"

"Precisely."

There are still too many gaps for it to make any sense. I glance around to the others, hoping to find that maybe they understand something I don't. But judging from their clueless expressions, they're just as lost as I am.

Except for Kalli. Always Kalli, her mind an ever-churning waterwheel, gathering buckets of information and processing them over and over into something profoundly useful.

"They needed something from the sirens to make their alchemy work," she says, voice distant and spellbound.

Esmond's finger points to her. "A penny for the wise Senator. Well, *former*," he corrects, his malicious grin widening when he sees my sister flinch at the reminder. His demeanor is swift to turn bored, flippant. "Yet another bit of intel that was shared too eagerly, too trustingly. Honestly, why would any mage, let alone a member of their precious council, willingly tell me, the Magistrate of Arcathain and a declared enemy, that they use siren scales to create the tonic used to infuse them with magic?"

Ryven's fingers tighten into fists at his waist. "Because we made a truce. You were allies."

Esmond spits. "I was never an ally to the mages. No true Arcathainian would be."

My lips part so that I might argue with him, but no sound comes out. I can't find the words, at least none that would be convincing. After what the mages did to Alphonse, to me, after they separated us from our friends and became at least indirectly involved in Dimitri's own capture and death, I'm not sure I could've ever trusted them. I knew we needed to for this, for today. But moving forward? If I doubt my own ability to trust the mages, to live in harmony with them, then how realistic is it to believe humans can do the same?

"I'm afraid you are wrong." It's Alphonse who speaks this time, his tone as resonant and powerful as the chime of the bell at Nigh. He strides forward like a man with a purpose, and stares down at his kneeling father. "Whether there had been a written or verbal agreement, Arcathain had declared a truce with the kingdom of Illashore, thereby making us allies. And you breached that truce. Tell me, Father, are you aware of the laws that govern your own country?"

"Silence, you pathetic imbecile. I will not be lectured by a bastard heathen, not even born of our own countrymen."

The venomous retort, one that would've wounded my fragile cousin before, only seems to embolden him.

"Oh, but you will, I'm afraid." Alphonse clasps his hands behind his back with the pompous arrogance only learned from being the son of someone powerful and important. "You see, you broke one of your own laws. You breached a peace agreement between our people and another that could've resulted in a catastrophic war. In fact, it would've, had Halira not been here to fix what you broke."

His eyes flick my way for a moment before returning back to his seething father.

"You have become a criminal. A terrorist. A traitor to your own country." Alphonse leans forward, hinging at the hips so they're facing eye-to-eye. The next words he utters are so quiet that I almost don't even hear him. "Welcome to being a nobody like the rest of us. We'll make sure that you're well taken care of in whatever cell you're dumped in."

Esmond's face burns as red as fresh blood. "You so much as try, and I will—"

The two bears standing on either side of him growl, their upper lips rippling and pulling back to reveal jaws of large, pointed teeth strong enough to turn him into one of the corpses surrounding us.

My thoughts retreat inward as Alphonse and Kalli start discussing the politics of it all. Something about Alphonse being his heir and therefore the rightful choice to take the seat of the Magistrate once we return.

As their conversation blends with the rushing sound of the waves, my gaze drifts across the beach. The tide glides over the shore, taking with it more and more of the mage carcasses as it tumbles back into the ocean. And it's only then that I notice one of the bodies is larger than the others. Beneath the damp robes, the ribcage is full. The legs and arms, meaty.

My curiosity piqued, I make my way across the beach and toward the fallen. I nudge the body with my toe to find it's plump with flesh and muscle. This mage wasn't devoured by the others. But why? The sirens feast on flesh. It was their greatest grumble about their retreat: having less food. I imagine coming here to lure the mages to their deaths was a feast fitting their wildest dreams. So then why was this mage spared death by devouring?

I kick the waterlogged person over, the hood of their robes falling away as they roll to their back to reveal a man. One I recognize.

Varyn's pale skin is as white as the long, wispy beard tangled like seaweed from his chin. Something catches my eye from his stomach. A crimson stain with something solid and protruding from the center.

I take to a knee to examine it.

"What is it?" Ryven asks, appearing behind me. "What did you—" He all but gasps. "The Head Mage. Why didn't they do to him what was done to the others?"

When I stand and show him what I've plucked from Varyn's stomach, a harsh line creases his forehead.

"Is that—"

"It's my knife." In my palm, I rotate Tor's dagger over and over. My fingers sing at the touch of the familiar weight of it, at the chinks and tears in the leather wrapped around the hilt. I don't ever want to let it go, and so even though I still wear the sheath it belongs in, I hold it firm in my grasp. "They left me my dagger."

Ryven's head shakes almost imperceptibly. "I guess they felt you fulfilled the end of your bargain."

"Yeah," I utter, the word clogging my throat like a stone. My eyes meet his, tears brimming. "But at what cost?"

The air is cool around us, almost like the dead themselves are watching.

He grasps my shoulders. "*This* wasn't your doing. You bargained for peace. You brought the mages, the druids, and the humans together. You returned the land. You restored the Pits of Bagamore *and* the Primordial. You were trying to make things better. You have!"

The leather hilt burns in my clutches the tighter I squeeze it. "It's not over though. What of all the mages who weren't here? What of the ones who remained at Aeysil Keep, or lived in some of the remote villages you mentioned passing through on your way to the Keep? Now that their access to the Pits has been destroyed, what will come next?"

Ryven leans his head in closer to mine. All I can see are his dark, mesmerizing eyes. They beg me to let them shelter me in their comfort, and I so badly want to. I want to bury my face in his chest and pretend that everything will be all right. But it won't. There are decades and centuries of rivalry between the people. There is blame, grief, and vengeance, enough to fuel generations to come.

"We will figure it out. Hey," he says, giving my shoulders a jostle when I start to look away. "Halira, today is still a victory worth celebrating, even as we mourn our losses. And even as we prepare for what lies ahead in our futures. But do not for one second blame yourself for these mages' deaths."

I open my mouth to speak, but I'm too exhausted. I know he's right. I know what we've accomplished has just saved tens of thousands of lives, maybe more. And after all the efforts we've put into seeing this possible future into reality, we should take time to celebrate our accomplishments. It's the only way we'll be able to survive the storms that are still to come.

Nodding, I finally concede. Ryven wraps his arms around me and tugs me against him.

My cheek rests on warm, bronzed skin, and it forces a strangled chuckle up my throat.

"You're…you're still not wearing anything."

"It is a bit indecent. Isn't it?"

My smile warms, and for fear that he might misconstrue my meaning and leave me to find clothing, I squeeze my arms around him tighter.

But just as the weight of the world is beginning to fall from our shoulders, someone gasps.

"Piss on a mage!" Fox chokes out. "Is that who I think it is?"

Alphonse is next. "I'll be blighted. It's—"

Kalli's cracking voice answers for him. "Tor?"

A DRUID'S CURSE

EASTERN COAST, THE UNITED REALM

My head jerks up to see what the others are gaping at. A dozen or more men and women emerge from the trees, naked as the day they were born. Their skin is slick, streaks of black scattered and sticking to their bodies like they climbed their way through the Pits of Bagamore to the surface.

One man stands out from them all.

Tor's hair has never been nearly as white as Kalli's and mine. It shines like it's spun with strands of gold that catch the sun's cheerful rays now that my storm has cleared from the sky. It's tied back into a loose, low-hanging ponytail. Just like it always was. But errant strands have strayed from its tidied place, dangling from his forehead and swaying past his cheeks, his jaw.

There is a ferocity in his gray eyes that is on par with Kalli's, but the usual carefree tilt of his mouth is gone. His lips wobble. His hands tremble, and though it's possible he might be chilled by the crisp, sea air, the hollow way with which he scans his surroundings tells me it's something more. A cold that runs bone-deep.

"Brother," Kalli says, casting her swords aside and

advancing on him with the grace of a newborn fawn. "Brother, it's me. It's your sister, Kalli."

My arms fall from where they were wrapped around Ryven. It's as if someone has cut them off because I can't feel them any longer. Nor can I feel my legs, or my tongue, or anything.

"K-Kalli?" he says, voice raspy and gravelly.

She tears the long, flowing fabric wrapped around her shoulders and throws it over him. It's so sheer, it likely doesn't do much for warmth, let alone modesty, but he clutches it tightly regardless. His fingers can't stop rubbing it, as if he hasn't felt anything like it in years. And I suppose he hasn't.

Just when I'm about to turn to stone—truly become cemented where I stand and unable to move for the rest of eternity—he speaks again.

"Halira. Where is Halira?"

It's the only awakening I need. Before he can even finish, I'm bolting back across the sands. He notices me running and flinches at first, but when recognition crosses him, he starts ambling toward me.

I collide into him like the ocean smacking into a cliffside. Despite his trembling, he stands strong, folding his arms behind me and lifting me from the ground.

"I can't believe it." The sobs wrack through me uncontrollably. "You're—you're actually alive. I knew it was possible, but I wasn't sure. I'd hoped but—You're really here. You're alive!"

I'm only dimly aware of Kalli appearing next to us until Tor opens one of his arms and jerks her into the embrace.

"It's so good to see you both," he says, kissing the tops of each of our heads. Resting his chin atop mine, he sighs. "Where are we?"

My sister is first to laugh, a tight-lipped chuckle that comes on gradually like a series of hums before finally bursting into a throaty, boisterous chorus. Soon I'm joining her. Because the question is so simple and yet so much more complicated than he ever could imagine.

Tor recoils from both of us, his disturbed gaze moving to the people behind us.

"I was…I was a demon."

"You were, brother," Kalli answers.

"But how is that possible…I should've died. I…I remember being bitten. A demon killed me."

Before the horror bulging behind his eyes can consume him, I jab him in the ribs. "You're lucky I didn't kill you. I've made it quite the habit to slay demons, just like we always talked about."

He's still staring down at his chest like he can't believe his own pale skin is there beneath his fingers. But my words snag his attention. "What do you mean *slaying demons*? Are you—"

Proudly, I nod. "I joined the Shadow Crusade. I told you I always would."

Someone snorts from behind us, and a second later, Alphonse joins us. "She *was* in the Shadow Crusade. Before you became a deserter."

I scowl at him, but he keeps his smug grin on Tor. "It's good to see you, cousin."

"You too." Tor shakes his head, a confused look about him. This all must be so much to take in. For two years he's been trapped inside the body of a behemoth. For two years he's been completely lost to the Blight. But my brother never was one to dwell on things, and so his confused expression quickly fades behind his casual, easy-going nature. "I bet our mother gave father an ear-full for allowing that. She never was too thrilled by my joining. How is she?"

We sober in an instant, and there's no recovering in time to soften the blow. Tor understands what our suddenly sullen expressions mean easily enough.

Dragging a hand through his disheveled hair, he curses. "How long? How long have I been gone?"

Kalli and I exchange a worried glance.

Tor was always resilient. The kind of person that could smile through a flood and find the bright side of a drought. If he had been around when our father housed refugees from Ashenvale, he would've said how fortunate it was that we were there to care for them, instead of worrying about how long we'd be able to. If he had been with us when we were imprisoned, he would've flashed a dazzling smile and said something like, "Well at least they're not executing us just yet."

But this? Coming back to life, essentially, after spending two years as a demon and discovering that your parents were killed. Who could endure such earth-shattering news? And that's not even including everything else that happened. The scourge on Gravenburg; mine and Kalli's exiles; I'm not even sure if he knows of his powers, let alone that he's a druid. Dimitri's death. The two of them had been just as close growing up as Dimitri and I were, the three of us as thick as thieves and always in each other's company. It seems unfair and cruel that on the first day of his return, we would bombard him with so much misery.

Kalli licks her lips, the heartfelt words struggling to leave. "Time seems so irrelevant when your brother has seemingly returned from the dead."

Sympathy exudes off him. Sympathy and guilt.

But Kalli holds up her hand. "There's no need for that. I just mean that...I think I speak for Halira and I both when I say that we are simply grateful to have you back. And that perhaps it would be best to fill you in on the details once we're settled somewhere a little more...private." She glances between us as she speaks, and I realize that for the first time in maybe forever, she is asking us for our input.

I nod, and after a long moment, so does Tor.

Considering it's been two years since I've seen my brother —one of my best friends—I embrace him a few more times for good measure.

When we're finally done though, I glance across the beach to Ryven. Throughout all of this, he's given me my space, and he continues to do so now. Or, at least that's what I believed he was doing. Looking at him now, seeing the pain rippling behind his russet eyes, I realize for the first time what Tor's appearance means to him. What it means for Ahl'Ro.

If Ryven hadn't killed him, if he hadn't intervened that day to rescue me, Ahl'Ro might still be alive. He could've been among the many to step out from the meadow, and Ryven could've been having a reunion with his own brother right now.

I muster a sad smile, one to let him know just how sorry I am for—for everything. His lips curve, but nothing squelches the sorrow in his eyes. I'm not sure anything could in this moment, but I walk over to him anyway and nestle back into his arms.

Elder Nebadri breaks the silence a moment later. "These people are naked. So many of them. The animals don't mind, but we should probably find them some clothes."

It is not as easy of a task as she makes it seem, for the only garments nearby are the ones drenched and tangled in bones, or drenched in blood back at Bagamore. We do what we can though, through tears and outbursts of confusion. We've been through worse. We've endured worse.

In a matter of a few hours, we have everyone clothed and calm, for the most part. Ryven and Elder Nebadri thankfully knew some of them, but there are those among us who seem to have been stuck as behemoths for years. Decades. Practically since the day the Shadowthorn was created.

We reach Bagamore again where Qaeus appears to be waiting.

"Will you be all right?" I ask her. For years she's roamed the earth, and for most of that time, she's had her sisters with her. Or her demon spawn. "You don't have to stay here all alone."

Her voice is warm where it permeates my mind. *"I will remain to protect Bagamore, and to aid those who need to be cleansed, until I am no longer needed here."*

"Cleansed?" I ask, but the answer comes to me before she can say it. "You mean the other mages? You can help them?"

She nods. *"If they come here, I can remove the darkness, and their lives will be their own again."*

This is great news, but a hitch in my chest makes me remember how fervently they've fought to retain their powers.

"I'm not sure they'll come peacefully."

A windy noise escapes her. *"No, some will not. But not all were living a life of their choosing. Some will want out of the bind they forced upon themselves."*

I believe she's right. Perhaps at one point in time they wanted magic. But at what cost? I imagine that once they discovered they could never stop injecting themselves for fear of death, some of them wished they'd never dabbled in it to begin with.

"We'll send word," I assure her, making a mental note to have Elder Nebadri send her birds with messages for the remaining mages at once. "But what about the ones who don't come peacefully?" Turning to Alphonse and the others, I say it again so they can hear. "We can't leave this place undefended. The mages will return to do exactly what they did before."

Alphonse shakes his head. "We won't let them." Glancing to Kalli, who nods, encouraging him to continue, he does. "I will be taking my father's place as Magistrate. I will make sure this place is well-defended. We would welcome some aid from the Eyve, as well."

My sister's head dips in time with Elder Nebadri's. It seems as if Kalli knows something that I haven't quite yet figured out, but that's all too familiar for us, so I don't think much more on it.

Instead, I let Qaeus know that she will not be left here alone, that we will never let the darkness take her again.

We leave a small party to keep the area guarded until Alphonse and the Eyve can send a more permanent force. And then, we leave Bagamore and embark on a new era for Arcathain. For the Eyve. For Illashore. For all of mankind.

EPILOGUE: ASCENSION

THE FORGOTTEN FOREST OF EYVE

"Are you sure this is what you want?"

My fingers curl around the crown of twigs and leaves, the bright yellow flowers reminding me of the beehives I once tended with my mother. It feels like so long ago now, like those memories might as well belong to someone else entirely. But they are what shaped me. Each and every morning that I evaded my household chores or absconded from my beekeeping and candle-making duties led me to where I am today. Standing beside my sister as she prepares to claim her birthright. The one passed down by our mother, and her mother before her, all the way back to the original Elders.

Kalli sucks in a breath between her nearly pursed lips and takes the flowery crown from me. She brings it eye-level, examining it, and I realize I've seen her look like this before. The day she accepted her position at the Senate, I'd never seen her look more regal and honorable. When the man swearing her in handed her the cape that marked her as a member of the Senate, she'd paused, much like she has now. She'd run her fingers over every thread stitched in the fabric. She'd stared deeply into the phoenix sigil as if it was speaking to her; and I think in some ways, it was. I think Kalli was reminding herself what it would mean to step into the role and making a promise to hold the title with integrity, justice, and loyalty to the people.

It had suited her well.

And I have no doubt that being an Elder will fit her just as snugly.

After a few moments pass, she finally rests the crown atop her head. "This is what I was born for."

A small breath of laughter brushes past my lips. I'm not even sure what provoked it. It's not that I'm laughing at her or doubting her, because I couldn't agree more. Kalli will be great at being an Elder. She will serve the people just as well, if not better, than any Elder before her.

I guess I'm just nervous. The last time I was in a ceremony, I was receiving my Shadow Crusade sigil.

Kalli glances at me, concern hinting behind her eyes. She takes the crown off, setting it back on the pillow draped in gauze.

"You know," she says, turning toward me. "I may have been born to become an Elder, but you? You were born to reunite Arcathain with the rest of the Broken Realms. Never forget that, Halira."

Suddenly, my cheeks are on fire. "Oh. I wasn't—I didn't mean—"

Her smirk is subtle, but her nose inching higher is obvious and deliberate. "Good. Because if you did, I'd have to cancel the ceremony and take you all the way across the Eyve and Arcathain to visit Drayfil, just so you could see for yourself just how immensely you've impacted the peoples' lives. We'd visit Uncle Adrien and Sai, living on our grandparents' land once again. Land that had been destroyed during the Great Rift but, with the aid of the druids, is thriving once more. We'd greet their neighbors—you might remember meeting them the last time we visited. Where are they from again?"

Begrudgingly, a laugh escapes me. "Illashore."

"Oh right! They used to be mages. But thanks to you restoring the Pits of Bagamore, and the Primordial cleansing those who would rather live than die, they are now living harmoniously, free of magic, in Drayfil."

"Okay. You've made your point," I say, swatting her away. "Don't cancel the ceremony."

A soft smile twitches the corners of her lips before she glances back to the crown. To *her* crown. "I wouldn't dream of it."

Silence settles over Imryll's home then. Outside these walls, the community is alive and frantically preparing for the big day, for Kalli to march the winding path from the base of the tree to the top, and take her place alongside the Elders. Judging from her calm demeanor, no one would know that the ceremony will begin in less than two hours.

"Have you heard from Ryven recently?" she asks.

My head bobs as I recount the last message I received from him while he was at Bagamore. Over the past few months, the two of us have volunteered a number of times to help guard the borders, as well as aiding mages who are interested in becoming un-tainted to access the cleansing waters.

It's still difficult for me to be at that place without feeling an overwhelming sense of guilt. Logically, I know I didn't kill the mages, and I know if we had let Qaeus roam, so many more people would've died. But my heart is still heavy regardless.

Ryven, however, can't volunteer his time enough. This was the dream that he and Ahl'Ro had been embarking on: to see the nations brought together in peace, or at least to strive toward it. There is still much work to be done, but he wants to be there for every moment of it, to carry on Ahl'Ro's legacy and make his death mean something.

"He's on his way," I tell her, joy threatening to choke the life from me. "I caught his message on the wind last night that he was no more than a half day's journey away. He should be here soon. I was actually about to go meet him at the border."

He's been gone almost two months this time already. And three months the time before that, although we were still together for part—if not most—of that trip. I've missed him tremendously, however the time apart has served an unexpected purpose. It's allowed me to find an inner peace, a quiet in myself that I've never really known, or at least, haven't known in the past year. Living in Gravenburg was loud. Our lives a busy, endless cycle of duties and chores and survival. Being in the Shadow Crusade, was much the same. We never had much time for rest, and when we did, we filled it with time spent with each other because our days were numbered. And after I fled the Castle of Nigh, I hardly had a moment of peace and quiet until Qaeus was restored, and we returned here. To what I can honestly say is the most peaceful place in all the United Realm.

And it's been here that I've found myself yet again. Now that the Shadowthorn is gone and the demons have disappeared, now that Qaeus is a benevolent guardian again, the way she was intended, it's in this place that I've discovered there is more to life than fighting and running. I can wield the chaotic magic of lightning at a moment's notice, or I can breathe in the fresh, calm air of the surrounding forest. I can spar with Ryven and hone my skills—both physical and magical—or I can lounge with him in the hammock outside his home, our hands intertwined and our laughter ringing up to the trees.

There is still much work to be done, but it's all worth it for the people we love. And I have so many people I love.

"Go." Kalli sighs, flicking her hand back at me while her gaze remains fixed on the mirror. She watches herself retrieve the crown and place it atop her head for the dozenth time. "Don't stay on my account. But I'll see you at the ceremony, correct?"

"Of course," I tell her. "I wouldn't miss it for the world."

I leave her before the mirror to finish dressing herself in the ceremonial garb the Elders have given her—the worn tunic and golden armbands that had been meant for our mother. But as I'm leaving our aunt's hut, just as I walk through the doorway and turn down the street, through the window carved on the side of the hut, I swear I hear Kalli mutter, "If the world needed you, I don't doubt that you would."

I'm smiling almost the entire way down the sloping path. At first because of Kalli's uncharacteristically supportive and uplifting mood, but then because the excitement of the Eyve becomes contagious, and the people are all too eager to congratulate me and my family on this big day.

By the time I reach the border, my cheeks are hurting almost as much as my thighs. We've been living here for six months, and I'm still not used to the daily climb. There are still many things I have yet to grow accustomed to, but I look forward to each and every one of them because this place feels like home. More than Gravenburg ever did. More than Nigh. More than anywhere I've ever been—and I can honestly say I've been almost everywhere.

I send a gentle breeze through the once-shriveled trees surrounding the Eyve that are once more thriving with glorious canopies of thousands of verdant leaves. The wind circles back to me, Ryven's cedar scent heavy in the gust.

Crossing the border, my gait is casual at first. I stroll through the trees like I'm taking one of my daily morning walks. But the closer he becomes, the more hastened my pace is. Soon, I'm running, bounding through the green forest without a care in the world because no longer do we have to worry about the creatures hiding in the shadows.

Suddenly, I stop. His scent disappears for a moment. I stare ahead, something like fear trying to claw its way into my chest, but I keep my hold on it. There is nothing to fear here. Not anymore. Right?

A whoosh drops from above. I duck and roll out of the way of the black thing leaping down from the trees. It's small at first. Its leathery wings flapping frantically, pushing air downward and saving it from the fall. But then a body explodes from it, bare flesh extending in legs and arms and that gorgeous face of his.

I shove myself off the ground, wiping away the dirt from my bottom. "One of these days you're going to get yourself struck by lightning."

A crooked grin inches up one side of his face as he strides toward me. He lifts me into the air, my legs wrapping around him on instinct. "I don't mind a little spark."

"Little?"

He chuckles against my neck, inhaling the scent of me. "I've missed you."

I lean into him, my hands digging into his smooth, warm skin. "I've missed you too. Why is it that you always find a way to get yourself naked?"

The sound he makes is part laughter, part animal. "If you don't like it—"

"Oh, I didn't say that."

When I lean back to gaze into his eyes, hunger stares back at me. It's more than just lust though. Being away from Ryven can sometimes feel like I'm being starved for air—which is saying a lot for someone who can command it. And whenever we are reunited, there is a surge of power between us, a wave of static that rolls over my body from head to toe and back again.

And that is the very same look he gives me now, one charged and fierce and all-consuming.

"How much time before the ceremony?" he asks, his voice low and gravelly.

I resituate in his arms, making sure to press into where his hands are cupping my backside.

"A couple of hours," I say.

"Perfect," he growls, leaning closer to lick my neck. "A couple of hours is a good start."

Our kiss is deep and powerful. Stars burst behind my eyes and the world melts away. After months of being apart, our bodies crave each other like their lives depend on it, and we don't stop them. Our hands, our mouths, they move over every inch of each other, in whatever ways they desire.

I give myself over to him, and he gives himself over to me.

Because there will always be work to be done. There will always be peace to strive for and people to appease. But until then, for now, in this moment, there is only each other. And each other is all we need.

Thank you for reading *Immortal Return!*

If you like gothic worlds and bloodthirsty demons, be sure to
check out my next release:
Blood and Magic Eternal!

Leave a Review
Indie books *thrive* off reviews! Help other readers find this
dark saga by leaving a review on Amazon, Goodreads,
Bookbub, or any other reading website. Even a simple "I loved
it!" can really help!

Social Media
Subscribe to my newsletter, or stay connected on social media
using the link here:
https://linktr.ee/jessaca_with_an_a

ARC Team
If you're someone who loves leaving reviews and you're excited
by the idea of having early access to all of my books, check out
my website for more information on how to join my ARC
Team: www.jessacawillis.com/ARC

BLOOD & MAGIC ETERNAL
Vampire Dark Fantasy Romance

Eighteen-year-old Charlotte Thorne was just a babe when the heroes of Nigh saved the realm from demons...or so they thought.

The Blighted may have shed their horrifying skins, but now they blend in with the masses, seemingly human, thirsting for blood and awaiting the Hunt.

Charlotte has three rules for evading their capture:
    1. Always carry a crossbow;
    2. Never—*ever*—trust the living; and
    3. Be as comfortable in the shadows as the monsters are.

But one day, she breaks every last rule...

When Charlotte recognizes one of the cries for help on the deserted streets of Gravenburg, she leaves the safety her hovel, sets down her weapon, and tries to free a childhood friend from one of the vampire's traps.

But Charlotte is the one ensnared.

Captured and bound, she will be released in the Hunt, a twice-annual feast of flesh and fear. No human has ever survived. They are too weak to overpower the hungry monsters that chase and terrorize them.

But Charlotte Thorne is not weak. She will outlast their sick games. And in order to do so, she will slay every single Blighted that hunts her...unless she falls in love with one of them first.

Blood & Magic Eternal is a gothic, dark fantasy series with devastating vampires, a stabby female protagonist, and a dark realm where humans are near extinction, and the Hunt is a brutal source of entertainment for those powerful and blood-thirsty enough to watch.

Grab your copy of *Blood & Magic Eternal* here!

*In a realm where murderers are taken by
the Councilspirits and forced into becoming Reapers,
one girl is on a path to redemption...*

Sinisa is a Reaper of Veltuur, an assassin born from the underrealm, with fatal magic coursing through their veins.

For three years, she's slain her targets dutifully. Now she just needs one more kill to ascend as a Shade, a coveted status of power. And when the King of Oakfall requests a Reaper to execute his daughter for an unforgivable crime, Sinisa is first to volunteer for the job.

It *should* be easy.

But when the Prince discovers his sister is in danger, he flees the palace with her, leaving Sinisa with only two options: journey through the mortal realm to find and slay her mark, or face the consequences of returning to the underrealm empty-handed.

It's no choice at all. She has come too far to stop now.

Besides, no one can outrun a Reaper… Or can they?

~Check out the Reapers of Veltuur Trilogy on Amazon~

Supernatural powers destroyed the world...
Now four unlikely heroes have to save it.

The world ended two years ago. They called it the Awakening: the supernatural event that gave some people powers and left others normal. Nations went to war and millions died.

Sean was one of the first to Awaken, but it wasn't until he walked in on his brother's brutal murder that he learned of the darker nature of his power: blood calls to him, and he to it. And in that moment, he showed his brother's murderers no mercy.

Now Sean must fight to keep his inner demons in check, and his path to redemption begins with the establishment of a sanctuary for people like him, people with powers: the Awakened.

But not even in the apocalypse are the Awakened safe...

Can Sean and three strangers unite the remnants of mankind when everything else has fallen apart? Can they face the darkest horror this new world has yet to offer?

~Check out The Awakened Quadrilogy on Amazon~

ACKNOWLEDGMENTS

"It takes a village" is a phrase I've always loved. Every time I hear it, or see it in action, I am overcome with just an incredibly warm, bubbly feeling that makes me wonder what a great world we would live in if we always felt that way.

Much like *Blighted Heart, Immortal Return* also took a village to finish, and I am eternally grateful for the village I've surrounded myself with.

My village knows who they are and hopefully they know how grateful I am for each and every one of them.

Jessaca is a fantasy writer with an inclination toward the dark, epic, and adventure sub-genres. She draws inspiration from books like the Nevernight Chronicles & ACOTAR, videogames like Dark Souls III, and television shows like Game of Thrones and The Chilling Adventures of Sabrina. She is a self-proclaimed nerd who loves cosplay, video games, and comics, and if you live in the PNW, you just might see her at one of the local comic conventions in one of her favorite RWBY cosplays!

www.ingramcontent.com/pod-product-compliance
Lightning Source LLC
Chambersburg PA
CBHW062311200726
48292CB00006BA/1961